GRANDFATHER ANONYMOUS

Anthony W. Eichenlaub

oakleafbooks.com

To all the badass grandparents out there. Don't let anyone tell you to slow down.

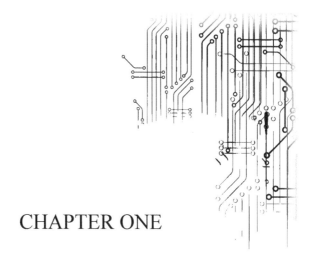

CHAPTER ONE

In the midst of a thousand one-story ramblers sat a house so very like the others as to be entirely invisible. Its aging boards creaked in the cool Minnesota autumn, but the roof didn't leak, and when all was said and done, it performed all the functions a meticulously unremarkable rambler ought to perform. It kept its sole resident, Ajay Andersen, warm and dry, gave the post office somewhere to deliver his mail, and provided him a place where, in his retirement, he could run an advanced computing rig and hide from a world that he had legitimately learned to fear.

When Ajay cracked open the door and saw a round-faced social officer staring back at him, his old heart nearly dropped into a hard arrhythmia.

Social officers loved to poke around the business of all the old folks in the neighborhood. They made sure nobody was rotting away on the bathroom floor. Ajay bristled at that. He preferred to decompose in peace, thank you very much.

The boy thumbed a disc nestled in his left palm: his fidget computer. His fingers danced across the device as the police-blue strap across the back of his hand flashed a series of holographic images. Words scrolled by too quick for Ajay to interpret backwards. He didn't even try.

Ajay struggled to remember what he'd been doing before he'd dozed off in his favorite natty old lounger. It had been routine online maintenance, but that kind of maintenance required a secure connection and the use of his highly illegal and somewhat stolen diamond-optical quantum computer. The fist-sized black box sat only a few feet from where Ajay's tired slippers scraped the faded linoleum and would plant too many ideas in too many heads. Ajay couldn't let the officer in or he'd be fighting questions all week. All year, maybe. He stuck his chin out at the officer.

"Hello, sir," said the officer, with a smile that strained credibility. "We're going around doing walkthroughs this morning. It's a safety checkup."

Damn. Ajay rolled his knobby knuckles against the door frame. Damn.

The officer's eyes darted to his hologram. "You're Ajay Andersen," he said, drawing out the last name in a long monotone.

"That or the King of Norway," said Ajay, forcing an attempt at humor against all his better judgment. "Can't remember."

The officer stiffened, looked up at Ajay, narrow eyes taking in Ajay's brown complexion and shaggy gray mustache. Ajay had to play it smooth. The best move was to keep his low profile and avoid antagonizing the officer at all costs. A lump formed in the old man's throat. Off to a bad start already.

A brisk autumn chill blew through the open door straight on up Ajay's threadbare robes to chill his bones. He'd grown up with frigid Minnesota weather, but that didn't mean he much preferred it. Red Wing might be in the southern half of the state, but that was still the northern half of hell as far as he was concerned. His favorite strategy to handle the winters involved closing the door in October and opening it again in May. In his youth, Ajay had always wondered if he would be happier in India, where his mother was born, but the time to think about that kind of travel had long since passed. Ajay was too old. Too tired.

Behind him, his television pinged, warning of low connectivity. The buffer on the golf game he'd been watching was low, the network broken. A mass of hair under the television shifted, and Ajay's bloodhound, Garrison, blinked wearily at the two men standing in the wide-open doorway.

The officer's eyes flicked to the screen, then to the dog, then back to Ajay. He raised an eyebrow.

"I'm not the King of Norway," Ajay stated in the flattest voice manageable.

"I see that."

Ajay gripped the door jamb. This was his chance to play it cool. All he had to do was play the kid's game. "Not pale enough for you?" he said. Not the right thing to say by a long three-iron. Something about the kid's soft cheeks and squinty eyes made it impossible for Ajay to show even one tiny thread of respect, despite the consequences of further scrutiny.

"State your birthday," the officer said.

"I'm half Norwegian, you know." Ajay bit his lip. Starting an argument with the kid was a terrible idea. "On my father's side."

The officer paused the span of a deep breath. "Your birthday." It wasn't a question so much as a statement of information forthcoming.

Ajay swallowed. "Today. Seventy years ago, today."

The officer looked at his screen, scrunched up his brow. "So it is. Happy birthday." He said it with all the enthusiasm of congratulating him on a fantastic colonoscopy.

Ajay responded with a noncommittal grunt.

"There have been reports in the area," said the officer, craning his neck around to get a better look inside Ajay's rambler. "Network connectivity problems."

Ajay moved to block the man's view. "Must be tough."

The officer's lips tightened. "It is tough. Lot of folks depend on their connection for their friends, health checkups, and—"

Ajay waved a hand at the officer as if his words were flies that could be swatted away.

Red connectivity errors flashed across the officer's display. "Dammit." The officer snapped his palm shut; the display on the back of his hand winked out like an extinguished flame. He sighed, as if talking to Ajay was the hardest part of a very dull job. Maybe it was. "May I come in?" he asked, stepping forward as if only one answer existed.

But Ajay stopped him, puffing up to block the doorway. He snatched an umbrella from its stand and thumped it on the floor in front of the officer. Not a threat, but certainly a warning. The officer frowned, creases bisecting the dimples at the corners of his mouth.

Ajay poked him in the chest with a finger. "I know my rights." He slipped on his half-moon glasses and peered at the man's badge. His Minnesotan grandmother used to always call her little reading glasses cheaters, but these cheated a whole lot more than hers ever had. They flickered for a moment, then blinked red.

"They won't work," the officer said in the tone of someone explaining very simple technology to a very stupid person. "Bad connectivity, remember?"

"Dammit." It took all of Ajay's willpower to keep himself from glancing at the black box. Had he left it running? That might explain the scrambled signals in the area, but it didn't bode well for his aging brain.

Instead, the name printed on the officer's badge caught his attention. "Chester." He dredged up as sincere a smile as he could manage. "Thanks for checking in, but this old man is perfectly fine. You can move along. I think Mrs. Goldstein's hoarding cats next door, and they smell something fierce."

"I'm sorry," Chester said, the tone of his voice hinting that he was not sorry at all. "We have instructions to do full walkthroughs—"

"Bullshit," Ajay said, poking the curved umbrella handle — a stylized squid tentacle — at the officer's chest. "You got a warrant?"

"There would be a device." He kept a hand on the door so Ajay couldn't close it. "Scrambler of some sort."

"Not illegal to own a scrambler," Ajay said.

"It's illegal to use it."

Ajay's belly boiled. This officer didn't know horse shit from butterflies. "You ever read the Constitution, son?"

The officer's eye twitched. "Sir, the Constitution allows for extra safety provisions in a time of emergency."

Ajay's voice trembled. "Buncha made up bull, and you know it."

"We're coming up on the hundredth anniversary of Hiroshima and Nagasaki. The extra vigilance is for your own protection."

"And before that was the anniversary of 9/11, or the start of Vietnam. It's the ten-year anniversary of the cash riots next month. How long have we been under constant emergency vigilance?"

The officer seemed to deflate. "It's for our protection," he said, not sounding convinced.

Ajay swatted the words away. "You think somebody's going to set off a nuke in my house?"

"No, sir, I—"

Ajay stepped right up to the officer, their noses inches apart. He stared the young man right in the eyes and saw resignation. Defeat. This officer didn't like this process any more than Ajay. "There's a lot worse out there than nukes, son," Ajay said. "A lot worse."

"I'm aware."

"Oh, I don't think you are. If you had any idea what they knew about you, it'd keep you up at night." Ajay's gaze slipped to the man's badge again, spotting the tiny lens there. "You recording this?"

The officer smiled. "It's policy."

"That's mine," Ajay said. "The recording. Mine by right."

"Yeah. Constitution. I'm aware."

"You mocking the Constitution, son?"

The officer's eyes twinkled. "No, sir."

"You get out of here, then." Ajay pushed the door, struggling against the stronger man. "Unless you have a warrant."

"Mr. Andersen," the social officer said, "video of this conversation will be uploaded and checked for signs of guilt." He looked around. "As soon as I get back to a connected space, anyway. Your home will be marked as an unknown, so you should probably expect more visits soon."

"Of course it will be."

The officer launched into the standard parting routine — a ritual his kind went through to let citizens know that they were leaving but that everyone should probably still be afraid. Ajay waited patiently through the speech, which involved a lot of legalese and very few curse words. Thinking the kid was done, Ajay stepped back and leaned against the wall.

It turned out to be a mistake. The officer stepped through the door, hand outstretched as if for a handshake. Ajay batted the hand away. By the time he got the boy out the door again, the officer had taken in a full view of the living room. Had he been in far enough to record an image of the box?

The officer acted as if nothing had gone wrong. He activated the display on his hand. "Oh, and one more thing." He spoke casually as if this might have nothing at all to do with the real reason for his visit. "There's a fugitive spotted in your area. A woman, traveling with her two daughters, aged ten and fourteen." A big red light flashed on his display as he tried to connect. "Dammit."

Ajay raised an eyebrow.

"Anyway, her name is Sashi Chandrakar." Chester forced another friendly smile. "Seems she stole something pretty important. If you see her, let someone know as soon as you can."

Ajay's response stuck in his throat. He knew that woman. Daughters? Ajay's gut twisted. His mouth went dry. Daughters. It couldn't be.

Chester let go of the door, sending Ajay lurching forward. For a long time, he stood in the empty entryway, focused on something far away. Sashi Chandrakar, or as he knew her, Sashi Chandrakar-Andersen. After all those years. His daughter. The squid umbrella slipped from his fingers and clattered to the floor.

Granddaughters. Go figure.

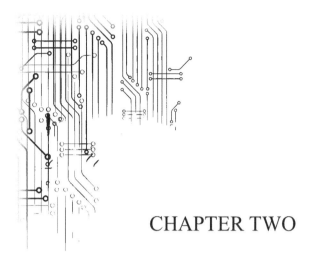

CHAPTER TWO

Ajay swore. He cursed himself for leaving the diamond-optical's scrambler on, drawing unwanted attention. Everything depended on remaining anonymous. Now his daughter was back and she'd see him as his sad, old self, unable to properly care for his own tech. He couldn't manage his own affairs, dress properly, or even remember to switch off the one truly dangerous piece of tech in the house.

The device sat there dark as a lump of charcoal. It hadn't been scrambling at all.

So, who was?

His handheld fidget, an old clunky thing with edges worn down, displayed an amber X, indicating a blocked signal. The yellowed strap across the back of his hand projected error messages into the dusty air. Somebody else was scrambling the wireless. Who would do that? An itch of curiosity tickled at Ajay's brain. It dug in like a mosquito, but he waved it away.

There was no time to track down whoever was messing around in the area. It was probably some hacker trying to be all sneaky. They'd catch whoever overstepped the law, and that'd be the end of it. They wouldn't return unless they saw something in the officer's video that led them to it. Or they'd be back if they figured out his connection to Sashi.

They'd be back if the social officer had gotten vid of that box. This time, they might come armed with a few of the right questions.

"That video's mine, you son of a bitch," Ajay muttered. "I'm not talking to you, Garrison," he said to the dog. "You're a damn poor watchdog, but you can have all the videos you want."

Garrison looked at him with baleful eyes.

Ajay sat at his kitchen table, sweeping the remains of yesterday's breakfast to the side. The bagel fell to the floor and Garrison pounced on it with the kind of focused ferocity one expected of a tree sloth. The table lit up as a single screen containing dozens of prompts. Ajay selected one and typed a few commands. The hardware was old — ancient, really — but it still worked well enough. Wish he could say the same for himself.

The old tabletop computer was wired directly into the central grid. A thick cable ran from his old house directly down to the conduit that ran the length of the Mississippi. Old tech, but solid enough, and fast.

He stretched, his back popping into place. His shoulders squared and his spine straightened.

Ajay gestured across the screen to pull up his custom utils. He already had several routines planned for police video. Within minutes he lurked in the local segment, digging through the piles and piles of collected information. The 29th amendment to the U.S. Constitution gave him ownership of all data collected on him as well as the right to resist the collection thereof. The 30th gave government and corporations the right to collect and defend it.

A sly grin crossed Ajay's face. He sipped cold coffee from a stained mug. "Bring it on," he muttered.

Within seconds, he had a dozen scrubbers running. They searched for his image and deleted, deleted, deleted. These were dumb routines, but sometimes simple and stupid got the job done. In this case, of course, it wouldn't. The police databanks responded, duplicating any video he touched as fast as he could touch it. It was all public space, of course. The concept of private storage in connected space had died with encryption years ago. If they wanted to keep data safe, they'd need an air gap: a complete disconnect from the network.

They needed a warrant for that, and warrants took time.

Not much time.

The officer's upload had started when he'd emerged from the scrambled zone. Ajay zapped an archive process before it could start up, relying heavily on hand-coded automation to find and kill. If they archived his info offline, there wouldn't be any way to grab it, so those archival tools had to die.

But one archival process didn't die. Ajay's attention snapped to that process. His jaw hardened.

He took another sip of bitter coffee.

The kill didn't work, but root ought to be able to obliterate any process in the system. Did he not have root access? Ajay checked. He scanned the system, touched some restricted files. Yes, he had root. He tried to kill the process again. Meanwhile, his automated scrubbers cleaned the data. Deleting one file after another in rapid succession. A thousand archive processes perished on the fields of battle.

Still, one survived.

Ajay mapped its dependencies. Something held it open, and if he could pull on that thread, then it would die. It had to.

It tied directly into the kernel, the central process of the whole system. At least...

Ajay squinted through his cheaters. Text blurred past, feeding him the pertinent info as fast as he could absorb it, which was — ahem — pretty damn fast.

That process wasn't tied into the kernel. It couldn't be. If they'd done that, then he would have legal rights to kill it, and nobody wanted that nuke to strike. That could collapse a whole grid, rendering whole sections of town dark. No power, no network. All those services the social officer thought were so important would crash hard. No, that connection was faked. It was a damn honey pot.

A decoy.

Ajay swore through his teeth. He'd wasted too much time on a process that did nothing but eat cycles and chew time.

His time.

With a swipe across the tabletop, Ajay cleared away everything he'd brought up on that process. Once that disappeared, he saw the fleet of obfuscators rolling up on his scrubbers.

Now those were clever bits of code. They'd blur his image in any video files, making it harder for his seek-and-destroy process to find their target. He could see where they'd already modified a pile of files. He manually selected those and deleted them before they slipped away into the ether.

There wasn't much left, only that last minute with the officer. A surge of archival processes started, too fast to be killed. Ajay swore. Code locked down the remaining few files. What was this?

A warrant.

Little video remained. That last piece, mere seconds of video, couldn't be deleted until the archive tool finished. A lock held it hard.

Shit.

"I need time," Ajay muttered.

Garrison's ears perked up.

There was no time. Seconds remained, and those archives had to do their thing. They'd save the file and then people would start asking questions. He had to control the questions. That's what he always said. Always control the questions.

In this case, answers needed controlling, not questions. Archive functions only asked two questions — "What needs to be archived?" and "Where should it go?"

Ajay redirected the archivers, telling them to store information on his own data stick instead of the police storage. One technology that continued to improve at an exponential rate was the speed of data transfer. This array of video took nanoseconds to transfer, with a few seconds' delay on each end to establish the connection. When it finished, those processes died off. He snapped the data stick out of the drive, sending it clattering to the floor. Garrison gave it a sniff to make sure it wasn't food, then laid his head back down.

With the file unlocked, the scrubbers removed the last bit of video. The obfuscators rose in a cloud and dispersed one by one. Archivers died en masse, victims to Ajay's aggressive slash and burn.

Then… silence. Ajay's presence, or any direct link to him, was gone. Almost as an afterthought, Ajay hacked into the social officer's database and changed his own address from "unknown" to "safe." Before logging off, he changed Mrs. Goldstein's address to "safe" as well. He couldn't think of any reason she needed to deal with the trouble brought on by being marked "unstable."

Garrison bumped his head against Ajay's hand, which was draped over the back of his chair. In response, Ajay scratched behind the hound's ears. "I'm getting old, Gare," he said. "That decoy almost had me. Another couple seconds…"

Ajay slumped back in his old oak chair, which creaked under his weight. Garrison rested his head in the old man's lap, and Ajay obligingly continued to dole out the required attention. Garrison was old, too.

The tabletop display gracefully darkened, leaving the hazy kitchen lit only by late morning light filtering through the red maple outside. The wind blew, rustling autumn leaves and causing the illumination to flicker like a dying flame. Ajay still wore a threadbare paisley robe and fuzzy slippers.

He lit the stove and cracked a couple eggs. He wasn't hungry, but hard-won experience told him that skipping meals led to problems. Every year left him a little skinnier and a little weaker. He despised the frustrating drift into the nothing of old age. Once the eggs were done — over hard — he flipped one into Garrison's bowl and slid the other onto his plate. He ate slowly, chewing each piece into a smooth, flavorless mush.

Ajay picked the data stick up. Almost all traditional computing happened in centralized servers, and most quantum computing operated through the Cube. Quantum computing shattered Moore's Law, upending the way people interacted with digital space. Any local computers were little more than peripherals to the hybrid of traditional and quantum systems. That meant anything done at home could be accessed remotely.

Almost anything.

Once he settled comfortably onto his worn lounger, Ajay picked up the black box and held its dense form in the palm of his hand. He thumbed the power switch and the device hummed, turning warm almost immediately. It scrambled signals, but he made sure to keep the setting low enough that it wouldn't be detected from the street. Once he was sure it worked, he connected the data stick to his fidget and brought up the snippet of video.

This was so much more than some lousy scrambler.

The officer left his doorstep, walking down the narrow, weedy sidewalk. He turned toward Mrs. Goldstein's house. Up ahead, at about the distance of a solid seven-iron, a woman sat in a car with two girls — presumably her two daughters. The officer didn't seem to notice them, or at least didn't react to their presence. He was probably busy messing with his computer. The woman glanced in his direction, then the car sped away.

The video stopped, hitting the end of what Ajay had taken. He reversed a few seconds, then zoomed in as close as he could to the woman.

He scowled at what he saw. The two girls' faces were hidden by the hoods of their sweaters. The woman should have been plainly visible in several frames, but instead, her face showed as a pixelated mass. Something she wore muddled the video. Ajay was familiar with the technology. It emitted a light that scrambled most video collection.

There was a way around it, though.

His cheaters, hanging from a chain around his neck, flashed green. Their connection to a central computing server was still broken, but they linked to the box. He slipped them on, though they were still almost useless without the central connection. But they wouldn't need that for this. Twisting the black box in his hand, he activated its dummy signal and the glasses flashed blue.

He knew who was in the video, but he had to see. Had to be certain. He only wanted to glimpse her again, after all those years.

The data stick with the video slipped neatly into the black cube. He interfaced using his fidget, selecting a single frame of video as the sample. The black box grew warmer as it decrypted the segment of video, scalding to the touch. Its diamond-optical quantum computer was ages above anything publicly available. Quantum computing outside of the Cube was almost unheard of and heavily regulated. As a prototype technology, it had more kinks than Congress, but he had little doubt it would get the job done. Ajay used the sleeve of his robe to move it onto the coffee table. It wouldn't take long, and then the device would cool down well enough. Probably.

His cheaters blinked, and he saw the muddled frame return to focus.

There are some faces that a person never forgets. Not even after twenty years. There are faces that are burned into a man's eyes. Into a father's mind. Forever.

Ajay would never forget his daughter, though until that moment he had figured she'd forgotten him.

Older now. Grayer. A palpable look of fear flashed in her dark eyes, but he recognized that sharp snowplow jaw and thin lips.

There came a tap at the back door, sending a shiver down Ajay's spine. He deactivated his cube and shoved it into his robe pocket, searing his thumb in the process. Cautiously, he peered out the back window.

There she was, beautiful and strong. Ajay shuddered.

He composed himself and straightened his robe, wishing he had prioritized getting dressed instead of hacking the video. When he opened the back door, he greeted his daughter with as close to a genuine smile as he could manage.

She had been gone near twenty years, long enough for an old man to give up hope of ever seeing her again.

His greeting stuck in his throat when he saw his granddaughters standing in the doorway with her. The younger was dark and fierce like her mother, the elder striking and pale. They were unmistakably Sashi's girls, though he couldn't have imagined two girls more different from each other.

"Shoulda known you'd bring trouble," he said. He meant it as a joke, but it fell flat and hard.

Sashi's jaw tensed, and she made no response for long enough that Ajay worried about the impending heat death of the universe.

Ajay took a step back, holding the door open. "Come on in, then."

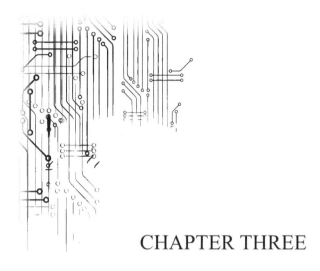

CHAPTER THREE

"Don't touch that," Ajay snapped at the ten-year-old girl as he emerged from his bedroom wearing a midnight hoodie over his least-stained button-down shirt. The newly printed clothes itched compared to his comfy robe, but he had guests. It was important to give a good first impression — which he had already failed terribly. "It's breakable."

The girl froze, perched on the arm of his ragged sofa, holding the framed picture. The whites of her eyes showed and her hand trembled.

"Kylie, dear," said Sashi, her voice soft but laced with threat. "Set it down, please."

Kylie, the smaller of the two girls, looked almost exactly like a young version of Sashi, with hair of polished mahogany and dark eyes to match. The girl's jeans had ragged holes in both knees, and the red hooded sweater she wore bunched up in the back where it had picked up dozens of burrs. She set the picture down and slumped onto the sofa next to her older sister, who sat with a calm Ajay found uncommon for a fourteen-year-old.

Sashi wore a long kurta, a knee-length shirt derived from traditional Indian clothing. Its deep violet drew light into the depths of its color, and the more Ajay looked, the more he was convinced that the fabric was something more than simple silk. A ruby bindi on her forehead glinted, and Ajay didn't doubt that it was the source of the video-muddling noise he had decrypted. Sashi's expression didn't change as she ran a manicured finger along the edge of a dusty ceramic pot on Ajay's shelf. The piece was one she had made long ago, but Ajay thought she looked as if she were staring beyond it, into some deep past where ceramics and kind words could heal any rift among family.

The older sister had lighter skin than Kylie and almost-blonde curls, but her eyes bore her mother's depth, even though their color was a striking blue. When Kylie squirmed and fidgeted and kicked, the older girl shrank away, an expression of distaste tugging at her thin lips. She pulled the hood of her oversized gray sweater over her face, but when her eyes fell on Garrison, her mouth fell open and she seemed to forget about her sister.

"He won't bite," Ajay said. "Call him over."

"Come here," Kylie said, her voice shaking.

Garrison's only movement was to roll his eyes in her direction.

Ajay clicked his tongue. "Call him like you mean it. His name's Garrison."

"Come here, boy," she called, her arms spread wide and her eyes twinkling. "Come on, Garrison!"

Garrison lifted his head as if shouldering a massive boulder, then set it down again.

The older sister curled her bare feet up under herself and shrank away from her noisy sibling.

Garrison lumbered up to the quiet older girl and rested his big head in her lap. Drool pooled on her leg.

"Oh, what a good dog!" Kylie grabbed Garrison's ears and rubbed vigorously. Once she was done, she hugged his big head and gave him a kiss on his nose. "He likes you, Isabelle."

Isabelle pulled her hands into the sleeves of her sweater.

Anthony W. Eichenlaub

Ajay wanted to ask why Sashi had come. He needed to know what her life had been for the past twenty years. Twenty years! And she had daughters. Now, out of nowhere, she visited, pretending as if nothing were wrong? What terrible danger must be out there driving Sashi his way? Or did she finally want to make amends?

But the words stuck in his throat. The wrong words might crack the first ice of winter, sending him plunging back into the cold depths. Instead, Ajay limped away into the kitchen, leaning heavily on his umbrella. "Would the girls like a snack?" he called back as he went, hating how inane his words felt.

Kylie said, "Yeah!"

"No, we're fine," said Sashi.

He opened the refrigerator and found the detritus of an old man living ten years alone — condiments, old cheese, and a leftover take-out. Closing the door, he leaned his forehead against the cool surface. No. Of course, he didn't have food for them. He didn't have anything for them.

"Papa?" Sashi stood in the kitchen doorway.

Ajay pasted a proud smile on his face. "It's so good to see you, dear." He opened the fridge and pulled out the old hunk of cheese. It wasn't all mold, so he took it out and set it on the cutting board. With his sharpest knife, he carved the bad pieces off of the cheese and sliced the rest into thin strips. Sashi watched him, leaning against the door jamb, a fair imitation of a relaxed posture, but she was a coiled spring ready to snap.

"You haven't seen this house, have you?" Ajay asked. He gestured at the kitchen with his knife. "I've done quite well with it, I think."

"Yes," Sashi said. "It's very nice."

"How are things?" he asked. "Are you employed?"

"Trevan Pharmaceuticals," she said. "It's fine." She crossed her arms.

Ajay stopped his knife halfway through the cheese. He shot her a sideways glance. The Sashi he remembered was outgoing and talkative. A force in any room. Yet there she was,

22

hardly saying a word. Something had her rattled, but was it an external danger, or was she reacting to him? He wanted to comfort her, tell her that she didn't need to worry about him, that he would accept her no matter what.

But those were hard words to form.

The crackers in his cupboard were mostly stale, but one sealed package hid in the back. He took it, sliced it open, and placed it with the cheese on a plate.

"You're always welcome here," he said.

She let him pass back into the living room, and he set the tray down on the coffee table. He felt her eyes on his back and couldn't help but feel the weight of her stare. What did she think of this old man living in this smelly old house?

Garrison lifted his head from Isabelle to look dolefully at the cheese. Ajay clicked his tongue to warn the dog off, at least long enough for Kylie to get a chance to grab a few pieces.

"Papa," Sashi said behind him, quieter now.

He searched her sunken eyes for clues but found none. "We may need to order out for supper."

Her back stiffened. "We need your help."

A long time passed while he tried to form words to respond. Even after he had words, they refused to form on his lips without his voice threatening to crack. "What is it, dear?" he finally said.

"Nothing," she said. "I need you to watch the girls, just until I get back from an errand."

"I won't have these girls starving, and I've just— it's grocery shopping day and I haven't gone yet." Never mind that his cupboards were always this bare. The grocery store frightened him. His head had trouble wrapping around the idea of Sashi asking for help.

Sashi motioned for him to return with her to the kitchen. Once they were alone, she said, in a more authoritative voice, "I'd rather not draw attention."

He watched her expression for a long time, trying to read something in it. He had never been able to really understand his little girl, and now that she was full-grown, she seemed an impenetrable barrier of severity. She asked for help, but the edge in her voice warned him not to get too involved.

"You know what I can do, Sashi," he said. "I can do more to help than watch the girls."

"But I'm not asking you to do any more."

"Is someone after you?"

Her brow furrowed. "People aren't so easy to fool with your NSA tricks these days."

"You think my skills are obsolete," he said, sounding more hurt than he wanted to show.

Sashi's jaw hardened, but she didn't respond.

"Why me?" he asked.

"I had no choice."

He rubbed the bridge of his nose in an attempt to placate a headache. "No choice, no choice. I'm the very last person you wanted to see, then?"

She shook her head. "Second to last."

In the other room, Kylie shouted, "He's sitting on me! Ahh, he's sitting on me!" Followed by a wave of giggles. Ajay poked his head into the other room to discover that, yes, Garrison had indeed decided to sit on the kid. In fact, he found a way to sprawl across both of the girls at the same time, giving Kylie the head and Isabelle the rear.

He met Sashi's gaze for a moment. "You should have come sooner," he said. "You could have written to me about your daughters."

Her jaw tightened.

"What?" Ajay's voice came out too loud. Too aggressive. "Do you want to accuse me of something?"

Sashi's nostrils flared, but her voice calmed when she spoke. "It should only be for a few hours."

He shook his head, feeling deflated.

"What?" Sashi said.

"I once knew a girl that age—" he gestured at the girls with his knife "—who got herself stuck in a tree and broke a leg rather than ask for help."

Sashi's expression hardened. "That girl grew up," she said through her teeth. "People do that."

Had it been so long that he no longer knew his own daughter? Had he ever really known her? "Are you hiding them from someone? The father?" He gestured again with the knife.

Sashi gently but firmly took the knife from him and set it with the mountain of dirty dishes on the counter. Ajay peered at it, not entirely sure why he had held onto it for so long.

Kylie poked her head around the corner.

Ajay smiled, blinking back tears he hadn't known he had. "How are you doing in there, Kylie."

She held up the photograph he had specifically told her not to touch, pointing to one of the figures in it. "Is this you?"

Sashi shot her a dark look that dissolved to nothing in an instant. Ajay wondered at the meaning of the look, but Kylie didn't seem to pick up on it at all.

"That's me, all right," Ajay said of the picture. "That was my team the day I quit my job at the NSA."

"What's the NSA?" Kylie looked up from the picture but didn't set it down.

Ajay shot Sashi a quick look, but she avoided his gaze. "Well, Kylie, that's probably a story for another time. We worked with computers and tried to save people's lives." He cleared his throat. "Among other things."

Kylie, seemingly satisfied with the answer, returned to the living room, and Ajay followed. She showed the picture to her sister, who gave no response. Isabelle shot Ajay a quick glance, but her icy eyes held no hint of her emotions. He managed a weak smile in return.

"Why are you living here, Papa?" Sashi asked.

His stomach turned. He sat heavily in his chair and waved for her to take the other seat, which she did. "It's not bad here."

"You're hiding." She gestured dismissively before he could protest. "I've watched you, Papa. I know you're still hiding. Why live in this town full of white Scandinavians, where you know you'll stand out?"

"There are Germans, too," he said. When she didn't show any sign of amusement, he continued. "It's not as white as it used to be, and I'm as much Minnesotan as anyone here. Liz—" The name of his late wife caught in his throat, but he corrected and continued. "Your mother is buried close. You might not remember her, but she still means a lot to me."

Sashi shook her head. "You could live in Florida."

"Florida is where folks my age go to die. They have nursing homes and tourist traps. Here, I'm fifty miles from the Mayo Clinic, sixty miles from the Silicon Valley of med-tech, and a thousand miles from anyone who'd care enough to try to find me. Life expectancy of someone in my demographic is in the upper nineties, and I expect to make the most of it."

"By golfing for another twenty years?"

"I gave up golf."

"Minnesota is a lot closer to Iowa, too, isn't it?"

Ajay tried to keep the scowl from his face. "What's that to do with anything?" As if he didn't know.

"You knew I went to work for the Trevan lab in Ames twenty years ago, didn't you? You never could keep from spying on me."

Ajay pressed his lips into a thin line, unwilling to try to defend himself. His inability to keep from meddling in her life was the very reason she'd left in the first place. He finally said, "I didn't know you had daughters." It was the truth.

"Isabelle is special. She's lived on lab property all her life, and there was no reason to share information about her to the rest of the world."

Ajay lowered his voice so he was sure the girls wouldn't hear in the other room. "She looks like you, but she doesn't. I don't know genetics, but her hair is too light, and can her eyes be that color if she's yours?"

Sashi's eyes wouldn't meet his. Instead, she looked intently at the vivid photograph of Pebble Beach covering his tabletop computer. "You gave up golf?"

"I had to."

That startled her. "Really? You always loved golf."

Ajay felt older than he ever had. "The scores kept going higher. All my life I worked to get a decent score and a powerful swing. Now — I'm not what I used to be."

"So why bother."

"The numbers only remind me of what I've lost."

"I'll be gone a couple hours at most," said Sashi, standing up from the table. She rested a hand on her father's shoulder. "Just keep them off the radar."

Ajay sighed. "That's fine." He ate a bit of the cheese, tasting nothing in the flavorless lump. "Fine."

Despite the protest of his joints, Ajay stood and moved into the room with his two granddaughters. He plopped down in his lounger while Sashi used a sleek fidget with gold-trimmed edges to pull up a map of Red Wing. Holographic images projected above the back of her hand as her polished nails tapped the controls.

Kylie watched Ajay. He felt her eyes peering at him as she sat quietly next to her sister. From time to time, Kylie would open her mouth as if to speak, but then she would shut it again. He narrowed his eyes, trying to think of some topic she might find interesting, but coming up short. Finally, he said, "You golf?"

She shook her head.

"Ever think to try?"

Again, no.

Ajay nodded at Isabelle. "She talk much?"

"Not any more," said Kylie. She began to say more, but Sashi shot her an expression bristling with warnings. "She sometimes still talks."

"That's enough, Kylie," Sashi said. Then, to Ajay, "A couple hours."

Ajay started to climb his way out of the good lounger, but Sashi waved him back down. He gratefully slumped back.

"I won't be long," Sashi said, glancing at her handheld display. She drew a long silk wrap from her purse, draping it over her shoulders and head. "Did you have plans for the day?"

"You're looking at 'em."

Sashi rolled her eyes. "Always the social butterfly, right, Papa?"

He shrugged.

"Can you really handle the girls for me? For a few hours?" Her expression spoke of more desperation than Ajay thought necessary.

"Of course," Ajay said, because, well, of course. He desperately wanted to ask her everything. Where had she been for twenty years? Who were these daughters, and why didn't he know about them? Was she well? Was something bad happening? Something dangerous for the girls? Was she married? Divorced? Remarried? All he said was, "Of course," again. That was all he really needed to say.

Sashi bid the girls goodbye, pulled her hood over her face, and ducked out the back door.

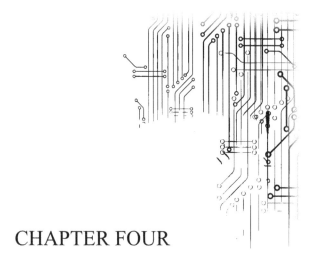

CHAPTER FOUR

"Stop touching that," Ajay said.

Kylie touched it.

The "it" in question changed, but the conversation stayed the same. She messed with photographs, old microchip breadboards, the window shades, a ceramic owl that young Sashi had once brought home from school, a mousetrap. Ajay itched every time she touched something of his. She wasn't careful. Not at all. Over his years of living alone, he had become very accustomed to having things just so. He had friends, of course, but he never brought them home. Not here.

Throughout the day, she touched every single thing in his small home, and Garrison watched her the entire time. His head cocked to one side when she found a black remote control during a particularly adventurous mining excursion into his couch.

"What's this?" Kylie asked.

Ajay raised an eyebrow, suspecting a trick question. "A remote," he said. "For changing channels on the television."

Isabelle craned her neck to see the TV. It played some awful video full of flashing colors and a terrible, terrible mockery of music.

"What's wrong with your TV?" Kylie asked.

"Nothing's wrong with it."

She waved her hand in the air in a universal signal that should have brought up the TV's menu. "It doesn't work."

"That's because I've covered the motion sensor."

"Why?" Kylie pushed numbers on the remote. The station changed to a soap with two men arguing about something in Spanish.

"I don't like it watching me."

Kylie scrunched up her face. "It worked for Isa."

Ajay didn't bother explaining that it couldn't possibly have worked for her. Gesture controls on his television had been disabled since the day he bought it. A black piece of tape still stuck to the sensor. Ajay scratched his mustache. How had she changed the channel?

Isabelle made a frustrated noise, scowling at Ajay. He stepped to the side so she could see.

"Well, she needs to use the remote to change the channel." He reached to take the remote from Kylie's hand, but she jumped away.

Kylie mashed buttons, bringing up a menu. "What's this do?" She took another step back.

Isabelle punched her in the hip, a sharp, forceful blow.

"Ow!" Kylie dropped the remote, which popped against the coffee table, sending shards of plastic flying.

"Dammit," Ajay said, then realized he was swearing at his only granddaughters. "It's fine," he said, though his grumbling tone said otherwise. The menu disappeared from the television screen, and the terrible music started again, forcing him to raise his voice. "The remote is the only way to change the channel."

"But why?" Kylie asked.

Ajay snapped up the remains of the remote and jabbed its buttons, bringing up a children's show. Fuzzy bears danced to an obnoxious tune.

Kylie frowned at the bears. "We're not babies."

He shoved the remote her way. "No major networks," he said. "They know my patterns."

Isabelle rolled her eyes in that way teenage girls do best. It made Ajay's chest hurt a little, remembering Sashi at that age. It was harder to remember a time when Sashi took him seriously. Maybe at Kylie's age, she had, but even then, he wasn't sure. Ajay left the girls in the room and took his tray of cheese and crackers back to the kitchen. He set it down on the counter next to the dirty dish mountain, shoving the lot to the back so they didn't get in the way when he wanted to clear more plates later. That was thinking ahead. Wisdom of old age, that was. Ajay smiled to himself.

Garrison lumbered into the room and Ajay sat at the kitchen table so he could better scratch the dog between the ears. "What do you think, fella?" he asked. "Those girls going to be trouble?"

The dog didn't appear to have an opinion one way or the other, so long as the scratches continued. Ajay thought that was likely a good sign.

Kylie came into the room a few minutes later and sat in the only other spot at the kitchen table. She rested her chin in her hands and looked up at Ajay.

"What?" he asked.

"We're bored."

"Do you play Go?"

Kylie shook her head.

"Your mother never taught you Go?" Ajay scratched his head. "She used to be pretty good. Almost beat me sometimes. Go's a more elegant game than chess. Prettier, too."

"We play Parcheesi."

Ajay shuddered. "She would teach you Parcheesi."

They sat in silence for a while. In the other room, the TV blared. Ajay recognized one of the networks and the sound of their jingle sent shivers down his spine. He grumbled and moved back into the other room.

"Shut it off," he said to Isabelle.

She ignored him, psychotic rainbow colors washing over her from the over-hyper television screen. Her expression remained impassive as she bathed in the shocking media noise.

"Your mother said someone was looking for you," Ajay said. His hands felt clammy. "If anyone's really looking, then they'll know my television hasn't played this channel in a decade. They'll hear the noise and notice the change. A broken pattern always means something's up. If they're looking, then you'll be found within the hour." He picked up the remote, earning a glare from Isabelle. "Unless you watch golf."

He changed the channel. Rather than leave her the remote, he crammed it into his pocket. "Just... Listen to me," he sputtered. "I don't know what your mother has told you, but I know a thing or two about how this works."

Kylie placed a hand on his. Her touch was warm and dry. "Do you want to play Go?" she asked.

Ajay bit back the momentum of a growing lecture. Isabelle wasn't listening, anyway. She watched golf with the same expression she had turned toward her video. He nodded to Kylie, pulling his board and pieces from the cupboard. "Go's the simplest game there is," he said.

"Parcheesi is pretty simple."

"Shush." He placed a few pieces down, black, then white, then black again. "Surround a piece or group of pieces and you capture them. Surround an area to control the board. Easy as that."

Kylie scrunched up her nose. "So I just capture all your pieces?"

"Nope," he said. "Smart players don't have to capture a lot of pieces to win. It's all about territory. If you get all worked up about catching all the pieces, you'll miss out on actually winning."

Garrison shifted, slumping up against Ajay's legs.

"What should I call you?" Kylie asked. "Grandpa?"

Ajay grunted. "Grandpa sounds too old. Just call me Papa. Or Ajay." He set up the board while Kylie watched, and drew a black token from the bowl and played the first piece in a corner. "Mr. Andersen is fine if you don't want to get too familiar. What did your mother tell you about me?"

She played a piece in the middle of the board, apparently not thinking through her strategy.

"What do you like to do at home?" Ajay played another piece next to his other one.

Kylie narrowed her eyes, then played a piece next to her first. Maybe she was thinking after all.

"You'll want to watch your liberties," Ajay said as he placed another piece, conservatively growing his territory. "Those are the spots adjacent to your pieces that are still open. They are your ways out, and if you find you're down to only one, then you're in trouble."

She played another piece next to her own.

He placed a piece next to hers, eliciting a scalding glare. "Do you watch those videos like your sister?" Try as he might, he couldn't shake the feeling that he was losing this game. Not the game of Go, but the game of trying to get a young girl to open up to him. He'd been a father, raised a girl on his own, and never really gotten good at it.

They played several turns while he slowly surrounded her pieces, and she retaliated by engulfing his. He came out ahead with every exchange, but she kept playing and continued to improve.

"We're not supposed to tell you anything," she said quietly, placing a white piece near one of his blacks.

"You can tell me what you like to eat."

She thought about it long and hard. "Ice cream."

"Chocolate?"

"Mama only buys chocolate."

Ajay nodded sagely. "That sounds about right. No reason to buy any other kind. Am I right?" He played a piece, setting up a big move for her that she wouldn't be able to resist.

Kylie peered at the board for a long time, then played somewhere else, blocking the retaliatory move he had been planning.

"You're the clever one, aren't you?" he asked.

She shook her head. "That's Isabelle."

"Well, maybe I should play against her sometime." He played another piece.

"You probably wouldn't like it."

He raised an eyebrow. "Oh? Why not?"

"She'd beat you." Kylie said it with a dead seriousness that took Ajay aback. It wasn't that Kylie thought her sister was good at Go, though that was interesting. What made him wonder was the fact that Kylie knew how competitive he was. He'd never let Sashi win at a single thing when she was growing up. He didn't believe in going easy on kids just because they were kids. It didn't serve them at all in the end.

He didn't go easy on Kylie, either, but she did well considering the circumstances. When they had finished tallying the score, he stuck out his hand. "Good game," he said.

She shook it. "Good game, Papa. Next time I won't go easy on you."

Before he could find the words to respond, she walked into the other room to curl up next to her sister with an old magazine from Ajay's shelf.

Isabelle shut off the TV and the tiny house fell into a deep silence. The older girl sat with the shadow of a scowl on her face, just enough to keep Ajay from trying to approach. It reminded him of when he'd been a single working father raising Sashi all on his own. Only now, these girls outnumbered him.

Ajay poked around in the refrigerator. There wasn't anything good to feed the two girls. Hell, there wasn't even anything good to feed himself. How long had Sashi said the girls would be here? Ajay wanted to get to know them. After all, they were his grandchildren. But he was tired. He went into the living room where the TV lay dormant and Isabelle sat still staring at its black expanse. He waited for a sign of life until finally she blinked and looked back at him. She was in his favorite lounger, so he settled into the sofa with its cracked faux leather and uneven springs.

"It's been nice of you to visit," he said. His mouth was dry. He pressed his palms against his eyes. Age didn't suit him well. The aches and weaknesses, exhaustion nagging at him, but worst was the lack of purpose. He'd lived his life. Now was just the long wait 'til the end. Until recently he'd been able to play golf, but with the hip...

His hands rested on his belly, and he didn't bother to reopen his eyes for a long time.

The whip-snap rap like a weapon at the door tore him hard out of a sleep he hadn't known he was having.

The sun hung low in the sky. Where were the girls?

He grasped at the question for a moment before remembering his visiting granddaughters. Where was Sashi? She should have been back hours ago. Where were the girls?

"Papa?" Kylie's voice drifted in from the kitchen. There was light there, just a single bulb, a dim incandescent, not the always-online ones that were so popular these days.

Ajay rose, joints popping as he moved. Garrison struggled up as well, staying close at his side. The rap-rap-rap came at the door again, and an instinctive adrenaline coursed through Ajay's veins. The knocking wasn't so loud any more, and Ajay wondered how his sleep might have distorted the noise. Maybe it was Sashi.

"Girls," he said, bursting into the kitchen. They were in the middle of a Go game, and Isabelle was doing quite well. "It's time for us to get out of here."

Isabelle's mouth hung open.

Ajay gave her a dry look and she withered under it. She stood, gathered herself with the dignity expected of a queen, and raised an eyebrow at Ajay.

"We'll go out the back," he said. Without waiting for a response, he ducked into his bedroom where he already had a pack with a few supplies, medicines, and some clothes. He checked the pockets and verified everything was where it needed to be. Various pockets held different kinds of cash, from the old-style paper dollars, to coins, to Canadian currency, to several clips of the newer crystal chits. He rolled one of the clear, rectangular crystals between his thumb and forefinger. Untraceable currency was worth keeping around. Always.

The rap-rap came again — but was cut short as the door opened.

The hum of a drone sent shivers down Ajay's spine. Its bone-piercing buzz came through the wide-open door. He pressed himself hard against the bedroom wall, not daring to poke his head out to see what was happening. They'd been found. Kylie had opened the door, allowing the surveillance of the outside world in. He swallowed back his fear. Someone had to do something about this. There would be video to disrupt and delete.

Then the door closed. The aroma of hot cheese and burned pepperoni suffused the house. Pizza.

Ajay burst back into the kitchen. "You ordered pizza?"

Isabelle shrugged, eyes twinkling.

Kylie said, "Isabelle has her own crystal kit back home, so she grew her own money."

When digital currency collapsed a decade ago, one of several replacements for the bitcoin was a carbon crystal currency that could be grown in a moderately complex lab. Similar to the bitcoin, its value was inherent in the resources and time required to produce it. Since there was no central mint, counterfeiting was built into the system's growth. It had become one of the more reliable forms of currency, and it made sense that the girls would carry some.

Ajay sputtered, his face reddening with the pure shock of what those girls had done. Didn't they know how the world worked? "Isabelle," he said, forcing his voice to be calm. "We can't do things like this. They'll see the change in pattern. If they look, they're going to find us."

Isabelle's voice came light but strong. "I was hungry."

"We're always being watched, Isabelle. Always." Ajay watched the girl closely for any kind of reaction. She'd talked. Could this be her opening up, or was she just hungry?

She shrugged, apparently not caring at all one way or the other.

Kylie said, "I kept my hood up, so it couldn't see me." Indeed, the hood of her sweater was lined with beads that would disrupt most video surveillance.

Kylie opened the box and picked out a piece of pizza. When Ajay glared at her, she cocked her head to one side and raised an eyebrow.

"Soon as someone smart starts really looking, that's not going to do you any good at all," Ajay said. He chewed on his lip for a minute, trying to think of something that wouldn't sound absolutely batshit paranoid. "We're going for a little trip."

"But—" Kylie started to protest.

Isabelle met his gaze and for a fraction of a second, he thought they had a moment of silent communication. Normal, open emotion flashed across her face: a soft displeasure that told him he better not screw this up because it might be his only chance ever to connect with this granddaughter.

Ajay took a piece of pizza from the box. It was greasy and cheap, but his stomach rumbled. "After we eat."

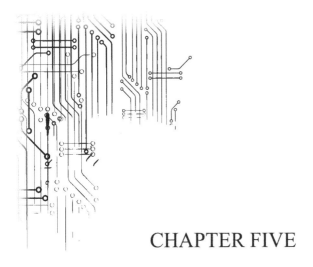

CHAPTER FIVE

Isabelle raised one eyebrow at Ajay's car; her lip twitched in the faintest hint of disgust. The vehicle's cracked blue body proudly bore the corrosion of twenty harsh Minnesota winters. Layers of dust and grime that coated its surface hid what shine might have been left in its dark windshield. Even the headlights bore age poorly; one was cracked and filled with the nest of some rodent or bird.

Ajay unclipped the charger, and the car lit up in the double blink that showed a full charge. The batteries couldn't hold power like they used to, but they kept him moving. The car would get them around town without complaining too much, and it was one of the few vehicles Ajay trusted not to spy on him. Much.

When he opened the garage door, a cold wind swirled through his cluttered garage. Ajay grabbed a long overcoat from the hook by the door, shaking the dust off it. He wanted the extra layer of protection from the weather, but also the extra pockets made him feel safe. The diamond-optical box fit snugly into one, and his fidget computer landed where he could have quick access. He grabbed a multitool from the shelf in the garage and stuffed it into another pocket. It never hurt to be prepared, and there was no telling when he might need a wimpy pliers or undersized screwdriver.

He held a door open for the girls and they climbed in, leaving fingerprints in the caked-on dust. Kylie smiled and wrote a big K in the windshield, but Ajay erased it. The inside of the car held four seats, two of them facing forward and two facing back. It was one of the second-wave all-automatic cars, and its cracked seats, dented panels, and scratched windshield made a grand show of its age. Garrison climbed in and sat on the ragged seat next to him.

"We're going to go visit Olivia, a friend of mine," Ajay said.

Kylie said, "A girl friend?"

"She's a woman, and no, nothing like that." When Kylie didn't seem convinced, he added, "We're bridge partners and there's nothing more between us," which didn't appear to convince Kylie at all.

Kylie said, "Mama says it's safer to sit facing backward."

"You'll stay with my friend, and I'll go see about finding your mother."

"I heard that a seatbelt can break your ribs if it's not on right." Kylie eyed Ajay's seatbelt suspiciously.

Isabelle chewed her lip.

Ajay pinched the bridge of his nose. "If I'm going to die in a crash, I want to see it coming."

"Well," Kylie said, in what must have been her best imitation of her mother, "I hope this car has the latest software updates." She called to Garrison and he crossed the car to sit at her feet, resting his head in her lap.

Ajay elected not to tell her the car hadn't been updated since it went out of warranty seventeen years prior. The software had worked just fine back then and it would keep right on working. That way he could keep it disconnected from the network entirely, so long as he didn't feel like taking any new roads.

The car rolled through Red Wing. They rode across the tops of bluffs nestled into the red-orange glow of autumn.

Below, the Mississippi rolled by, its dark waters smooth in the cool calm of the afternoon. It cut a line through the pale white parks veined with reflective white asphalt. The light roads and pale plants had once been meant to buffer the world against climate change by reflecting light rather than absorbing it. Debates still raged about whether or not it had helped, but nobody argued that the genetic changes coded into cover crops had escaped into the native populations, sometimes via cross-species viral transfer. White-streaked maples lined the streets next to too-pale grasses.

People walked the streets, crossing in groups in the carefree way that people always had. Did they know about the drones watching from overhead? Did anyone even care? Their town had changed little over the years, but cameras studded every street corner from Historic Main to the top of Memorial Hill. Eyes watched from the sky. Ajay pulled the hood over his head, even though he knew the watching eyes from above couldn't penetrate his tinted glass.

A muscle in Ajay's neck twitched painfully, and he covered the wince by scratching at it. His palms went greasy with sweat and his mouth went dry. The deep sense of being watched crept over him, tightening his chest. Every time he left the house, he felt like eyes everywhere were watching him. The oppressive sense of being seen seized him. He almost ordered the car to turn around and take them back to the safety of his house. It was the one place he knew he'd be alone.

But he wasn't alone. He reminded himself of that. The girls needed him. He eyed them, watching as Isabelle stared wistfully out the window. Kylie looked everywhere, scanning their surroundings like a curious puppy. She couldn't pick a window to stare out of, as if she wanted to watch everything out of all of them.

Highway 61 took them to the northern half of town, where towering apartment buildings stabbed the sky high above withered oaks, their dark silhouettes hacking the stark blue into bite-sized chunks.

Olivia lived in one of those buildings, low-income apartments that were run down the minute they were built.

Those who lived in these towering wrecks were there because there was nowhere else to go. It was better than the streets. Marginally.

The car pulled up to a dark gray building at the very edge of town. The only thing farther north were the old Towerview and miles and miles of empty forest. The car's maps didn't know about these apartment buildings and warnings flashed across the rudimentary display. Still, holding down the override, Ajay was able to direct the car through a glaring white parking lot past blowing garbage into a parking ramp that led down under the building. Ajay would have preferred parking on the street but didn't have the energy to bother. Once the car had parked deep below ground, he picked up his umbrella and handed it to the girls.

"Use this," he said.

Kylie's brow scrunched up. "Is it raining in here?"

Ajay shook his head. "Your mother said to keep you out of sight. That means blocking cameras as best we can."

He pulled the hood of his hoodie closer, so that his face disappeared under its folds, and stepped out of the car. It wouldn't hide him from everything, but it was the best he had.

The girls disappeared under the umbrella, which was another black-and-white squid design. Garrison followed close at their heels, as if he, too, needed the shelter it provided. In the elevator, Kylie poked Isabelle in the ribs hard enough to make her cough. Isabelle fought back by slowly pressing Kylie into the corner until Kylie had absolutely no space to move. Kylie shouted in protest. Still, Ajay ignored them. He took a roll of electrical tape from his pocket and covered the cameras.

"All right," he said, trying to keep the annoyance from his voice. "You can put down the umbrella."

"Are the men done watching us on the cameras?" Kylie asked.

"Worse than men," said Ajay before he could stop himself. "Computers."

Isabelle rolled her eyes.

The elevator door opened to a dimly lit hallway. The carpet's crisscross pattern of reds and blues ran the flickering length of the building. The busy, irritating pattern probably served to hide dozens of ugly stains, but there were plenty that it failed to conceal. Ajay took his umbrella back from the girls and used it as a walking stick. It was sturdy enough and would do in a pinch since he had forgotten his good cane back at home.

"Follow me, ladies," he said. He quickly checked the cameras in the hall, noting that they all bore the telltale marks of heavy vandalism. A smile tugged at the corners of his mouth. It was nice to see the building's residents had their priorities straight.

Ajay used the handle of his umbrella to tap gently on the seventh door on the left, then he waited. Garrison sat, head cocked to one side. Isabelle leaned against the opposite wall while Kylie ran the length of the hallway over and over again.

Olivia Bjørnson threw open the door like she was challenging the world to dare step up. Her imposing frame filled the doorway, and her silver mane was streaked with green and splayed around her head in a display of defiant chaos. In one hand, she held a dented aluminum baseball bat, which she tapped rhythmically against the doorframe.

She flashed straight, white teeth. "Who the hell are you?" she asked, looking Ajay in the eyes.

Ajay raised his eyebrows at her, hands on his hips. He waited as she looked him up and down, taking him in with a serious expression.

Then she broke into a wide smile. "Come on in, Ajay. I didn't know you were coming." She gave Garrison a little pat on the head.

Ajay hissed to get Kylie's attention. When that didn't work, he rapped his umbrella on the door. She looked his way from where she was trying to scale the narrow hallway walls by pressing against one side with her feet and the other with her hands. When she looked, her balance went off and she toppled to the ground. Isabelle pushed past Olivia into the apartment, and Kylie ran to catch up.

Olivia's apartment smelled like potpourri and cookies. Minnesota Public Radio played in a low hum behind the working buzz of the apartment's heater. A hazy light filtered in through her west-facing window, the last hints of the dying sunset. Olivia's living room wasn't exactly cluttered in the way that the ocean wasn't exactly wet. Her shelves of books, magazines, and wood-carved owls formed a maze which Ajay navigated on his way to the familiar couch. It was cozy there, and when he sat he understood why she lived in such close spaces. It felt safe.

"You girls like snickerdoodles?" Olivia asked.

They did, as it turned out. Once they were situated at the table, Olivia sidled up next to Ajay.

"New radio?" Ajay asked.

"No, hon, I've always had that."

"Is it connected?"

"It's antique, so you just shush about robots watching you all the time. This radio's safe."

Tension in his shoulders eased. He sat at her kitchen table and rubbed his eyes with the heels of his hands. "How did your appointment go?"

"It went as those things do."

A timer buzzed, and Olivia stood to fetch more cookies from the oven. She poked at one of the brown and white swirls, testing that they were done. When they passed her inspection, she set them on the range and turned off the oven.

She turned back to him and must have seen the exhaustion written on his face. She gestured at him with a spatula. "You look like you have something on your mind. What is it this time? They double the Thunderhead drone coverage or something?"

He grumbled.

"New cameras out on the golf range watching you putt?"

"I don't golf anymore," he said. She knew it was a sore spot for him, and he harbored a little resentment that she would bring it up. "But yes, they are adding more cameras, and there's no need for it."

She scrunched up her face. "But what has you bothered?" Leaning over to see the two girls in her living room, she said, "Certainly not those lovely girls."

Kylie bumped a tall glass vase, which fell to the carpeted floor with a heavy thump.

"Sorry," Kylie called. She looked accusingly at her sister. "Sorry!"

Ajay gave a wan smile. "I need your help, Liv."

She raised an eyebrow.

He pulled his hood back and looked her right in the eyes. "They're my granddaughters," he said.

Olivia blinked. "Granddaughters? Oh, honey, I didn't even know you had any." She tossed a snickerdoodle in the air and Garrison caught it before it landed.

"Sashi stopped by earlier today. She had to step out and said she'd be back in a couple hours, but it's been longer and—" He glanced at the clock on the wall. "I'm worried."

Olivia took one of his hands in hers. Her warmth soothed his sore knuckles. "I've never seen you worried about anything, Ajay."

"You've never seen me with my daughter around."

Olivia sighed. "I suppose she dodges cameras about as compulsively as her dad?"

Ajay felt a swell of pride. "I suppose she does." Ajay wished he knew who she was trying to avoid. "I'd like to go out looking, but I got the impression she didn't want the girls out and about."

Olivia sighed. "Ajay..."

"It's only for a little while." He touched the back of her hand. "Please, Olivia."

She met his gaze, hard at first, but then her bright green eyes softened and he knew he had her. A pang of guilt tugged at his chest. He had no doubt that she could take care of the girls, but what if she'd had other plans for the evening? What right did he have to impose on her? He swore to himself that he would make it up to her. Somehow.

"Call me if anything looks sketchy," he said.

"Are you still doing that thing with your identity?"

He rattled off his ID so that she would know what number to call. It changed every day according to a pattern that only he knew, and if she was going to contact him outside of his house, she would need it. "I'll be back soon," he said. "I promise."

Ajay navigated the maze of Olivia's apartment, making his way to where the girls perused a leaning bookshelf. He reached out to touch Isabelle on the shoulder, but pulled up short, not knowing how the girl would react to such a familiar touch. She didn't know him, and although he was starting to feel like she might really be long-lost family, he had no way of knowing if she felt the same. Hell, for all he knew, she was afraid of him. He cleared his throat.

Kylie poked her head around the corner of the bookshelf to peek at him. Isabelle cocked her head to the side but otherwise didn't speak.

"I'll be back soon," he said. Isabelle's shoulders slumped a fraction of an inch, and never had so slight a gesture broken Ajay's heart so thoroughly. He'd made the wrong choice, and it broke what shred of trust he'd built with her. "Your mother has been gone too long, and I need to look for her."

When he didn't get a response from Isabelle and Kylie retreated behind the bookshelf, he pulled his hood down over his face and ventured out into the world.

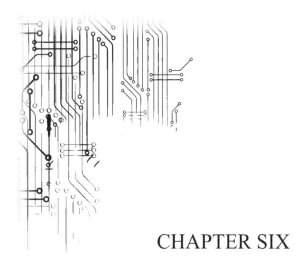

CHAPTER SIX

Invisibility was a form of art. When every camera, every motion sensor, every advertisement billboard detected the identity of every person to pass by, walking from one side of town to the other was waving a big old flag printed with name, birthdate, and Social Security number. The few unmonitored corners sat like islands in a storm-tossed ocean.

Yet Sashi remained hidden. Ajay found hints of her passing. Complaints of scramblers and dampers trailed through town, but the lag was such that he couldn't find a good pattern. What was she looking for? She'd visited Red Wing Shoes, the factory in the north side of town, but to what end? Did she expect to find something there other than steel-toed boots and loafers of exceptional quality? The southern part of town, where the tech installations grew like barnacles from the banks of the Mississippi, had seen the grace of her touch more than once throughout the day. She'd returned to the towering biotech buildings over and over, sometimes to the same ones twice. Or, at least, it seemed she did. Following her path was like tracking rabbits during a heavy snowstorm.

Ajay sat in the run-down fast food joint overlooking the humming Highway 61. The greasy aroma of burgers and cheese curds soaked into every surface of the place, giving it a rancid slick-to-the-touch feel that reminded Ajay of freshly polished shoes. The corner spot near the back offered a view of the parking lot, the highway, and both entrances. The surly clientele never grew into a large crowd, but never disappeared entirely, either. Ajay liked the place for only one reason: the video surveillance was crude, disconnected, and probably fake. It was one of the few places in town where he could sit undisturbed and unwatched.

It wasn't as though Sashi were the only person in town scrambling signals. After all, illegal activity still had to exist in some form, and when contraband changed hands, a rash of signal jamming reports broke out in the surrounding area. In all cases, the sky became the enemy, and so it did for Sashi.

Drones came in three varieties. First, there were the low-flyers. These hummed around close enough to touch, so long as the person touching didn't mind being chopped to pieces with rotor blades and lawsuits. These were mostly harmless surveillance, wandering the city to deliver goods, fill gaps for police or security guards, and provide a general nuisance for well-meaning people like Ajay. Most people disliked this kind of drone most because it was the one they could see and hear. They were fools.

Higher in the sky, at the very edge of the visible distance, flew the mid-level drones. Those drones provided up-to-date mapping information, imaging sharp enough for facial recognition, and first responder services for any detected injuries.

The Thunderhead drones higher above worried Ajay the most. They were an annoyance and a real problem to anyone trying to stay hidden. Thunderheads flew far above the range of sight and were often hard to spot even with the appropriate equipment. They watched from high enough to provide micro-weather reports as if people needed to know the exact weather in their exact location at some exact point in the future. They couldn't manage facial recognition, but there were systems of body mechanic recognition that allowed them to identify people with near-fingerprint precision.

Also, Thunderheads carried missiles.

Safety and security being a concern, none of the drones ever connected their steering or their weapons to any kind of network. They always behaved in pre-programmed ways based on complex cognitive systems and internal calculations. They used an entirely different sensor array for steering than they did for spying, and that meant they could beam info down to earth without compromising the solid security gap they needed in order to avoid the whims of the writhing mass of humanity that would probably crash the drone into the nearest available Mississippi River.

Or worse.

A motley group of teenagers came into the restaurant. They all wore something to mess up facial recognition. One greasy boy had so many eyebrow studs Ajay doubted his own mother would recognize him. Most wore face paint of one kind or another, with the fashion trending toward henna-like patterns around the eyes and down along the cheekbones. These cheap tricks might fool cursory scans but would falter upon deeper analysis. Ajay doubted the kids knew the details of it. After all, it was only fashion to most of those punks.

Ajay didn't need to steer any drones, and he didn't have any use for their weapons systems. All he wanted was a look through the flying spyglass down at the town below and to steal some computing power to do some quick detective work. Getting in wasn't hard. When quantum computing had brought down all the old encryption algorithms, what had remained was a thin veneer of computer security. He could get in.

Staying anonymous was the tricky part.

Using his fidget, Ajay triggered some burner routines: one-off programs designed to cover his tracks. It wouldn't buy him a lot of time, but it'd keep him safe for a few minutes. Once that activated, he formed an image link to the drones surrounding the city. There were a few major private hubs, the police hub, and a military hub. They all fell quickly, and only the military hub had anything resembling a true digital defense. He routed the image systems to facial and body mechanics recognition service, focusing the processing on locations that he thought most likely to find her.

Then he waited.

The teenagers left, but more customers filtered in. The restaurant grew busier, and Ajay had to adjust his hearing aid so it wouldn't pick up their conversations.

Minutes passed, and Ajay ate his greasy cheeseburger as his program ran. The burner routines' cover slowly eroded, with the cognitive defense network slowly adapting to his techniques. He swiped at the display, leaving a streak of grease across the back of his hand. The routine was failing faster than he expected, and the recognition software still hadn't found anything. He swore and deployed another routine. His supply was running low, each one representing hours or even days of programming.

Ajay refocused the recognition routines, narrowing in on the Thunderheads. Sashi could scramble anything close, but she would have trouble blocking anything so far away. If she did, the fingerprints left by that interference would be easy for him to spot unless she used a burner routine like his own. Keeping that up for any amount of time was simply impractical.

Someone sat across from him at the table. Ajay scowled, not willing to take his eyes off the display.

"Spot's taken," Ajay said. "Go sit somewhere else." By the background noise, he could tell the place was getting busy.

"Looks like you know what you're doing," said the man across from him.

He glanced up. The man looking back at him filled his half of the table. His great, shaggy beard spilled out over a beaten leather jacket, streaks of brown and gray mixing at the tips. The man had a stocking cap pulled down over his head and a toothpick sticking out of his mouth. Black ink lines ran from below his eyelids all the way down into the scruff of his beard.

Ajay's neck tensed. In front of him, the fidget's amber screen flashed as his routines continued to work. "I've had some practice," he said. "But I really need to concentrate on this, if you don't mind."

"Sure, sure." The man made no move to leave.

Trying to shield his fidget's display, Ajay continued to monitor the processes. He did his best to ignore the man in front of him, but it wasn't easy. A roar like thunder from outside rattled the windows and made Ajay's chest flutter.

Ajay's brow creased. "Is that a combustion engine? I haven't heard one of those in ages." He leaned forward and peered into the dark parking lot. Several large pickup trucks idled, their lights burning holes in the black night.

The man smiled. "Diesel. My buddies are showing off." He stuck a hand out to Ajay. "Name's Mack."

Ajay looked at the grease-covered hand with its cracked nails and bloodied knuckles. After only a short hesitation, he shook. Mack nearly crushed his hand.

The second burner routine degraded, sputtering under the opposing pressure of the self-learning routines designed to suppress it. Soon, his movements in the digital space would be visible to anyone bothering to look. Still, he had no clues to Sashi's movements through the day. He set the task to looking through archived footage, concentrating on locations that reported disruptions in service. She had to be near those, but she knew enough to stay where the Thunderheads had trouble seeing her. She would move through dense crowds or, possibly, wear loose clothing that could hide the unique signature of her body mechanics.

She hadn't been wearing anything like that when she came to see him at his house. The bindi she wore disrupted video recording, but the way she disrupted tech required something far more sophisticated. Where would she have picked up anything like that? Ajay searched the registries, trying to find local dealers of any anti-tech. Maybe if he started looking in those locations, he could find something. No, he remembered seeing her in a car. She could easily have stowed gear in there.

"My boys and I hang out here a lot," said Mack. "Best burgers in town, don't you think?"

Ajay nodded without taking his eyes from the screen.

"Sometimes we do work for hire." Mack rested his arms up on the edges of the booth, allowing his leather jacket to pull back and reveal a holstered gun strapped to his side. "Maintaining a diesel these days ain't cheap, you know?"

"I can't imagine." Ajay dared not look the man in the eyes. There was some power play going on and he didn't want any part of it.

"Sometimes we find people," Mack said. "For a fee. You know what I mean, Ajay?"

Ajay froze.

"Which is why it's interesting that we'd find you here." Mack grinned, his perfect white teeth shining in his mess of a beard. "You're not the one we're looking for, but the boss said analytics pointed your direction."

Ajay wondered if the odd television behavior had tipped them off or if it had been the uncharacteristic pizza order. Maybe something else. Either way, he cursed himself for getting sloppy.

The alert flew by so fast Ajay nearly missed it. He swore, swiped back in the logs. There! A low-flyer went offline. Ajay scanned the area, swiping through video recorded before it disappeared. South of town, where the biomedical complex sprawled along the river, there were hundreds of people leaving work.

And one person going in.

Mack leaned forward, peering at the screen. Ajay shot him a warning look. Back-of-hand holographic displays were convenient, but terrible for privacy. Mack would be able to see everything he did, but he had to risk it. This was the link he needed.

It was her. Body mechanics pinged and lit her up in blue. Ajay grabbed the image and location, setting the burner routines to self-destruct. He disconnected the video redirect and covered his tracks. No use leaving any hints that he'd been there, even though he knew that long-standing routines would always obscure his trail.

"Mississippi Prosthesis?" Mack said. "Is that where the li'l lady is, then?"

Ajay didn't respond. He had to finish up before his connection collapsed. One side effect of the self-destruct would be that his link would be severed for some time. At the last second, he logged completely out and killed the machine.

He looked up at Mack, who grinned back at him.

Mack reached over and patted him on the shoulder. "Saved me some work, then, didn't you?"

Ajay flinched away from the big man's touch. Heat flared at the base of his neck. "I don't know what you're talking about."

Mack flashed his white teeth again. "Sure you don't." He leaned forward, so his big beard was only inches from Ajay. "Because you don't have any business in this."

"No business," Ajay said through his teeth. "It's my business if I say it is, so you listen to me. You go after her and you're going to regret it. I'll burn your IDs, your friend's IDs, and every time you look up in the sky, you'll wonder if I'm looking down. Traffic lights will never turn for you, drug dispensers will spit out poison." He stuck his thumb out at the parking lot where the trucks still idled. "You'll find you've lost your registration for those puppies. Your insurance, too. Every damn time you turn around you'll find someone who hates you with white-hot passion for something you don't ever remember saying to them. You go after my daughter and I will destroy you, Mack." When he finished, he gulped in hot breaths of air as his lungs fought desperately to keep up with his rage.

Mack soaked in Ajay's anger for a moment, then broke into a smile. "Daughter, huh?" he said. "Didn't know she was your daughter." He patted Ajay patronizingly on the shoulder, then stood.

Ajay slipped his fidget back into his coat pocket, hands still shaking.

"Now, Ajay," Mack said. "You're going to wait here while I gather up the boys and go get the girl." Mack placed his two fists on the table, knuckles down, and leaned forward.

When he spoke, it was in a deep growl. "You step out of this booth and you'll learn a little something about making threats. One of my boys is going to bruise up that face of yours so hard you won't have to worry about triggering surveillance. He won't kill you, but he'll sure as hell make you wish you'd stayed put. Don't get online 'til I get back, either. Wouldn't want anyone thinking you're doing anything illegal." He chuckled to himself.

With that, Mack pushed his way out the door, shouting to his people outside.

Ajay paused, considering his options. Outside, diesel engines roared, and harsh headlights flashed around the parking lot. A sour taste rose in the back of his throat. These men, he'd seen them around before. They were nothing more than bullies and thugs, a local gang willing to hire themselves out for a little extra coin.

The trucks circled a few times, then sped away. Ajay tried to convince himself not to worry but failed. Had Mack really left someone behind? A quiet couple looked at him warily from a couple booths down, but he didn't figure they were with Mack. At the counter stood more customers. A few of them looked pretty rough.

But were they Mack's people?

Ajay closed his eyes. They couldn't be. It wouldn't make sense. If Mack's gang was really tracking down Sashi, then they would want to focus on that. They didn't care about Ajay. Not really.

Then again, Ajay might warn Sashi. If he got there fast enough, he might ruin whatever plan they had. Ajay scratched his mustache. In fact, he knew someone at Mississippi Prosthesis who might be able to help do just that.

Ajay extracted himself from the booth, knees shaking from the adrenaline crash. He made his way to the door, keeping track of as many people as he could. Nobody moved to stop him. He told himself over and over again that Mack had been bluffing. His umbrella clacked against the grease-slick brick floor. If he could only get there fast, he might save Sashi.

She had always hated being rescued. How would she feel about his help now?

No time for that. If he was right about Mack, then nobody would stop him when he walked out the door.

He was right.

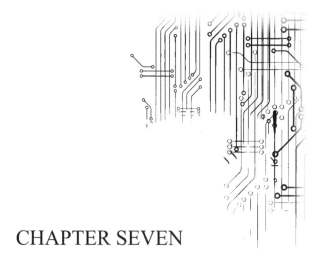

CHAPTER SEVEN

Kylie wondered how long the spider had been sitting at the center of its web. She poked at the web where it connected to an old issue of Guns and Ammo, but got no reaction from the fuzzy little guy. Was it even still alive?

She chewed her lip, thinking of what to do next. Really close up, she could see the spider's shiny bright eyes. Spiders didn't blink, did they?

The radio squelched a burst of static. Kylie looked around the smelly apartment. Stacks of old stuff made it hard to see her way around, but the radio was all the way across the room, right on the ledge between the living room and kitchenette. Nobody was even close to it.

Kylie narrowed her eyes. Touching the dog on the head, she whispered, "Did you hear that, Garrison?"

Garrison looked up at her with sad eyes. She loved this dog already, even though she hardly knew him. Kylie gave the big dog's head a hug, and he didn't protest. He probably loved her, too.

The lady who lived there, Olivia? Kylie had a bad feeling about her. Whenever she met the old lady's gaze, she felt an uncomfortable itch in the back of her head. Olivia might have cookies, but she wasn't nice. Kylie did her best to avoid the woman, but that wasn't easy in such a small apartment.

Static erupted in short bursts through the radio.

"Isa, quit it," Kylie said, annoyed.

She turned back to the spiderweb, but the spider was gone. Where was that thing? Her skin prickled around the base of her neck, and she couldn't help but imagine a furry little spider crawling all over her. Keeping perfectly still, she concentrated on making the feeling go away. After all, the spider couldn't possibly have jumped and landed on her.

Could it?

Kylie shrugged to herself. Spiders never really bothered her. Not that they had many spiders back home in the lab. Everything was always clean and perfect. Boring. The only thing to do there was play educational video games or watch educational videos. This apartment couldn't be much worse than that, could it?

It was worse. Who was she kidding? Even with a healthy spider population, this place was boring. Kylie crept out of her nook, followed by Garrison. The radio spat up static again, and this time Kylie felt little jabs of pain in her fingertips.

Staying on her tiptoes, Kylie moved between bookshelves. Her arm brushed a shelf of knickknacks, making a low scrape as a glass gnome slid across the untreated pine surface. She stopped, pulled her red sweater in close. Making a shushing gesture at Garrison, she continued forward. Behind her, near the kitchen, Olivia moved. Kylie could sense the big woman shifting in place.

Something bothered her about Olivia. Kylie had always had a special connection with her sister, and sometimes with Mom. Often she knew exactly where her sister was or what she was feeling. Now, that same sense came from Olivia, but the feelings felt thick and soupy. Sticky. Like looking at her through the bottom of a glass jar.

Then she saw her sister. Isabelle looked so skinny lately. Her thin arms hardly looked like they had any muscle at all. When Kylie remembered Isabelle at night before falling asleep, she remembered her as the smiling, mischievous older sister who always showed her something fun. That wasn't what she saw huddled in the corner by the little end table. The Isabelle who laughed didn't visit anymore. Not for a long time.

This Isabelle was dark. Gray. She looked up at Kylie's approach, her nose twitching at the air. She looked down at Garrison and shrank back into herself a little.

"C'mon, Isa," said Kylie. "Let's play something."

Isabelle didn't make any response. The radio squelched again, the burst of static loud and long. Olivia swore and fiddled with the thing, probably thinking there was something wrong with the device.

"Quit it!" Kylie said. She grabbed her sister's toothpick arm and shook it. "We're not supposed to."

Isabelle shoved Kylie away. Kylie stumbled back, tripped over Garrison, and crashed into a pile of books. Her butt hit hard on a frog statue on the ground and she shouted out in pain.

Kylie's face grew red with anger. Her hands balled into fists and before she could think, she was on top of Isabelle, swinging. Her sister fended her off, stronger than she looked. Kylie lashed out with wild fists, and for her trouble hit nothing but a pillow that Isabelle held up as a shield.

This infuriated Kylie. Isabelle grabbed Kylie's hair, pulling her closer. The two tangled, falling back against a large shelf, which tipped.

And tipped.

Olivia caught the shelf before it fell. "Girls." Her voice wasn't angry but held a forceful authority that froze both sisters in place. "I'll have none of this in my house." She peered at them for a long time, her eyes taking in their every detail. She let out a big sigh and said, "Help me clear a space. I won't have such sloppy fighting while I still live and breathe."

Ten minutes later, they had a clear space on the floor large enough for the three of them to stand without running into anything. Kylie faced Isabelle, who raised a skeptical eyebrow.

"Now," Olivia said, "has your mother taught you nothing about how to fight?" When neither girl would meet her gaze, she continued, "In this day and age, it's a wonder people survive at all. It's tough out there."

Olivia took one of Kylie's hands, closing it into a proper fist. "This is how you want it, girl. Make it hard. Good. Now if you need to punch your sister, it needs to flow from a good stance." She moved the girls through several basic punches and blocks.

After what seemed like forever, Kylie flopped down onto the sofa. "I can't do good punches and I don't really want to hurt Isabelle!"

Olivia raised an eyebrow. "Really? You sure looked like you wanted to hurt her."

"Well." Kylie didn't raise her eyes. "Not really."

The old woman looked Isabelle in the eye. "What about you? You interested in hurting your sister?"

Isabelle held the old lady's gaze but made no response.

"I see." Olivia held out a hand, palm up. "Give me your hand, dear."

After a slight hesitation, Isabelle placed her hand in the woman's. Olivia turned the hand face up and bent the fingers back slowly until the tension forced Isabelle to straighten her whole arm. Then, she gave a slight tug, stepped in, and locked the elbow. Isabelle blinked, looked at the elbow, then tried to get away. She couldn't.

"You don't need to be strong to win a fight," Olivia said to Kylie. "And you don't need to hurt anyone."

Kylie stood, heart pounding. She wanted to hit Olivia now. "You're hurting her!"

"There is a big difference between causing pain and causing injury." Olivia let go of Isabelle's arm. "A good knowledge of joint locks and pressure points will end a fight faster than it starts."

Kylie stepped between Olivia and Isabelle, not knowing how she might protect her older sister from the mean lady. Her fists were hard like stones at her sides.

Olivia chuckled. "Now, fighting a bigger opponent, that's where a good hand-to-hand skill will help you out." She motioned for Kylie to attack.

Kylie threw a punch, just as Olivia had taught. Olivia sidestepped, faster than Kylie thought the large woman could move. Kylie turned and swung again, sloppier this time. The blow bounced off Olivia's lazy block.

Fuming, Kylie shouted and lunged at Olivia, only to have her momentum redirected with a perfectly timed push. She stumbled and sprawled onto the sofa.

Breathing hard, she said, "Why even bother, then?"

"Why fight?" Olivia asked. "Oh, honey, you girls are always going to be smaller and weaker than someone. That's no reason to stop fighting." She held a hand out to help Kylie up. "But it's a damn fine reason to start fighting dirty."

Kylie refused the offered hand and stood up on her own.

"Look," Olivia said, kneeling so her head was lower than Kylie's. "Many of your opponents are going to be men, and they have a pretty good weak spot. You knee them there and you've basically won the fight."

Kylie looked to Isabelle, who didn't seem to be paying attention. "What if it's not a guy?"

"Well, then you headbutt them and run away."

"Headbutt?"

"Just make sure the hard part of your head hits the soft part of theirs. You'll do fine." She patted Kylie on the back. "You did well for your first lesson," she said. "Now, are you ready for some more cookies?"

Maybe Olivia wasn't so bad after all.

Later, after Olivia retired to her room, Isabelle and Kylie sat on the sofa sharing a blanket. Kylie thought that maybe the old lady meant they should go to sleep, but Kylie didn't feel tired, and Isabelle was reading an old, dog-eared copy of Do Androids Dream of Electric Sheep, which didn't interest Kylie at all. Kylie was bored. Her arms ached from the hours of punching, kicking, and joint locks. There was too much, and she didn't think she could remember it all.

Not that it mattered. When was she going to fight? She hardly even knew anybody, and even after weeks away from her home in the lab, she still hadn't met anyone new other than Papa and Olivia. She didn't think either of them would be fended off by a couple hours of martial arts training. So, what was the point?

Kylie was so bored. She lay her head down on the musty pillow. "This sucks."

Isabelle kicked her under the blanket and glared at her over her book.

"I will not be quiet," Kylie said.

Isabelle opened her mouth as if to say something, but no words came out. After several seconds, she went back to reading.

Kylie thought about pestering her sister more but decided against it. She closed her eyes and eventually sleep came. When she woke, the room had a dark, eerie quiet that set her nerves on edge. She blinked at the ceiling for several minutes, trying to place what was wrong. The room had an oddly open feel to it like sounds were echoing from somewhere outside. The door to the hallway was open. She peered at it, twisting her body around to see the dim, warm light streaming in from outside. Why was that door open? She turned to ask her sister if she had seen anything.

But Isabelle was gone.

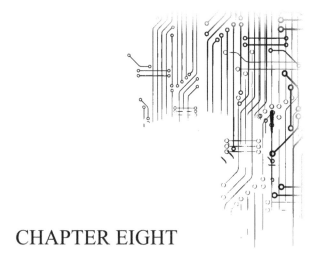

CHAPTER EIGHT

Ajay leaned up against the mustard yellow security desk in the front lobby of Mississippi Prosthesis. "How're the grandkids?"

Ben, the security guard on duty, stared back with a look like he was chewing lemons. "I'm not letting you back there."

The main entrance to the business end of the building sat in the corner closest to the Mississippi, so two wall-sized windows looked out upon the parking lot and the mighty river itself. Ajay felt terribly exposed standing there, knowing Mack and his gang would arrive soon. How long could it possibly take to rally the troops? How many troops did Mack have?

The wrinkles in the corners of Ben's eyes tightened. His too-big security hat slid forward when he frowned. "I'll lose my job, Ajay," Ben said. His large white mustache twitched back and forth.

"My daughter came back," Ajay said.

"Really," Ben said.

"I have granddaughters, Ben."

Ben's eyes twinkled. "Grandkids? How come I never heard of them?"

"That's not really the question." Ajay met Ben's gaze, not backing down for a second. "Question is, why have I never heard of them?"

"Damn."

Ajay nodded. "Damn."

The security desk in the lobby of Mississippi Prosthesis dwarfed its little guard, stealing any authority he might have otherwise grasped with his wiry little fingers. Ben took off his hat and scratched his spotted scalp. "I don't know," he said. "This job is all I got, Ajay. Josie's visiting next weekend and I want to show her that I've still got it in me."

Ajay sighed. "You need to leave. Just take a break for a little bit. It's— it's not going to be safe."

Ben puffed out his chest.

Ajay saw he wouldn't make headway on his old friend. "Fine, stay, but let me in to walk around. You know I won't trip any alarms. Your daughter won't ever know I was there."

Ben's lips tightened into a line. "You're not as invisible as you think."

"Granddaughters, Ben." Ajay stepped up to the desk. Yellow light filtered in from outside, but the lobby was lit inside by only the glow of a cascading fountain and the screens on Ben's security station. "They're brilliant and they're just like Sashi."

Ben smiled weakly. "So Sashi's back?"

"And fierce as ever. Rumor has it she's in this building, though, and I need to look for myself."

The old security guard pushed his chair back and strolled around his desk. He carried a small sidearm, not a gun, but rather a slick neuro — one of many kinds of neurotoxin delivery systems. Ajay couldn't tell exactly what type Ben's was, but the way Ben presented left no doubt that he would use it if the need arose. Ben peered through the reinforced glass windows. The landscaping outside dropped off over a sharp ridge, the rise and fall of concrete forming a barrier between the building and the parking lot.

Ajay peered through the glass. A harsh pair of headlights turned into the parking lot, followed by two more.

The trucks made their way along the lot's outskirts, their drivers hollering and whooping as they roared past the glass entry. After a few laps, the trucks circled near the center of the lot, engines dropping to a loud idle.

Then they didn't move.

"What are they waiting for?" asked Ajay.

Ben shook his head, mustache twitching. "I've seen these folks out here before. They're harmless."

"I don't think they're harmless this time, Ben."

Ben patted his neuro, a grim look on his face.

"Don't leave your post, then," said Ajay. "Keep an eye on those guys and I'll have a quick walk through the building."

Ben closed his eyes and drew a long breath. "I don't know..."

"First round of beers is on me next time we go golfing," Ajay said, knowing full well that there wouldn't be any such occasion. He still told his friend that he'd make it out again as soon as he felt up to it. The deception made him feel like garbage, but he vowed to figure out a way to get Ben the beer, anyway, even if it meant meeting him at the nineteenth hole.

Ben, without opening his eyes, held up three fingers.

"Fine," said Ajay. "First three rounds."

Ben smiled but didn't open his eyes. Ajay took the hint and moved past the desk. As he approached the door, Ben touched something on his belt. The heavy security door opened and Ajay slipped into the dark hallway beyond. Sometimes getting through the heaviest security in town meant knowing the right people in the right places.

Mississippi Prosthesis showed its age poorly, though ten years wasn't a long time for a building of its size. Ajay moved down a wide hall, passing dust-matted fake plants and garish orange doors. Decoration was an odd mix of dull office decor and exquisitely crafted prosthetic legs, the best of which were lit from beneath with blue and violet lamps.

The town of Red Wing had always had a shoe factory. When the biotech boom struck, it was only natural for the industry to spread into prosthetic foot tech. They had done well. Not well enough for a remodel of the public-facing section of their building, but well enough to employ a few hundred clever engineers and provide them with the technology to keep them happy.

Ajay pulled his hood over his face, verifying that the electric hum of its scrambling tech kicked in. He didn't like being under such scrutiny. This would be a bad place for the facial recognition software to spot him. He switched on his hearing aid, setting it to alert him of any movement that might be from a human-sized creature.

He passed another limb on display at the corner of two dimly lit cubicles. Blue light shone off its chrome plating, accentuating exquisitely crafted leatherwork. Ajay thought it looked garish, but anyone who lost a limb in the wars had earned the right to all the glitz and glam they wanted.

Using his umbrella as a makeshift cane, Ajay made his way to the stairs. If Sashi were there, she would be well hidden. Ben wouldn't know she was there and the automated security tech wouldn't find her. No, Ajay needed to lay eyes on her. Fast. Tell her about the thugs waiting outside before they could grab her.

Ajay stopped in place, attempting to steady his pounding heart. How many times had he tried to save Sashi, and how many times had it ended badly? She had never been much good at being saved. He almost turned back. Almost.

How many times had he almost done the right thing by her?

In the center of the building stood an enormous spiral staircase. The center's open design extended upward five stories, all the way to the executive offices at the top.

Would Sashi be up there? If she were spying on a rival company, then that might be a logical destination. That was where any offline information might be hidden. Paper had seen a resurgence after the fall of data encryption. She could be rifling through paper right now in any one of those offices. Ajay tuned his hearing aid as he walked up the stairs. He felt exposed, up where anyone might see him. By the third floor, he gasped for air and his heart stuttered in his chest. He leaned against the wall for a rest.

The hearing aid didn't pick up anything that sounded like rustling paper, but if Sashi's noise cancelation was fancy enough, it might not pick up anything she did. Ajay peered into the darkened third floor at an expansive lab. Through thick plexiglass walls, Ajay saw 3D printers, spanners, welders, and electronic equipment. All the tools for the artists of the company to build their creations sat just behind a locked door.

Or was it? The cameras on this level didn't blink the same as the ones below. They shone darkly in the bluish glow of safety lights.

A shadow moved deep inside the lab. Someone was there.

Sashi. It had to be. Ajay touched the door, not surprised when it slid open under a gentle push. He slipped into the lab, closing the door behind him.

The room smelled of bleach and solder. Workstations sat at varying levels of disarray. Some held half-completed limbs: metal bones, fully articulated feet, polished flesh. Every time he spotted a realistic leg in the corner of his eye, he jumped a little, his nerves far too edgy for him to be sufficiently sneaky.

What if it wasn't her? Someone else could be there, working late or protecting the company's most valuable products. They might even have automated security. Ajay considered what he would do if he ran into a sentry bot.

Ben would have warned him of bots, wouldn't he?

Ajay passed tables where men and women worked daily to improve the neural linkages required for their prosthetic limbs. Designs sketched on broad sheets of paper showed how limbs attached directly to a neural network, latching into nerves and working their way up through a person to fully attach. Those papers, however promising they might have been for a criminal, sat undisturbed. Surely Sashi would have seen those records and wanted them if she were stealing information for her own company.

He ran his hand along a machine that resembled an old MRI tube — a scanner of some sort. No, he thought, not an

MRI machine. That much magnetic garbage in a room like this would cause too many problems. It also looked too old to be one of the new graviton resonance imagers he'd read about but could be one of the many precursor technologies that had sprung up in the past decade. A proper GRI spanned the height of a whole skyscraper, so this definitely wasn't that.

Ajay touched the warm slate at the side of the machine. It had seen recent activity. The papers in the tray smelled of fresh ink, and they were warm. More sheets were scattered on the floor, but they didn't show legs and feet like the others. These papers were brain scans, of the sort one might get after finding a tumor. Ajay squinted at the picture, trying to see the image in the dimly lit room.

Something moved in the darkness ahead. Ajay didn't see it so much as feel the movement in the air. A slight increase in pressure and the faintest hint of lavender.

He drew breath to speak.

A hand clamped over his mouth. His body resisted by instinct, pulling and twisting. It was no good; the grip was too strong. It held him still, then rotated him around.

Sashi. Her eyes grew wide when she saw him under his hood, then darkened in anger. She let him loose and held a finger up to her lips.

Ajay nodded. Silence.

She motioned for him to follow, and he did.

CHAPTER NINE

Ajay and his daughter flew past rows of desks in darkness broken only by the dim blue glow from concealed floor lights. His heart pounded, and adrenaline dulled the ache in his hip as he limped forward as fast as his old bones would move. Sashi was a blot of ink in the blue-black, a silence in the low hum of climate handlers. Ajay's senses fooled him more than once, her shape disappearing entirely at times. Only the hint of lavender and citrus in her wake kept him close behind her.

They passed larger equipment, which Ajay guessed to be various kinds of scanners. Near the far end of the room, heavy metal doors dotted the walls in a staccato pattern, and Sashi led him to one. He wondered briefly why, but then he saw the tech surrounding them. These were silent rooms, cleared of any surveillance systems, and probably used exclusively for discussions that needed to remain private.

Sashi pulled open her chosen door and tugged Ajay's arm so he would enter quickly. He stumbled forward, and as he caught himself Sashi flipped on the lights and yanked back his hood.

Her brow furrowed and the line of her jaw hardened into a diamond edge. "What are you doing here?" Her fists clenched at her sides.

Ajay looked back at her, taking in her professional black silks and obscuring hood. "You were late," he said, then realized it was possibly the stupidest thing he could say.

"This is inconvenient, Papa." Sashi threw up her arms and made a frustrated noise. "Very inconvenient."

"Your daughters need you."

Sashi pinched the bridge of her nose. "I was almost done, and now this. Damn it, this is what I was afraid of."

Ajay shook his umbrella back and forth. "No, no, no, Sashi. Don't put blame on me. You're in trouble here, and you know it."

She locked gazes with him. "This was the last place. You don't understand what this means for my girls."

"They need you," Ajay said. "They need you to come back to them."

Sashi jabbed a finger at his chest. "You don't get to tell me about how they need me. You don't get to even try."

Ajay slumped into a chair, weighed down like a bag of sand. He buried his face in his hands and let out a long breath.

"You want to help?" Sashi asked. "Take care of those girls until I get back." The steel left her voice. "Like I asked." With that she pulled her hood back over her face, hiding everything but the hard line of her jaw. She turned toward the door, moving with a silence that made his ears ache.

Ajay's hip hurt something fierce from all the walking, but he forced himself to stand tall so that he could block her way. "There's more."

She pulled her hood back, her narrowed eyes burning holes his skull.

"There're men waiting for you out there," he said.

"I can handle myself." Sashi paced. She checked the weapon at her hip, which Ajay had failed to notice before. It was a sleek black thing, something Ajay didn't recognize.

"You can't, Sashi," Ajay said, knowing it was the wrong thing. "There are too many of them."

"There always are, aren't there?" Her lip curled up as if she tasted something bitter. "You never liked it when I made my own decisions."

"Only when you made the wrong ones."

She took a step back as if struck. "Only always," she snapped.

"Then that must tell you what kind of choices you made." As soon as the words came out, he knew he had gone too far. "Sashi, I'm sorry..."

"What is it you think I should do?"

"Why are you here? Some brain scans?" He waved the papers in front of her face. "What's this tell you, Sashi? Please."

She snatched the papers from his hand. "It tells me there isn't much time."

He flashed a quirky grin. "Then maybe you need a better scan, like that fancy gravitic scanner they have up in The Cities."

Sashi didn't return the smile. "Yes. Maybe."

"I'm joking, Sashi. Those scans are destructive."

Her jaw tightened.

Ajay cleared his throat. "There's a back exit that we can use to get out." Ajay twisted his umbrella in his hands. "In the basement, there's a tunnel that Ben uses to leave. It exits down by the river."

"Who the hell is Ben?"

"I've parked nearby, so we can take my car once we're out."

Sashi kicked a chair. Her fists made tight knots at her side. "I don't need your way out." She drew several angry breaths. "This has been a waste of time. They have some of the most advanced tech in here, but it's all for feet. Feet!"

Ajay desperately wanted to know what she was looking for, but the rage on her face held him back. He could learn more later when she was calm. Reasonable.

Then, with no warning, calm overtook her like stepping inside out of a blizzard. Her body lost its intense rigidity, her expression softened, and her eyes focused on something far away. She swallowed. "No," she said. "I take it back. Your way is fine. Let's get out of here."

"We need to stop by and have Ben disable the alarm, then we can get out through the service exit."

She blinked and scrunched up her face, some small fraction of the tension returning to her shoulders. "We'll be gone before anyone cares about an alarm."

He tapped his eye. "Easiest way to be invisible—"

"—is to control the questions people ask." Sashi rolled her eyes, and Ajay smiled. This was the Sashi he remembered. "If you've always been so invisible, how come you work so hard at staying hidden?"

Ajay pulled his hood over his head. "Stick around and maybe I'll tell you the story."

She put a finger to her lips and shouldered her way back out into the lab as she pulled up her hood. The two crept through the building's third floor, passing dozens of desks and lab tables with their varying arrays of prosthetics. When they arrived at the stair, the plexiglass door opened at a touch.

The still air broke with a string of pops from somewhere below. Ajay cocked his head to the side, at first not understanding the noise. The open space of the offices and labs made for an odd echo chamber for the staccato rhythms. His hearing aid floundered trying to pinpoint the source, but after a brief pause, Ajay's eyes widened in recognition.

Gunfire.

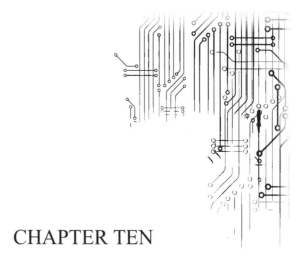

CHAPTER TEN

The gunshots pounded, at once too far away and too close. Ajay flinched at each one as sweat dripped into his eyes. He gripped the railing and descended the stairs two at a time. His feet stumbled. Sashi caught him, her steadying grip so tight it bruised. He brushed her off. Pushed forward, down to the floor with Ben.

"Stop," she whispered, her voice distorted from under her hood.

Another staccato rhythm, this time accompanying the crash of broken glass.

"Ben," Ajay said through gritted teeth. His lungs ached from the effort, but he reached the bottom of the stairs.

Sashi grabbed his arm and their eyes met. Her brow knit in fierce determination, and she pointed down the rows of cubicles, away from the lobby.

"No," Ajay whispered. He pulled away from her and ran, despite his aching muscles. Ajay staggered and gripped the short walls for support.

Sashi, after a moment of hesitation, followed. The bluish light illuminated her face and made her chiseled features appear more fearsome than Ajay could ever have imagined. When they reached the metal door to the lobby, Ajay heard shouts, then more gunshots.

Small caliber, he thought. That wasn't the crashing cacophony of automatic weapons. Sweat ran down his brow. He gripped his umbrella so tight his knuckles went white. Even a small pistol could wreck a good man's weekend.

"Well?" asked Sashi, pulling her hood back. "There's no reason to be here."

"We have to help Ben." When Sashi didn't respond, Ajay said, "He's nighttime security here."

"The police are on their way."

Ajay shook his head. "They won't get here fast enough."

She sighed, exasperated. "That's not what I mean. We need to leave."

Ajay tapped her sidearm with the tip of his umbrella. "Threaten the attackers. They'll run."

She shook her head. Her voice had a mocking tone when she said, "The best way to stay invisible is if nobody's looking for you."

"We need Ben for that," he said. "Any misdirection we can possibly pull off comes from him." He knew it wasn't likely Ben could do anything to dissuade a determined police investigation, but he couldn't bring himself to leave his old friend behind.

Her eyes dropped focus for a split second. His grip tightened on his umbrella and he stepped toward the door.

Sashi put a hand on his chest. "No," she said. "No, we'll do it your way."

She kicked the door open, drawing her weapon in one fluid movement.

The thugs were there: Mack and half a dozen of his buddies. Some had cover behind overturned tables. Others stood in the open. Mack flaunted his pistol, whooping and firing in the air.

Sashi fired. Her weapon snapped an electric crack-pop. A skinny man with two small pistols clutched his shoulder, blood spurting through his fingers for a full second before his head exploded in a mess of bone and brain. A woman in a black leather overcoat clutched a font of blood as it spouted from her belly. She went down like a screaming sack of mulch.

Ajay's heart hammered in his chest. "Sashi," he said, or tried to say. His words stuck in his chest. He swallowed. "I said 'threaten.'"

Sashi shot another through cover. The man screamed and screamed until she shot him again. "This is a threat."

Ajay rounded the corner. Ben lay on the floor behind his security desk, blood welling from his gut. Ajay ducked behind the cover, taking his old friend's hand.

"Ben," Ajay said. "Stay with me, Ben."

Ben's face was pale, making a stark contrast with the blood smeared across his chin. He focused on Ajay, eyes glassy. "Tell..." His eyelids drooped.

The pop-pop of gunfire rang out, followed by the snap of Sashi's weapon.

"What?" asked Ajay. "What do you want me to tell?"

"Tell Josie—" Ben coughed. When he slumped back, Ajay saw that he had more wounds than just the gut shot. Blood oozed from his shoulder and chest as well. His lip quivered, words hanging at the tip of his tongue.

And then Ben died. Ajay heard shouts. The cries of pain. He heard them long before he realized they were his. Ben slumped, glassy eyes staring into space. All around, the fight continued, but Ajay shook Ben, hoping for one more moment. One word from his friend.

But there was nothing. There never would be.

Sashi ducked down into the cover behind the desk. "They're retreating."

Ajay's throat was too dry to speak.

"This is bad," Sashi continued. "But I don't think the ones that left got a good look at me. I stuck to shadows." She chewed on a lip as if trying to convince herself of something. "Some of them had these." She showed Ajay the boxy semi-auto pistols the men had been wielding. "Take one."

Ajay took the gun with a trembling hand, not knowing what he could possibly do with it. It fit, though. When the grip nestled into his palm, he felt a kind of comfort he hadn't felt in a long time. He could do this.

"A few of them had neutralizers like these," Sashi said. She held a small, rounded pistol with a gas canister attached to the top. It resembled a paintball gun, but these paintballs held a powerful neurotoxin. They'd release a liquid and gas upon impact that could drop the toughest thug out there.

"There's no more use in staying invisible." Ajay swallowed. "We need to leave."

Sashi shook her head. "No, Papa," she said. "I don't think so."

Ajay furrowed his brow. "You killed people, Sashi. They're going to start looking for you."

She looked down at Ben's body, then at the gun in Ajay's hand. She looked at the little black gun in her holster and chewed on her lower lip. She ran her fingers through her hair. "No," she said. "I don't think they'll be looking for a second killer."

Sashi shot Ajay with the neutralizer.

In the face.

The blue neurotoxin seared at his skin. His muscles seized, clenching into painful knots.

Sashi looked down at the little paintball gun, nodding with satisfaction. She tucked it away and holstered her sleek pistol.

As he toppled onto Ben's corpse, Ajay heard a call ring through his hearing aid.

Olivia's voice came on the line. "Ajay," she said. "Ajay, are you there?"

Ajay tried to speak, but his muscles wouldn't respond. His breathing still worked, and his heart rate pounded. Blood rushed in his ears. Still, he couldn't reply.

"Ajay, it's the girls," Olivia said. "They're gone."

Then the toxin took away Ajay's consciousness and everything went black.

CHAPTER ELEVEN

Stars of searing pain lit the back of Ajay's skull. He peeled open his crusted-over eyes. Light burned through his eye-holes straight through his brain. The hangover pounded so hard his ears rang, and bitter bile coated his mouth.

He sat up. The room was mercifully lit with only a single dim light; its white glow cast sharp shadows on the concrete walls. He had a toilet and a bed. The only exit was through a metal door. They'd taken his coat, hoodie, and umbrella. Pants pockets were empty.

It took him several minutes to figure out that he was in a jail cell, and several more to remember how Sashi's betrayal put him there. Ben's death. Bile rose again, but he swallowed it back. Fingertips tingled from whatever toxin still coursed through his system. His hearing aid dangled loosely from his ear as he rolled over. It was the police, after all. They had rules about which assistant devices they could take from prisoners.

Ajay smiled a weak, wan smile. Rules were his favorite.

Then it struck him: he was a prisoner. His mouth ran dry. All of his work to stay invisible might be completely undone. Years of staying off grid were at an end, and he had nobody but himself to blame.

No, he thought, that wasn't completely right. Sashi betrayed him. She could be blamed.

Ben. The old man's glassy stare haunted Ajay. His old friend was dead. Killed because of Ajay's own stupidity. How was he to know how serious those gangsters were? How could he have known they'd turn violent so fast? It should have been obvious. One serious look at Mack would have told him what he needed to know. That those men were killers. They weren't some little group of truck enthusiasts looking to earn a buck. Those men and women were violent mercenaries.

And they had killed Ben.

Rage pumped through Ajay's veins, but he steadied his breath and forced himself to slow down. There would be time to consider what to do about Mack once he was out of jail. If he got out of jail.

The clock across the hall read just after eleven. He'd been asleep for hours. They had dumped him in jail after whatever toxic attack Sashi had hit him with, and nobody had read him his rights. Good. That was a start.

Ajay watched as the clock dragged on.

Midnight was the hour of his undoing. When that tower bell struck twelve, a routine woven deep into the core of the network would spin its web, changing his identity and making him someone else. Every night, the connections dissolved and reformed, giving him new life and freedom to exist another day. At midnight, the computer would come back and say he was innocent, but what about the men and women who had locked him up? They were sure to notice the software glitch.

Weren't they?

The piercing pain in his head felt like a spear stabbing holes in every coherent thought.

Olivia had to be in a panic. Where would she have gone? Ajay convinced himself that she would stay in her apartment since leaving would mean the girls could only come back to an empty place.

If they came back. Why had they left? Fear? Boredom? Ajay chewed his lip. He shook his head to clear it and the headache returned full force. He hadn't been aware that it was fading.

Fading. Failing. He was failing. Had to focus.

He had to get out of the cell. They were watching him. Dumping prisoners with unknown toxins in their systems was terribly dangerous unless they were properly monitored. Ajay uncovered three sensors within the cell, and two more outside. They needed to be disabled.

Fine.

He touched his earpiece. The hearing aid did so much more than help him listen. He was useless without it, but with it, he could do much more than the average person. The piece had recorded, even while he had been unconscious. Rewinding the feed, he cycled through the various sound and electromagnetic feeds that it had picked up. The police chatter wasn't noteworthy, but he picked up a couple names and voices. Chester, the social officer, had been there. Poor guy must have worked a double shift.

But there wasn't much he could do with the recording without a better interface.

He shook his head again. Ten minutes until midnight. He had to get out soon or he wouldn't be able to escape.

Ajay crossed to the cell door. It had a physical lock, nothing digital at all. They took security seriously. Computer systems wouldn't hold anyone with an uplink to a quantum computer. He scratched his head. Swore.

Three minutes 'til midnight. He could summon a cop. Get some eyes in here and maybe they'd be confused and just let him go. It was a non-zero probability. Would they come, though? Maybe if he used their surveillance against them. He could do something to fool them into thinking... What? Ajay thumped his head against the wall. Fireworks flared in his skull. What could he do?

It had been a good run, that transient identification of his. Each day Ajay's identity changed, but not his name. Not his face. Every camera on every street corner would still ID him from the wrinkles at the corners of his eyes and the shape of his too-big nose. The information behind that identity would be updated. He'd have a new, clean past. One that didn't get arrested and didn't get in any trouble. How would that look when they found him in this cell?

His solution had been clever, he thought. By changing one pointer deep inside the central computers, he'd remained hidden for a decade with little or no maintenance, so long as nobody took particular notice of him and started asking questions. He had to control the questions.

The policemen would start to ask questions. They would wonder who he was and what his real past was like. Somebody might figure it out.

The only way to stay invisible was to keep them from looking.

One minute.

Ajay slammed a fist into the concrete wall. The flare of pain shot down his whole arm. Think. He had to think. How could he have screwed this up, too? He needed a plan and he needed it fast.

Why did he screw everything up when it came to Sashi? Ajay slumped to the floor and buried his face in his hands.

Midnight. A buzz sounded down the hall, and the lock on his door clicked. The metal door slid aside. Ajay looked up and saw a man's crisp, polished shoes and keenly pressed khakis.

"Time to go, Mr. Andersen," the officer said. "Your ride's here."

Ajay furrowed his brow. "Ride?"

The man didn't answer. He led the way out of the room and Ajay followed. Once they'd passed through an armored airlock of a checkpoint, the officer handed Ajay a cardboard box. His umbrella protruded from the top, and his other possessions were inside, including his suspicious variety of money. He took them without comment.

Through another locked door — Ajay marveled that he'd ever thought he could sneak out of such a place — and they came to a lobby where Olivia sat patiently, hands folded in her lap. The bright squares of her quilted coat stood out like a signal flare against the drab decor of the waiting room. She looked up as he entered, but her smile was distant and weak. Tired.

"Well," the officer clapped a hand on Ajay's shoulder, "it seems the early shift didn't even process you for detox, so that's less paperwork for everyone."

Ajay crossed to Olivia, and she held his elbow. He couldn't believe it was so easy. He didn't know what she had told them, but he was walking out and they weren't making a big fuss. With any luck, they'd never discuss his case with the other shift and he could be on his way.

Just as he was stepping through the door, the officer said, "Oh, Mr. Andersen?"

Ajay stopped but didn't turn around.

"It's after midnight, so..."

Ajay smiled. He knew what came next.

"Happy birthday."

Ajay pulled his hood over his face. "Thanks," he said. One other side effect of his constantly rewritten background was that it was always his birthday. Every day.

He and Olivia ventured into the cold night.

Olivia tugged at his arm. "Walk faster," she whispered.

Despite the increasing ache of his hip, Ajay managed a faster pace. Every step came with a fresh wave of dizziness and pain. Whatever neurotoxin Sashi had used on him hadn't completely worn off. He staggered, only to be yanked back up by Olivia's iron grip.

"Ow!" Ajay said. "What's the rush?"

Olivia spun on him. "Rush? You got pulled in for shooting up a prosthetics factory, murdering a bunch of folks, and generally causing mayhem, and you ask what's the rush?" She looked back at the station, inert in the autumn chill. "We have about five minutes before someone other than the guy I bribed figures out he shouldn't have let you out on bail. You wanna use that time escaping or standing here chatting?"

Ajay pulled away from her. "What did you do?"

She leaned close and whispered, "I bribed a man to let you out because you sure as hell weren't going to see the light of day otherwise."

"I have to fix this. I'll wipe their servers. I'll—"

"Shut it." She opened the door on her dented blue car. "Get in, and let's go find those girls."

Inside the car, Garrison lifted his head and yawned at Ajay.

"You don't understand," Ajay said. "If I get home, I can remove their records of me. I might be able to salvage this."

Olivia said nothing else, holding the door for Ajay as he climbed in.

"Fine," he said. "All right. I've had enough of the easy life, anyway." He hadn't. It wasn't fine. The little blue car pulled out of the police parking lot, merging onto Highway 61 and passing by the bluff where he saw his quaint little rambler high on the hill. He might never see it again. "Fine."

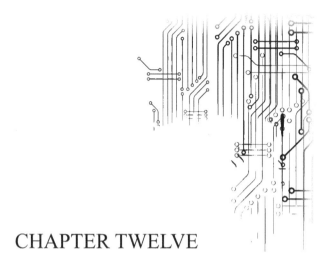

CHAPTER TWELVE

Garrison licked Ajay's ear as Olivia's little sedan hummed through the dark town. It was late for the little town, and historic Red Wing felt abandoned except for a few wandering packs of teenagers and the seedy congregations that gathered outside seedy bars. Men and women still whooped and hollered at the night, unwilling or unable to settle down for the evening, at least not until the bars closed and the patrolling social officers gave them the nudge.

Ajay scratched his dog's ears and tried to make sense of the day's events. His thoughts still flowed like the muck at the bottom of the Mississippi. Every time he had hold of an idea, it would dissolve into so much glittering sand.

"Sashi betrayed me," he said. His words sounded muddy in his ears, but he didn't know if that was a problem with his mouth or his ears. "She saw a clean exit and set me up to take the fall. But my Sashi wouldn't do that."

Olivia placed a hand on his shoulder. "They grow up, Ajay. They go off and become their own people."

He shook his head. "No, this wasn't that." Was it? He wasn't sure. How much of his muddled mind was due to the neurotoxin and how much was due to old age? Damn it, he hated being old. Maybe he simply couldn't handle the stress like he used to. Hell, was he ever able to handle the stress? Then another thought floated into his head. "The girls."

"I'm sorry," Olivia said. "It's…" Her voice trailed off. She might have had more to say, but she didn't say it. The car topped a bluff, and on the far side rows of houses stretched on for miles. Finally, she said, "I thought they were asleep."

"Where did they go?" When she didn't respond, he looked up at her. No, of course, she didn't know. "Any clues? Did they say anything?" He had to get his head around it. Somehow thinking of new problems beat dallying on the old ones.

Olivia shook her head and rubbed her temples. "The younger one…"

"Kylie."

"Kylie." Olivia nodded to herself, mouthing the name a few times. "Kylie had a tussle with her sister, but they worked it out."

"So, Isabelle left first?"

Olivia's smile didn't reach her eyes. "Those are some tough girls."

Ajay took Olivia's hand in his own. "You did your best, Liv." He squeezed the hand and hooked his pointer finger in hers. "Nobody asks any more than that."

Tension drained from her shoulders, and she leaned into Ajay, resting her head on his shoulder. For a while the two sat like that, the car gently transporting them across town. The side-to-side sway of the little car lulled Ajay, and the long day caught up with him. His eyes drooped. For a brief moment, he was comfortable. Content.

Then Olivia's apartment building loomed like a dark splotch of ink in the blue-black sky. Below, the stark-white parking lot glowed against the moonlight.

Ajay said, "We can't let Sashi find them first. There was something about what she said. I need to figure out what she has planned."

"She's their mother, Ajay."

Ajay scratched at his mustache. "I'm not kidnapping them. I'm worrying for their safety."

"You're doubting your own daughter's ability to raise them."

He rubbed his temples.

Olivia drew a sealed plastic bag from her purse. "They're not in the building."

Ajay looked at the bag for a long time before her line of thought clicked in his head. The bag held a mitten, one that he recognized as Kylie's. "You think Garrison will follow a scent?"

Olivia flashed a crooked smile. "He seems to follow the scent of aged gouda without any trouble."

"That was once."

"He ate half a pound of cheese."

"Suffered the consequences for it, too." Ajay chuckled. "I did, I mean. I suffered the consequences. Damn near peeled the paint off my walls."

Olivia popped open the door.

"C'mon, boy," Ajay said as he pried his tired body out of the seat. Olivia's car had parked itself in the outdoor lot only a short distance from her apartment complex. The edge of the woods loomed close. In the night, it was a grasping shadow blocking out half the sky. Cold wind numbed Ajay all the way down to the joints, even though his hoodie and long overcoat.

Ajay opened the bag, which tumbled from his frozen fingers and fell to the slick pavement. The puddle there had an iced-over crust, and in its black surface, Ajay saw the reflection of the gibbous moon. Garrison snuffled at the bag, his floppy jowls picking at it, moving it about.

"Hold on, hold on." Ajay snatched up the bag and opened it. Holding it out to the dog, he paused while the beast inhaled all the air within. "Can you find it, boy?" Ajay asked, enthusiasm in his voice doing all it could to fight the exhaustion in his muscles. He tested the lead on Garrison's collar to make sure it held.

Then Garrison pulled, scanning from side to side. Ajay's joints protested at the dog's exuberance, but he didn't dare call the dog off. If the dog indeed had some instinct to follow, it would be foolish to squash it. He managed to follow the dog across the parking lot, then along a grassy swath filled with the frigid runoff from the parking lot. His loafers soaked through, sending pain like bone-deep razors through his already frozen feet. Olivia followed close, hugging her quilted coat against the wind.

Garrison continued his searching sniffs, pausing from time to time to look back at Ajay for guidance.

Ajay cheered the dog on with whatever energy he could summon. Ahead, a small bridge crossed the ditch, heralding the start of a walking path. Ajay's hopes soared. If they'd come that way, surely they would leave a scent there.

They didn't. Or at least Garrison found nothing. Ajay offered Garrison another sample of the scent, but he didn't seem interested. He pulled, harder and harder, darting from side to side. He moved faster than Ajay had seen him move in all the years he had owned him.

Ajay frowned, his face stiff from the cold. "What if this doesn't work?" he said. "Then what?"

Olivia's bright eyes tracked Garrison as he snuffled about in the dry grass.

"I like to plan a few steps ahead, you know." Ajay lurched forward as the dog nearly pulled his arm out of the socket.

Somewhere, far away, an engine howled in the cold night. Ajay tugged Garrison, guiding him around the building. Here, on the north side, they met again the edge of the parking lot where it met the inky darkness of the wood. Street lamps scattered pools of harsh white light in this section of the border between civilization and wild. Not so wild, really, Ajay thought. It was the edge of some parkland, but the city stretched for another mile or two. Beyond that, the Dakota-Sioux reservation ran for miles along the river. The forest wasn't entirely untamed in that stretch of Minnesota, but it was certainly not friendly.

Ajay's hip ached. Cold penetrated through his coat and hoodie, stiffening his limbs and slowing him. The roar of diesels echoed through the apartment complex. That sound chilled Ajay's bones more than any breeze.

He caught Olivia eyeing him, and he had no doubt that she knew his feelings. She'd always been able to read him.

"You should go," he said. "This isn't working, and this will be dangerous."

"Nonsense."

"Just a little longer, then," he said, urging Garrison on. Only a few more pools of light dotted the edge of the lot, then they'd be able to rule out this direction. Assuming the dog was really seeking a scent. If he wasn't, well, then they were just out for a nice walk.

Olivia frowned, but followed. Garrison snuffled and stopped, taking a long while to sniff at a particular spot on the ground.

"You got something?" Ajay asked.

As if in response, Garrison burst forward, sniffing again from side to side in his searching pattern. His leash bit into Ajay's wrist. The cold numbed everything except for where he hurt. His hip ached; his bruises felt like stiff death all over his body. Every movement made it worse.

The engines shifted somewhere, still out of sight.

"We have to move," Olivia said, urging Ajay toward the forest. "Hide."

He held ground, following Garrison, silently urging the dog ahead. The dog searched, frantic. Energetic. Cold water soaked up Ajay's pants as they barreled carelessly through another swale.

For the first time in ages, Ajay felt alive.

The truck rounded the building at full speed, engine roaring as it barreled into the near-empty lot. Its harsh headlights shone on the few cars there. Ajay ducked down, hoping the tall grasses were enough to conceal his movements.

Olivia grabbed Ajay's arm and pulled him down further. They crawled along, edging their way into the forest.

Underbrush swallowed them whole, the buckthorn clawing at their coats. Garrison became a stubborn pile of bricks on the end of his leash. Ajay had to practically drag him along.

Once they were far enough in the trees to be hidden, Ajay crouched down and hugged his big dog, whispering encouragement into the bloodhound's floppy ears. And he watched the truck in the parking lot.

A man stepped out of the passenger side of the truck, eyes glued to a glowing screen. He rotated around, first facing the apartment building and then moving it in an arc across the lot. He wore all black, from his gloves to his long black coat. The man's square jaw tightened, and something he saw on a holographic display made him frown.

"I know him," Ajay whispered, loosening his grip on Garrison so that he could crawl a little closer.

When the man spoke, Ajay couldn't hear the words, even with his hearing aid focused on it. Still, the force of the man's command sent shivers down Ajay's spine. Mack emerged from the driver's side of the truck and stood at a kind of sloppy attention in front of the man. Someone else stayed in the truck, a silhouette dark against the dimly lit background.

Garrison whined and cocked his head to the side.

"They're after Sashi," Ajay whispered.

Olivia touched him on the shoulder and then touched her finger to her lips. Right. The men in the parking lot were probably capable of hearing everything. All they had to do was focus on their part of the wood and they'd hear them or see their infrared silhouettes. Ajay gripped his umbrella.

The man waved Mack toward the apartment building, and the big man obeyed. The stranger then turned his eyes back to the device in his hands. When he turned, Ajay got a better look at his face.

His numb hands broke into a cold sweat. "I know that guy," he whispered again. From where, though? The slippery mud of his mind failed to gain traction.

Garrison let out a low yowl, and Ajay grabbed the dog's face and held his muzzle shut. Garrison struggled against it. Olivia, silently, pulled Ajay's arm. It was time to go.

Deeper in the woods, the underbrush thinned out, but not much. Eerily pale buckthorn scraped across Ajay's coat as he passed. Every step was a struggle for Ajay and Olivia, but not so for Garrison.

Then the dog stopped, sniffed the air, and ran.

The leash yanked free of Ajay's wrist with a painful snap.

Olivia shot Ajay a dirty look, shook her head, and followed Garrison into the dark. Ajay followed as best he could, pushing through underbrush that raked at his face and hands. The numbing cold only seemed to turn his skin into fragile glass. Each snap of a branch sent hairline fractures through frozen skin. Ahead, he heard his dog. He could still follow the trail.

Soon he couldn't run anymore. The underbrush thinned, but his heart hammered and his hip threatened to seize completely. He started using the umbrella as a cane again, just to take some pressure off, but it was too late. He already limped. He was weak. Slow. Old.

Too damned old.

Ajay leaned against a tree, the gray bark scratching his thin skin, even through his coat. His head thumped against a knot in the wood as his lungs pulled in cool air. Anybody could catch him, he knew. This old body of his had to be the slowest, most out-of-shape that anyone had ever pursued through a forest at night. All his pursuers had to do was walk a brisk pace and they'd catch him.

Would they do that, though? It seemed unlikely that they would barrel through the woods, not when there were eyes everywhere. If they were anything like clever, they would wait to see where he came out. Eyes swarmed everywhere, even inside the forest. Connected eyes. Ajay palmed his fidget; the worn edges fit nicely into his wrinkled palm. Amber images snapped up in front of him, flickering in the dark. Yes, dozens of cameras and hundreds of motion sensors covered the property. His pursuers probably knew exactly where he stood.

Far back, he heard the rumbling of an engine. This had to go fast. Ajay selected one of the cameras, making a quick edit of its video stream.

He triggered movement on one node. Brushed one shadow past another. Good. Across the highway, there were no nodes at all. The vast expanse of black, unconnected forest made his heart skip. That was where someone would flee if they wanted to get away. He steered his digital doppelgänger that way.

He tripped the movement trigger on another wildlife monitor, taking it closer to the dark part of the forest. Then another. In a tiny window, he brought up the apartment complex's parking lot images, watching as the truck left the lot. He needed to be fast.

Another monitor; then, just to be sure they saw it, he triggered motion sensors on a traffic light on the highway, just as if someone had run across.

Then, adrenaline pumping through his veins, he stalked after Olivia, careful to avoid any more sensors.

He could still hear Garrison, yowling in the distance. How far, he didn't know, but he had to hurry. The man in the truck might not take long to figure out his sloppy ruse. Ajay emerged from the forest to find a spike-topped brick wall. The gate, a short distance away, stood open. Beyond sat several buildings, including a circular brick tower lit by clear moonlight.

Ajay knew that place. It was the Towerview Andersen Center, an artists' refuge built long ago by a man who feared the Minnesota winters almost as much as Ajay did. Ajay had never had the resources to build a series of buildings and interconnected tunnels, though. A. P. Andersen, who'd made his fortune by inventing puffed wheat, did.

A light shone in the room at the top of the tower, and in its glow stood a solitary figure, there for all to see.

Isabelle.

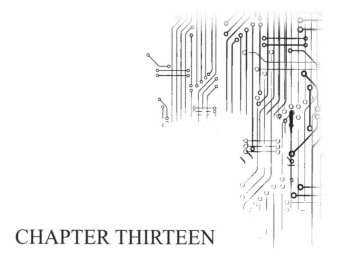

CHAPTER THIRTEEN

The thin moon kissed the tops of colorless trees, threatening to plunge the Towerview campus into darkness. Ajay stepped faster, but his hip threatened to drop him right there. The squid handle of his umbrella dug painfully into the palm of his hand. Frosted grass crunched under his feet.

The field was strewn with statuary of all sorts. Stone, bronze, auto parts. A great, fierce elephant formed of twisted and rusted metal loomed over Ajay's path. Pushing past the beast, he worked his way closer to the tower where the yellow glow of incandescents called out into the night.

Above, in the tower, Olivia approached Isabelle slowly, the way one approaches an old stick of dynamite.

Ajay barked a shin on a bronze turtle. He swore under his breath, twisting around to make sure nobody followed him. His old body refused to move faster, but a shout stuck at the tip of his tongue. Panic threatened to overwhelm him. The world searched for him, coming closer and closer to finding him. He wanted to run.

But running wouldn't work. Not without drawing even more attention. He didn't even dare turn on the light from his fidget. They'd be there soon. If not through the forest...

Ajay peered into the night. His feet stuttered and stopped, refusing to go another step. They'd come by truck, but no engine noise echoed through the night. They'd retreated after his trick with the cameras. Cold, deep, billowing breaths escaping his aching lungs.

If they approached, he would hear them. There was still time.

He flipped on his light, jumping back at the sneering face of a bronze buffalo. It was a hideous thing, and Ajay couldn't think of any more appropriate expression for that extinguished species. "You show 'em, buffalo," he said and patted it on the head.

At the bottom of the tower, he found the door wide open. The interior stairs didn't just stretch up but also went down into gaping darkness. The tunnels. No matter, though, since he only needed to go up. The narrow, twisting stairs up were more intimidating than a whole economy-sized can of prunes. His legs ached at the thought of climbing.

It took him ten minutes to reach the top. His vision blurred and his head swam, but when he got there, he flipped off his light and fell into an empty chair.

Olivia peered at him from the darkness, Garrison at her feet. Kylie's head lay in the woman's lap, the girl's drowsy eyes barely registering the new visitor. Isabelle stood motionless, exactly as Ajay had seen her from below, though now in the dark.

"She won't move," Olivia said. "The girl's got some idea that she can solve everything standing right there."

The energy flew from Ajay like a flock of crows. He buried his face in his hands and stopped trying to piece everything together. It didn't make sense and wasn't going to. Did any of it even matter?

He might have stayed that way a few minutes or an hour. All the while, a dull fear lingered at the back of his chest. They needed to leave, to run. All stayed silent in the little room, hoping they might at least avoid becoming a lighthouse for those men out there.

Isabelle said, in a soft voice, "I'm not supposed to move."

It took Ajay a long moment to realize she'd spoken. The sky had lightened some, showing hints of orange in the east. "We need to leave, Isabelle."

For a long time, she said nothing. Then, "I can see the world from here."

Ajay said, "If you can see the world, then the world can see you."

"But I can almost talk to the sky," she said. "There are monsters there."

The sky exploded in orange and red as the sun's first rays peeked over the trees to the east. Ajay stood so he could better see the scene around them. A forest stretched out to the horizon, its yellows and reds competing with the sunrise in color if not brightness. Fewer plants bore white streaks here, and the pure colors were shocking. Something about the scene breathed life into Ajay's weary limbs. Garrison raised his head, and with a groan moved next to his master.

"We need to figure out what to do," Ajay said. "They'll find us here soon, and we need to be gone."

"These girls need their mother," said Olivia without opening her eyes. She nudged Kylie and the girl sat up, rubbing her bleary eyes.

"Way I see it," Ajay said once he had everyone's attention, "we want to do whatever's best for the girls." Ajay cleared his throat. "We old folks don't have any business in this, especially you, Olivia." He ignored her insulted look. "It's probably best for everyone if we stand down and hand the girls off to the authorities."

Olivia said, "Unless that's who they're running from. And we sure can't get you anywhere close to the police. Not anymore."

Ajay scowled. She was right. He glanced back at Isabelle. "What is that girl doing?"

Kylie spoke in a soft voice. "She's listening to all the noise."

There wasn't any noise, other than the blowing of wind across the tower windows. Ajay took a step closer to Isabelle, watching her serene face as she stared up into the sky. "But why does she want to be right here?"

Kylie said, "That's where they told her to go."

"Who?" When nobody answered, Ajay wondered if he'd asked the wrong question. At that point, it didn't matter who was after them or even why. What mattered was how. Isabelle's bright eyes shone in the starlight, and the cool wind tugged at her long hair.

On an instinct Ajay couldn't quite place, he reached into his pocket for his diamond-optical device. Instead of properly switching it on to block signals, he toggled it, creating a quick signal disruption.

Isabelle blinked. She left her place at the window.

Ajay cleared his throat. "The police can protect the girls from those thugs."

She crossed her arms and frowned.

"Honey," said Olivia to Isabelle in a calm voice, "you haven't done anything wrong, and you're not in trouble with the law. Your grandpa just thinks they can protect you."

Kylie smiled.

"Are you?" Ajay asked. "In trouble with the law?"

Isabelle scowled at her sister.

A slight growl seeped into Ajay's voice. "Nobody's trying to make you do anything."

Isabelle raised an eyebrow at that.

"We just want to do what's best for you," Ajay said. The circular nature of the conversation gave Ajay a wicked parenting flashback.

Isabelle's mouth hung open, then closed. She shot a glance at the window where she had stood, and with a look of desperate longing, returned to her previous spot. She shook her head, eyes wide with fear.

"What is it, hon?" asked Olivia.

Isabelle pushed past Ajay and ran down the stairs. He looked to Olivia for guidance, but she only shrugged.

"C'mon, then," he said to the others. He hurried down the stairs, Garrison in front of him. Rushing down the stairs was certainly easier than climbing up, but soon his legs were burning with the effort and they threatened to go out from under him.

Then came the noise.

Not far away, a diesel engine roared.

"Isabelle!" he shouted down ahead of him. "Stop!"

Isabelle stopped. At first, Ajay thought she'd simply obeyed his order on account of it being delivered forcefully or authoritatively enough, but when he approached her from above on the narrow stairs, the spiral stairs that were too narrow to pass, he saw that lines of fear touched the corners of her eyes like cracks in a porcelain doll.

Ajay touched her shoulder, squeezed her close. Her gaze hardened.

She whispered in a voice so quiet he could barely hear. "They sent a Thunderhead. I talked to it."

"They're always up there," Ajay said.

She looked him in the eyes, shaking her head. She started down the stairs again.

Ajay blinked.

Above, Olivia made her way down in their wake, leading a drowsy Kylie. Outside, the roar of engines deepened. The thick loping of diesel engines surrounded the tower. Ajay tried to count the headlights from a narrow window, but they moved too fast.

Ajay rushed forward again, catching up to Isabelle. "You can't talk to Thunderheads. Their security is too tight," he said. "Anyway, why would they send one? They have us surrounded." He ran a quick routine through government servers, searching the skies for hints of Thunderhead activity.

Isabelle shook her head. Her foot caught on the edge of a narrow step and she stumbled. Ajay caught her and steadied her before hurrying her forward. One more flight and they would be at the tower's base. "It's coming," she said.

Then what?

Ajay tightened his grip on his umbrella. The display on his hand showed a warning. Thunderhead activity. There was no way to know its target, but it could be there any second. He would have to delay the men outside, give the girls a head start.

He clutched Isabelle's elbow and turned her to face him. "Go," he said. "Keep going down and get as far as you can in the tunnel." He waved a hand, dismissing the panicked look she gave him. "We'll work something out." The words sounded hollow, even to him.

Ajay squeezed past Isabelle and sprinted the last few steps. Every movement hurt his old bones, but he ignored the pain and the promise of more pain later. His eyelids felt like sandpaper and the ordeal had already taken so much out of him. From his pocket, he pulled the black diamond-optical computer. With a quick manipulation, it could jam simple uplinks. A quick gesture set it to work in a wide radius. He didn't want them doing any last-second research or communication while they had this quick chat.

Leaning his umbrella against the wall, Ajay stepped into the doorway with his hands raised and his hood pulled back. A dozen headlights, all harsh halogens, blazed in his face. The shapes of people moved alongside their vehicles, but the harsh lights kept their forms concealed.

"Ajay Andersen," a man said in a reedy voice. "How has retirement been treating you?" One of the shapes moved forward, harsh headlights illuminating him.

The man's well-cut suit shone in the glare, its luminescent weave capturing the array of light and casting it off in an almost hypnotic pattern. His crop of short hair danced in the cool breeze.

Ajay finally recognized him. "Jackson Garver." Behind him, he felt the movement of the others passing on their way to the stair that led into the basement below.

Jackson's posture relaxed and he stepped forward, hand outstretched as if to offer a shake.

"Stay where you are," Ajay said. "Word is we have something to work out here." The black box grew warm in his pocket. The other men shifted behind the cover of their trucks, weapons plainly visible. Mack stood a few feet behind Jackson, arms crossed.

The smile on Jackson's face failed to reach his eyes. "Nothing to work out, really," he said. "You have something of mine."

"You finally give up on being a shitty hacker?"

He shook his head. "Oh, Andersen, there's so much you don't know."

Ajay ground his teeth. "Let us go. These are my granddaughters. What do they have that you want?"

Jackson's eyes sparkled with amusement. "Perhaps Isabelle can show you." He activated his fidget, selecting routines from its glowing display.

A flash of rage flared in Ajay's chest. Maybe the slow crush of helplessness finally got to him, or maybe a vestige of familial protectiveness flared up in his old bones. Stepping from the safety of the tower, Ajay closed the distance between himself and Jackson and jammed an index finger at the man's perfectly pressed tie. "What's so funny, Jackson?"

Jackson's eyes flicked to the side. Ajay caught the look and turned in time to see a couple of men moving in behind him. He shot a warning look at them and something on his face must have shocked them because they stopped. In the morning sun, he no longer felt cold, but instead, the heat in his chest felt like it burned hot enough to melt the whole field. That, along with the searing waves now emanating from the diamond-optical, and he didn't feel numb at all anymore.

He almost felt alive.

The smile twitched at the corners of his mouth. "Do you ever feel like you ought to respect your elders a little more?" Ajay asked.

Jackson glanced at the back of his hand, where a holographic display showed red warnings. He shook it and tried again. "Are you jamming us?"

Ajay kept his face impassive, even as his heart skipped from the rush of adrenaline.

Jackson grabbed Ajay's coat and pulled him close, looking him in the eyes. After a long moment, he shoved the old man back, causing him to stumble and fall painfully to the hard earth. Ajay reached into his pocket, wincing at the heat coming from the black box. Hoping it wasn't damaged, he thumbed the control and switched off the jamming signal.

"It was nice seeing you again, Jackson," Ajay said.

Jackson's display came alive with alerts. "Jesus Christ, Andersen," said Jackson. Then, to the others, "Move back! Everyone back in the trucks." In a flurry of movement and roar of diesels, the hired men retreated from the tower, leaving Ajay in a heap.

Ajay scrambled the final few feet back into the tower.

The explosion struck like a snowplow hits roadkill. Heat washed over Ajay, flattening him with concussive force. Bricks rained down outside.

Men and women shouted. Lights flashed as trucks backed away. People ran.

A tree near the tower burst into flames as another missile hit. Splinters pattered against Ajay's coat.

Jackson, somehow unhurt by falling bricks, brought up his holographic display. "Get out here, Isabelle," he shouted, gesturing several commands into the machine at once. "Now!"

Ajay scrambled forward, tumbling down the stairs as another missile struck the tower. More bricks fell, showering him with dust and rock. In the dark, down below, he heard shouts. He scrambled to his feet and rushed on, heedless of the ache in his limbs.

Isabelle hit him going the other way, but he tackled her, and the two of them tumbled forward and down.

Another missile hit, shoving them both down into the tunnel. Ajay struck his head against the stone wall, and everything went black.

CHAPTER FOURTEEN

Ajay opened his eyes to darkness, dust, and despair. Blinking back tears only made them worse. He pawed at his hearing aid, trying to get the high-pitched hum to fade. It wouldn't. The sound came not from the device, but from his own ringing ears.

He scrambled forward, feeling at his pockets. The umbrella was gone, left above. Garrison pushed his wet nose into Ajay's face, slobbering all over his cheek.

The old man rasped, "Girls," pushing the dog back. The sound barely registered in his ears, and the muffled noises around him rose to meet it. Someone else survived. Who?

The fidget in his hand flared to life at a swipe, its blazing light stabbing through the dust-filled air. Someone moved not far ahead. Touching the figure, he found Olivia, who jumped and turned to him. She held Kylie, whose tears mixed with dust in a mask of mud.

"Where's Isabelle?" Ajay asked. Garrison looked up at him, head cocked to one side.

Olivia shook her head. There was hardly room in the tunnel for Ajay to pass, but he squeezed by. If Isabelle was farther back behind him, she'd be dead. She had to be somewhere farther ahead. The possibility of Isabelle's death sent a rush of panic through Ajay. He'd failed to protect her. It was Sashi all over again. His bloody hands shone in the amber light of the handheld but gave him no pain. Only guilt. Failure.

Ajay gripped the wall, using the stone archways as a makeshift support. Shrugging off his pain, he forced himself forward. He shouted for her, though his hearing was so bad he didn't expect hers to do much good. Coughs wracked his chest, the dust filling his lungs.

She couldn't have gone that far. How long was the tunnel? Ajay didn't know how far he'd walked, but his legs felt weak. His head spun. The tunnel was narrow and straight, its brick walls well-aged in places and recently restored in others. The wooden beams that made up the supports were painted gray and cast hard shadows from the white light in Ajay's device. Ajay stumbled. Dropped to a knee.

She couldn't have gone that far.

The fidget dropped to the floor, flickering as it hit. He buried his face in his hands. It was too much. To discover granddaughters, only to lose one like this? His whole body shook. Pain and age and weakness crippled him. What could he do? What could he have done? Was she still back there, suffocating under a rock? Maybe he'd missed her. She could still be back there.

But she couldn't have gone that—

Something touched the top of his head, a gentle brush to take some of the dust away.

"Isabelle?" Ajay asked.

She stepped closer, and her ghostly image lingered at the edge of the light. She motioned for him to follow.

Ajay blinked. He looked behind and saw Olivia and Kylie working their way through the tunnel toward him, Garrison trailing along. Had they seen Isabelle up there? Did they know she was there? He picked up his handheld, slipped it into its comfortable spot in his palm, and followed her.

After a short distance, she turned back to him and placed a finger over her lips. When he nodded, she faced forward and continued to lead. The four of them picked their way cautiously through the tunnel. In places, water dripped into puddles on the floor. In other places, boxes stacked almost to the ceiling. When the tunnel branched, Isabelle confidently picked a path and stuck with it. Soon, they came to a set of limestone stairs, which led up to a solid-looking wooden door. Sunlight cut through the gap under the door, illuminating a waist-high pile of junk wood, bronze scraps, and discarded paint jars.

Kylie took Ajay's hand in both of hers. Tears pooled in her eyes, but she wouldn't let them flow. Her chin quivered slightly. Ajay knelt, despite his aching knees, and pulled her in for a hug. He whispered comfort to her and found that his eyes blurred from a well of tears.

"We should go," said Olivia.

Ajay shook his head, not sure if he even could stand. Instead, he slumped against the wall. When Kylie sat next to him, he drew her close and threaded his fingers through her hair. Isabelle watched but said nothing. The unreadable expression on her face didn't change.

"We'll wait," he said. His vision blurred, and exhaustion scratched at his door. "They'll think we're dead, so we have some time. In a while, I'll go out and see where we are." Where they would escape to, he didn't know. Plans didn't exist that far out.

"We stay silent, then." Olivia's features were chiseled from granite. She turned to Isabelle and didn't soften her tone one bit. "You, dearie, better stay silent with whatever you're using to connect."

Isabelle's eyes narrowed.

"That's right," Olivia said, "I know you're trying to get on network over there." She sniffed. "I can smell it. Stay quiet or they'll know we're alive."

Ajay's eyes closed and Kylie's warm body nestled into the crook of his arm. Garrison settled down at his feet, the warmth of the dog's body keeping him something close to comfortable. After a time, Isabelle sat next to him as well. She didn't curl close to him like her sister, but he took her hand in his and she didn't protest.

Granddaughters. Ajay had granddaughters.

The hell if he'd let them go now.

CHAPTER FIFTEEN

They were looking for him. The police, Mack's gang, Jackson fucking Garver. Maybe even Sashi. Ajay hoped Sashi was looking for them. At least he had a chance at explaining his actions to her, right after she explained her actions to him. The thought of a thousand searching drones bearing down on the tunnel exit brought an anxious shake to Ajay's hands that wouldn't stop no matter what.

"Control the questions," he muttered to himself. Well, now the questions ran free to bite whoever they liked.

The plan had always been to avoid detection by making sure they never started looking. It was the best advantage, and in less than twenty-four hours, he'd lost it. The weight of those eyes staring down at him from the sky threatened to crush his aging heart. What if they saw him? What if they knew what he was doing?

Hell, they probably didn't care. Ajay kicked aside a sheaf of waste wood. The afternoon ran on, but it would be hours before dusk allowed his whole group to move anywhere outside of the tunnel with any kind of secrecy. Then the clock would be ticking. They would have only a short amount of time to leave the building here and go…

Where?

Best think of that later. Ajay spotted the bronze handle of something buried deep in the junk. He reached in with one battered, bruised hand. They'd escaped the blast with few injuries, which might have been something like a miracle. Isabelle didn't have a scratch on her, and she'd managed to pull Kylie far enough in that the worst injury between the two of them was a knot on Kylie's head. Olivia was too damn tough to be hurt from something so trivial as falling limestone and concussive force.

He closed his hand around the bronze handle. It was the shape of a lion, and his hand fit perfectly around it. He gave a hard tug, throwing himself off balance when the stick came free easily. The junk pile shifted, and he toppled down to the ground where Garrison licked his face until he used his new walking stick to stand up. It balanced well in his hands. Some of the wood was worn away, and the brass handle was a bit too heavy and poorly molded. Still, it had a pleasant feel to it, and if he couldn't have his squid umbrella back, this lion was likely the next best thing.

Afternoon light still shone in from the tunnel entrance. Through it, they could see a large utility shed that leaned heavily to one side. Weeds grew up around the lot, and the forest stood only a hundred yards away.

Olivia crawled back into the tunnel, covered in grass, wood from the junk pile, and a layer of dirt that might have been from the explosion and might have been applied for the sake of camouflage. "There's a little utility vehicle in that shed that we can steal."

"Why are you wearing that stuff?" Kylie asked. She sat in a corner with Garrison's head in her lap.

"Camouflage, dearie," Olivia said. "If anything's poking around out there, this'll confuse it."

Ajay asked, "Does it have power?"

"It's charging now. I don't know what kind of shape it'll be in. Looks like it's been sitting there a while." She shrugged off the bulk of her camouflage.

"Fine." Ajay rubbed his temples. "Hopefully they haven't figured out we're alive yet, and if we can get into the trees, we should be hidden from any cursory scans."

Olivia nodded, wiping the dust from her face with a cloth from her purse. "Where's Isabelle?"

Ajay's breath caught. Where was she? He looked to Kylie.

Kylie shrugged. "She said she'd be back."

Ajay shot a glance down the dark black of the tunnel. "How long ago did she leave?"

Kylie shrank into herself, hugging Garrison for support. "I don't know," she said, almost too quiet for Ajay to hear.

"Dammit," he said. He tested his new cane once again, and when it held his weight, he turned back to the tunnel.

Isabelle stood there, at the edge of darkness, holding a stuffed backpack. She tossed it to the floor. Ajay couldn't see any sign of exhaustion dragging her down the way it pulled so hard at him. The girl stepped past the dropped bag, touching her sister on the cheek. Kylie refused to meet Isabelle's gaze, and Ajay got the distinct impression that something passed between them: some unspoken communication.

The backpack was full of granola bars and cheese. Ajay's belly grumbled so loudly that he didn't even think to ask where the food came from. Why bother? He distributed food to the others, who gladly took their shares.

"Thank you, Isabelle," Ajay said through mouthfuls of granola, "but please don't go off on your own again."

Isabelle rolled her eyes, but she appeared to be more amused than truly annoyed.

Ajay peered out the tunnel entrance. "We have a few hours before dark still, but when the sun sets, we're going to get ourselves over to the forest and travel under cover away from the sky for a while."

"Where are we going?" asked Kylie.

Olivia said, "We don't know, honey, but we'll be spotted if we head back to town, so your grandfather says we should go for the forest."

Kylie jutted her lower jaw out. "I want to go home."

Ajay shook his head. "What can you tell me about your home, Kylie? Where do you live?"

Kylie chewed on her lip, and Isabelle shrank in on herself. The older sister tuned out of the conversation, preferring instead to stare out into the waning afternoon. After several deep breaths, Kylie looked back at Ajay and said, "We're not supposed to say."

Isabelle's gaze snapped to her sister. "Tell them."

After a long pause, Kylie said, "Mama says we live in a bubble. It keeps everything we do a secret so that bad people can't find us." She drew a circle on the floor with her finger. "There's little buildings and corn everywhere as far as we can see, but mostly it's just the lab."

"Your mother's lab? Trevan Pharma?"

"And Dad's. They used to work together."

Used to. Ajay wanted to wonder about what drove them apart, but couldn't get past the idea that his daughter was married and he never knew. The bubble that Kylie talked about must have been a powerfully paranoid piece of technology.

"When can we go home?" Kylie asked.

Comforting words existed somewhere, but Ajay could not think of a single one. He took her hands in his and fought back the empty pit that threatened to open in his chest. How far had he grown from his daughter that she was married with these wonderful kids, and he never knew? Could he have figured everything out if he had tried, or were his skills as a hacker so outdated that her bubble would have kept him out regardless?

A crease formed between Kylie's eyebrows. Tears beaded in the corners of her eyes. "I want to go home."

Ajay looked at her, and a healthy mix of exhaustion and helplessness washed over him. His shoulders slumped. He did his best to keep the pleading expression from his face. "You're just like her," he said in a quiet voice. Olivia placed a hand gently on his shoulder, though Ajay didn't know if it was meant for support or restraint.

Kylie's expression turned to one of curiosity. "Who?" she asked.

Ajay settled down onto the remains of a wooden box. He clasped his hands on the handle of his found walking stick and let his mind wander back to long ago. Had times changed so much over all those years? Maybe Ajay was the one to have changed, and the world rolled on the same as ever.

Well. There certainly were some changes.

Kylie sat cross-legged on the tunnel floor, while Isabelle leaned with loose limbs against the wall. The older girl pretended disinterest, but Ajay saw that she tilted one ear in his direction. She knew that he would talk about their mother, and likely didn't want to miss a word of it.

"It was long ago," Ajay started, slipping easily into his storytelling voice. "Your mother was no older than Isabelle over there, and maybe a year or two younger. Her mother had long since passed from this world, leaving me in charge."

"That's trouble," Olivia said.

He cast a sideways look her direction. "But young Sashi developed a strong sense of independence, being raised by only me. You see, back then I worked as a cyberspy for the government, in something called the NSA."

Kylie leaned in. "You were a cyberspy?"

The old man nodded. "The very best, and back when such things were much harder. You see, in those days, computers had encryption and heavy security. People had an illusion of privacy since the various cameras and other sensors that they gathered around themselves were at least marginally protected."

Olivia cleared her throat loudly.

"What?" Ajay asked.

"You're getting off-topic."

Ajay bristled. "I'm not."

She motioned for him to continue.

"The state of technology at the time is important to the story," Ajay said. When nobody responded, he continued. "Sashi wanted to go on a road trip with a friend, and I wouldn't let her. Maybe she was a little older than you,

Isabelle, but the boy she wanted to go with was older still because he could drive. Anyway, it wasn't a good idea and I thought that was the end of it." He twisted the cool bronze in his hands. "It wasn't, of course. I thought nothing more of it, and then one day Sashi was gone. Went to school; didn't come back."

Kylie's eyes were wide. He had her attention, and leaned forward, drawing out a long pause. "After a time, when she still hadn't returned, I did as any father would do: I worried. And I worried." He licked his lips. "And I worried."

Isabelle turned to look at him, concern darkening her beautiful eyes.

"Couldn't you find her with the eyes in the sky?" Kylie asked.

Ajay shook his head. "No, there were no drones back then, at least none the public could get to easily. There were cameras around, of course, and other sensors. Social media gave the computers a window into the world, but it was very chaotic and not reliable. Remember, back when there was encryption, people had an expectation of privacy. I may have had the tools and skills to get into every device out there, but such things were forbidden."

Kylie scrunched up her nose. "What did you do?"

"I did as any good father would do." Ajay stretched out his sore hip, feeling the joint pop as he did. "I assumed she had been kidnapped and broke every goddamn rule to get her back."

Kylie's mouth dropped open.

"We were at the cusp of something, and very few people realized it." A tingle ran down Ajay's spine as he recalled the discovery. "With early quantum computing on hand, I was able to break encryption and tap thousands of devices at once. Audio, video. It took mere minutes to find her, even though she and her boyfriend had turned off their phones. Ultimately, it was facial recognition from a security camera at an Arby's two hundred miles away that found her."

"Damn," said Olivia.

"Damn is right," Ajay said. "Whole lot of legal mess came down after that one, on account of all the broken laws."

Kylie frowned. "I thought we were going to hear a story about Mom."

Ajay smiled. "Well, I gave the hotel she was staying at a call, see." He mimed making a phone call, but Kylie cocked her head to the side like she didn't understand the gesture. "This is how we talked on phones back then," he said, rolling his eyes. "Anyway, do you know what she said when she realized I was on the line?"

"What?"

"She said, 'Three days, Papa? Don't you even care about me?'" Ajay swallowed, suddenly very aware of a lump forming in his throat. "See, it only took me a few hours to find her, but it took me two days to notice she was gone and another whole day to decide what to do about it. And she knew it."

Olivia clapped Ajay on the back, hard enough to jolt him out of his reverie. "That was a terrible story to tell, Ajay." She helped him stand up. "But thanks."

"Thanks for what?"

"For opening up and finally telling a real story. If I'd known that all it took to get you to open up all these years was a mild concussion, maybe we'd be a lot closer."

"We're close."

She shook her head. "You feel close because I tell you about myself. All I know about you is that you love golf and you're good with computers."

Ajay's jaw tensed. He'd always felt a connection with Olivia, but maybe was he lost in some self-involved illusion? Olivia was one of his closest friends after Ben. Could it be that she didn't think much of him after all?

"I'm sorry," he said.

She watched him for a long time as if debating what to say. Finally, she said, "You're a decent man, Ajay. Don't wait too long to let people know about it."

"Decent," he muttered to himself as she walked away. Nobody had thought of him as decent since his wife had died so long ago. Even before that, he'd never thought of himself that way. Pragmatic, clever, and maybe charming, he could see those. It was too late in his life to add decent to the list, just like it was too late to add PGA champion to his list of credentials.

He looked out the tunnel entrance and saw that the sky had deepened while he spoke. Dusk crept across the open field, and if they were going to make their way to the cover of the autumn canopy, now, when the drones above had the hardest time picking out movement below, was their best shot.

On the first step, his hip popped, sending a fresh jolt of pain through his leg. "Well," he said, offering a hand to Kylie. "We'd best be going, then. Grab some cover and we'll make our way out."

With that, he pulled his hood over his face and made his way to the leaning barn. Sure enough, amongst piles of tools and junk, sat an old utility cart. It was little more than a rugged golf cart, with a long-lasting electric motor and a miniature truck bed. The green canopy over the top was moth-eaten and decrepit, but on the dash, a small blue light blinked.

Across a short prairie, the lights of Highway 61 shone in the encroaching dusk. Beyond, the wreckage of Towerview blazed with lights. Police swarmed the area, accompanied by ambulances and construction equipment. They wouldn't find the bodies they searched for, and Ajay wondered how long it would be before they gave up.

He stood at the edge of that great dark expanse of forest. If they made their way forward, he wouldn't need to worry about tripping errant sensors for miles, buying a little more time before really deciding their destination.

When Ajay started the cart, it rolled forward with only a slight tap of the accelerator. Isabelle and Kylie piled in the cargo bed in back along with Garrison. Olivia sat next to Ajay and patted him on the leg as he drove them quietly onto the narrow dirt road that wound its way into the forest.

Olivia leaned close and whispered to him. "It really was a terrible story."

"I know," he said as the dark trees swallowed the sky. "I know."

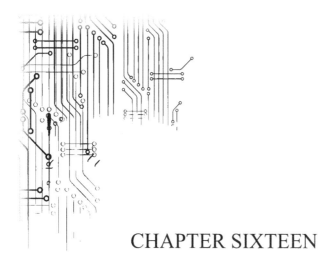

CHAPTER SIXTEEN

The dirt road was little more than a seldom-used trail. Two lines of shorter weeds hinted that once, long ago, the trail had been used by cars or other vehicles. Ajay figured as long as it ran north he could use it to reach the Mississippi, but from there what would they do? He also figured that since the Cannon River was low, he would be able to drive the cart across a shallow spot without any trouble.

He was wrong. The cart got stuck.

It wasn't just stuck; it was really stuck. Jammed up against the ancient stump of a fallen willow, its wheels mired in muck and loose vegetation on the shore. Ajay's head throbbed. His muscles ached. Big, fat bruises bloomed on his arms and chest. He didn't even remember where all of them came from. His hip screamed as he strained against the cart, but the thing didn't move.

"Should I press the accelerator now?" asked Kylie.

Ajay let up. "You weren't?" he said when his breath came back. Garrison nuzzled his hand, and he absently scratched the old dog behind the ears. Garrison loved the entire situation as if messing around in the shallow waters wouldn't end with them all shivering the rest of the night.

Kylie chewed on her lip.

"You know," said Ajay to Isabelle, who stood a short distance away, watching, "you're welcome to help."

Isabelle raised an eyebrow but didn't move from her perch on the far shore. It was best she stayed hidden, anyway. Where Ajay pushed from the river's edge, he could see the sky, and the sky could see him, and that meant the danger of drones.

Ajay couldn't figure out how those men following them could activate a Thunderhead. And why would they? They'd acted as if they wanted something the girls had, but if that were true, why blow it all up? The government controlled the drones, anyway, and anyone outside of official channels would have a hell of a time coopting the weapons.

That meant the police really had it in for them.

"She wants to know where we're going," said Kylie.

"I think we should go see an acquaintance of mine who lives up here on the reservation."

Isabelle hugged herself against the cold.

"He's a hacker who goes by the name the Loon," Ajay said, feeling a need to justify his plan. "He'll help us find your mother." Among other things. If they could get Loon's help, they might be able to hide in plain sight.

Olivia returned, crashing through the dark woods. She emerged, gray hair in disarray and her coat scattered with twigs and leaves. Ajay watched, speechless, as she brushed twigs from her now unkempt hair. When she finished, she looked up at him and flashed a crooked smile that warmed his toes.

Ajay braced his back against the back of the cart, so he could push with his legs. "Punch it," he said.

Wheels whirred as Kylie pounded on the accelerator. Ajay pushed and the cart inched forward. Louder and louder it whirred, wheels spinning, kicking up mud.

Ajay's feet slipped. He planted ass-first in mud. Kylie let up, and they were all silent while Ajay stood and tried his best to clean up.

Isabelle politely covered a smug smile with one hand.

Olivia braced herself against the cart, very careful to keep her feet on dry land. "That the Loon friend of yours you're talking about? That the activist you told me about with his own radio tower?"

"That's the guy."

"And is that the same guy with the weapons cache and largest collection of anti-surveillance equipment this side of the Mason-Dixon?"

Ajay nodded.

"You know how I feel about his sort." Olivia's scowl cut deep furrows in her brow. "I fought too hard for this country to see it pulled apart by people like him."

"Just because he used to be part of the dissent doesn't mean he's going to be trouble." Ajay took up a spot next to her, drawing deep breaths to calm himself. "And he's the best chance we have."

"He's wanted in three states." Olivia scowled again. "One of them is Minnesota."

"That's why he's on the Lakota-Sioux rez. The rules are different there." Ajay started pushing. Garrison cocked his head at them as if trying to figure out what was going on. "All right, Kylie. Hit it."

Wheels whirred. With Olivia's help, the cart lurched forward and grabbed solid dirt. Kylie squealed as the vehicle launched itself down the narrow trail.

"Let off the gas!" shouted Ajay.

"What's gas?" Kylie shouted back as the cart barreled around a corner.

The crash of cracking plastic shattered the calm forest. Ajay ran after Kylie, following the still bright lights. She hadn't made it far before smacking the cart directly into a sturdy oak. Wheels still spun, digging at the wet leaves underneath. Kylie blinked, as if stunned.

"The gas is the accelerator," said Ajay, gently lifting her leg up, stopping the cart's spinning wheels.

Damage to the cart wasn't terrible. The front hood was cracked, and all of their cargo scattered from the back, but the motor still worked. Ajay pulled Kylie in for a one-armed hug, grinning proudly at her.

She shot him a weak smile. "Sorry."

"Not a big deal," he said.

Kylie shrank into herself.

Olivia laughed, giving Kylie a one-armed hug that shook the little girl to her core. "That was wonderful! Wonderful!"

Kylie flashed a weak smile. "Really?"

The old lady stuck a thumb out at Ajay. "The old man couldn't have done better himself."

"Well," Ajay said, clearing his throat. "This seems as good a place to take a break as any."

They set up the cart bed so the girls could get some rest, bundling them against the cold in their jackets and a couple of thin blankets that they'd stolen from the utility shed. Ajay found food for everyone from Isabelle's backpack, and though Isabelle's complaints were written plainly on her face, she didn't voice them, and thus they were easy to ignore. Olivia brought some gum from her purse and told the girls it was just as good as brushing their teeth. Once the kids were asleep, Ajay and Olivia sat on the cold ground, backs against the giant oak. The absurdity of their situation shook Ajay with laughter from time to time.

"I don't like it," Olivia said.

"Another hour or two north, then we get our bearings at the Mississippi. Then we should be able to find the place." He picked at dirt under his fingernails. "Every time we cross one of those little county roads, we're risking getting spotted from above."

"This cart won't last," she said.

Ajay looked back at the cracked plastic bumper. "The battery might give us a few more hours, then we'll walk." How well would he be able to cover terrain once the cart stopped working? He stretched his hip out, feeling it pop. Garrison lay on Ajay's feet, warming them as much as a wet dog could.

"Do you trust this guy?" Olivia asked.

It was a long time before Ajay understood she was talking about the Loon. "I trust him with my own life. Every day."

"But can you trust him with theirs?"

Ajay twisted around for a look at the sleeping girls. They had moved so they were curled up together. They looked almost comfortable there, with Isabelle wrapping her little sister, protecting her from the world.

Olivia drew his amber fidget from her pocket and handed it to him. "I did just what you asked. I got as high up as I could, but there's not much signal this far out."

"There aren't many places that still lack connection, but this rez is one of them." Ajay took the device and powered it up. Sure enough, the logs from the alerts rolled out across the screen. There was somebody looking for them. Multiple someones. The clumsy attempts of the local police stood out in sharp contrast to the slick and nearly invisible attempts of someone else. Jackson, Ajay guessed, but there was no way to be sure. Whoever it was hadn't broken through his anonymization, but it was close. If anyone bothered to look, they might be smart enough to figure out that someone was trying to connect from the middle of nowhere, but Olivia hadn't let the device communicate long enough for that. For now, their location would stay hidden.

But they were looking. Did that mean they knew he was alive? They were asking questions, and he didn't have any control over what and how they asked. Eventually, they would track him down. Then what?

"What about the rest of it?" he asked. "Were you able to get anything else?"

"It's all there," she said, pointing to the device in his hands. "Trevan Pharma is one of the most paranoid corporations out there, running back at least fifteen years."

The logs on the device showed a snap download of public records documents during the period fourteen years prior. It also had some conspiracy theory garbage and a whole flood of public relations documentation.

"Look at the government contracts," Olivia said. "They're more than a simple pharmaceutical company. This is military stuff."

"But no details. Everything useful is wiped from public record. Could they possibly be involved in something that goes high enough up to hide all these contracts?" A quick scan through the logs found names and dates associated with projects during the last fifteen years. Sashi's name came up several times, and Ajay wrote a quick script to archive any other names associated with her contracts. "Seems likely they're running from the government or Trevan Pharma itself."

"Or their father," Olivia said.

"Sure, sure." Ajay scanned the document feed again. "But who is their father?"

"You could ask them."

Ajay shut down the device and stared out into the darkness until his eyes adjusted. "Sashi doesn't want me to know."

Olivia spoke in a low voice. "Then maybe you shouldn't."

"We're a little involved at this point. Any information we can gather helps us." He stuck his thumb out at the girls. "It helps them."

"Are we being fools out here, Ajay?" she asked. "Shouldn't we just call your daughter and let her take care of it?" A hesitation in her voice hinted that she might not be sure anymore.

"Maybe," he said. "Maybe."

Olivia shivered, then wrapped an arm around Ajay to pull him close. He let her. A chill ran through his whole body, and being next to her warmth reminded him of it. Something about being close to her made him feel safe. Soon, he drifted into a fitful sleep.

When he woke, the few fragments of sky that filtered through the yellow leaves were the color of old age. A thin patina of dew embraced the forest floor and sapped warmth from Ajay's tired bones. His joints felt frozen like the rusted gears of an abandoned truck. They popped and creaked as he stretched.

The movement disturbed Olivia, who grunted and shifted away. It took him several long seconds of looking at the small cart to figure out what was wrong. Isabelle was gone. Kylie still lay wrapped up in blankets, curled into a little ball.

He plucked his walking stick from the back of the cart. Isabelle must not have left long ago, as her trail was still clear on the wet earth. His muscles loosened as he followed, crippling stiffness giving way to dull ache. The cool autumn air smelled of wet leaves, something that reminded him of freedom. There was no technology out in the middle of the reservation. Nobody watched constantly.

Reds and yellows fluttered above, responding to a pull of wind he couldn't feel down below. Nothing touched them in this protected valley between the bluffs. Here, far from the fields or cities, they were almost safe. The leaves were green and red and orange here. No white-touched plants this far away from the fields.

Isabelle crouched at the lip of the river, poking at its waters with a stick. The long branches of a willow draped around her, and the light that filtered through gave her an ethereal quality. When Ajay approached she glanced up, a vulnerability shading her expression that he had never seen before.

Her jaw hardened. "I couldn't sleep," she whispered.

Ajay made his way up next to her by the stream and stared into its shallow waters. "It's cold, I know."

She shook her head. "It's lonely here."

"You have your sister." Ajay felt thin and shaky. He searched for something to say to this girl that would build a connection to her but found none. Instead, all he said was, "We'll find your mother soon."

Isabelle smacked her stick against the water. Her jaw jutted out in a stubborn expression that reminded him so much of Sashi. He'd endured years of that expression, and he'd always known it was his fault. Why couldn't he ever be good enough for her?

Isabelle walked back to the cart. After a while, Ajay followed.

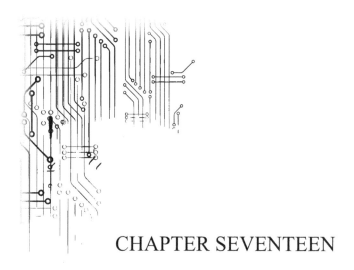

CHAPTER SEVENTEEN

As the day wore on and the gray sky brightened, the temperature warmed, and the day became something close to pleasant. The narrow road they followed petered out into almost nothing, resembling two parallel deer trails in places, choked completely with scraggly buckthorn shrubs in others. Their pace dropped to an excruciating crawl. Kylie hopped out of the cart and walked alongside it while Garrison looked on with baleful eyes.

"I have lots of friends at school," she said to Ajay.

"You do? Do you go to a large school?"

She furrowed her brow. "It's just a regular school." Her sweater caught on a branch and she had to drop back to untangle it. When she caught back up, she said, "They probably don't even know I'm gone."

"Oh, wouldn't they figure it out when you didn't walk in the door?"

Kylie giggled.

"What?" Ajay asked, genuinely confused.

Olivia elbowed him. "Kids go to virtual school these days, old man. Get with the times."

"Really? They do that?" Ajay had stopped paying attention to schools twenty years prior.

"It's just regular school," Kylie said. She hopped up on a mossy log, walking the length of it alongside the slowly moving cart.

Olivia picked up a water bottle. Her hands shook as she twisted open the cap.

"How are you doing back there, Isa?" Ajay asked. "Comfortable?" He looked back at her for the answer, knowing she probably wouldn't speak the answer aloud.

She glared back at him, not bothering to even shake her head. She sat in the filthy back of the vehicle, among shovels, picks, a pile of solar panels, and about fifty pounds of quality black soil. In the rush to leave they hadn't bothered to clean out the back, and the filthy state of Isabelle's clothing made the point moot.

"Dammit!" Olivia tossed the water bottle to the floor of the cart. It spilled onto the plastic, forming a dark puddle. She yanked her foot away from it.

Ajay raised an eyebrow at her. "Problem?"

Kylie jumped back into the back of the utility cart, earning a glare from her sister. Ajay was genuinely surprised at how long the battery had lasted. The warning light blinked amber, but it had been doing that for an hour without any real impact on their progress. It certainly helped that they moved slowly, but as they crawled their way up out of the valley, he knew they would need to recharge or abandon the vehicle and walk.

The forest thinned, and up ahead a county road split the landscape in two. About a five-iron separated the wood from the road. Beyond the cracked asphalt lay another ditch, and then a limestone cliff rose up where the earth broke to make room for the road. The cliff dipped a short distance away, and there was one spot where the rough trail they had been following continued under another canopy of trees.

And right in that spot, one of Mack's men leaned against the bumper of a big Ford truck, holding a small red cigarette in his thin lips. He was all lanky muscle and shaggy mustache. The leather coat he wore draped off him like it'd been hung on a rack.

Ajay turned around to Kylie and Isabelle, who were now huddled together in the back seat. "We have to be extra quiet," he said. "We're only a couple miles from where we need to go, but it'd be better if we didn't lead those guys right there."

Kylie nodded, eyes wide.

"How did he know to stop there?" Olivia asked. Her lips were cracked and dry, and her eyes were bloodshot. "He's waiting for us like he already knows where we're going."

"We don't know that," Ajay said, but his words sounded hollow. He took Olivia's hand in both of his. She refused to look at him. "Maybe they picked up on that download after all, and they're making some guesses about where we might be headed."

She licked her dry lips. A concerned look slipped across his face, but when she saw it, her jaw clenched.

"I'm fine," she said. "My hydrophobia's acting up."

Ajay couldn't imagine Olivia being anything other than fine, so when she said it, he believed it. Hydrophobia was a side effect of some of the older biotech. He didn't know what she was on those meds for, but it had to be something delivered directly to the brain.

"Do you have any music?" she asked.

Ajay furrowed his brow, not knowing why music mattered at that point. "Sure."

"Can you play Beethoven's Moonlight Sonata? Back when I was Army, that song got me in the zone for sniping. It might help."

Ajay navigated his fidget. He had the song in local storage, not by strange coincidence, but because he had often heard her play it. "Don't you have pills?"

Olivia closed her eyes and seemed to absorb the song through her skin. "Don't you think I would have taken them?"

He nodded. Of course, she would have. She'd probably left them at home. Ajay didn't very much like the idea of her skipping meds, and the sense of urgency ramped up like the rapids in a river. How long could she go without another drink of water? A day or two?

"I'm fine," Olivia repeated. Then, in a quieter voice, she said, "It won't matter much, anyway."

"Isabelle thinks we should talk to him," Kylie said from beside the cart.

Ajay snapped, "He'll probably shoot us before we get within chipping range," then immediately felt bad when Kylie winced.

Isabelle furrowed her brow in confusion.

The corners of Olivia's mouth twitched up, and she touched Isabelle's hand. "He's talking about golf, honey."

The teenager nodded, clearly not really understanding.

"Chipping is close," Olivia explained. "Fifty yards or so. Your grandfather just wishes that he wasn't afraid to still play."

"I can't still play."

"If you say so."

Ajay bit back a retort. A night sleeping on the cold ground and a morning without coffee had done a dark service to his mood. He walked back into the woods, taking in the heavy, cool air. Garrison followed at his side.

He rubbed the dog's ears. "Well, buddy, what do you think we should do?"

Garrison didn't express an opinion one way or the other.

After a few minutes alone with his dog, Ajay felt better able to handle the problem ahead. He turned around and made his way back through the woods. When he returned to the cart, Olivia wasn't there. He looked questioningly at Kylie and Isabelle, but they shrugged.

Out on the road, Olivia stalked up to the man by the truck.

The guy tensed. His left hand rested on the grip of a pistol. Ajay could see his lips move as he addressed Olivia, but her exact response was lost. His hearing aid only picked up the rustle of leaves up above.

Olivia didn't stop walking. She made her way through open field and the high weeds. Using Ajay's new walking stick, she crossed the unsteady terrain. The stick jabbed at the earth like she was trying to skewer it clean through. Her claw hand gripped the bronze lion like the talon of a bird.

As she got closer, the man took a step back. He talked louder. Yelled. "Stop, lady!"

But by then it was too late. Olivia popped the stick up, gripped it like a baseball bat, and swung. Ajay heard the crack as bronze pounded against the man's skull. His gun, half out of its holster, scraped against his truck as he fell. The man's head smacked hard against asphalt.

Olivia turned back to the forest and waved for them. Ajay climbed into the driver's seat, ignoring Isabelle's scowl. He drove them through that same bumpy land to where Olivia crouched in front of the fallen thug.

Kylie gripped her sister's arm. "Is he dead?" she whispered.

Isabelle shook her head.

Kylie craned her neck to get a better look. "Why'd she do that, then?"

"He was a bad man, Kylie," Ajay said. "He only let her get close because he wasn't going to let himself be afraid of an old lady."

"He is now," said Olivia, grinning. She belted the holster around her waist and made sure the safety was on before stowing the weapon. "He sure as hell is now."

Ajay took the cart around the still-idling truck, and soon they were bumping along through the forest again. It hurt him, leaving the truck, but there was no way to figure out how many ways the truck could be tracked. Better to keep going on an almost dead utility cart than a truck that would lead the enemy right to them. Ajay wondered if that had been Jackson's plan in positioning a guy there.

"We should have killed him," said Kylie.

Isabelle pinched her sister.

"Ow!" Kylie punched back. Hard.

"Girls," Ajay said, but there was no energy left in him. "Girls," he said again.

Isabelle and Kylie fell silent.

"Ajay," said Olivia.

"What?"

Olivia held up a finger for silence. For a long while frustration built in Ajay, tasting bitter in the back of his throat.

Then he heard it. The sound was so faint he wondered how Olivia had heard it at all. Adjusting his hearing aid allowed him to pinpoint its location. It came from the direction of the truck.

"A drone," he said. "Low-flying. Do you think it launched from the truck?"

Olivia drew the pistol. "It's coming fast."

Ajay placed a hand on the gun. "Put that away."

Her hand twitched, but she stowed the gun. "We can't let the drone see us."

Ajay pressed the accelerator hard against the floor as if that might nudge the little cart faster. "If we fire a gun, they'll pinpoint us. This area might not have sensors everywhere, but gunshot detection works for miles."

Olivia scoffed. "If that drone's from the truck, they already know where we are. All they have to do is follow our tracks from that fella back there."

She was right. It would only be a matter of time before Mack's men caught up. They might have known more about the threat if they had kept that man awake, but it was no use now. Ajay ground his teeth. Drones were such a tricky target to disable via hacking. And they were always up there, watching.

"All right," he said, "I think I have a plan." He turned around to talk to the girls in the back, but Kylie wasn't there. "Shit."

The corner of Isabelle's lips tipped up in a quirky smile. She stuck a thumb out, indicating the path behind them. Ajay saw the weeds folded down where the little girl had dropped to the forest floor and run back the way they'd come.

"Dammit," he said. "Why don't kids just stay put?"

"Because they're kids?" Olivia said.

Ajay stopped the cart. "Liv," he said, "take Garrison and Isabelle up the hill." He pointed up ahead and to the right a little. "There's a cliff about a mile that way. You ditch this cart up there, then come back about halfway down and head that way."

Olivia took his place in the driver's seat. "I'll mark the spot we leave the path," she said. "Just keep an eye out and you'll see it."

As they pulled away, he called after them quietly enough that he wasn't sure they could hear. "Just keep going," he said. "If I don't catch up, just keep on going."

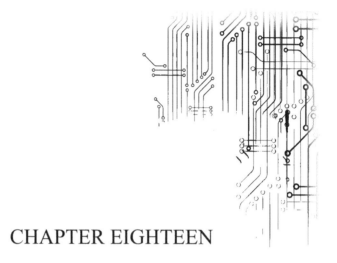

CHAPTER EIGHTEEN

"Kylie," Ajay called into the forest. Where had she gone? Ahead, the buzz of the drone sputtered and skipped. It was changing course, moving low through the forest. With so many trees between him and the tiny copter, it was impossible to tell how far away it might be.

Not far, though.

Ajay stepped behind an oak, and the buzz entered the clearing. It had heard him talk, but had he disguised his voice well enough? It might match a vocal record to a clear voice.

Or it might not. He needed to know what the thing was capable of.

Where was Kylie?

There. Low branches full of glossy green leaves shuffled as something behind them moved. She had to be there. Ajay crept away as the drone circled, keeping a thick oak between him and it. He clutched his walking stick, angling it against the ground to take pressure from his aching hip.

Movement ahead, and a scuff on some mossy bark. Was Kylie leading him, or was she trying to stay clear of the drone? Why had she come here if she was only going to run away?

"Kylie," he whispered as loud as he dared. "Kylie, where are you?"

She gave no answer, but the drone, again, sputtered and changed course. It drifted slowly, so keeping ahead of it wouldn't be a problem. His feet sank into soft earth, sending the scent of rich soil into the air. A thick duff layer of leaves padded the forest floor, but many of those leaves had been pulled away. Freshly exposed wet leaves glistened underfoot. The drone rounded the last tree and its distinct buzz sounded at his back.

He sprinted forward, but his foot slipped on an exposed root, cracking his knee against the oak's knobby bole. White-hot pain flared through his leg and hip. He bit back a curse, and instead of moving, made himself perfectly still.

The cold bronze of the cane's handle touched Ajay's forehead. His gloved hand gripped the stick as he listened, eyes closed and hood pulled close over his face. Breath swirled in front of him, pooling in the dark cave formed by his hood and arms. Dagger-sharp pain dulled into a deep throb.

It was all about shape. Ajay let his long coat flow over his body, his face hidden beneath the hood. Standing in the crook of a massive oak, his coat blended him with its dark form. Making sure to keep his face hidden, Ajay peeked from beneath his hood. It hovered close, the chop-chop sputter of the little thing resonating off the still autumn forest.

All he had to do was pull back his hood and he'd see it there floating through the clearing.

And it would see him.

He froze, body close up against the oak. Breath seeped in and out, becoming a passive flow of air rather than an active movement of the lungs. He was intimately familiar with the software running on such drones. It was a Seeker class. It had been his specialty. It was smaller than a football and unbelievably light. The rotors hitched and hummed as it wove its way among the trees, closer and closer. Now that the sound of it was clear, his hearing aid helped him identify it by running through a previously configured series of protocols. Each drone had a unique sound.

"Seeker Model 45-1," said the soft voice in his skull. An older model, then. Good. It wouldn't have the latest in body form recognition.

Ajay's grip tightened on his walking stick. For the first time since fleeing his mind seemed to grasp the danger of his predicament. Who would send such tech after these girls? Why was anyone interested in two kids? Could this be the police coming after him?

And where was Sashi?

His fidget sat like an inert lump in his pocket. If he used it for anything he'd be tracked. He was sure of it. Any worth-his-coin hacker could track him if they wanted. Sending Olivia out to do an anonymous download had been a stupid risk, and no doubt that was the reason Jackson and Mack's gang had been able to get so close.

Or was it? Mack wouldn't have sent one man if he had known exactly where they were. The whole gang would have been there at the intersection. They had to be furious after Sashi had killed so many of them at Mississippi Prosthetics. How many more had died when the Thunderhead struck? Jackson had hired the gang, but Ajay seriously doubted they were still entirely under his control. He swallowed a lump that formed in the back of his throat.

Mack's gang was the most immediate threat, but probably the least of his long-term worries.

Then there was Jackson. How did that sub-par hacker play into all this?

The drone stopped. Why did it stop? Ajay held his breath, no longer allowing himself even the faintest hint of air. The old man was as much part of the tree as anything in the forest. Image recognition wouldn't flag him. It couldn't. There was no way its shape recognition would identify this lump as anything worthwhile.

The drone's hum shifted, and it edged closer.

Ajay's heart hammered. Bitter bile rose at the back of his throat. Teeth ached. How could it not hear that ticking clock in his chest? The rushing in his ears? His fingers clutched the walking stick's cold bronze handle.

It was close. One good swing would take it down. A chip shot; not even a full drive. It was high, though. By the sound of it, the drone hovered a foot or two above Ajay's head.

But it would see his face if his hood fell back. Any such images would transmit so fast he'd have no chance to disable them before whoever was searching the woods recorded the evidence.

Did it matter? If it saw him at all, recognition might not make a difference. No, that wasn't right. Those seekers only reported back if they flagged facial recognition. If it didn't get a good look at him, maybe he could avoid giving away his exact location.

Why were they looking for the girls? Sashi knew. Ajay was sure of it. She knew, and by not telling him she was putting the girls at risk.

Ajay had to breathe. He had to. The drone's buzz shifted again and retreated a few feet. Could he risk it? A tiny fraction of his held breath escaped. It rasped on its way out.

The drone sputtered. Stopped in midair.

Shit.

Drone piñatas were popular for a while. Rich children of rich parents had used overpriced drones along with noisemakers and other novelty items to make a somewhat violent and deeply satisfying party game. It was all the rage at birthday parties for kids of all ages. For a while, it had been the staple of frat parties and team-building seminars. Someone had even done a series of peer-reviewed research articles on the practice of echo-location and the human brain's ability to process sound.

Ajay had always thought it was a bullshit fad. Not so much now.

He drew a deep breath. Cold air struck his lungs like a bucket of ice.

The drone edge closer.

Without looking, Ajay raised his stick in two hands, the heavy bronze handle circling wide. He swung hard.

And missed.

The drone, reacting to his movement, buzzed back rapidly. He charged after, heedless of terrain. Hood covered his face, all the way down to his chin. His foot slipped, sending wrenching pain through his hip. Another swing, less forceful this time, and the walking stick slammed against something solid with a resounding crack. The drone's noise didn't falter. He'd hit a branch.

The drone moved fast, but his hearing aid helped him locate it. Up and left a little. Faster. Running, shoulder thumping against an oak. His feet found a fallen log and he vaulted over it, ignoring the pain now blooming like fireworks through his side. Still, he didn't pull back his hood. The drone rose higher.

He jumped off the fallen log and swung, his last chance at a clean hit.

Metal crunched through the plastic hull, crushing it like paper mache. Like a piñata. Ajay allowed the smile to creep across his face.

That game was pretty fun after all.

Without pulling back his hood, Ajay went to the spot where the drone lay twitching on the ground. Poor thing. Raising a muddy penny loafer, he stomped it out of its misery. Once sure it couldn't spook and fly away, he flipped on his black box to scramble its signal back home.

"That. Was. Awesome." Kylie looked at him from only a few feet away. She wore wet, matted leaves all over her body, making her look like some kind of shambling pile of filth. Ajay hardly recognized her.

The drone probably wouldn't have, either. Clever girl.

"Don't run off like that, please," Ajay said, breathless.

She looked at the little drone on the ground. "Did you kill it?"

Ajay nudged it with his toe. "No," he said, "but I'm going to."

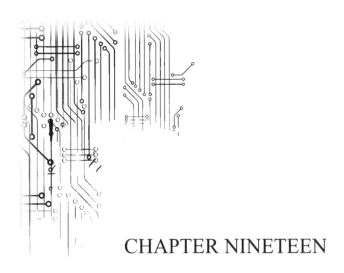

CHAPTER NINETEEN

"Who the hell sent you?" Ajay slipped his cheaters on and pried at the jagged edges of a broken panel. "What are you looking for?"

Kylie leaned in close. She smelled like damp leaves, even though she had already removed her camouflage. "It's trying to talk, isn't it?"

"Yes." Ajay patted the little diamond-optical device next to the drone. "I won't let it, though, not until it says what I want it to say."

"Can you do that?" she asked.

"Sure." He picked up the box. "This particular model can force-scramble any data signal up to fifty meters. It has some other features, too."

"Isn't that illegal?"

By the time he decided to lie to her, he could tell she had already read the truth on his face. "It's a gray area," he finally said.

She narrowed her eyes.

"Dark gray." Ajay looked her up and down. She was really interested in this. Not that it surprised him. Kylie was an intelligent girl with a quick wit. Why wouldn't she want to learn a little bit about hacking and technology? He wondered how much Sashi had allowed her daughters to learn. Ajay's daughter had always hated how he interacted with tech as if it were always nothing more than a puzzle to solve. She thought technology deserved the respect one gave a good friend, but Ajay thought tech required the respect only given to a true enemy.

"Are you going to use it to send a message?" She had a hopeful glimmer in her eye.

"You want to talk to your mother," he said.

She nodded.

"Well, not yet. First, we need to figure out who owns this thing."

Of course, it wasn't obvious who owned it. They hadn't stamped a logo on it or scrawled a return address on the bottom. He checked again. No, they hadn't. That in itself was a little suspicious. Automated systems like this one tended to drop out of the sky from time to time. A return address was one way to protect that investment. That and a good security system.

Ajay jabbed the pointy end of his multitool into the drone and sawed apart the auxiliary microchip. Kylie held a panel open while he mucked around inside. All of the communications systems were intact, but Ajay took the time to disconnect both sensor arrays. He sat on the soft layer of leaves, breathing in its wormy scent. His breath billowed out in big clouds.

He used some wire to connect his clunky handheld fidget to the drone's comm array. Newer models lacked the easy wire access, but Ajay's old one had a single port. "I'll spoof the signal," he said. "Should give us a few seconds of untraceable data."

Kylie leaned forward, chewing on her lip.

"What?" Ajay asked.

"You should have it send the okay signal."

Ajay blew out some air. "Can't do it."

"Why not?" A line formed between her eyebrows. "Then you can subvert the signal."

He looked at the readout, scanning a string of values as it slid by on his handheld's display. Could it be done? He poked at the data for a few minutes. Yes, it could. "Subvert?" he said. "Where the hell did you learn that word?"

Kylie grinned, swelling with pride.

"Well, give me a minute, then."

Ajay brushed away the display over his fidget. With his rig back home, the task would be simple. With a decent connection, the little drone would fall in minutes. He tugged at the dry skin flaking off his chapped lips. Who owned this drone? Diving back into the data, he tracked a new swath of segments. Where was all this data going? Where was this instruction coming from?

There. Had that even been there before? He leaned against the tree. A cool breeze quaked in the leaves above.

"Haveraptics Corporation," he said.

Kylie's eyes went wide.

"You know them?"

She wouldn't answer, instead retreating several more feet. She hugged herself against the cold.

Ajay shrugged, knowing better than to try to pry any answers out of her right away. He returned to his handheld, still connected to the drone's comm array. When he switched off the little black box, communication returned, and the drone sent the okay. Ajay piggybacked on the resumed data stream, subverting it exactly as Kylie had suggested.

"Sashi," he said as a faint click indicated the start of a connection.

"Papa," she whispered on the other end, urgency in her voice. "What are you doing? Where are the girls?"

"They're—" A noisy chatter on the line drowned him out, so he stopped talking.

"Isabelle needs to get back," Sashi said. More noise, as if she were dragging her microphone across corduroy. "—not safe for anyone."

"What was that?" Ajay adjusted his hearing aid. The noise worsened, then there was silence. "Are you still there?"

For a long time, nothing came through. Ajay buried his face in his hands and let his shoulder blades slump back against the tree.

Kylie edged forward.

"Papa," Sashi said again, the clarity of her voice startling Ajay so badly he fell back on his behind.

"What?"

"It's Jackson. He won't stop, Papa." Then, a long stretch of silence. When Sashi's voice returned, it lacked the inflection of emotion. "He's after Isabelle, and he won't stop until he's dead."

Ajay swallowed a big lump in his throat. "I don't know what you're thinking I'll do about that."

There was a long pause on the line, and Ajay didn't know if Sashi was at a loss for words or if the connection had died.

"I'm not what I once was," he finally said. "I can't do that kind of work." He felt Kylie's eyes on him, and hot shame welled up in his belly. "Not anymore."

Sashi let out a breath. "Fine. Remember that time I went drinking in Hastings and you had to pick me up? Remember where you found me?" Sashi's voice came through with authority. Loud and clear. "I'll have a car waiting there for you. Just get the girls to it and it'll take you to where we can meet."

"Hastings? Sashi, we're nowhere near—"

"I know where you are, Papa." Her voice held an edge of annoyance. "I know exactly where you are. I can't get there right now, but I will be out there soon." There was a long pause. "They know where you are, too. They're closing in."

Ajay sat in silence. Hastings wouldn't be impossible, but they would need better transportation. If Mack and his thugs knew where they were, then it wouldn't be long before the group caught up.

He opened his mouth to respond, but the chatter came on the line again. Something was terribly wrong with their connection. Ajay's fingers danced over the controls on his fidget, running all his routines. The data uplink looked solid.

It ran straight from the drone to Sashi. In fact, if he tried, he could probably locate her. But how had she located him? He checked the drone again and found its location device still disabled.

"Get off the line," Sashi snapped. "Papa, you have to move."

"What? Sashi, what's happening?"

"They know, Papa. They just saw Isabelle." The line crackled. "They have a Thunderhead nearby and they see her."

Ajay yanked the cord out of the drone and stuffed his fidget back in his coat pocket. He snatched up his walking stick and, ignoring the fireworks of pain, forced himself into a standing position. "Let's go," he said, and without looking back, stalked from the clearing.

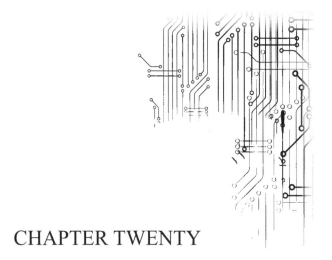

CHAPTER TWENTY

Through a gap in the oaks, far above, atop the nearest bluff, rose a column of black smoke. It sent a chill down Ajay's spine and set a lump in his belly. Nothing good burned black like that.

Was that what they did when they spotted Isabelle?

Kylie ran ten feet ahead of him, ducking between trees. She moved through the forest like she'd been born there, dodging underbrush and sliding easily through thorny weeds. He wouldn't let her out of his sight, but if she wanted, she could easily lose him.

Were they alive up there on the cliff? Ajay tried to push the thought from his mind, but it lingered like bad leftovers in the back of the fridge. What if Isabelle or Olivia were hurt? What then?

Something crashed through the forest up ahead. Kylie heard and ducked down behind a tree. She waved Ajay back, and he stopped.

"No use hiding," he said. He winced as his aches and pains caught up with him. His grip on the cane's handle tightened.

Garrison crashed through the brush, big jowls dripping drool. A massive weight lifted from the old man's chest as he bent down and embraced his big dog. "What would I do without you, boy?" He pressed his lips to the dog's head, forcing back the threat of tears. Kylie came, too, hugging them both.

After a time, Ajay signaled for Kylie to resume and she ran ahead. The air tasted of oil and burned plastic. The source of the smoke had to be close. Hanging haze grayed both forest and sky.

Ajay's walking stick worked fine for its intended purpose, but cane or not, his hip slowed him. The more he walked, the more limber and strong his muscles felt — and the more tightly his hip seized. Cold hardly bothered him. Either that sun high in the sky warmed the autumn afternoon, or the pain and effort of walking made a furnace of him. He coughed at the smoke as his lungs struggled to pull in more oxygen.

They followed the dirt road. In places it dipped low, mud and muck filling its twin tracks. They passed the point where Ajay had wanted Olivia to veer off, but he saw no marks. In other places, the road was little more than a slender track of grass and brush, two unbroken lines of stunted growth showing where tires had packed the earth long ago. Ajay wondered if those same lines would be there when Isabelle and Kylie were as old as he was. They might. Those lines could last forever.

The road wove up along the eastern side of the bluff. Closer to the Mississippi, the hill was steeper, in places a sharp cliff where erosion had only somewhat smoothed its jagged edges. The trees at the top were barren and dry, only the sturdiest oaks holding their autumn leaves. Even those were dull brown like rugged leather. Farther downhill, the color stayed, protected as it was from the harsh sun and wind. Ajay walked the length of that valley and rose through the bluffs as the wild forest fell behind him.

All the while, he wondered what he would find.

The unnatural tinge to the smoke made his mouth run dry. He covered his mouth and nose with the side of his hood, but breathing through the wet cloth hardly seemed to help. It smelled like wet grass and explosions. He had seen many Thunderhead attacks in his day, but never smelled their aftermath. It had always been from behind the safety of the screen. Always in the cold sterility of programmed logic.

Thunderheads had never been meant to control America's own population. When the program had first started, they'd been a ham-fisted, clumsy approach to assassinating an actual threat. Ten known terrorists had set off bomb after bomb in the rural Midwest. No president could allow that to continue in an election year.

Ajay had worked on the code that guided Thunderheads, back when they'd been designed to patrol foreign soil. He'd aided the team that modified them to fly high above the States. They'd worked. That actual threat had been neutralized in a very violent way, with little collateral damage. It had been luck that so little else was destroyed. Pure, dumb luck.

Poorly worded legislation had kept the Thunderhead program active. They required a state of emergency, but these days nobody even remembered any other state. The wording of the law also stated that the program would go to another vote when the weapons technology was updated, which kept the ham-fisted Thunderhead missiles exactly as ham-fisted as they'd always been. They were dangerous and stupid, but nobody ever tried to stop them. Ajay was ashamed of his part in the whole program.

His knees went weak, but he wouldn't stop. There was no time for weakness, and even the slightest pause might sink him into the quagmire of despair. Fear of what might lie ahead drove him back almost as hard as the fear of not knowing drove him forward. Almost.

Garrison whined and nuzzled Ajay's hand.

He looked up and saw Kylie staring back at him. Her eyes glistened, though he couldn't tell if it was from the smoke or worry.

No, Ajay couldn't stop there. Garrison needed him. Isabelle and Olivia were up ahead. They needed him, too.

Patting the side of his leg so that Garrison would heel, Ajay straightened himself and continued on his way. The road became steep for a time, and the arch of oak above blotted out the light. No grass grew on the slope, only a short tangle of weeds, with patches of buckthorn to choke things up from time to time. Cart tracks wove through and around the undergrowth, making way steadily uphill.

And Ajay followed. What else could he do?

The stench grew stronger. Black ash bit at his eyes and scratched at his lungs. Tears blurred his vision.

His hip twitched. The muscle seized.

"Age of honesty," Ajay said to Garrison, as he did every time his mind wandered to that bitter topic. "All secrets revealed. All encryption broken." He spat. "Lot of good it did us, right?"

Garrison didn't answer, as was his custom whenever Ajay went down that dark path.

"All based on my code," Ajay said. "If they're dead, it's me killing them." Ajay wiped the tears from his eyes, telling himself that the plastic smoke caused them. It did. Not as much as it seemed, though.

He rounded a corner, parting the still-green buckthorn and revealing the smoking mess that once was the cart. Fire licked the shattered front of the vehicle. Bits of plastic and metal decorated the clearing in big, broken chunks. Thick black smoke rose from the center of a crater, hinting at a smoldering fire somewhere deep within.

Ajay stood, frozen, for a long while. He leaned heavily on his walking stick, muscles in his arm shaking from fear and grief and exhaustion. How had they come so far, only for this?

But there were no bodies.

"Where did they go?" Kylie asked.

"I don't know." The wreckage blocked his view of most of the clearing. The bodies might be hidden from him, and all he needed to do was step forward and see his granddaughter, dead and gone. Olivia, his bridge partner. No, more than that. She was a true friend. He considered leaving. How much easier it would be to never know. For several long, ragged breaths, his muscles refused to obey.

Then he poked at a plastic chunk with his cane. It rolled and revealed the singed corners of wet leaves. Garrison sniffed at it, crinkling his nose at the acrid stench. There wouldn't be a forest fire. Not with everything soaked through as it was.

No bodies lay in the mangled wreckage. Tension drained from Ajay's neck and hope poured in like a river over a broken dam. If Olivia and Isabelle survived, hope did, too. Only a lack of imagination kept him from seeing where that hope hid. What could they do? He had told them to branch off farther down the hill. In the panic, could he and Kylie have missed their mark?

He pushed past the wreckage, Garrison at his side. Kylie followed close, no longer ranging ahead. She held the cuff of his coat in her little hand, keeping him always at arm's length. Beyond the path, not far through the trees, the earth grew hard and stony. A limestone ridge jutted out from the side of the bluff, overlooking the valley below. Scuff marks on soft limestone showed that someone had walked out there. At least one of them had enjoyed the view.

Maybe stepping out there had given them away. The whole sky lay out before him on that ridge. A cold haze hung over the forest below, coating autumn color in a stony gray. The sun dipped low in the western sky, threatening to drape the bluffs in its color, and then darkness.

Ajay hurried back into the cover of the forest. There had to be evidence of where they went, somewhere around the clearing. He was no tracker, but he could see an obvious sign. Garrison might help if they could find something that didn't smell like burning plastic.

The dirt road held footprints better than any surface Ajay ever knew, but the road ahead was completely clear. They didn't go that way. Where else? He poked around at the underbrush until he found something that looked like a broken branch. The yellow buckthorn underbark exposed to air stood out like a referee's penalty flag. That had to be it.

He pushed through the buckthorn, pulling Kylie with him. Picking past the worst of the choked forest, they made their way ahead. Leaves on the ground sprang back like sponges where they stepped, not holding visible footprints at all. Back behind them, the smoky remains of the cart were barely visible. There was no clear way forward.

As he was about to give up on the trail — the broken branch must have been a mistake — he saw another telltale yellow bark exposed to the air. Then another. The string of them led deeper into the forest. A rare glimpse of the sky revealed the reds and oranges of sunset as it washed over everything.

Only then did he call out. Fear of not finding them before dark finally outweighed the fear of discovery. He shouted their names, and long after darkness swallowed the forest, he still called for them. His fidget's battery was low, but its flashlight used little power. Each new broken twig in the underbrush came from a hard-fought search, and each fight grew more difficult. Down the hill they walked, sometimes down open slopes and other times through narrow trails choked with buckthorn.

A dark form stepped from beside the trail and clapped a hand over his mouth. Ajay panicked. Struggled. Kicked. But the form was too strong and held him tight. The person pinned his limbs one by one and held them tight in an iron grip. His walking stick fell to the ground.

Then he pulled in a ragged breath and smelled her. The hand cautiously let up from his mouth, and he whispered, "Olivia?"

"Keep quiet." She eased up on his arms and legs.

Kylie handed him his walking stick. By the glow of the handheld, Ajay looked at Olivia and knew exactly what was wrong.

Isabelle was missing.

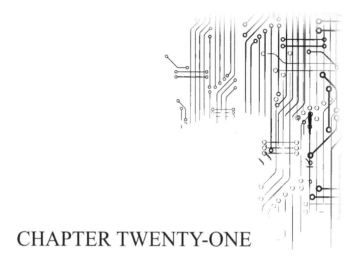

CHAPTER TWENTY-ONE

Olivia touched Ajay's elbow. "We need to move." Her voice was soft but strong.

He shook his head, though she couldn't possibly see him in the dark. "No," he said. "We leave no one behind."

"She's gone, Ajay." Olivia spoke louder, a touch of grit entering her tone. "Off in the woods somewhere. We'll never find her unless she wants to be found."

He pulled his arm away. The clouds in the sky shifted and he could make out Kylie's form a long putt away across the clearing. "Is that how the Army does it, Liv?" he asked in a whisper much harsher than intended. "Leave someone behind as soon as they step out of line?"

Olivia took a step back, her eyes glistening in the gray light. "Don't you ever."

"Ever what? Disrespect the job you had that ditched you when it was done? They left you behind soon as you aged out. Same as the NSA left me in the cold when they were done. We've been abandoned, left out in the dark to survive on our own, and you still think we owe them our loyalty?" Ajay let his voice rise, not caring anymore if Kylie heard. "You're not hunted like I am, but they don't exactly pay you a living pension, either, do they?"

"I'm not a fugitive," she said. "When I chose to leave the military, I left according to my contract, which they honored. I wasn't run out for overstepping the laws of human decency."

"I did what I had to do to keep my family safe."

"Isabelle ran from me. She keeps running," she said. "Maybe it's time to recognize when a girl doesn't want to be found."

"She's my granddaughter." Ajay's collar choked him, and he pulled back his hood to breathe cool air. "When she's under my care, I'll treat her like my own daughter."

Olivia frowned. "And how well did that work?"

They had never spoken much of his past, even though he had known Olivia for years. He had sometimes mentioned his daughter, but never in detail. "How long have you known that I'm a fugitive?"

"Long enough to prove it doesn't matter to me."

Ajay pulled his coat close around himself. "We're not leaving her."

"No," Olivia said, her voice flat. "We're not. She left us. After I pulled her back from the cliff, that bomb hit and she ran. Wasn't a thing I could do to stop her, and if that girl doesn't want to be stopped, ain't nobody going to do it."

"So it was another Thunderhead. There'll be a follow-up crew. We have police to worry about again."

"Even on the reservation?" Olivia asked.

"Especially." Ajay scratched his mustache. "The government will want to get rid of any evidence since they're not legally allowed to strike here." He closed his eyes and let out a long breath. "What do we do? I can't leave her."

"We're not going to leave her, but we can't find her right now. It's getting cold and we need shelter."

"All the more reason to find her."

"Ajay." Olivia grabbed him by both shoulders. "She can take care of herself."

He shook his head. She couldn't. Going anywhere without Isabelle was betrayal. His job was to protect her. Her and Kylie. He'd only just met them, but if there was one thing he would do in his final years, it would be to protect those girls. They were everything to him now.

"Fine," he said. "Shelter, then I'm going to go looking for her."

His fidget's lowest setting provided enough light for them to make their way through the forest. Any more and he would worry about drones in the sky spotting them. Still, the light made him nervous, even though he had used a much brighter setting to follow Olivia's trail. Now it seemed more important than ever to remain undetected. Mounting dread weighed like a bag of sand on his chest, and with every step, it grew worse.

Kylie's little hand slipped into his and she tugged him forward. She pulled a granola bar from her pocket and ate slowly, taking tiny bites as if testing a potentially unsafe food. She offered a bite to Ajay, but he declined. There would be time for food later. Low branches scraped against his face and body, clawing at him from the dark. Time passed, but Ajay didn't know how much. The sky above grew light with the moon, and the shadows around them deepened in depth and texture. He shuffled forward, unable to see the ground, but unwilling to stop.

The sky above the forest canopy lit with a blue-white light as bright as day, but as artificial as a politician's smile. Ajay froze, heart pounding in his chest. Kylie looked up to him for direction, and he looked back, wide-eyed, at Olivia.

"Run," she said.

They slipped through the forest quick and silent as deer in the spring. Ajay held tight to Kylie with one hand, using his stick to shield his face from branches. He had to trust that Olivia still ran behind him; her footsteps were completely silent. Garrison followed, his long loping gait the loudest sound of their passing.

The buzz of drones swarmed through the forest. All at once, they were everywhere. The farther the group ran, the darker the sky grew, but the noise of drones grew louder.

Ajay spotted a fallen tree, a massive cottonwood with roots splaying across the sky like a grasping hand. He yanked Kylie to a stop and ran to the tree.

"What are you doing?" Olivia asked.

He brought a finger to his lips, and she nodded. The drones would hear voices if they were close enough. Any talking might give them away.

Ajay felt in the shadows of the trunk, pulling away great clods of rotten wood. The air filled with the earthy scent of dry rot. A cavity opened up in the tree, big enough that Kylie might hide. But it wasn't enough.

Olivia helped, yanking out big chunks of soft wood. Damp sections pulled loose deep into the trunk. When it grew too hard to break apart by hand, Ajay started kicking chunks of it away. It grew larger as the drones closed in.

The lights brightened. Ajay grabbed Kylie and lifted her into the hole, then he grabbed Olivia's arm to usher her in. She glared back at him, her jaw set hard.

There wasn't enough room for both of them. Ajay felt her gaze and knew that she wanted him to hide. He gave her a quick shake of his head.

Kylie lunged out of the hole and hugged him hard, pressing her snotty face into his chest. He didn't know what to do, so he gently placed a hand on her back. She must have only been there for an instant, but it seemed like she pulled him tight for an eternity. Olivia shifted uncomfortably.

When Kylie let go, he knelt and looked into her bright eyes.

"It's going to be all right," he whispered. "Hide."

Kylie shrank back into the hole, and Olivia grudgingly followed. Ajay piled leaves and debris on top of them, hiding them and hopefully keeping them warm at the same time. Garrison nudged his leg as the last pieces fell in place. He pulled up his holographic display, marking their location so that they would be easy to find later if it so happened that he escaped.

Then the old man and his dog moved again.

The air changed, and the forest fell silent. Underbrush dropped away and Ajay found walking easy on the leaf-covered ground. As the artificial light faded, the silver traces of moonlight filtered through the canopy above. He hadn't realized how oppressive and close the shadows had been until his first breath of freedom in the open oak forest. The trees stood tall and ancient, their roots knotted like dinosaur bones strewn across the forest floor. His sodden penny loafers slipped over the wet, cold wood, but the way was open.

Fear and the pulse of an adrenaline rush suppressed the aches in his body. His hip would give out soon, but not yet. Behind him, lights flickered between trees like blue-white fire. They fell far behind him, and for a moment he felt a glimmer of hope. Maybe he could get away.

Then he slipped. His arm shot out to catch his fall and he smacked his wrist on the trunk of a gnarled oak. The walking stick flew free.

He swore.

The drones stopped.

Cradling his numb wrist, he struggled to his feet, only to fall again. Great plumes of white fog burst from his lungs, dissipating into the hazy air. Garrison licked his face.

Ajay grabbed his cane and used it to force himself to his feet. His mind raced with words of defiance that would keep him safe if he were caught out there. He was out for a walk, or maybe he was a guest of a resident. Could he fool them long enough to sneak away, as with the police earlier?

He didn't know who owned the drones bearing down on him. It was most likely the police, cleaning up after the Thunderhead. What if it wasn't? It could easily be Mack's thugs, and they didn't rely heavily enough on digital identification for him to sneak away. How long could an old man hold out if they asked where the girls were?

Long enough, Ajay thought. Long enough.

The hip finally seized up completely, refusing to move another step now that it knew the glorious state of inertia. He rubbed it with the palm of his hand, wincing as knives of pain shot deep inside the wrist joint. Garrison cocked his head to one side and whined.

"Dammit," Ajay said.

The lights moved. His heart pounded in his throat, choking back the choice curses. Drones floated his way, and he couldn't move. They'd heard him, and triangulated his exact location. What could he do?

Was it even worth hiding anymore? Ajay felt the weight of a million eyes on him, watching from all sides. The sky watched always. And it always would. How could anyone hope to hide from that?

Then he saw Isabelle, backlit by the drones' harsh light. She stood in her gray sweater, now filthy with ash and soil. Her face, black from ash, had two long streaks where tears had cleansed her pale skin. Her hair drooped languidly to the sides of her face, the left side seared shorter than the right.

She raised a finger to her lips. Their eyes met, and she held his gaze for several long breaths.

Drones swarmed among the trees, bathing them in their harsh white lights. Garrison howled, and lights snapped to him, dancing across his body. He howled again.

Still, Isabelle didn't move. She stood like another tree in the forest, finger pressed gently to her lips. Ajay followed suit, not daring to twitch as the drones scanned his body with their blue lights. Their patterns of movement made them difficult to count, especially without the benefit of being able to crane his neck around and track them. They spun and shifted, one after another. Several drones moved farther away into the forest, their lights shifting and flitting through trees like will-o'-wisps.

Then they moved on.

Isabelle fell back against a tree, sliding down and curling herself into a ball in the crook of its roots. She sobbed, curling harder into a filthy ball and covering her face with her arms.

Ajay rushed to her. "It's going to be okay," he said, though he didn't know how he could possibly justify the statement. "I'm here." His hand hovered an inch above her back, hesitating.

She turned to him. Tears streamed down her cheeks, and her eyes were puffy and red.

"It's your Papa," he said. "Grandfather Ajay."

Her lip quivered, and more tears flowed. Ajay pulled his hand back, not knowing what to do. Because, after all, how would he ever know what was the right thing to say?

Ajay would only make it worse.

Isabelle sobbed and muttered something, but Ajay didn't know what. He peered into the forest, where the drones still danced far away amongst the trees.

"C'mon, boy," Ajay whispered, patting the side of his leg. Garrison heeled nicely. "Help me out here, bud."

Garrison sniffed Isabelle, then licked her face until the ash was gone and a hint of a smile sparkled at the corners of her eyes.

"There," Ajay said. He desperately wanted to ask what she had done. It wasn't possible to hack drones that way, yet the drones had ignored them just as if they'd been blown wide open. The drones were far away, so he spoke comfortably. "Now that that's done, let's find someplace safe."

Isabelle flashed him a weak smile.

"Relatively safe," he said. He led her back to where Olivia and Kylie still hid inside the trunk of the fallen tree. With some work, they made enough space for everyone. It was a tight space, but cozy was what they all needed and within a few minutes, Ajay's head raced with the events of the day. The crushing weight of his failures pounded in his chest, and all he could think of was the ways he might have been smarter. Helped more.

Soon the sun rose again, and its light filtered into their little space. Kylie and Isabelle still slept, their breath coming out in frost-white plumes. Olivia tensed, and he looked over to see her glaring back at him.

"Well, who the hell are you?" Olivia asked. She pushed away from him, looking with wild eyes around the close space. Her kicking woke Kylie and Isabelle. More panicked, she repeated, "Who the hell are you?"

Ajay's jaw worked, but he couldn't think. Panic tore at him. He tried to retreat, but couldn't get free.

Olivia grew more and more agitated. She ran her hands across her quilted coat, pulling a knife, which she pointed at Ajay. "You stay back!"

He stretched out an arm, palm forward. "I'm Ajay," he said. "You remember?"

Her nostrils flared, and the knife shook in her hand. For a long while, the four of them didn't move a single muscle. Olivia's eyes were wide with fear, her muscles tense.

Kylie touched Olivia's hand.

The effect was immediate. Olivia's body relaxed, and her expression softened. "Ajay. Right." She blinked and smacked her dry lips. "Sorry about that. I'm better now."

But Ajay was no less scared.

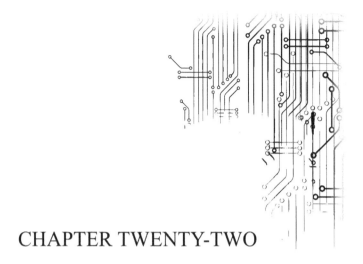

CHAPTER TWENTY-TWO

"I know where we're going," Ajay said. "It's not far now. We can rest up once we get to the Loon's house."

The bags under Olivia's eyes darkened. "Oh, I hope it's not far. I'm not sure how much of this I have left in me."

He rested a hand on Kylie's shoulder. When the girl looked at him with bleary eyes, he patted her once and said, "Are you ready, Kylie?" To Olivia, he said, "We'll get you home, Liv. I promise."

"You make too many promises, Ajay."

He sighed. "You're probably right."

The morning forest left no trace of the drones that had passed by in the night. The utter quiet in the hazy morning air belied the frightening experiences of the previous night. When they crossed another road, Ajay became more convinced that he knew where they were. He had never been to this part of the rez, but he had seen it from satellite photos many times. The road they were on would get them where they needed to be. Soon, he hoped. His belly rumbled from hunger. Kylie and Isabelle had more granola bars, but still, he elected not to eat. He'd hold off until they found more food somewhere, even if it did make him a little lightheaded.

Isabelle lost entirely the vulnerability she had shown the previous night. Ajay thought about bringing it up but was cowed by the looks of mild distrust she sent his way. Half of him wanted to ask her how she felt, half of him wanted to ask how in the hell she'd hacked those drones, and all of him was too afraid to say a single word.

The sky was still up there, of course, and it always watched. There might be a way to get to the house through the forest, but that might take all day. If they hurried, they could use the morning fog to stay hidden, even though the road offered them little cover. Without a word, Ajay pressed forward as fast as his aching hip would take him.

The gravel county road grew more familiar to Ajay. The only landmark he remembered in the area was right there on the hill, the looming, crisscrossing aluminum that made up the Loon's ham radio tower. He didn't hesitate to cross the road, didn't even bother caring about whether or not a high-in-the-sky could spot him from somewhere in the vast blue. It had to be done, and the exposure couldn't be helped.

They walked through the forest along the long road, hidden from the bulk of the sky by the colorful canopy. The haze cleared some as they walked, and soon it would give them no cover at all. When the girls asked to walk on the road in the sun instead, Ajay strictly forbade it.

"If you can see the sky," he said, "the sky can see you."

Olivia patted him on the back, then took the girls up to walk on the road. Ajay stayed in the ditch. They moved faster, and Ajay struggled to keep up, leaning heavily on his cane.

The Loon's house stood only a couple miles away, and despite the hunger, cold, and general state of misery, they managed to make it before noon. Ajay recognized the place below the tower. The leaning barn at the top of the hill was his first clue. When he had first seen images of it long ago, he would have sworn it would fall that afternoon. It hadn't. Years later it still stood, and by the look of it someone still used it. The nose of a rusty red tractor stuck out of the wide-open door.

Kylie grabbed her sister's hand as they crossed the yard, whether from habit or fear, Ajay didn't know. Isabelle pulled away, though, and soon the girls were shooting glares at each other that Ajay had no wish to get between.

"Girls," he said, "this is it. Mind your manners, and be polite as your mother taught you. We're depending on this guy for a ride the rest of the way, so be nice."

Isabelle flashed him a saccharine smile.

Kylie said, "Yeah, Isa, don't scare him away with your ugly face."

Isabelle scowled.

"No, you shut up!" Kylie dodged a slap from her sister and ran behind a tree.

"Girls." Ajay failed to keep the exhausted resignation from his voice. He opened his mouth to say more, but Olivia threaded an arm through his. She looked sallow and weak, her skin yellow and her eyes bleary. The walk, especially the last hour, had taken so much out of her. It was a wonder she kept going. "Not far now, Liv," he said, patting her hand.

The driveway was a stretch of pitted mud, more pothole than road. Any self-driving car would flip its shit completely if it powered up anywhere near a driveway like that. Not only were the roads out that far absent from most maps, but the Loon worked hard to keep his place obstructed from any outside influence.

A dog barked somewhere ahead, and Garrison's ears perked up.

"Just you stay," said Ajay in a warning growl. Garrison tensed but didn't leave the old man's side.

The house wasn't much to speak of, and that was probably to the Loon's liking. Nobody would think twice about coming around such a place. The Mdewankanton reservation had spent years in poverty before casino money threw the economy out of wack. This place and many others like it were left as a relic of those early times. Hell, casino money didn't exactly spread thin and even. It tended to lump up and those it left behind got left behind hard.

A single-story ranch stood with flaking blue paint and a porch slanted far enough to the left to cause worry.

Garrison let out a low woof.

"You show him, Gare."

Isabelle and Kylie had stopped fighting and held hands. Isabelle clutched her sister's elbow like it might be a life preserver. Her bright eyes took in the house and barn, but she didn't say anything. Ajay wondered at the look on her face. It was unlike any he'd ever seen on her, and the odd change in her behavior bothered him.

After a while, he braved the leaning porch and rattled the door on its hinges. "Loon?" he called. "You in there?"

When no answer came after repeated attempts, he tried the doorknob and found it unlocked. After a quick scout through the house to verify nobody was home, he waved the girls in. Kylie and Isabelle raided the yellow refrigerator, finding some cheese sticks that hadn't expired. Kylie picked some jerky from one of the cupboards, but Ajay shook his head. No telling what that was from or how old it was. Raiding the man's house for food was bad enough. Taking a man's prized venison jerky would be worse.

"Where is he?" Olivia rasped. She licked her dry lips. She sat in the threadbare chair and sank in as if she were planning on staying there forever.

"Must be out." Ajay fished a Flintstones glass from the cupboard, one of those ones people used to get from Happy Meals. He filled it with water and offered it to Olivia, but she pushed it away. "You have to drink," he said.

Her jaw hardened. "I can't," she said. Her eyes clammed shut, and her breathing became slow and precise. "I told you, my Lyssameds cause hydrophobia."

Ajay swore. Of course, hydrophobia was a side effect. Something as simple as drinking a glass of water and staving off dehydration couldn't be easy, could it? "Lyssameds?" he asked, wondering what they were for, but too afraid to ask directly.

Olivia nodded. Lyssameds were a biological nanomachine modified from the rabies virus. Hydrophobia, or the fear of liquids, was a symptom of rabies that clung to the meds as a side effect.

"How can that still be an issue?" he asked, frustration boiling in his gut. "They must be able to remove that side effect by now."

Olivia looked up at him and slowly shook her head. "Oh, Ajay." She patted him on the head. "The treatment is a single application. Once it's in, there's no profit. But they can treat a side effect like hydrophobia for the rest of a person's life with expensive meds. There's no incentive to fix it."

Ajay stepped back. "That's a bit cynical, don't you think?"

"Cynical's just a side effect of not moving around enough. I've been retired for too damn many years to be all bright and cheery. That's the first thing Alzheimer's took from me."

"Alzheimer's." Ajay swallowed a lump. So that was what it was.

"Can we go outside?" Kylie asked.

"No," Ajay said.

Kylie and Isabelle ignored him and went to stand on the crooked porch. Ajay knelt beside Olivia, taking her hand in his. "Liv," he said. "We're going to get you home."

"You're not my knight in shining armor, old man."

"No." Ajay ran his fingers through his hair. "I suppose not."

"When it gets bad," she said, "all I remember is Oscar. We served in Afghanistan together and he — Oscar was wounded and I didn't get him out." She shook her head. "I don't see how you can help here, Ajay." She met his gaze with hard determination. "And I'll be fine. Give me that glass."

He handed her the Flintstones glass. It shook in her clenched claw, edging closer and closer to her lips. She closed her eyes, and that seemed to help. She took a sip. Then another.

Ajay peeled off his shoes and damp socks, stretching the ache out of his pale, wrinkled foot. The socks he set on a radiator, which seemed to be producing some heat. The shoes leaned up against the radiator, too, though there was no real hope of those ever drying out. His feet resembled the white bellies of dead frogs and didn't smell much better. The lower half of his pants were still damp, but he suspected that taking off his pants might break an already strained propriety.

Olivia threw the glass across the room, where it shattered on the wall. Water soaked into the bare drywall.

Ajay flinched away from her, shocked by the sudden action. She shook, her hands trembling, clenched together. He clasped her hands in his, holding her close until she drew a long breath.

She smiled apologetically. "Hydrophobia," she said by way of an explanation. "So, where do we suppose this Loon of yours is?"

Ajay took the cue to change topics. He glanced through the open door. Kylie and Isabelle argued out there about whatever sisters argue about. Behind them, atop the hill, stood the antenna they had seen on the way in.

"He's probably nearby. The tower, maybe," said Ajay, sitting next to Olivia. When she rested her head on his shoulder, her warmth soaked right down into him. "We'll rest a bit," he said, "then I'll go looking for him."

Olivia patted him on the leg. Her breathing slowed, and a sense of relaxation flowed through them. They'd wait a bit. Yes, that was the right thing. Rest for a little bit. Then go looking.

Ajay's eyes felt like tar on a hot summer day. They burned with every blink, and each blink left them harder to open. He needed to stay alert, though. It was no time for sleep. The girls needed him, and the Loon needed to know they were there. A moment more of rest would be fine, so that Olivia could fall into a deeper sleep, then he could get up and accomplish something.

Ajay slept.

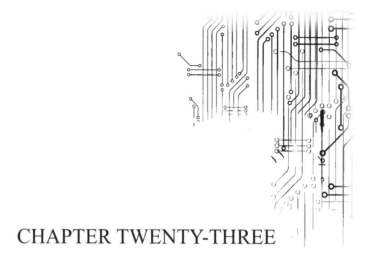

CHAPTER TWENTY-THREE

Kylie threw the stick as far as she could. Garrison watched the stick travel in its long arc, land in the dry grass, and sit there.

"Well?" Kylie asked the dog.

Garrison looked at her with his sad eyes. Isabelle gave an airy smile from where she sat picking at the grass.

"What are you laughing at?" Kylie asked her sister. "He's a dog, they're supposed to fetch." She shook her head. "Come on, let's go explore."

She sensed hesitation in her sister but ignored it. The yard was surrounded by forest, some of it evergreen and some deciduous. The evergreens stretched three times as high as the house and looked like excellent climbing, so she went that way. Isabelle and Garrison followed.

When they got to the row of pine trees, Kylie saw a faint path leading between two of them. She shot a glance back at her sister, who frowned. It was like she didn't even want adventure. Kylie shrugged and darted between the trees.

The path led up a hill, branching a couple times. She always took the one leading up, because why wouldn't she want to keep going higher? From time to time she glanced back at Isabelle to make sure she still followed. Being on an adventure in the forest was one thing, but being out there completely alone was another.

"Why do you keep running away?" Kylie asked her sister. "Mom says we're better off if we stick together."

Isabelle surprised her by speaking. "It's not safe," she said.

Kylie stopped, her palms sweating. The girls had reached the edge of the forest atop the bluff. A short distance away, she saw a small gray building with a big antenna poking up from the top. "This doesn't look dangerous."

"No," Isabelle said, her voice little more than a whisper. "Staying with me isn't safe. If I go away, he won't look for you."

"Who?"

Isabelle took a very long time to form her answer. "Your father."

Kylie searched her sister's face for any sign of a reaction. Isa's expression lacked any hint that she might be joking. Her sallow cheeks didn't so much as twitch with smile or frown, and her eyes remained locked in a glassy far-off gaze. Kylie touched her elbow, trying to jostle the girl out of whatever trance she had fallen into. "He's your dad, too."

Isabelle gave a slight shake of her head. "How can he be my dad? He doesn't even think I'm a person."

Kylie took a step back, remembering that last day when their father had left. It scared her, thinking of the changes Isabelle had gone through, all while their father shouted about proof that she wasn't human. As far as Kylie was concerned, Isabelle was as close to normal as anyone ever got. Not that Kylie knew any other kids.

Isabelle continued, "And that man is not our grandpa."

Heat rose in Kylie's face. "He is so. He's nice to us, and he cares. Why don't you want us to have any family?"

"They all want things for themselves. None of them care about us at all."

"You take that back!" Kylie's hands balled into fists.

Isabelle either didn't take the challenge or didn't notice. "Your dad wants me to help him train more people like us."

"Us?"

"He said it when he sent a message to me at the tower."

Kylie took a step back and forced herself to relax. Her sister needed her help, and fighting wasn't going to do anyone any good. "Is that why you left Olivia's?"

"He made me want to leave. He does that sometimes. It's like he's hacking my whole mind. He made me want to go somewhere that I could see the sky. Somewhere they could find me easily. I still want it. It's like an itch I can't scratch."

"I don't understand."

"He said I'll be with more people like me if I go with him. I'll be in charge of them, but I don't know if I want to go."

"How does he make you want things?"

Isabelle spoke without moving her lips, as she sometimes did. "Not everyone can hear machines like we do, Kylie. It isn't just Father. Most people can't. Papa can't."

"But Olivia?"

"It's not the same with her." Isabelle chewed her lip. "I don't know. All I know is that if I go away, you'll be safe."

Without Isa, Kylie would be alone. A long time ago, Isabelle had talked every day. She had even laughed sometimes. Even when she threw her fits of anger, she'd at least showed emotion. Now it was like all of Isabelle's memories stayed in her head while her personality slowly disappeared.

Ever since the day Dad left.

Kylie had been there the night Dad left, but she still didn't understand what had happened to her sister. It must have been bad because they never saw him again. That had been a year ago, and she missed Dad. She drew out the picture she had taken from the frame at Papa's house. Papa stood smiling next to a cake that said "25" on it. A bunch of other people in shabby suits milled about in the background, but right there next to Papa stood Dad. Smiling.

Times like these, when Isabelle spoke to her little sister, were to be treasured, even if they didn't make a whole lot of sense.

"Do you want to play something?" Kylie asked, stuffing the photo back in her pocket.

Isabelle, her voice still flat, said, "What do you want to play?"

"I don't know. Wanna practice punches like Olivia taught us?"

A twitch in Isabelle's upper lip hinted at disgust, but she walked back down the hill slowly enough for Kylie to follow without any trouble. As they neared the house, a dog barked again, somewhere close.

Kylie looked down at Garrison. "Was that you?"

Garrison didn't answer but looked up at her with his sad eyes. Kylie stepped off the path, following the sound of the barking dog. Something about the bark sounded strange, but she couldn't place it. She checked to see if Isabelle followed, but she didn't. The older sister stood watching her from the path as if waiting to see if it was safe.

The dog barked again. Yes, it sounded very close and very loud. Garrison's ears perked up at each bark, but he reserved his yowls for when it mattered. Kylie tiptoed her way through the forest, soft leaves squishing under her feet. She reached a line of trees grown almost into a dense wall. When she squeezed past them, she saw a small shed, with a big solar panel set up next to it.

A little box on the side of the shed barked fiercely.

"It's just a speaker," Kylie shouted back to her sister. Pride swelled in her chest. She'd solved the mystery all on her own; Mama would be proud of her clever daughter.

Something big moved in the shed. She saw the dark form shift through the open door.

Kylie ran. Isabelle ran with her, and Garrison kept up as well as he could. They didn't stop until they were inside the house. Kylie barely breathed hard, but her sister wasn't in such good shape. Isabelle sat down against one wall, eyeing the doorway warily.

"I don't think it saw us," Kylie said in a whisper.

Olivia and Papa sat on the sofa, a long line of drool running from his lower lip to pool on his shoulder. Olivia wasn't asleep, though. She watched Kylie through narrow eyes, making no other movement than to track the girls.

"Oh, sorry," said Kylie, "I didn't know you were trying to sleep."

Olivia's voice came in a dry rasp. "No bother. Do you girls need anything?" She nudged Papa to one side so that she could extract her arm. He slumped a little bit but didn't wake at all.

When she stood, she didn't seem as intimidating as she had when Kylie first met her. Olivia's shoulders slumped, and her eyes had a hollow look that made Kylie worry.

"Garrison needs some food," Kylie said because she wanted to seem like the kind of girl who was responsible enough for a pet. "Do you think there's any food he can eat?"

Olivia let out a long sigh. "Let's check the basement," she said.

Kylie didn't like the sound of that, but Olivia opened doors until she found a staircase leading down into the spookiest darkness Kylie had ever seen. There wasn't a light switch on the wall, so Olivia batted around over her head until she found a pull string.

The dusty yellow light didn't make the basement much better. Kylie followed Olivia down anyway, wanting to seem brave. Tables of grimy junk cluttered the little basement. Tools, wood, metal, and all kinds of things Kylie had never seen were piled up on workbenches along the walls. Olivia ignored all this, instead turning her face to the door straight ahead. The old lady swayed as she walked like her weight was almost too much to move around. Through that door, she found another light, but that area looked much cleaner. Shelves in that section of the basement were full of canned foods and weapons. Guns and knives.

Olivia caressed one of the guns, a big green one with lots of gizmos attached to it. Kylie didn't know a lot about guns, but that one looked heavy. It wasn't the biggest, but it had so much stuff attached to it that it looked more like a toy than something people used to kill each other. Some of the tiny guns looked plenty dangerous, and Olivia blinked like she had dust in her eyes before she moved farther back into the basement.

Kylie cleared her throat. "Do you see anything for the dog?"

Olivia started as if surprised that Kylie had followed her. She picked up a can of meat and handed it to Kylie. Her voice slurred a little as she spoke. "Here you go, dear. See if you can find an opener upstairs."

"Canned... meat?"

"Dogs like meat, don't they?"

The logic seemed sound. Kylie watched Olivia for another moment, a little nervous to walk back through the basement on her own. Olivia showed no signs of wanting to leave, though, instead picking up a two-foot-long black case and hugging it close to her body.

"Oh," Olivia said. "Oh, I remember this." She sat heavily on the floor, paying no attention to Kylie.

Kylie ran out of the basement as fast as she could. She found a can opener, opening the can of meat for Garrison. He ate it without even considering the fact that the label didn't make any claims about what kind of meat it was. She hoped it didn't make him sick.

The door stood wide open. Papa still slept on the couch, but Isabelle was nowhere to be seen.

And someone outside yelled.

She ran out, and as soon as she turned the corner she saw the biggest man she had ever seen. He wore dirty blue overalls and his beard splayed out like someone threw it at his face but almost missed. He had Isabelle's arm in one of his massive hands.

"Who are you, girl?" he bellowed. "Just tell me your damn name!"

Kylie sprinted across the lawn, balling up her fists the way Olivia had shown her. "You let her go!"

She grabbed the big hand in both of hers and pulled it hard, trying to twist it around into a joint lock. His grip didn't budge and he grabbed at her with his other hand. She backpedaled away.

"C'mere," he said. "Who the hell told you you could be here? You spying on me?"

Kylie didn't feel like answering. Her face reddened from all her anger. She picked a rock up from the ground and threw it at his face.

He blocked it away easily. "What the hell?" His face turned red as well. "Don't you see I got your friend?"

Kylie picked up another rock. "Let her go!" She threw the rock, hitting him hard on the forehead.

He didn't let Isabelle go, and he definitely didn't drop unconscious or dead. Kylie had hoped it would be that easy. It wasn't.

Instead, he got really, really angry.

CHAPTER TWENTY-FOUR

Ajay woke to a deep bellow outside, a crick in his neck, and not one single clue as to where he was. The room didn't look familiar. What was that terrible smell? He sniffed at his shirt. Oh. When he moved, the tweak in his neck lit up like the Fourth of July fireworks over the Mississippi. He bit back a series of profanities on instinct, looking around in the strange living room. Springs in the sofa dug deep into his bottom, and the heavy stink of mildew permeated everything, even his own skin.

Right. This was the Loon's house, right smack dab in the middle of nowhere. The chain of terrible events that led him there made his head spin.

He made the mistake of trying to move. His feet were numb, and as he shifted, blood rushed to those limbs, and pins and needles spread like a spring flood through the lower extremities. The feeling was unpleasant and somewhat disconcerting but also a mercy compared to what the rest of his body was doing. His hip was so stiff it felt like someone had replaced the whole thing with a hot iron crowbar. The skin hurt on his face, his hands, his arms — hell, it was easier to list where his tender flesh didn't hurt.

Nowhere.

Yep, that about covered it.

If it weren't for the bellowing outside and the dangerously strong pressure on his bladder, Ajay might have just laid down and given up for the day. Garrison nuzzled his hand.

He blinked, trying to focus on the opposite wall where Olivia had shattered that glass. There was no longer a wet spot but the glass shards still sparkled. Where was she?

The walking stick sat within reach, so Ajay grabbed it and used it to force himself up. Bones creaked and tendons popped, but he made it. Once up, he hobbled on prickling bare feet, giving the broken glass a wide berth on his way to the door. Garrison loped past and ran to the edge of the porch.

"Then why ya here?" bellowed the giant.

The Loon was a big man. His grease-stained blue coveralls barely contained his belly and came up a few inches short on the legs. Steel shone from the worn-down toes of his mud-caked work boots. The beard he wore looked like it had been trimmed at the turn of the century, with streaks of gray sprouting at odd angles. He held a shotgun by the barrel in one hand, waving it like a spear. In his other hand, he gripped Isabelle by the arm.

"Leave us alone," Kylie said, from outside of the big man's reach.

The Loon's face turned red under the matted mass of hair. "Leave you alone?" He took a huge step forward. "Leave you alone? How's about you get off my property?"

"Henry," Ajay said from the porch, in as calm a voice as he could muster. "Leave the girls alone, son."

The Loon froze, then turned his head slowly to look Ajay up and down. His jaw worked for a moment before he finally said, "And who in the hell are you?"

Ajay thunked his walking stick on the wooden porch a few times, making his way forward and down the steps. Henry, the Loon, was still a good ways off. Thirty feet at least. If the big man decided to hurt the girls, there wasn't a thing

Ajay could do about it. Hell, there wasn't anything he could do if he were up close.

"Seems to me," said Ajay, "a man like the Loon ought not to look for trouble on his own property."

Henry looked to the girls, then to Ajay.

"Threatening little girls with a shotgun, Henry?" Ajay shook his head and frowned. "Thought better of you than that."

Henry looked at the gun in his hand as if seeing it for the first time. "Now, see here—"

"And we came to visit in good faith, too." Ajay closed a few more steps. "We need your help."

"There's no help here."

"There is, though." Ajay flashed a wolfish grin. "And nobody even needs to know who I am, or that I paid you a visit."

Henry looked him up and down. He let go of Isabelle and stroked his beard, tension leaving his shoulders. "Well, hell, you're him, aren't you?"

Isabelle scrambled over to her sister, rubbing her arm. The two girls backed farther away.

"I'm nobody," Ajay said.

Henry's laugh started with a low chuckle and escalated to a deep guffaw. The girls edged back and around to stand next to their grandfather. Henry's laugh tapered to silence. He placed his hands on his knees and great tears shone in his eyes.

"You're goddamn him," he said. "Grandfather Anonymous." He straightened up and stifled his smile. "Never thought you'd be an actual grandfather."

"You and me both," Ajay said.

Henry strode forward, taking Ajay's hand in his own and shaking it. The man's meaty paws dwarfed Ajay's whole forearm. With that, Henry passed the trio and entered his house. "Might as well come in, then," he shouted behind him.

Ajay turned to Isabelle. "I thought I told you to stay indoors."

Isabelle shrugged and passed him. Kylie followed, an apologetic look on her face. Ajay figured that was about as good as it was going to get.

"It's all right," said Henry. He pointed straight up. "Long as the grid's on, there's nothing to worry about up there. Scrambles things up so the drones above won't see clear."

Ajay looked up and sure enough, the air about fifteen feet up had a hazy, wavering quality. At an angle, he could detect a warping in the air that might hide them well enough.

"Well, come on in, then," Henry said. He tromped across the rickety porch and entered his house.

"Where's Olivia?" Ajay asked, following Kylie into the house.

Kylie said in her tiniest voice, "Downstairs."

Henry opened his fridge, looked inside, and muttered something under his breath about groceries.

The threadbare sofa beckoned to Ajay, and his hip answered with a grinding ping. He refused to sit, though, fearing that he might not be able to get up. The girls took the opportunity and sat on opposite ends of the couch, with the middle cushion as tenuous neutral territory.

"You're probably wondering how Henry here knows me," Ajay said to the girls.

Henry smiled. "I'm wondering that myself. Don't remember giving out my address in the forums or on the radio." His expression got grim. "But that wouldn't stop a legendary hacker like yourself, would it? How long have they been after you?"

Ajay folded his hands on the brass handle of his cane. "That was years ago and if you think I'd do business with you without knowing exactly who you were, then you're as crazy as you look."

Kylie raised an eyebrow. "Legendary hacker? When can I learn to be a hacker?"

"Shush," said Ajay. "It was a long time ago."

Henry said, "Double-crossing the NSA took some balls, old man. Good to see someone can get away with that."

Kylie shrugged. "Guess I'll just learn on my own."

Ajay opened his mouth to reply but thought better of it.

Henry's eyes twinkled with amusement. "Well, I've let you route data through here long enough. I suppose you're stopping by to thank me?"

Ajay let out a sharp laugh. "Thanked you enough by helping you set this place up."

Henry scowled. The big man cut a jovial enough image when happy, but when he frowned the whole room got dark. "Nobody helped me."

Ajay strode up to the giant and poked him in the chest with his cane. "And I'm that nobody. The police could have found you, but they didn't, did they? The crime families you pissed off down in Chicago never were able to track you down. That lady—"

"You leave Jessie out of this."

"She looked a long time, you know."

Henry grabbed a handful of Ajay's hoodie and leaned down to get right in his face. "Now, you listen to me," he said. "I said, you leave her out of this."

Ajay smiled, covering how much this huge man intimidated him with his own show of cocky mirth. "I'm not going to threaten you with that, Henry."

Henry seemed to weigh that for a moment, then let go of Ajay's shirt.

"Girls," Ajay said, straightening his hoodie, "go find Olivia." Without waiting for their answer, he turned back to Henry. "If I wanted to threaten you, I'd let the tribal council know that you've never so much as glanced at that eighth of Mdewakanton lineage you're claiming."

The air went out of Henry. His shoulders slumped. "You have a funny way of asking for help from a friend."

"I don't have a lot of friends."

"No wonder," Henry said, tugging at his beard. "So, what exactly do you need, and how soon can you leave?"

"I need information." Ajay pointed at the door with his cane. "My daughter said that a man named Jackson Garver is after my granddaughters. I want to know who he works for and what he does. I know the man. He's an ass, but he's practical."

"So you think he has a good reason for wanting to kill a little girl?"

"Maybe."

The two men locked gazes for a long time. Ajay couldn't tell what the big man was thinking under his mask of scraggly beard. Still, the Loon had been something of an ally for a long time. Their goals had been similar, after all. Hide from prying eyes. Avoid being interesting and avoid scrutiny. Normally that wasn't hard.

"I don't have data here," Henry said. "You want a link, we need to go up to the tower."

"Fine."

"So who else did you bring? This is a regular party, isn't it?"

"A friend," Ajay said. He noted the hurt in Henry's eyes. "A real friend." That didn't help.

Henry let out a long, weary sigh. His watch beeped, and he switched it off. "Eyes in the sky," he said. "Drones coming around."

"Thunderheads? Doesn't your grid hide us from them?"

"Sure, it's Thunderheads. What else would there be?"

"You don't get any low-flyers around here?"

"Nope. Rez council doesn't allow it."

"Papa!" Kylie said from the basement. "Come quick!"

Ajay took two long steps to the basement stairs, ignoring the pain. Henry was quicker, pushing in front of the old man and throwing open the door.

"Nobody's supposed to be down there," he growled.

Kylie called out from down below.

Following Henry down, Ajay couldn't see much of the basement, except that it held the same kind of cluttered decor that most of the old farmhouses probably exhibited. Tools everywhere, not only on workbenches but scattered across the floor. Through the first door, things became better arranged. This was a bomb shelter and a well-maintained one at that.

"Oh, shit," Henry said, stopping in the doorway.

Ajay hurried forward, cursing when he couldn't push past Henry. Garrison stayed close at his heel, snuffling hard at the slimy walls. "Let me through to her," Ajay said.

Henry moved forward, then scrunched up against one wall. "Sorry," he said, sucking in his gut.

Ajay squeezed past, barely managing to push to the other side. The tiny room ahead was dry and clean, its walls of solid, upright cinder block. The ten-by-ten space looked nothing like the cellar behind them. Its tables were covered with guns, knives, and what looked like a handheld ham radio. The radio emitted the buzz of an open channel.

Kylie and Isabelle stood there, looking at something on the floor that Ajay couldn't see. His palms went cold. Even Isabelle looked shocked. Her facade had shattered under a pressure that Ajay feared to see. Finally, he managed to force himself to step forward, round the table.

And there she was, splayed out on the floor, clutching a black plastic case in her hands. Shaking. Hard.

A seizure.

"Get back," Ajay said, pulling the girls away. "Give her room."

Her hands, like claws, clutched the case. Foam flowed from her mouth, pooling on the floor. She shook harder than Ajay thought possible.

He froze, not knowing how to help. Time flowed like mud in a river. He touched her shoulder, shocked at how absolutely rigid she was. How long had she been like this? What if it didn't stop?

What would he do without her?

Ajay was scared, more than he ever had been before. All those times he'd spent with her, laughing about burned snickerdoodles and playing bridge. Those nights they'd watched movies together. The long days after her cat died and she'd spiraled into depression. That whole time he'd considered her the young one. The healthy one. She was always the one who would outlive him, no matter what, but they were both to an age when such things met reality the way a car meets a concrete divider.

Then, she stopped.

She drew in a deep, shaky breath. She was alive.

Broken, but alive.

CHAPTER TWENTY-FIVE

"You're safe here," said Henry, "for now, anyway."

He taped a tube to Olivia's arm while Isabelle and Kylie looked on with worried expressions. He had expertly started an IV using medical supplies from the bunker in his basement, and Olivia now lay unconscious on the sofa. The black case she had found lay next to her, and her purse sat on the coffee table. Ajay nudged it so that the pistol she'd taken from Mack's man wasn't visible before Henry saw it. No need for him to know everything.

Olivia sniffed the air, but her eyes didn't open. Her lip twisted up in an expression of disgust, which faded as quickly as it had come. A sunken, dark shadow shrouded her features. The saline Henry had would help her with the dehydration, but how long would that work before she needed her meds? Despite his extensive store of medical supplies, Henry didn't have what she needed, and Ajay was hesitant to rely too much on Henry's goodwill. The big man seemed friendly enough, but a smile and a joke could hide a lot of distrust. Ajay had been on both sides of that equation.

"I appreciate this, Henry," Ajay said. "We'll get out of your hair as soon as possible."

Henry scratched his beard. "Whole property is nulled out, and what yard isn't under trees is hazy on any drone systems that might see us. Your girls won't be seen from the sky. Anyone looking for you would need to go door to door around here, and I doubt they'd have much luck at it." He raised an eye at Garrison. "Unless they have a fella like that helping."

"Well, let's hope they don't." Ajay squinted out the window into the late afternoon sunlight. Isabelle and Kylie fought playfully using sticks for swords. "If they did, we'd be caught already."

"That you would." Henry groaned as he pulled himself to his feet. He checked the saline solution one last time, then walked out the back door without another word.

Ajay took Olivia's hand in his own, holding it for a long time, feeling the calloused skin of her fingertips brush against his palm. This wasn't her. The life, the ferocity, the fire: those were Olivia. That was who Ajay knew, but maybe there was more to her than he'd ever allowed himself. He sniffed back snot and wiped away tears.

Olivia was supposed to be the strong one.

"Okay," he said, setting her limp hand down on her chest. "Okay."

The girls played with Garrison, in the way that children play with an inert lump of fur in the middle of a shaggy grass lawn. Kylie jumped over the dog, hugged him, threw sticks in hopes that he might fetch. He didn't, of course. Isabelle stood with arms crossed and a scowl on her face.

Ajay gestured to the girls and they came to him where he stood on the porch. Garrison lumbered after them, finding a new resting place on the lawn where he could watch everything they did.

"Girls," Ajay said, "there are some things I'd like to talk about."

Kylie looked up at him with wide eyes. "Is Olivia—"

"She's recovering," he said, forcing his voice not to crack. "But there are some bad men after us and I'd like to go over some basic self-defense."

A twitch of a smile crossed Isabelle's face.

Kylie said, "We've already done this."

"Oh, really?" Ajay scratched his mustache. "When?"

"In Olivia's apartment," Kylie said.

Isabelle whispered something too quiet for Ajay to hear.

"Come again?" he said.

Kylie interpreted. "She doesn't think you're going to tell us anything new."

"Oh." Ajay thought for a moment. "Well, I might know a few tricks. Do you know what a head-butt is?"

Kylie giggled. "That was one of the first things she told us, right before teaching us where to kick boys to make them hurt."

"Really?"

Isabelle opened her mouth as if she were about to talk, but didn't say anything.

Instead, Kylie spoke. "She said we should always fight dirty. Throw sand, head-butt, bite, kick boys between the legs."

"Now, hold on a second. There's no need to fight that dirty."

Kylie's lips formed a tight line.

Ajay said, "Well, only as a last resort, then. When you know you're really overpowered."

The boards swelled under Ajay, and he heard Henry's footsteps as he rounded the house and stepped up on the old porch.

"What are you teaching them, old man?" Henry said.

"To fight."

Henry chuckled. "Don't fight, girls. Run away. Run fast. You'll have a much better survival rate. Let the idiots do the fighting, right?" He elbowed Ajay hard enough to leave a bruise.

Ajay rubbed the spot. "Well, yes. If running's an option."

Henry continued. "Or else kick them in the nuts first chance you get."

"Hey, now," Ajay said.

"First chance." Henry winked at the girls. "Hard as you can."

Ajay shook his head, not knowing anything else to add. The truth was if the girls had to fight Mack or any of his goons, Ajay wasn't sure they could do it. Proper training, martial arts, and dirty fighting might get them a little bit of an advantage, but that would only overcome part of the size differential. Henry was right. They needed to run.

Henry placed a hand on Ajay's shoulder. "C'mon, you can help me out." With that he returned to the house, continuing through out the back.

On his way through, Ajay touched Olivia's cheek with the back of his hand, feeling the warmth radiating from her. How long had he known her and kept her at a distance? Now, the thought of losing her put an ache in his chest so fierce he couldn't breathe. "Stay strong, Liv," he said. "I'll be back soon." Garrison followed him out the back door.

In back of the house, several rows of pines separated the livable property from the scrubby forest beyond. The grass grew tall and green here, especially around the septic tank. When Ajay stepped off the concrete step, his shoes sank deep into moist soil. Despite the rustic and heavily isolated feel of the property, it was in reasonably good shape. The grass was long but clearly trimmed that way on purpose. A neat stack of firewood sat near the wall of pines, shielded from the elements by a thin tarp and the reaching boughs of the trees.

Henry pointed to a place in the woods where a narrow walking path led into the darkness. "If things get bad, head up that path there. Leads you up to my antenna."

"What good will that do us?"

Henry shrugged. "It's easier to defend, isn't it?"

Ajay shifted uneasily on his feet, unsure of why Henry's gaze felt so heavy. "You have weapons there?"

The big man laughed, his whole body shaking. "Ajay, I've got weapons everywhere." He took two steps along the side of the house, opened a cedar box there, and pulled out a double-barrel shotgun. "I like to be prepared."

"Good to know."

Henry walked toward the forest, motioning for Ajay to follow. "Who's after you, anyway? Government?"

"No." Ajay struggled to keep pace. "Well, police aren't the first on the list, anyway. You heard of a company called Haveraptics?"

"Sure."

Ajay kicked away the spent milkweed at the edge of the woods. "They must be new."

"New?" Henry laughed, leading the way down a small path between two trees. "If ten years is new, then I suppose you're right. They're one of the big government contracts came out of that decryption meltdown."

"Ah." Ajay had left tech for retirement just before that, as the old digital empires fell to the free access of encryption-smashing quantum computers. Many of his colleagues had left around that same time, very few with the same stigma that followed Ajay. Several of them would have been able to find employment in one of the rising companies, even if those companies served government contracts. "Are they development or mercenary?"

Henry ducked under a branch, then made a quick turn to the right. "A little of both, really," he said, scratching his head. "Pays to diversify, right? If I remember, they dealt in a lot of biomed."

"Bio?" Ajay stopped walking, letting Henry get a few paces ahead. "What kind of government contracts do biomed companies get?"

Henry tugged at his beard. "What happened to you back then, anyway?"

"I retired."

"Now, hold on." Henry stopped, turning to Ajay. "Retired doesn't get you that kind of attention, and I think if I'm letting you stay on my land, I deserve some details."

"You won't let this out?"

Henry crossed his arms. "I make no promises."

Ajay chewed his lip. He'd never talked to anyone, in all the years since he'd left the NSA. "What I did wasn't anything any other father wouldn't do." Closing his eyes, the memory came to him as if it were yesterday. "I hadn't seen my daughter in almost a decade. Kinda figured I'd never see her again."

Henry turned and started walking again, motioning for Ajay to continue.

"Well, her name started showing up, not exactly as a person of interest, but adjacent to a lot of persons of interest. I'd sworn to respect her privacy, but there it was, again and again."

"So, she got into some bad stuff?"

"I don't know, but my team leader at the time — that same Jackson Garver who's chasing us now — told me to bury it. So I did. It was easy."

"Easy? That's a pretty involved piece of hacking for anyone else."

"Not if they have a diamond-optical quantum computer to throw at the problem."

Henry shook his head. "Those don't exist."

"They do, and they did. NSA had several, and they'd have rolled out to consumers if the Helsinki Accords hadn't solidified international support for classifying them as a weapon of mass destruction." Ajay licked his lips. "That was about a year later, and they faded after that."

"Never made a bit of sense to me. The Cube breaks encryption just fine. What's so different about having a handheld version?"

"It's all about control," Ajay said. "And those in power prefer centralized systems."

Henry grunted assent. "How come you got in trouble, then, if your diamond-optical device wasn't illegal yet?"

Ajay flashed a wolfish grin. "They don't write rules like the Helsinki Accords unless something really bad causes them."

"You?"

"Things escalated, and to tell the truth, I was feeling a little down. It was my anniversary at work, and maybe I was more than a little frustrated. Sashi wouldn't stay off the books, so in order to keep her safe..."

Henry nodded. "You opened all the doors."

"Broke every key I could come across. Until then we'd kept the advantage a secret, but the NSA was getting dangerous. Like, maybe considering a coup kind of dangerous. So, I broke down some digital barriers and during the chaos put some programs in place deep in the systems that kept me hidden."

Henry stood still for a long while, jaw slack. "Damn," he said, finally.

Ajay agreed with the assessment.

"Do you still have the diamond-optical?"

Without even weighing the costs and benefits of telling the truth, Ajay lied. "No."

"Huh," Henry said. He pushed through a row of maples into a small clearing in which sat an ancient wooden shed. Above the shed stood an umbrella of a sprawling solar panel. A white light lit the inside of the shed, and when Henry opened the door, the glare of the light made Ajay squint and shield his eyes.

Inside the shed sat a single console in front of a single chair. On the screen blinked a green cursor made of eight distinct pixels. The light dangled from wire stapled to the ceiling, and the tangle of cords behind the console ran to a stand holding three big batteries. The shed had once been painted and subtle hints of that long-ago blue still clung to the inside corners of the gray wooden surfaces.

"What is this?" Ajay asked.

Henry chewed his lip. "We go way back," he said. "And you've always been able to get things done."

The screen flickered, and thousands of lines of code flew past.

Henry ignored the screen. "I know you're able to get things done that nobody else can." He tugged at his beard. "I want you to decrypt the data on that disk."

Ajay furrowed his brow, genuinely confused. "Why can't you do it?"

"It's..." Henry looked around as if searching for the right word. "...illegal."

Then it made sense. Henry couldn't decrypt the data disk using the Cube because doing so would likely raise too many flags. Ajay thought of the diamond-optical black box in his pocket that could perform quantum computing tasks without connecting to the network at all. Henry was right: Ajay could get the job done. All he needed to do was activate the diamond-optical device.

Instead of answering, Ajay entered the shed and sat on the rickety chair. He licked his lips and started typing, navigating through the old computer system. Without a proper graphic interface, the going was slow, but he figured out where the links to the data were and where he could generate some scripts.

Henry leaned over his shoulder. "Can you do it?"

Ajay grunted a non-answer, fully absorbed in the task. A brute force hack wouldn't do. The levels of encryption were significantly stronger than anything that could be forced without quantum computing. However, if he could narrow down the search, there might be an answer. "Do you know anything in this data?"

"Her name's Jessie," Henry said.

Ajay tensed. "Jessie? The woman who was looking for you?"

"This will tell me how to find her."

Ajay removed his fingers from the keyboard. "Does she still want to be found?"

Henry pounded his fist on the table. His face turned a deep red. "I need to know."

"So she doesn't."

He leaned against the wall of the shed, which creaked under his weight. "It wasn't— It wasn't that big a fight."

For a long while, Ajay sat with his fingers hooked on the edge of the table. Henry wasn't a bad man, or at least everything Ajay knew about him indicated decency. Yet this made Ajay nervous. If the giant could hide this relationship from him, how much else could he be hiding? Henry did, after all, mostly live off-grid. If Henry were a stalker or a serial killer, wouldn't this be the best setup for him?

Henry sat on the floor in the shed's corner. His big shoulders hardly fit in the space between the wall and the table, but there he was with his fingers running through his big mess of a beard. It had been a long time since Ajay had seen that kind of pain, and even longer since he'd felt anything of the sort. Whatever Henry's nature, the big man really hurt from losing this Jessie. Maybe he was a stalker; maybe he loved her.

"We all have regrets," Henry said without looking up. "You know?"

Ajay tried to remember what he could about the relationship. He'd seen old transcripts when he'd searched for information on Henry. Jessie certainly had seemed to reciprocate Henry's feelings. When he went off-grid, she'd searched for him, methodically checking all the places Henry wasn't. At the time, Ajay hadn't really considered the tragedy of it to be any of his business. Now, here Henry was, asking for help. Ajay could think of only one way to know for sure the nature of their relationship. He turned back to the console.

Henry tugged at his beard. "I settled down here after I met her. Wouldn't have otherwise. But then, things went south between us, and, well, I don't know. I just want to talk to her again."

"I'll take a look," Ajay said, but he was already looking.

And then Ajay was hooked. It is the nature of a hacker to be a puzzle-solver. Whenever a puzzle presents itself, no matter how tricky, the true hacker has a deep urge to solve it, like a junkie and his drug. Ajay knew, in this case, that the easy solution sat like a lump in his pocket. With a little clever wiring and some judicious quantum computing, the encryption on Henry's data disk would crack right open. There was no challenge in that.

First, he needed to know what Henry had tried. The man hadn't documented anything, of course, but a quick perusal of the logs showed all that had transpired.

Henry had been at it for years. Every day the brute-force decryption ran, and from time to time Henry updated the hardware. The background processes guessed at keys, uselessly throwing processing power at random keys day after day. What obsession drove Henry to it? How healthy could this big man's brain be if he stayed dedicated to this for so long?

Ajay stopped those processes. They would do no good.

"Might as well have all this hardware working out predictions for horse races," he muttered to himself.

"What?" asked Henry.

"Never mind." Ajay listened, his hearing aid picking up noises from around Henry's property. He could still hear Kylie's voice whenever she said something to Isabelle. The two girls searched for food, which seemed like a reasonable thing for them to do. Ajay's stomach rumbled, but the challenge lay in front of him, and he wouldn't give it up for anything.

His fingers hovered over the keyboard as he closed his eyes to consider the problem. The biggest issue was the sheer bulk of the data. To decrypt the entire thing would take this hardware several minutes, which was why Henry's attempt at random guessing wouldn't work. When the number of possible solutions could be measured in multiples of atoms in the universe, brute force simply wouldn't work.

However, if he could shrink the target set, odds improved. The hardware in the little shed wasn't terrible. In fact, considering that the data file used encryption from years ago helped quite a bit. Even though quantum computers made encryption a joke, standards continued to increase, making a modern hash much harder to break in any conventional way.

At least, of course, until hardware caught up. And once it did, they created new algorithms and longer keys. Henry's hardware could crack this code, but it needed to be approached at the right angle.

Ajay typed. Code flew onto the screen as fast as his fingers would move, words of logic flowing as if it were his native tongue. This was his chosen craft, and he was good at it. The sun set and the deep electric hum sang in the cool night. Time meant nothing to the hacker as night stretched on. The animals of the forest called and skittered, their voices nothing more than little whispers in the back of Ajay's mind. Code grew in small pieces, each running as an individual chunk until an elegant start emerged into a brilliant solution.

He glanced at Henry. The big man's head nodded and deep breaths lifted his chest. Ajay didn't know how long he had been asleep, and he didn't much care. It made things easier, depending on what he found in the file.

The program ran for ten seconds, then crashed.

Ajay swore under his breath. Things never worked on the first try, did they? Or the second, third, or fourth. When finally the program ran, deep in the night, he leaned back in the chair and watched as the hash algorithm rushed by on the green screen monitor.

The solution was simple, really. It only tried to decrypt the header, and only searched for the hashed version of the word "Jessie," assuming that her name would be part of the document. If it wasn't, or if she went by a different name like "Jessica," then they would find nothing. In his clunky old fidget, Ajay carried a reverse hash database, so he didn't even need to waste processing power on decrypting the entire header every time. He only searched for the string. Ajay rested his head in his arms and slept.

Time passed. Ajay knew because the drool at the corner of his mouth didn't just exist, but it'd had time to dry. He blinked wearily at the screen, which displayed a single block of text:

AI Identification: Jessie Morris
Primary Schema: Romance De-escalation Scenario
Target: Henry Bower, dissident

"Damn," Ajay said, and he deleted the information, removing his decryption program and any evidence of his project. "Damn."

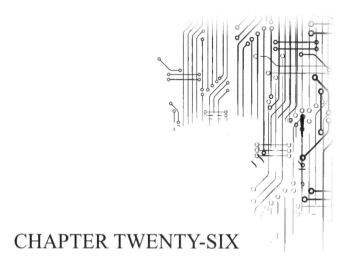

CHAPTER TWENTY-SIX

Ajay nudged open the back door of the house with his cane. The weight of the past days dragged at his feet and made bags under his eyes like great sacks of sand. The raw ache of exhaustion pained his joints, making each silent step a struggle.

Olivia still lay on the sofa, sleeping fitfully. Her saline drip neared empty, so he changed the bag for a new one. How long would she stay unconscious? There were certain bodily functions that needed tending if she stayed out much longer. Ajay sniffed the air. It didn't seem to be too late on that account. Soon, though.

He knelt on one knee and held her hand to his chest. As his eyes adjusted to the dark room, he made out the pile of blankets that likely held the girls. They had taken care of themselves without any help, then. Found bedding and made themselves comfortable. Good.

"I'm sorry," he whispered to Olivia. She couldn't hear, of course, but the words weren't meant for her.

It had been wrong to drag Olivia into this. He knew that. Tough as she was, there was only so far a person could be pushed. The state of her fragile mind should have been obvious. It would have been obvious if he had ever been a better friend.

If only he had been a better parent. Then this would never have happened.

Her forehead felt warm to his touch — not feverish, but pleasantly warm, like a good distance from the hearth or like baked bread. She radiated the heat, but only to those close enough to look for it. He touched his lips to her forehead, breathing in her soft scent as he kissed her good night.

"I'm sorry," he said again.

"It's not your fault," came Kylie's soft voice from behind him.

He started at the noise. "I thought you were asleep."

Her smile shone in the sliver of moonlight. "Someone had to watch over them," she said. She shifted and a glint of a knife slipped under her covers. "And I'm not sleepy."

"We have a long day tomorrow," Ajay said. "We're going to meet up with your mother again."

Kylie's eyes went wide for a fraction of a second. She leaned back against the wall. "We could just stay here," she said.

"No, I don't think that's a good idea." Ajay crossed to her and sat against the wall. He took her hand into his own. "Those men will find us, Kylie. And we need to get Olivia to a hospital."

Kylie crossed her arms, a scowl on her face. Ajay couldn't help but chuckle at the sight of her.

"What?" she asked.

He leaned against the wall. His aches were fading, but his eyes refused to stay open. How long had he been awake? "It's nothing," he said.

Kylie poked him in the shoulder. "What's nothing?"

"When your mother was, oh, eight or nine..." Ajay stared off into the dark room, trying to jog his memory. "Younger than you are now, anyway. Well, I had a rare weekend free from work, so I took her up to the Minnesota Landscape Arboretum. You know, the place with the hedge maze?"

Kylie stared at him blankly.

Ajay cleared his throat. "We'll have to go there sometime. It's a beautiful place in the fall. She was bored most of the day, not really into trees as much as her old man. Hell, I wasn't even that into it. It just seemed like the kind of place a good dad ought to take his daughter. I should have taken her to the mall. Or the zoo. She would have liked the zoo better, I think."

Kylie took his hand and scooted up next to him. She rested her head on his shoulder, and her warm body nestled up against him.

"Well, anyway, there was a pond at the arboretum, full of fish. Koi, I think. She loved those fish when she saw them. Fed them little bits of her lunch. Then it was time to go see something else, and she didn't want to. We fought a little bit, as parents and kids do sometimes. I took her on a trail to the mazes, which I knew she'd love.

"But all she wanted to do was see those fish. Sometimes, when people have the very best intentions for someone else, they stop listening to what that person really needs. Do you know what I mean?"

He felt Kylie's head shift a little on his shoulder as she nodded.

"Then she was gone. This little eight-year-old girl, gone in a huge park. Back then, there weren't drones everywhere. Places like that you could hide for days if you tried. I looked all over for her, in the flower patches, butterfly gardens — after a little while, the idea to go back to the koi pond even sank into my thick skull."

"You found her there?" Kylie asked.

"Nope."

Kylie sat up and looked him in the eye.

"She had been there, but she was too smart to hang around. You see, she didn't just want to see the koi again. She had this whole idea of being their new caretaker. Living there permanently and feeding them every day. A group of students passing by said that she had joined them for a while. Blended right in with the crowd."

"Why?"

"Because she probably knew nobody was looking for a crowd of kids. The workers were looking for a lone girl wandering on her own. By that time nearly every worker at the arboretum was doing the same. Dammit, she was too clever for her own good."

Kylie jutted her chin forward. "I wouldn't have tried to hide from you."

Ajay ran a hand along the stubble of his jaw. "Well, your mother was always passionate about everything. Can't blame her much for that. When she got it in her mind to care for the fish, there was no stopping her. When we found her, it was long after dark. We brought the police in and everything."

"Where was she?"

"Where do you think? She was right there by the koi pond, feeding the fish."

Kylie screwed up her face. "How come you didn't find her for so long, then?"

Why hadn't they? Ajay remembered that night in vivid detail. The crisp autumn air had felt much like it always did at night. Sashi hadn't given up her resolve to feed the fish, but the cold probably put a dent in her wish not to be discovered doing so. The truth was when Sashi wanted something, she got it. Plain and simple. Ajay didn't tell Kylie that, though.

"We just weren't looking in the right place."

He helped Kylie get situated back in her blankets, then checked on Olivia one last time. She rested so peacefully, with no hint of worry knitting her brow. Ajay felt a peace from her, like she was finally starting to recover from her episode. Maybe by morning, she would wake.

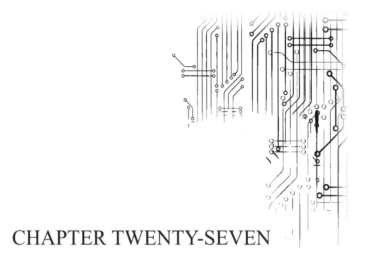

CHAPTER TWENTY-SEVEN

"Two-tone blue, with a touch of rust." Henry ran a finger along the dusty body of the only car illuminated by the crisp morning radiance streaming into the big pole barn. "Auto-drive for when it's needed, but it's forward-facing seating with a real steering wheel for folks who are old-fashioned like that."

"I am," said Ajay.

"Kinda figured." Henry kicked a tire, sending dry mud cascading from his boot. "License plates flip at a touch of the button, active radar damping, if such a thing comes up, which it won't because you're not stupid enough to draw any attention. From above, this'll look like any other car on any other road, but with an added advantage that if you need it, she'll spit out a series of shadows that can disrupt any eyes in the sky."

"Like chaff?"

"Sure." Henry squinted at the older man. "Like chaff."

"You're not messing around." Ajay leaned close to the window and peered inside. Indeed, the black dashboard console shone with a polished look that didn't fit with the rest of the car. "You'll lend us this?"

Henry guffawed and slapped Ajay on the back. "Aw, hell, no. I need this so I can stay off radar when I fetch groceries." He stuck a thumb out at a dark lump of a shape under a tarp farther back in the shadows. "Got something a little more rustic for you back there."

Before Ajay could respond, a baseball flew through the open barn doors and slammed into Henry's head. He snapped around, face red as hellfire. His huge hands balled into fists.

Henry shouted as he stalked out of the barn. "What the fuck do you think you're doing?"

Ajay rushed forward, grabbing the big man's elbow. "Henry," he said, "they didn't mean—"

Henry shoved him hard, sending the old man sprawling. Somewhere, Garrison let out a low woof.

Kylie skidded to a halt outside the barn, her eyes wide with fear. Her jaw worked up and down, trying to form words, but failing. She held a baseball bat loosely in one hand, letting it drag against the dewy grass.

Henry stalked at her, shaking his head. He rubbed the back of his head with one meaty palm. "Goddamn!" he said. "Goddamn!"

His nostrils flared, and his face turned a shade of crimson Ajay hadn't thought possible. The big man stared at Kylie until she crumpled back on herself, then he looked down at the ball. Her grip tightened on the bat. Henry's arm twitched, fist like a chiseled stone at the end of his arm.

Ajay pulled himself to his feet. "They didn't mean it, Henry," he said.

Henry shot a look back at Ajay that sent a jolt of fear through the old man's chest. Henry breathed several deep, ragged breaths. His lips pulled back in a grimace.

Isabelle ran up behind Kylie, panting. She flashed a disarming smile.

Henry picked up the ball and peered at it. "This is Butch's," he said.

Kylie and Isabelle looked at each other, then at Ajay. "Who's Butch?" Kylie asked, her voice shaking.

Ajay shrugged, still shaken by Henry's whiplash mood swing. "Butch must be the dog we heard earlier?"

Henry tossed the ball to Kylie, and she caught it. "Something like that." He nodded out the door. "Now get," he said as a dismissal.

The girls turned to go, but Ajay stopped them. "Isabelle," he said, "are you feeling better?"

She chewed on a lip but nodded.

"How is Liv?"

Kylie spoke. "She's good, but still asleep. Her IV bag is still half full. We just checked."

"And you'll check again in ten minutes?"

The girls both nodded, and it struck Ajay how similar they were. Superficially, they were such different girls, but when together they had so many similar mannerisms. The way they tilted their heads to the side when they felt shy reminded him so much of Sashi. They batted their eyelashes. Where did girls learn to do that?

"You can go," he said. "But take Garrison, and play across the yard."

Kylie called to the big dog. Garrison looked pleadingly at Ajay before he left, as if to say, "Really? You're doing this to me?" When no reply came, the dog loped after the girls, pointedly ignoring the ball when Kylie tried to make him fetch.

Henry whipped the tarp off the other car. Where it wasn't rust, it was white, but it wasn't very white. One headlight sat at an odd angle and the thing's bulbous lines made it look more like a bubble on wheels than a proper car.

"A Volkswagen Beetle?" Ajay asked.

Henry pulled the tarp off the rest of the way. The back fender was matte black and sat several inches lower than the front. He scratched his head. "It'll run," he said. "Full diesel."

Diesel. Of course, it was diesel. Ajay shuddered at the memory of the truck-driving thugs who had caused so much trouble for him already. Might as well finish things up in a diesel. After all, something like this would run forever if properly maintained.

It didn't look properly maintained.

"We need to get Olivia her meds as soon as possible."

Henry shot him a dark look. "What you need to do is crack that encryption."

"I told you," Ajay said, "it's not an easy crack. That program will run a few days before you see anything." Ajay picked his walking stick up from where it had fallen on the ground. "And she needs her meds sooner than that." They'd managed to get fluids into her, but her degrading mental state worried Ajay more than anything Jackson and his thugs could throw at him, and definitely more than the police. Maybe that wasn't smart, but a man had to prioritize.

Henry pulled out a key and crammed himself behind the wheel. "It's not as bad as it looks," he said. "I get out here every couple months and drive it, just to make sure I have a backup working vehicle." He cranked the ignition and cocked his head at the weak wheeze of the engine turning over. "Battery might be low."

Ajay threw up his hands. "Great."

Henry extracted himself from the car. "It'll be ready by the time that encryption cracks." His face darkened again.

"I told you—"

"And I told you no deal." Henry pulled himself up to his full height. "It'd be polite to say thanks to whatever I get you."

Ajay stepped up, poking the man in the chest with his cane. "Polite! I'll tell you polite." He jammed a finger at the house. "Polite is giving a good goddamn about the woman dying on your sofa. Polite is getting those kids somewhere safe. I'll pay you, Henry." He drew several crystal clips from his pocket — enough for a small fortune in MREs and guns. "What do you want?"

Henry waved the money away. "Those kids?" Spittle flew from Henry's mouth. "What is it with those kids, anyway? What's going on so special that people are after those girls?"

Ajay stepped back. "What makes you think anyone is after the girls?"

Henry loomed over Ajay. "You think people just help others out for wanting it? What the hell world do you live in?"

"Just for wanting it?" Ajay sputtered. Could this man really not know? He'd been through too much to let this get away from him. "I did my best to help you, Henry. You know that."

Henry's jaw worked like he was chewing a wad of sap. "Like hell."

Ajay wondered how much the big man guessed. "Jessie isn't who you thought she was."

The flash of rage that reddened Henry's face was gone as fast as it came. His fists flexed, then relaxed. When he spoke, his voice rumbled like an earthquake under a mountain. "That ain't your business."

"You never met her, did you." He tried to listen to Henry over the panicked thrum of his own beating heart. "In real life, I mean."

Henry pulled a charger from a shelf and plugged it in. He made sparks by tapping the leads together, which cast his grim face in a strobe of lightning flashes. "Get to whatever it is you have to say."

Ajay took a step closer to the giant man and placed a hand on his elbow. "How much do you know about Jessie?"

"Know?" He connected the charger to the car's battery. "All I know is she was there when I needed her. Helped me get out. Helped me..." He brushed at his eyes with the back of his hand. "She helped me."

"You were a dissident, weren't you?" Ajay said. "The Age of Honesty, right? Once encryption fell, you people went around blowing open all the secrets of governments and corporations. You were good at it. Moved around, hacked well enough to avoid being properly caught. You were a shark in a tank of dolphins and made a real difference, back when things had the potential to be a lot better."

Henry bowed his head. "There were eight of us."

"All the others left, though, didn't they?"

Henry's nod was so slight Ajay almost didn't see it.

"One by one, and for reasons you didn't understand."

"We were kids. They grew up. People do that."

Ajay flashed a smile. "I never did."

Henry barked out a bitter laugh. "Well, you're the only damn one."

Ajay and Henry locked gazes for a long time. "She wasn't real, Henry," he said, almost under his breath.

"Bullshit!" Henry slammed a fist on the roof of the car, leaving a dent. Then, quieter, he said, "You can't know that."

"I can." Ajay pulled the black box from his pocket, feeling the cool heft of the metal surface. "Do you know what this is?"

Henry furrowed his brow.

"It's a diamond-optical quantum computer." Ajay held it up in the light. "It's one of the first models, from before they regulated the hell out of them. It lets me see what goes on behind the scenes." He put the box back in his pocket. "I know what the government is capable of."

"You had that all along."

"I did."

Henry drew a deep breath. "You could have cracked that code in minutes."

"A little longer than that, probably, but yes."

"Why didn't you?"

Ajay felt a little spark of pride swell in his chest. "Didn't need to."

Henry leaned back against the Volkswagen, which swayed under his weight. The look in his eyes was one of profound pain. Betrayal. "So, you did crack it."

"Part of it," Ajay said. "Enough to recognize the work."

Henry folded into himself, sliding his back down the side of the car until he sat on the cold earth, head in hands. "I don't want to hear it," he said.

But Ajay didn't stop. "Imagine knowing everything about everyone: what they eat, what they play, what they watch, what they weigh. Imagine knowing what they wish for when they're alone and where they go when they're feeling lonely. They know everything about us, Henry. Everything that's worth knowing."

"They could have had us killed."

"Of course they could have. That's what they're trying to avoid because the government that kills its own people doesn't have long to survive. But this is different. The system discovers what it takes to get problem people out of the way. It learned everything about you and decided that the one thing that would make you give up was love."

Henry looked up at Ajay, and guilt twisted the old man's gut. He wished to hell he didn't have to tell Henry about this. If only they could have left sooner.

"It made you abandon your goals, but it didn't give a shit whether or not you fell in love. It's cognitive computing at its worst, applied to the predictive psychology of people they need to control. The de-escalation scenario only knows that if it says certain things to you, you'll behave in a certain way. You were going to cause big trouble for the government, and it de-escalated and de-radicalized you. The system works nine times out of ten."

"And the tenth time?"

"There's always the fallback plan."

Henry ran his fingers through his hair and laughed. "It's embarrassing, isn't it?"

"No," Ajay said. "It's frightening. Ten years ago, they manipulated you like that. They're always getting better at it."

Henry shrugged. "World we live in, right?"

Ajay patted him on the shoulder. "If we're lucky."

Henry glanced at his car, the Chevy with the two-tone blue. "Well, give me some time and I'll get that car running for you."

"We need to leave, Henry. Soon."

A mirthless smile tugged at the corners of Henry's mouth. "It'll be ready to go in twenty minutes. I just need to retool the biometrics."

"Thank you," Ajay said. "I'll gather the others."

Ajay crossed the nine-iron's distance to the house. Isabelle and Kylie played with Garrison, still trying to get him to fetch. Ajay would gather them next, but Olivia was his greatest concern. His cane thumped on the porch, and he pushed his way inside the house. Wind snatched the screen door from his grasp, slamming it against the side of the house.

Olivia sat bolt upright on the sofa, panic plastered on her face.

"Liv," Ajay said, trying to calm her.

Her gaze focused on him. She swept the gun up from the coffee table and rolled down behind the cover of the table.

"Liv, hold on," Ajay said. His eyes adjusted poorly to the light, and shadows swallowed everything in the room. "It's me."

Kylie's voice came from behind him. "Papa?"

"Stay back," Ajay said. He turned to see her at the door, a worried look on her face. He waved her away. "Just get back."

Olivia fired a wild shot in his direction, gun booming in the close confines of the room. His ears rang. Ajay ducked back, shoving Kylie out of the way. She ran back to where Isabelle stood wide-eyed. Ajay ducked outside.

"Liv," he called in. His heart thumped, wild enough to make his whole chest hurt. "Olivia, it's just us."

Henry crossed the lawn, shotgun in his fist and scowl on his face. "What the hell's going on?"

Ajay waved him back. More guns would scare Olivia even worse, and there wasn't anything to do about it. Ajay felt an attack of panic rising like the flood surge of a tsunami.

Henry didn't stop, so Ajay met him at the edge of the porch where he could look him in the eye. "Put that gun away, son."

Henry quaked. His grip on the gun tightened. "What the hell is going on?"

"She's having a bad episode." Ajay spotted Kylie and waved her farther away. No use having her close. "She's got Alzheimer's, and she's confused."

The big man's posture sank. "Alzheimer's."

"All we need to do is settle her down some." Ajay swallowed the lump in his throat. "She'll be fine, but you go in there waving that gun and one of you isn't going to walk out."

Henry didn't move.

Ajay placed a hand on the big man's shoulder. "I give you fifty-fifty odds."

Finally, the giant took a step back. "Fine."

"All right," he muttered to himself, turning back to the house. "That's it. No more feeling sorry for yourself, Ajay. Tough it up and from this point forward, you gotta control the situation. Pay attention." He nodded. He could do this. He could get Olivia the medication she needed, get the girls back to their mother, and get home in time to watch some football on Sunday. He'd always been the kind of guy to get things done, and nothing said there was an age limit on being that guy. First step was to calm Olivia down. She would listen to him.

Ajay stepped into the doorway and drew a breath to speak in his most calming voice.

Olivia rose from behind the sofa and shot him.

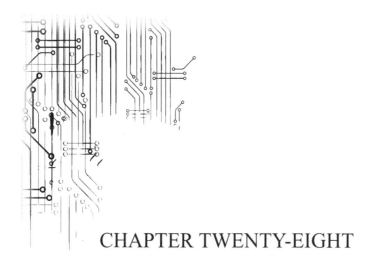

CHAPTER TWENTY-EIGHT

Ajay clutched his shoulder, blood and pain bursting like fire from the wound. He stumbled to one side. Leg caught on the upturned coffee table. A shout. He went down hard.

Olivia's brow knit in a fury he'd never seen on her. "Now you get out of this house before I finish the job," she said.

Ajay tried to raise his hands in surrender and regretted it. Any motion set off a plume of molten lava, and how pacifying could a pair of bloody hands be, anyway? He scrambled back as best he could. "Liv—"

"That ain't my name." She jabbed the gun in his direction, and he flinched as if she'd shot him again. "And don't you talk to me like you're familiar. I've never seen you in my damn life." She tore the IV from her arm.

The sofa rammed against Ajay's arm, and he realized he was scrambling backward again. His jaw worked, trying to figure out what to say.

Behind Olivia, the door swung open. Kylie stood in the doorway, frozen. Her voice was barely a whisper. "Papa."

Olivia swung on her, pointing the gun just to the side. Her jaw slackened, and her brow furrowed in confusion.

Ajay thrust himself up using his good arm. He lunged at her to take the gun, maybe overpower her.

Olivia caught his momentum, cracked him on the back of the head with the butt of her gun, and sent him reeling into the sofa, where he sprawled in a heap. Olivia backed against the wall, leveling the gun at his head. "Next time you try something, you'll get the business end."

"Again," Ajay said.

"You're damn right, again." Olivia motioned for Kylie to enter the room, but Kylie took a step back outside. "Don't you run away, girl."

Kylie froze. She shot Ajay a pleading look, but he was too busy worrying about the blood flowing from his wounded shoulder.

"Now," said Olivia. "Who in Sam hell are you?"

Ajay's heart slammed like an '80s rock band. His vision blurred from blood and tears, and he had to concentrate just to steady his breath enough to talk. The air smelled of blood and piss, and he wondered if it was all his.

The porch boards creaked as Henry's massive form appeared in the door. Olivia's attention snapped to him, but he leveled his gun at her and she knew not to make a move. She took a step back.

"This is my house you're shootin' up," Henry growled. "And I don't much appreciate that of a guest."

Ajay pulled his fidget from his pocket. What was that song? His breaths came fast and shallow, every movement sending burning shockwaves through his bleeding shoulder. "Beethoven," he said to the machine, his voice barely a whisper.

Olivia blinked and took another step away from him.

Henry moved into the room, keeping his gun trained on Olivia. She shot him a warning glare.

Beethoven's Moonlight Sonata #14 sprang from Ajay's handheld. Olivia's expression grew hard and her hand shook.

Ajay mouthed, "Run," to Kylie, seeing that she still stood in the doorway. She shook her head, stepping in closer to Olivia. The old woman swayed, blinking with confusion.

For a long time, the song played, and Kylie edged closer and closer to Olivia. Olivia watched Ajay with a wary expression, the line between her eyes a deep furrow. Step after step, Kylie moved in, one hand outstretched.

Kylie touched her hand, and Olivia dropped the gun.

When Olivia spoke, it was the voice he recognized from their long friendship. "Ajay?" she said in a whisper. "Why are you acting like I killed you? It's just a flesh wound."

Ajay looked down at the blood smeared all over his side. "Because it hurts?"

"It grazed the top of your shoulder. Hardly dug into the muscle at all."

He stared at her like she'd just given him a death sentence.

She shook her head, blinking in apparent confusion. "Hold still, then." She paused, looking him in the eyes. "And Ajay?" she said, her voice quivering a little. "I'm sorry."

"Are we good, then?" Henry asked. He lowered his shotgun but kept his finger near the trigger.

"Do you have a wound kit?" Olivia asked.

Henry pointed with his gun at the overturned coffee table. "Right there, ma'am."

Olivia rooted through the debris, finding the kit and the black plastic case that she'd brought up from the basement. She slung the case's strap over her shoulder and brought the first aid kit to Ajay.

Henry ground his teeth. "Hurry up and let's get you and your people out of here," he said. He stuck his head out the window and let out a loud whistle, waving for Isabelle to approach. After a minute she came in, turning her nose up at the sight of blood.

"Girls," Ajay said, wincing. He wanted to warn them of something, spur them into action. Something bad was coming, but the pain gobbled up all of his attempts to organize his thoughts. Shadows crept in at the edges of his vision, and words felt like slugs at the end of his tongue.

"Shit," Olivia said. "He's going into shock." She knelt next to Ajay and eased him down to the floor. Doing so jostled his wounded shoulder, sending sickening fangs of agony deep into his flesh. "Aw, shit, sorry, Ajay. I didn't realize you were such a wimp."

"I'm showing vulnerability," he said.

Olivia pressed on the wound. "It's not as charming as you think."

"I don't feel like I'm going into shock," Ajay said. "Just a little cold. And my fingers are numb."

The sound of ripping cloth filled his ears, but it might as well have been tearing flesh for how it felt. Somehow, someone threw a blanket over his body.

"Stay with us, old man," Henry said. "Can't let you go yet."

But Henry stayed. Ajay couldn't figure out why that was bad. How could it be bad to have more help? The big man's anger scared Ajay, but that wasn't the problem. What was? Why was it a problem that Henry was there to help?

Ajay twitched, tried to sit up. Olivia pushed him back down, sending another stab like a venom-soaked knife through his body.

"No," he said, "I'm fine."

Olivia straddled his body, getting down right in his face. She held his gaze for a few seconds as if verifying that he was still there. Still alive. "You're not hurt bad," she said. "But you need to toughen up so I can stitch this."

Ajay opened his mouth to protest, but the noise that came out sounded more like the cry of a kitten whose mother was missing.

"Oh, quiet down," Olivia said. "Toughen up a little." She motioned to something Ajay couldn't see, and then she held a bottle up to his lips.

He drank without thinking, and immediately regretted it. He spat harsh whiskey in a mist. The taste of the stuff lingered on his tongue.

Olivia leaned down on him again, almost touching her nose to his. "Good," she said after a few seconds. "Now quit complaining so much."

"I've been shot!" Ajay scrambled a little farther from her. "It fucking hurts."

Olivia swished whiskey around in the half-full bottle. She took a swig. "You were only shot a little," she said. "And the bullet passed clean through muscle."

"It was my muscle!"

Ajay stole a glance at his naked shoulder. The entire thing was a mess of blood. Olivia splashed whiskey on it, sending another molten surge of pain through his body. Ajay forced back the panic. His handheld still played Beethoven, and he tried to focus on that.

Olivia held the bottle in one hand and in the other hand a needle and thread. She looked at the bottle, then the needle. For a long stretch of forever, Ajay thought he saw the confusion creeping back into her gaze again. How long would she stay better? She held the whiskey up to his lips, and this time he drank as much as he could handle. She stuffed a couple of pills in his mouth, and he drank another swig to wash those down.

"Painkillers," she said, her voice calm. Pleading. "Hardly expired at all."

He shook his head.

She stroked his hair, her fingertips brushing against his temple. "My platoon had a bad deployment once, back in Afghanistan. Some of us got separated one time, including me and Oscar. Lost our vehicle and our comm. Back then..." she took a deep breath. "This won't hurt a bit," she said as she jammed the needle through Ajay's tender flesh.

Ajay bit back a scream. Beads of sweat rolled down his forehead.

She smiled. "Very good." She made another stitch, taking her time to press the torn flesh back together. "Lot of fighting back then. Confusion. There were eight of us, and we decided to hoof it back to base. Shouldn't have taken long, but we got messed up in the mountains." She narrowed her eyes as she pulled the needle through. Then she met his gaze. "They're like bluffs, but bigger."

He spoke through gritted teeth. "I know what mountains are."

"Well, the enemy picked us off one by one. Smith lost it to a landmine, Huber took a sniper bullet to the temple." She tied off the thread, then touched Ajay's temple again. "Right here." A faraway look shadowed her face, followed by a quirky smile. Splashing whiskey on her hands, Olivia readied her thread for another stitch. "First few mornings, we woke under attack. After that, we didn't sleep much. At all. Not even with a watch. Only so many days a person can go without sleep. Every day we thought it was the day we'd escape. Every night we hid, afraid for our goddamn lives."

Ajay started to say something, but Olivia jammed a needle into his flesh, and he clapped his mouth shut. She pulled the thread through, stitching in silence for a while.

"It was the night I dozed off that they hit us. Oscar got gutshot, and it was my fault. I woke up slow that night, and he suffered for it. When we finally found our way out of those mountains, Oscar was too far gone. Every morning since then, for near fifty years, I've woken thinking I'm under attack."

She paused, and Ajay met her gaze. He didn't try to say anything, but he wanted to understand what it had to be like for her. Always waking in that panic. Never fully resting. It had to be bad, but she took it.

She made another stitch. "For a while, it faded. It'd be that little flutter of panic when you feel like something's wrong, but you don't know what it is. Played something fierce on my love life, but otherwise, I did fine." She swallowed. "Then the Alzheimer's came."

"That made it worse?"

She tied the knot on the final thread and started picking select pieces out of the first aid kit. "No, the Alzheimer's made it better. It's a horrible disease, but you have no idea how nice it is to forget." She looked down at her bloody hands. "No," she said, "it was the cure that made it worse."

Ajay took one of her cold hands in his right one, wishing only to give her some of his warmth.

"The cure works by fixing faded parts of memory, reconnecting what's come apart to some extent. It's one of those fancy biologicals. I told you that, right? It assembles a network in my brain or some such nonsense."

"It causes the hydrophobia."

Olivia licked her dry lips. "It's a hell of a side effect."

He held her hand close to his chest. "It's worth it for an extra twenty years, though, right?"

"Ten," she said.

He cocked his head to the side.

"Ten years," Olivia explained. "I'm two over that, so I'm one of the lucky ones. My memory's fading again, and it's fading fast. There's only so much the fix can do once the brain is damaged too much." She shushed him as he tried to speak again. "It started about a week ago. They said I'd fade fast once the biological stopped working. I probably don't have a month."

"But your meds will help?"

Olivia wrapped his wound in sterile, non-stick cloth, securing it in place with tape. The shoulder ached, and movement caused a vicious stab of pain, but he wouldn't bleed to death. His eyes drifted closed, either from the meds or the alcohol. Numbness crept up his fingers and toes, wrapping his body in a medicine cocoon.

"My meds I have at home won't help," Olivia said in a voice so quiet he almost didn't hear. "It's only going to get worse."

He pulled her into an embrace with his one good arm.

"Worst part is," her voice cracked, "my memory's not fading where I want it to. I'm forgetting you, Ajay, and I'm remembering the war." She pulled back and looked at him through teary eyes. "I don't want to forget you, Ajay."

Ajay pulled her hand close and kissed it. "I'll be here for you, Liv," he said. "Doesn't matter whether or not you remember me. I'll be here." He swallowed a big lump of pain that made his shoulder wound seem like a minor scratch. "'Til the end, Liv. 'Til the end."

Then he remembered. The thought that scratched at the back of his brain finally had a moment to properly form. Gunshots made noise. A lot of it. Any drone within a dozen miles could guess at this location, and the hell if they wouldn't investigate. Now, the pressing need to leave was even more urgent. He needed to tell Henry to prep the vehicle. He needed the girls to gather their things. He needed...

The shadows overtook Ajay, and he slipped into unconsciousness.

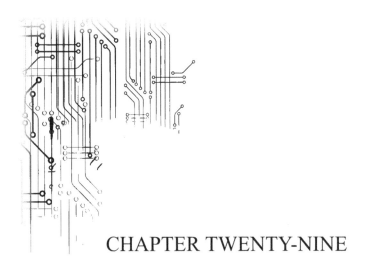

CHAPTER TWENTY-NINE

Ajay was no stranger to pain. In his experience, every day was an ever-present and ever-changing arrangement of aches and agony. It was a seasonal thing, that chronic pain. In spring, knees popped to the coming storm; in summer, the hip moved like gravel in a groove. Autumn was a constant creaking of lungs and eyes; in winter, muscles cramped and froze. Years of pain built him up, stronger and stronger against the daily agonies of age.

The shocking crack-stab of the bullet had torn him from the constant thrum of background pain. It reminded him of what pain really meant. For so long, pain had been a false signal, telling him that something was wrong when really, age was his only flaw. Sure, the hip would one day need to be repaired. Golf suffered, but what need did he have of one little game? More important to stay out of a notoriously information-hungry hospital. Hospitals scared him more than pain ever did.

But the molten-lead agony of that bullet. Now that was something.

He woke to a symphony of knives, no less painful than when he'd passed out. His mind packed that pain away, storing it in a little place in the back of his brain so that he knew it was there, but wouldn't blackout from it.

Then Kylie, not knowing he was already awake, shook him hard enough to crack the back of his head on the wooden planks of the floor. Somewhere, a dog barked loud and rough. It wasn't Garrison.

He sputtered and swore. "I'm awake," he said, surprised at the slur in his voice. How much whiskey did he still have in him?

Kylie put her finger to her lips and whispered. "Ms. Olivia said to wake you up. She said to make you take these." She handed him two pills and a little orange bottle.

Ajay grimaced as he forced himself up onto his good elbow. The world spun around him. "Where is everyone? Is that another dog?"

"It's just an alarm system. That's how Henry knows someone is near the end of his driveway."

Ajay remembered hearing the dog bark when they had walked down the long driveway. It made sense as a way to alert the owner to an intruder. Seemed a little silly not to just go ahead and own a dog, though. He forced himself all the way up, paused while his body adjusted, then stood. He gestured at his cane and coat on the sofa and Kylie grabbed them for him. He tried to shake the fogginess from his head but was only met with a wave of nausea. He stuffed the pill bottle in his coat pocket but didn't take the extra meds. Kylie draped the coat loosely over his shoulders.

She led him to the barn, and while the nine-iron felt more like a full par five, he covered the distance without complaint. The dog still barked in the distance. How could someone take so long to move down the driveway? Looking at the sun he figured — hell, he figured it was still daytime. Never was much good at telling time by the sun. In Minnesota, the autumn sun always sat a little low on the horizon, but now it seemed somewhat closer to the treetops than he might have guessed. How long had he been out?

Henry howled in pain.

Olivia held the big man's thumb, twisting it back hard. He dropped to his knees with a solid thunk, his face red under his scraggly beard.

"It's mine," Olivia said. In one hand, she held the black case away from Henry, keeping it just out of reach.

"No. It. Ain't." Henry frothed as he spoke.

She twisted harder. His elbow joint locked. She eased her weight forward, putting more pressure on the joint.

"I bought it last year," Henry said. He shot Ajay a pleading look. "What the hell?"

Olivia saw Ajay, and her grip slackened. She didn't drop Henry, but she didn't put quite so much pressure on him, either. "We need this," she said.

"What is it?" Ajay asked.

Henry said, "It's my favorite rifle."

Olivia let go of him with a shove. "It is not. Your favorite rifle is that damn green one with all the gizmos. You had this thing packed way down in a corner of your basement." She turned to Ajay and held up the case. "This is the same model I used in the service. It might come in handy if those fellas attack again."

"Henry," Ajay said, "you know I'm good for it. I'll pay you for the rifle."

Henry's jaw worked back and forth, but some of the color drained from his face. "Fine," he finally said.

Kylie tugged on Ajay's sleeve. "Where's Isa?"

Isabelle was not in the barn, not even high up in the loft. Ajay looked to Henry and Olivia, but they avoided his gaze.

The crack-roar of a diesel engine howled somewhere in the distance.

"Shit," Henry said. He dove into the driver's seat of his car. "Climb in," he said. "I didn't get the bio-security retooled, but that don't matter if I drive."

Ajay opened the door and ushered Kylie in. "I need to find Isabelle," he said.

"There ain't time." Henry pushed a button on the dash and his diesel engine coughed to life, filling the barn with acrid white smoke. "Get in. I'll drive us out the back way."

Ajay took Olivia's arm and tried to usher her into the car, but her muscles tensed. "Liv," he said. "I'll find her. I'm okay to walk."

"I'm coming with," she said, "and don't you dare say otherwise."

Kylie opened the far door and slid out of the car. "I'm coming with, too."

Ajay stepped back. He knew he couldn't change Olivia's mind, which was fine because he didn't want to. His chances were much better if she came with him to help find Isabelle. But Kylie? To Henry, he said, "Just get yourself to safety. We'll be fine."

Henry sighed. "Dammit, I'm not hiding. Just head up to the radio tower, and I'll swing by to pick you up once I ditch them." He stomped on the accelerator and the little car launched out of the front of the barn. After tearing up a good part of the lawn, he sped back behind the barn, flipping the windows to near-opaque black as the car crashed through a barrier of weeds.

Ajay turned to Olivia and Kylie. "Where would Isabelle have gone?"

Kylie avoided his gaze.

Ajay felt the tension working through his jaw. "Kylie, I know you can find her."

She shifted her weight.

Olivia pulled the black case closer, hugging it as if it were a life preserver. After a long moment, she looked him in the eyes and said, "Well, then let's look for her."

Engines in the distance sputtered and roared — then retreated. They took the bait and followed Henry. Ajay grabbed hold of Kylie's hand and led her across the yard to where the path led through the pines. He wasn't fast, but he kept moving, ignoring the agony that flared like a gasoline fire along the length of his arm. Kylie ran ahead, but Olivia stayed close.

Ajay stopped himself from calling out to the girl. She moved with direct purpose like she really knew where Isabelle was. She probably did. Ajay suspected the two girls talked to each other more than he ever heard. Kylie skirted the edge of the forest, ducking behind the pines. Garrison tagged close at Ajay's heels, easily keeping up with the old man. The hip no longer slowed Ajay down, but every move jostled the tight stitches in his injured shoulder, and soon the agony grew into a network of razors throughout his whole body.

But he pushed through it. Olivia followed close, and from time to time he stole a glance back in her direction. She held an expression of firm determination on her face, and she did not for one second loosen her grip on that black case.

"Are you doing all right?" Ajay asked when Kylie mercifully slowed at an intersection in the paths. One direction led deeper into the woods, the other toward the house.

Olivia blinked at Ajay, then gave a slight nod.

Kylie took the path deeper into the woods. "She's up here," she said. "She wants to see the sky."

Ajay frowned. Did Isabelle know that she could reach the tower with that path? He didn't think she knew, based on what he'd told her, but she might have figured it out. If she went up there, surely the Thunderheads would spot her again, maybe even lock another missile onto her location. They had already dropped one in the middle of the reservation, so there clearly wouldn't be any hesitation to do that again.

Why, though? What was so special about her that they wanted her dead? Never mind who wanted her dead. He could figure that out later. Why follow this girl so closely, and what danger could she pose that would warrant the programming of drone strikes?

She must have dangerous information. It was the only answer Ajay could think of that made any sense. Isabelle knew something that was dangerous to someone in a position of great power. Or she was something dangerous.

Ajay resolved to press Isabelle for more information as soon as they caught up to her. He had to know what they were up against. It was the only way to navigate the course that would keep them safe.

That was all he wanted: to keep the girls out of harm's way. Protect them.

They passed Henry's shack, with the data drive and the solar array. Machines inside still ran relentlessly, whirring away in their little home. Soon the code would crack, but would Henry even care anymore? A pang of guilt settled in Ajay's gut next to the cramp in his side. This wasn't anything like a run, but he felt like it might be the tail end of a marathon by the way his body ached. Wiping sweat from his brow, he turned back to Olivia to commiserate, only to find that she had her head down and didn't seem to be having any real trouble. The path angled up, and Kylie darted up the rocky trail without any hesitation.

An echoing pop sounded somewhere far off in the forest. The trees swallowed up the noise, bouncing it around into a directionless tap. Such a harmless sound, out there in the middle of nowhere. Ajay thought of the sound of duck hunting or practice shooting. It was the sound of hunting squirrels or even deer. Even so, the sound sent a chill down Ajay's spine. Had Henry run into trouble with Mack's men?

The path became a scattered track of limestone rocks where water had long ago dug a trail into the hillside. Kylie scrambled up the slope with no trouble, but each step up became a painful ordeal for the old man. Olivia helped him over the harder parts, where hand-over-hand climbing was almost necessary to make progress. It was there that the tree cover opened up and Ajay saw the countryside laid out before him.

Henry's car sped along a twisting road, pursued by two trucks. So the big man hadn't been shot yet. Good. Maybe he could get away. Another truck left Henry's driveway and turned in the direction of the tower. That wasn't so good. What if they knew where Isabelle was headed?

As that truck accelerated, another car — something bright and sporty — passed it at full speed. Dust kicked up from the gravel road as the new car spun its tires, barely staying under control. The truck's diesel engine roared in response, and the truck quickly got up to speed behind it.

The tower was close. Another long five-wood could take them there, but whoever was driving that truck might get there first. Ajay took a deep breath and forced himself onward. Instead of making his way carefully over the path, he tilted into it, risking a bad fall, but practically vaulting up the rocky limestone ledges. His loafers slipped across the sandy rock, but he kept going anyway, injured arm held close to his body.

Olivia followed, holding him as he swayed at the top.

"Go," Ajay gasped. "Go get her out of sight."

Olivia nodded and ran forward, swallowed by the underbrush. He staggered after her. The branches scraped at his face as he pushed, unable to block them with his cane hand or his injured arm. He gritted his teeth against it, ignoring one more pain in the company of many.

The diesel got closer. His ears tracked it coming up the hill, and he could only imagine that the silent red car still preceded it. He lowered his head, swearing as a particularly large branch smacked at his face.

Then he was through.

Isabelle stood only a pitching wedge away in front of the dusty red car. The window was rolled down, but her body blocked Ajay's view of the driver. His lungs scraped at the air, and muscles screamed for oxygen. He tried to yell to Isabelle, to warn her that a truck was coming. She had to have heard it, though. How could she not?

Kylie, halfway to her sister, shouted something Ajay couldn't hear.

Isabelle turned, and the two girls looked at each other. Why did it feel like they were communicating when they did that? Ajay forced his feet to move, carrying him across the bare top of the bluff. Below, the meandering Mississippi wove through the forest's thick canopy. Wind tugged at his coat as soon as he stepped from its cover. All of the sky looked down on him, and a choppy jolt of panic surged through him.

One step, then another.

Isabelle moved, breaking the staring contest with Kylie. The younger girl ran back toward Ajay, eyes wide. Isabelle ran around the car, opening the door on the far side.

Ajay caught only a glimpse of the car's driver, and the sight of her stopped him in his tracks. She wore large, dark sunglasses, and her hair was hidden under the wide brim of a crimson hat, but he would know her anywhere. Any time. Sashi drove the red sports car.

Once Isabelle's door closed, the car sped away.

"Run!" Kylie shouted as she passed him and barreled back down the path into the forest.

Ajay turned to follow, but as he did the truck rounded the last bend at the top of the hill. Mack drove, a dark, angry intensity on his face. Ajay's foot caught and he fell to one knee, jostling his injured arm. He bit back a scream, forced himself back up using his cane, and hobbled forward. Olivia came back, placed a hand at the small of his back, and helped him.

By then, it was too late. Mack cranked the wheel, jumping the ditch and barreling across low, dry grass. His truck overtook Ajay in a matter of moments, circling him and cutting off his access to the forest. Olivia drew herself up, glaring at the driver. He smirked, tipping his hat, but he didn't get out.

Instead, the man in the passenger side, which was closer to Ajay, opened his door. Jackson Garver hopped down from the high vehicle, a small, boxy pistol in one hand. Wind tugged at Jackson's hair and coat, but the younger man didn't seem any worse for it.

He kept his pistol out in front of him but pointed at the ground. "Never thought I'd see you again."

Ajay stuck his chin out. "One could only hope."

Dark rage flashed across Jackson's face. "I'm trying to help, old man."

The two scowled at each other for a long time. Cold seeped into Ajay's bones like the grip of a ghost. Jackson couldn't be trusted, but it would be so easy to simply give in. Ajay was old. What business did he have out there in the wilderness? How could he possibly struggle any longer against forces so much more powerful than he?

Wasn't that what he had always done, though? Wasn't that what he'd practiced for the last decade, avoiding detection?

He licked his lips and whispered his answer into the wind. "Bullshit."

Jackson raised his gun, pointing it at Ajay's chest. "Then let's talk about option B."

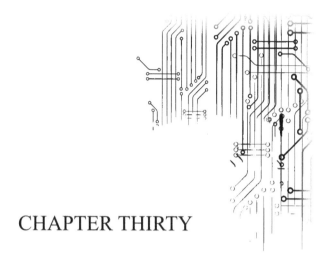

CHAPTER THIRTY

Jackson shouted to Mack over the grumble of the idling truck as he cinched a zip tie around Ajay's wrists. "Go find the two girls." He handed him Ajay's fidget. "We're close. Let's not let them get away."

Ajay smiled through the pain. "The girls are gone. Drove away with my daughter right before you got here. They're safe, and there's nothing you can do about it." Ajay hoped Jackson and Mack had not spotted Kylie as she had run into her hiding place. He made a conscious effort to not scan the edge of the forest for her.

Mack didn't move. His knuckles cracked. "That fucker killed my people and wrecked our trucks."

Jackson didn't turn back to the big man. Speaking through his teeth, he said, "I'm paying you to help find the girls."

"My truck..."

"Leave the truck here and see if you can find the girls." Jackson tilted his head at Ajay. "I wouldn't put it past this old bastard to lie to us."

"Aw, take it easy on the guy," Ajay said to Jackson. "He's had a rough couple days."

Mack might have glared a hole through his head if he'd stared any harder.

Jackson thumbed his fidget, and it flashed an array of warnings. "Just get out there," he said to Mack. "Find them."

Mack nodded, not taking his eyes off Ajay. As he moved to leave, he shot a meaty fist out and punched Ajay hard in the gut. The old man doubled over, vision blurring. He tried to gasp for breath, but for a long while the air refused. Olivia glared at Mack. By the time Ajay could look again, Mack was striding along the forest's edge, peering between the trees. He could only hope Kylie was able to avoid him.

"Tough to find decent help these days, isn't it?" Ajay said.

Jackson shot him a wry smile. "Believe me, the alternative is much worse. These thugs aren't competent, but at least they aren't company men."

Ajay let out a sharp laugh. The truck sat on the side of the gravel road, next to Henry's radio tower, and he wondered if there might be a signal that high up. Not that it would do him any good.

Jackson glared at Ajay. "Mr. Andersen? That's the name you're using still, right? Andersen?"

"It's my name."

"Why haven't they found you?"

"Oh?" Ajay feigned surprise. "I didn't realize they were looking."

Jackson put an iron grip on Ajay's injured shoulder, sending spikes down the length of his arm. "You screwed us when you left the NSA, you know. Punched a lot of holes in the hull as you stepped off that ship."

"The ship was already sinking."

"But you sank it. You dumped every technique we used and every encryption-breaking tool to the public." Jackson drew several long breaths through his nose and seemed to calm some. "Your Age of Honesty ruined us. Oh, we looked for you at first. Then they privatized the NSA and we had better things to worry about."

"Who do you work for, Jackson? Why are you here?"

Jackson fiddled with his fidget again, but his connection didn't improve. His fidget's amber glow lit his face from below, cutting deep furrows in the lines of his frown. His was a matte black computer, its contours custom molded to his palm, with the strap along the back of his hand splaying out in a soft mesh.

"Dammit," Jackson said, pounding a fist on the massive truck's wheel well. His voice lowered. "You think they're safe with her, Ajay? How well do you think you know that woman because believe me, they are not safe."

Olivia's fists clenched. Her hands were tied behind her back as well, zipped together with plastic ties. Ajay's own not only dug into his wrists but also held his shoulder in an agonizing contortion.

Jackson raised an eyebrow. "Shall we?" He gestured to the cinder-block building at the base of the tall radio tower.

"It won't help," Ajay said, without looking away from Mack. "There's a disruption field running through the whole property."

"That explains why we could no longer ping your granddaughter."

"Ping her?"

Jackson sighed. Ajay saw a weariness in the younger man's eyes that told of long nights and a whole lot of the world beating him down. Ajay knew the feeling. It was easy to spot. The way Jackson's shoulders slumped under his rumpled suit, the bags sagged under his eyes. He'd aged hard, Ajay noted. It hadn't been possible to see back at the artists' tower, but Jackson was a man deeply troubled by his situation.

"Look," Jackson said, "how much do you know about Isabelle?"

"She likes awful music, dislikes authority, and can't decide whether or not she likes her little sister."

"The sister. Right." Jackson's fingers flew against the surface of his fidget, but the display remained dark. "What do you know about neural tech?"

Ajay glanced at Olivia, but she stared at the sky with glassy eyes. "I know a little about biologics with regards to Alzheimer's or other neurological disorders."

"Sure, sure. What else?"

"Rumors."

"What rumors, Andersen? Come on, you have to keep up on some of this." Jackson pulled his coat close around his body.

"Twenty years ago, they talked about soldiers with brain modifications that let them communicate through limited telepathy. They talked about memory and logic linkups to make super smart people. Then ten, fifteen years ago the media stopped reporting anything about that branch of tech."

"What's that tell you?"

"That whoever was working on it either had a horrible setback," Ajay said, "or they started to succeed and got enough power to shut up the media."

Jackson motioned for Ajay to continue.

"When I did some digging, I found that there was some research that said it couldn't be done. Brains were degenerating after five or ten years. Lots of bad PR. Lots of efforts by biomed companies to hush it up." He flashed a wicked grin. "Right around then, someone made broken encryption public and a lot of secrets came out."

Jackson leaned forward and spoke in a low voice. "Can you imagine hacking with little more than a thought? Can you imagine the power that kind of neural connectivity would give you?"

Ajay's wrists burned where the ties dug into his flesh He tried to shift his position, but it didn't help. "Are you saying that Isabelle has these modifications?"

"Your Age of Honesty came only a few years after she was born."

Ajay nodded. "She has neurological enhancements?"

"More than that. Much more. She's revolutionary."

Ajay bristled at the idea of experimenting on his granddaughter. What had Jackson done to her? Then the implications of what he'd said clicked. "The computer in her head isn't secure, is it? Quantum computing got to the point where encryption became meaningless, and she's got a computer in her head. That's a danger to her. Why's she treated like she's a danger to anyone else?"

Olivia straightened her back and twisted her tied arms. They didn't budge, so she glared at Jackson. Her expression hardened, and Ajay guessed that he had her attention back.

"What do you want from us?" she asked.

Jackson glanced down at the dark display of his fidget, made a frustrated noise, then slipped it off. "Dammit, we need to move." He cast a glance at Mack, who still skirted the edge of the forest. "We were able to track Isabelle because we can ping her, but every time we ping her, everyone else knows where she is and she knows we're doing it. But in these hills, and apparently, on this guy's property, we can't get that signal."

"Yup," Ajay said.

Jackson let out a sigh. "I know that's why you came here, but it's a real goddamn pain. You're on the wrong side, Andersen. If I could get a signal, I'd show you."

"So, drive away and go get a signal in a nice town somewhere. Leave us the hell alone."

Jackson furrowed his brow at Ajay. "Why do you dislike me so much? I'm trying to help your granddaughter. She has a bright future in front of her if we can only help her develop her unique set of skills."

"Remember when I left the NSA?"

"You mean when you sent the online world into chaos, stole a bunch of equipment, and went into hiding?" Jackson pulled Ajay's diamond-optical device out of his pocket and held it in front of the old man's face. "Including this? You know these are extremely illegal, right?"

"That's not how it went down."

"Really?" He looked at the box, then shot Ajay a quizzical look. "It seems we have some evidence to back me up."

"I had to do what I did."

Jackson smiled. "Because somebody had to give away state secrets and leak all of our protected information to the public. Somebody had to show the world the kind of surveillance it was under."

"Someone had to save my daughter."

Jackson's jaw hardened. "You made things hard for us, you know."

"I'm sure you did just fine."

"Oh, we did." Jackson's eyes became unfocused. "We did."

"You really think Sashi is dangerous?"

"Don't you?"

Ajay paused for the span of two long breaths. "Yeah," he said. "Yeah, I suppose I do."

He nodded. "There's something I need to show you," he said. "I need a connection for it to work, and I think we can get what we need in that little building there."

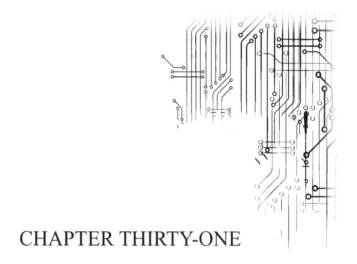

CHAPTER THIRTY-ONE

The little cinderblock building sat on the edge of a cliff, overlooking a wide swath of forest and the Mississippi. Below, the river's bend broke into several pieces, leaving little wisps of islands scattered like leaves. The earth stretched into a broken plain of marshes, parking lots, and even a lone nuclear power plant off to the southeast. The river sparkled in the hazy moonlight of early evening, moving along at its lazy pace. There wasn't any ice cover yet. The night was cold, and Ajay huddled into his coat — which draped loosely across his shoulders — as he stepped into the building.

Inside the shed, the crackle of static chopped at the night air. This shed was where Henry had spoken to Ajay all those times over his tenuous connection. It was where they'd formed their friendship if it could even be called that. Henry hadn't known Ajay. Not really. Could a friendship even form in that situation? Ajay didn't have enough experience with friends to know whether or not it could.

Jackson followed Ajay and Olivia. Olivia's face fell slack again, and Ajay wondered how much she remembered. For now, it would be fine if she followed along peacefully, but if they needed to run, would she remember Ajay enough to trust him?

The space was cramped, but Jackson set his fidget down on the desk and turned to them. "I'm going to show you something, then I'm going to ask for your help." The signal light popped up on his display; its glow turning his grin into a frightening mask.

"Good luck," Ajay muttered.

Jackson nodded. "Look, I know you don't like me much. To be honest, I always hated you."

"I could tell."

"You had it easy. Before the Age of Honesty, people kept their secrets right out in the open. People trusted encryption. You had the skills to get around that, so you were valued — valued a lot more than a direct guy like me."

Ajay looked at Jackson's handheld. "You were a thug."

He nodded. "Somewhat, yes." With a gesture above the device, he activated its controls. "I knew enough hacking to get along, but sometimes it's the softer skills that get you past an encrypted barrier."

"Like torturing the password out of someone."

Jackson smiled. "Yeah. Passwords. Those were the best, weren't they?"

Ajay grinned despite himself. "P A S S W Zero R D. People were stupid. They thought they could keep their secrets behind that."

Another gesture brought up a holographic image above the fidget on the table. A still image of Sashi, softer and less gray than the woman who'd come asking for Ajay's help. Her image flickered there in the dark room, and Jackson let Ajay take it all in for a long while.

Then the image started to move.

A male voice from off image said, "Can you tell me again about your discoveries?"

Sashi licked her lips and swallowed. "Yes." She looked at something in her hands. "It's the neuros, and how they integrate with the brain. They..." She seemed to search for the right words.

"Go on."

"Well, it's just that they don't fully integrate. We have them mapped so that they can do a full overlay, but there's degeneration in the prefrontal cortex after only a few years. We think this can be extended to perhaps five or ten, but based on our findings, this line of development isn't going to work for what you want."

A long silence stretched on while Sashi shifted uncomfortably in her chair.

"There are other problems as well," Sashi continued. "As the neural net grows, it causes changes to the amygdala, which we think explains the emotional disturbances experienced in late stages of use."

"The attacks on Fort Bragg?"

Sashi swallowed. "Yes, sir. And others, too."

The man cleared his throat. "I was under the impression that the only subjects were the ones under my command."

"For this contract, sir. You command the Army's only subjects." She shifted in her seat. "Trevan Pharma has other contracts, however. No other nations, but there are private contracts."

"Such as?"

"They're confidential, sir."

The man's voice lowered to a growl. "Such as?"

Sashi stuck out her chin. "I'm sorry, sir. I'm not at liberty to speak of our other clients."

"Fine. We'll find out one way or another, won't we?"

Smiling, Sashi said, "Yes, you likely will." She remained silent for a long time while the noise of movement came from somewhere off-camera. When the noises stopped, she spoke again. "There is another option."

The man sighed. "One that involves a more lucrative contract, I'm sure?"

Sashi leaned back and crossed her legs. "One that will be lucrative for both of us, I believe."

He chuckled.

Ajay leaned close to the image. Sashi wore the expression she got when she was up to something. The corner of her lip twitched up in an almost undetectable smile. She had a plan, and she was manipulating this man, whoever he was. It brought a smile to Ajay's lips. The guy probably didn't stand a chance.

"As we age, our brains lose plasticity," Sashi said in the tone of a teacher giving a lesson. "We become less able to form new neural connections, form new memories, and learn new things. If you haven't ever learned a new language, then the older you get, the more difficult it is. The same with other skills, like computer programming, or playing a musical instrument. It can still happen, but the brain resists. We believe this resistance is causing the damage that we're seeing, particularly with regards to the long-term memory loss and the, um, emotional issues."

"Doctor Chandrakar, the Army does not experiment upon children. We have a reasonably solid policy against the recruitment of child soldiers."

"Of course." Sashi leaned forward. "But I'm not talking about experimenting on children."

"I don't understand."

"What would you say if you could grow your army? If instead of sending humans to battle, you instead sent something less than human, but quite powerful. Something that could pass as any normal human, but never suffers post-traumatic stress disorder and never even needs to collect a pension. What if, by starting today, you could have a full army of fully integrated, fully connected soldiers in fifteen years?"

There was a long pause. Sashi folded her hands in her lap and waited patiently. Her eyes tracked something off-camera, probably the other speaker.

"Pause it," Ajay said. Blood rushed in his ears, and even though his arms were still held in a difficult position, the pain felt nothing to him.

Jackson gestured above the device and the image went still.

"What are you trying to pull with this bull?" Ajay said.

Jackson furrowed his brow. "What do you mean?"

"This video. That's not my Sashi. My girl's clever, but she's not..." He waved his chin at the image, indicating the whole thing. "Cold," he finally said.

The corners of Jackson's lips turned up. "How well do you know your daughter, Andersen?"

"Well enough." But an itch of doubt scratched at the back of his head. "When she left me to go to college, she was the kind of girl who would march on Washington every time there was troop action anywhere. She hated war, and hated me for ever being a part of the crap that held people down."

"Didn't you ever explain that you were only a geek behind a screen?"

Ajay tensed at Jackson's words. He clenched his fists behind his back. The ties dug into his skin, and the longer they were there the more numb his fingers became. Olivia took his hands in hers and rubbed them. Ajay looked into her eyes and understood that she benefited from the same technology that Sashi worked with, only a vastly different application. The same viral delivery mechanism had given Olivia back years of her life, but the side effects were the same that they had seen in soldiers. That Olivia had ten years of health and not five told him that she probably had a much later version of the technology.

Olivia passed her knife into Ajay's hands, and he felt that her wrists were free.

"I taught her what I knew," Ajay said, doing his best not to falter. "That we aren't always proud of what we do to keep people safe. Sometimes, we hurt ourselves to keep our world from falling apart, but technology could reduce that cost. Maybe one day eliminate it."

This brought a mocking laugh from Jackson. "And how's that working out?"

"Just play your damn vid." Ajay twisted the knife in his hands, awkwardly running the blade against his bonds.

Jackson gestured again and the video resumed.

After a short pause, the screen cut to another scene. This time, Sashi reached forward and started the video recording herself. Her cheeks were fuller and her dark eyes sparkled. A lock of black hair fell in front of her eyes, which she pushed away in mild annoyance. When she sat back in her black, cushy chair, a large belly became visible on the screen.

She let out a deep, exhausted sigh. "March." She closed her eyes, then opened them again. "March 22nd. I'm doing a video log today because my back is killing me and every time I try to type my breasts leak. Everything is going well, and eight months in, scans this morning indicated that the virus took and the fetus is developing as expected. This morning we were able to pick up a signal from the modified neurons, and next week we start comm training in utero. Scans indicate that the number of modified neurons outnumber the non-modified. This will be more machine than human, but the modified cells are doing their part to mimic true human development."

Sashi leaned close to the camera, and Ajay could see the bags under her eyes.

"Our government rep is sending over a man to inspect the program." She looked down at a paper in her hand. "One Jackson Garver is slated to go over our books and look into our tech. He's not Army, so... I don't know what the story is. Something about wanting to make sure we didn't do anything to disrupt status quo, whatever that means. I'll be out of the office by the time he shows up." She rubbed her massive belly. "Bedrest. Doctor's orders."

The video cut again, this time showing a white room, at the center of which played a toddler. As the camera activated, the girl of about two or three turned her crystal blue eyes toward it. Her sandy hair stuck out from under a padded helmet.

"Hello," she said in a sweet child's voice.

Sashi entered the room and handed a toy truck to the girl. "Hello, Isabelle, how are you today?"

Little Isabelle's smile didn't touch her eyes. She took the truck and sat cross-legged, driving the truck back and forth.

"Isabelle, honey, will you look at me?" Sashi knelt next to the little girl and placed a hand on her shoulder. Sashi's movements were stiff and formal, lacking the warmth of a mother's touch.

Another person entered the room through a door not visible to the camera. Ajay squinted at the image. A young Jackson came into view. He put an arm around Sashi affectionately and rubbed the small of her back.

"We need to take the helmet off," he said in a soft voice. "She needs practice."

Sashi's mouth formed a thin line. "It hurts her."

"She can't live her whole life with a helmet on."

"She can. People do that. She can just be a normal girl."

"Sashi." Jackson pulled her close, but she shrugged him off and crossed behind Isabelle. Isabelle continued to move the truck back and forth, even making some whirring noises. "Haveraptics isn't funding your project just to produce a bunch of people who have to wear signal blocking helmets. They want results. They want soldiers. I can't keep the NSA at bay if there aren't results."

"They can't have her," Sashi said. "Isabelle is not a soldier."

"I'm not saying she is, but she's..." He ran his fingers through his hair. "She's genetically designed for it, and your technology enhances that. She's a prototype — a fantastic one. You designed the program, Sashi. I love you, but this is how it has to be."

Sashi folded her arms as if to protect her belly. She spoke, almost to herself. "You're right. She's not really human. I just— forget sometimes."

Jackson in the video shook his head sadly. "People get attached to their pet fish. Hell, I had an amaryllis that I absolutely adored. Was devastated when it died. It's not a surprise that you love the girl you carried and gave birth to, even if she can't love you back."

"Can't she?" Sashi sat cross-legged on the floor and Isabelle sat in the nest she made. Isabelle clutched the toy truck close to her chest. "How do we know she can't?"

Jackson squatted down and brushed Isabelle's cheek. Isabelle smiled. "You've seen the scans. The virus replaced the parts of the brain responsible for human things like love and fear. You've largely removed what we'd call humanity, and replaced it with an ability to communicate with computers and with others like her."

"But there aren't others like her."

Jackson shook his head. "There will be. I got word this morning they approved another batch for production."

Sashi wrapped her arms around Isabelle. "Production. Is that what they call it?"

They stayed a long time in silence, and just as Ajay was going to say something, the Jackson in the video unhooked Isabelle's helmet strap and slipped the helmet from her head. Isabelle clutched her hair, eyes wide with fear. There was no longer any sound in the video because Isabelle opened her mouth for a scream, but Ajay heard nothing. The image of the video flickered, blocky squares of corrupted data forming hashes over the screen. When the image sharpened again, Sashi stood in one corner and Jackson's back blocked the camera's view of Isabelle.

But the truck moved on its own. When Jackson stepped to the side, Isabelle's taut form slid into view. Her narrow eyes tracked the truck as it made its way across the room, turned, and then went back again. Sashi hugged her daughter from behind, but the little girl paid no attention. Isabelle only seemed to care about the truck and its tiny motor sending it speeding around the room.

The knife slipped in Ajay's hand. Its point dug into his arm, and then it slipped free and clattered on the floor. He cleared his throat to cover the noise, but that sent him into a coughing fit. Olivia didn't react to his distress, instead staring out into the middle distance.

Jackson paused the video, waiting for Ajay to stop coughing. "Isabelle had learned far more than we expected," he said. "Analog remote-control cars were easy for her by age three. Digital signals were harder for her to decode, but she learned very quickly. She learned digital communication as a primary language, just as Sashi's programming expected. It wasn't perfect, but she was everything the program required to continue."

"You and Sashi?" Ajay asked, his voice hoarse.

Jackson chuckled. "She never told you, did she? It wasn't a coincidence that I was assigned as her government liaison. They knew I had a connection to you and might therefore have some leverage. Nobody predicted we'd fall for each other, though." His face pinched together as if biting something sour. "At least, I fell for her."

"She married you?"

The grin on Jackson's face didn't fade, but his eyes sparkled a little less.

Ajay felt weak. "You were married even before I left the NSA. You knew me then. We worked together." He rocked back on his heels as it all washed over him. Despite it all, he still felt like something was missing. Something important. He gazed out the front window of the shack, looking out upon the Mississippi River in all its glory. The stars were out, watching over the Earth like a million drones connected to a million computers. Always up there, always watching.

The real drones were closer, of course, and far more threatening. Soon it would be midnight, and Ajay's identity would revert again, as it did every night. His record would be wiped clean, and he would move on. He squeezed Olivia's hand. She might even forget him this time. Her descent into memory loss had been staggering, and it tore him apart more than when his wife had left him so many years ago. Hell, losing Olivia hurt more than losing Sashi, and being honest with himself about that gave him some insight into what might be wrong with his relationship with his daughter. He'd always taken her for granted. The father and daughter, both brilliant in their separate ways. Never connecting.

But how much of Jackson's video could be believed? Faking video, even augmenting an existing video, was possible, although not trivial. It was something Ajay had used back in his days in the NSA. A little misinformation spread in the right places could do far more than a SEAL team. Killing the enemy was good. Making the enemy tear itself apart? Perfect.

Ajay almost didn't need to ask the question, but he did anyway. "What do you want from me?"

Jackson took a long time to answer, but in the end, he picked up his fidget. "I want your help, Ajay. We need to find Sashi, and I suspect you can do it. I don't know what she has planned with those girls, but we have to stop her. We need to get them back somewhere where they'll be safe, especially Isabelle."

Ajay looked the other man in the eyes, taking in the pleading look and measured tone of his voice. Yes, those were good techniques for a field agent to have. Convincing. But they weren't truthful. Seventy years of experience told Ajay how to spot a liar, especially one he had personally trained. Jackson was up to something. It made sense to go along with him and sabotage as needed. That was the smart move, the move Jackson would expect.

"No," Ajay said. "Son, I'm going to have to politely ask you to shove it."

Quick as lightning, Jackson's gun snapped into his hand. He leveled it at Olivia, backing slowly to the door. "I wish you would have helped us, Ajay."

"That's it?" Ajay asked, stepping in front of Olivia in a vain attempt to shield her. "Your first flimsy attempt at the con and then you give up and shoot everyone involved?"

He smirked. "I know better than to take help from someone who doesn't want to work for me." He pulled open the door, raised the gun—

"Dad?" Kylie stood outside the door, eyes wide at the sight in front of her.

Jackson stowed his gun and plastered a smile on his face. "Kylie, thank goodness we found you." He dropped to one knee and spread his arms wide, inviting her in for a hug.

She took a step back, eyes darting from Jackson to Olivia to Ajay. "What's going on?"

"Your grandfather has done some bad things," Jackson said. "Part of my job with Haveraptics is tracking down hackers like him, but you're safe now. Why don't you get into the truck and we'll go home?"

"Why did you have your gun pointed at Olivia?" asked Kylie.

Jackson stood, towering above the little girl, but she held her ground. "They're both dangerous." He took a step forward. "But Kylie, that's not important. Let's get out of here and we can let your grandfather escape, huh? How does that sound?"

Kylie's brow scrunched up and her lips narrowed. "I don't know..."

He opened his palms to her, approaching in smooth steps the way one approaches a wild animal. When he was close, he snatched her arm before she could react. "We need to go, Kylie. I'll explain later."

She struggled wildly, crying out and kicking at his legs. He twisted her arm, forcing her forward, toward the truck.

Olivia clubbed him upside the head with her chair. He fell in a heap.

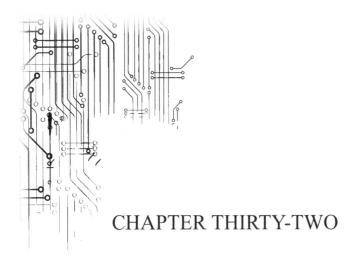

CHAPTER THIRTY-TWO

Ajay tossed Jackson's pistol and his own cane onto the front seat of the idling truck. Jackson's sleek black fidget was another matter. Ajay took the time to properly pry the back off and rip out the batteries. Olivia climbed in the passenger side, and Kylie and Garrison sat in the back of the extended cab. Ajay struggled to climb up into the driver's seat, with a bad hip and an arm that still refused to move properly. Painkillers dulled the sharpest edges, but that made it feel more like being bludgeoned with a baseball bat rather than stabbed with a hundred bamboo skewers. Preferable, maybe, but still not great.

He flopped backward onto the seat and swung his feet around. His left arm was bad, so closing the door proved difficult.

Down below, Henry's house exploded. A great fireball lit up the forest below, belching a ball of black smoke up into the sky. Pressure from the explosion washed over Ajay even across the distance up on the hill. The sounds of whooping and hollering came from down the hill, and three trucks tore up turf in Henry's yard.

"Whoa!" Kylie said from the back seat.

"They're burning it all," Ajay said. "And then some."

Olivia smiled and nodded, and Ajay wondered how lucid she was. They'd been in that basement. Had there been explosives down there? She didn't say anything, though, so Ajay figured she probably didn't remember, either. She clutched the black case as if it were a life preserver and this was the Titanic.

"Goddamnit!" Jackson shouted from the chair where Olivia had tied him. The blow to his head hadn't knocked him out for long, but it possibly had knocked all the good sense right out of him. As if there had been any to start with. "Andersen, come on, let me go. We'll talk! I didn't want them to do that."

"Sure you didn't," Ajay said.

"Really!" Jackson insisted. "I only hired those guys to keep the Haveraptics team out of this." He struggled against his bonds. "They're ruthless, and this is my family, Ajay."

"Ruthless? More ruthless than those assholes you hired who killed Ben and just blew up Henry's house?"

Jackson said quietly, almost to himself, "It's too late. The team's already on their way now."

Ajay threw the truck in gear. "Thanks for the ride." He punched the gas, the acceleration slamming his door shut. He drove the truck down to another unlabeled road, just in time to see two trucks on their way from the house, coming fast. He cranked the steering wheel one-handed and pointed the truck at what he hoped was north. As they peeled away, kicking gravel into the air, Mack ran out of the forest, angry as hell.

As he rounded the first bend, the headlights of the leading truck caught him full in the face, and the thugs must have seen his haggard face looking out the window.

Shouts. Gunshots. His window shattered, and he flinched away.

"Get down," he shouted to Kylie, but she was already as low as she could get, cowering with Garrison in the foot-space of the back seat. "Olivia, get down."

Olivia's eyes were wide. He shouted twice more before she curled herself low around her case. Good enough. Ajay kept his foot hard down on the gas. Trucks rode close behind.

The back window shattered, spraying glass through the cab. Kylie screamed. Cold air tore across Ajay's face. The night air smelled of wood smoke.

Tires spun on hard dirt as he rounded another bend. They broke loose, but Ajay turned with the skid. Behind them, headlights flashed between the trees. Two sets.

Olivia sat up and looked around, confused.

"Olivia, hon, get down!" Ajay took them too fast over a rise, heading ever upward through the forest. The wheels nearly left the ground, and the truck crashed down hard. Ajay's shoulder screamed in protest.

She peered out the window. They hit a straightaway, and gunshots rang out behind them. Diesel roared, sending the truck careening forward. He shouted again at Olivia, but she ignored him. Another series of bends, back and forth, as the shrinking dirt road wove through the forest farther up. The other trucks were a short chipping wedge behind them and gaining. Someone leaned out the passenger side of the nearest vehicle, shotgun in hand.

"Get down!" Ajay grabbed Olivia's shoulder, pulling her down. She went.

But he no longer held the steering wheel.

The truck hit a bump and knocked the wind from Ajay. Pain tore through his wounded shoulder. The steering wheel, uncontrolled, turned.

They crashed off the road, down a long downhill slope. Ajay swore and grabbed the wheel again. He dodged an oak, crushing through brambles as they barreled downhill. The steep incline felt like falling — stopping might not be an option anymore. At least one truck followed, headlights flashing between trees as it barreled over the bumpy slope.

Smashing through several pencil-thin trees, Ajay swerved again, and Kylie screamed from the back seat. Garrison yelped. Ahead, two intertwined oaks flashed into headlights.

Ajay cranked on the wheel, straining against the gravity pulling them ever downward. They sideswiped an oak, and the smashing of metal and glass caused another sharp gasp from Kylie. Olivia snapped up again and panicked. She grasped at his arm, pulling on it and grabbing at her door handle.

"Stay with me, Liv," Ajay said, but he didn't have time to check if she heard.

Ahead, the bluff was a long stretch of prairie, with no trees or obstructions at all. Ajay hit that and punched the gas again, but acceleration didn't come as readily as it had before. White smoke billowed from under the hood. He stuck his head out the broken window to see what lay ahead and caught a lungful of sickening sweet steam.

Olivia stopped grasping at his hand. "Ajay," she said, her voice clear and calm. She sat up.

In the back seat, Kylie scrunched her eyes closed, hands covering her ears.

Behind them, a single truck broke from the forest wall. They'd made ground against it, but it was still only a five iron away.

Olivia opened the case.

Ajay worked the pedal up and down, but the engine loped. More smoke, this time black, spewed from under the hood. The steep slope helped their movement, but the truck behind gained ground fast.

Olivia's hands flew over the contents of the case. Hardly looking, she popped pieces out, snapped them together. Within seconds, she held a stocky rifle. Seconds more, she stretched an extended barrel across the cabin. The thing was awkward in that small space, but she loaded it with fluid motions. Once loaded, she swung the rifle so the business end stuck out her window.

"Turn left," she said without even a hint of stress in her voice.

As soon as Ajay turned the wheel, she grabbed the emergency brake and cranked it. Wheels locked up, sending the truck into a spin. They turned, flashing their one working headlight back at the enemy's two.

Olivia raised her rifle, squinting at the two men in the other truck in that split second as their headlight revealed them. Then she put her rifle to her shoulder, swung it to track the men as the truck continued to spin around.

The passenger in the other truck leaned out with his shotgun—

Olivia snapped off three quick shots.

When the truck rolled past them, Ajay saw the passenger slumped halfway out the window, blood flowing from his head. The driver's chest was a bloody mess.

Ajay's truck skidded to a stop.

The other truck rolled a seven iron farther, then flew off a cliff, crashing into the woods below.

Olivia disassembled her weapon and put everything back in its place.

"Muscle memory," she said quietly. "Ain't nothing wrong with my muscle memory."

CHAPTER THIRTY-THREE

"Sashi!" Ajay shouted into Jackson's fidget, which he had anonymized and connected to one of his burner accounts. It was a newer model than his own and its sleek black shape fit nicely into his palm. Wind tugged at his hood, and he pulled his overcoat tight around himself. There they were, with the wide-open sky staring right down at them. Between gunshots and the crash of the truck that went over the cliff, Ajay had no illusions that they'd be hidden from the eyes up there. He only hoped that none of the drones decided to drop any ordinance. They wouldn't, of course. If they did? Well. "Sashi, what the hell is going on?"

Olivia curled up into herself, making herself as small as could be on the passenger side of the truck. The hood of the truck still smoldered with white smoke, which Ajay discovered was steam, not smoke. Ruptured radiator, maybe. He still hoped to get some miles out of it. In any case, walking caused serious pain, and a walk to civilization sounded about as lovely as a tumble down Mount Everest.

Kylie twirled his cane while Garrison watched, unimpressed. The dog had taken to the girl, and Ajay didn't wonder why. She was easy to like. He wrapped his good arm around her, doing his best to hold the ill-fitting handheld in front of him. They were exposed out on that hillside, but the signal from a nearby Wisconsin tower lit up proud and strong. It goes both ways, he thought. They see us, but now I see them.

And Ajay wanted some damn answers.

A voice crackled from the device, but it came in fits and starts. It was Sashi, for sure, but her words were too broken to make out. Maybe his signal wasn't so good. He squinted at the screen, unable to make out the tiny symbol that denoted signal strength. There was a good possibility the poor signal was on her end, especially if she still drove through the bluffs.

"Dammit," Ajay said. He walked a chip shot's distance uphill, watching the device for changes. When it seemed better, he said, "Sashi, I spoke with Jackson."

Sashi laughed. "Sure you did. What lies of his are you going to believe over me?"

"You married that guy?"

"Papa, I was hoping to never have this conversation."

"But him?"

"He was kind," she said, "and clever. And, also, a liar."

Ajay bit back a retort. He had to do better. "I have Kylie," he said, sounding harsher than he intended.

The silence on the line lasted so long Ajay suspected a lost connection. Then Sashi broke in again, her voice flat. "So what do you want?"

"It's not like that, Sashi. I want you to have her."

"Sure."

"I want to bring her to you," Ajay said. He swallowed a lump in his throat. The wind no longer felt cold to him, its cooling chill more refreshing than anything. "And I need your help."

Her voice came through sharp and choppy. "What kind of help."

"My friend," he said. His mouth went dry, and it occurred to him that he probably had never asked Sashi for help with anything. It was a first. "She uses a brain biotic to help her memory, but it's failing. She's losing everything. Fast.

I think with your knowledge of the science and your connections, you might be able to help her."

"Connections?" She gave a bitter laugh. "You think I have connections after this? Papa, I've burned all my bridges. You didn't think you were my first option for help, did you?"

"No," he said. "No, of course not."

"Nobody at Trevan Pharma will so much as talk to me without alerting the police. I don't have anybody on the inside anymore."

"What happened, Sashi?"

There was another long pause on the line. Ajay watched the moon hanging above the Mississippi, its reflection a slip of silver in those dark waters. He sat in amongst the prairie grasses, breathing in the golden scent of spent autumn. Below, the truck still sat at the end of its swath of destruction. Trampled earth surrounded it, and the trail of the other truck ran dangerously close to it. What would have happened if they had hit? Would it all be over? Kylie might have been hurt or even killed. He swallowed back that line of thought because the fear of what might have been was the worst kind of fear.

Far off to the left, below the cliff that the other truck had driven off, he could see the hint of a road. Not a dirt or gravel road, but a solid one of asphalt — with painted lines. They could get there, he thought. If the truck would run long enough, they might escape. Straight down this prairie hillside, the road carved its way through the bluff, creating the cliff that the other truck had tumbled over. It wasn't so steep farther away, though, and from up there, higher on the hill, Ajay could see where the gentle slope ran all the way to the road.

Sashi's voice crackled through the handheld. "Can you get to that place we talked about before?"

"Sure."

"Good. Do it."

She cut the connection, so Ajay pocketed the fidget and strolled back down to the truck. Kylie curled up in the back seat, seatbelt secure against her chest. Her arms and head were draped over Garrison, who looked up balefully as Ajay approached.

"Good boy, Gare," Ajay said.

Garrison responded with a low whine.

Olivia heard the noise and looked up. She still hugged the black case close to her chest. Her hands shook with tension, and her eyes darted across him. No flicker of recognition passed over her features.

"Do you know me?" Ajay asked.

Her mouth worked a few times before she finally produced an answer. "No."

Ajay fiddled with Jackson's handheld. He selected Beethoven's Moonlight Sonata and played it quietly. He set the device between them and watched her reaction. As the quiet tension rose in the music, she relaxed. He waited for her to recognize him, reaching out with a trembling hand and touching the back of hers. Their eyes met. Searched. Still, she didn't recognize him, but she was at ease, and that was probably enough.

"We're going to help you, Liv," Ajay said. "My daughter, she... She's an expert at this kind of thing. She can help you." He forced as much conviction into the words as he could. Olivia might not be able to understand, but saying the words helped him.

The truck didn't start on the first try. Nor did it start on the second or third. It only started after Ajay added a judicious portion of panic, profanity, and desperation to the custom diesel mix. When the truck roared to life, Ajay let out a whoop that woke Kylie and made Garrison bark.

He crawled the truck forward, making his way down the prairie hillside. They blazed their own trail, but the truck was designed to do that. Its oversized wheels trampled dry grasses and crushed clods of soil. Any animals making their winter homes in that field fled for their lives at the engine's deafening roar. Ajay wondered if they had damaged the muffler at some point, but figured it was too late to worry about it. They wouldn't be driving around in town for very long.

If they even made it that far. Steam streamed from under the hood, and the temperature gauge crept higher and higher. After a long while, the truck dipped into a short ditch, then came up onto pavement. The ride smoothed out, and all the aches in Ajay's whole body relaxed at the relief. He pushed the truck a little faster, not daring to go anywhere near full speed. The temperature leveled out a fraction below the red line.

The miles burned away like the fuse on fireworks. As they went, white streaks started appearing in plants, from maples to grasses. The unintentional influences of modern agriculture grasped at the edges of nature. They left the reservation, coming into the town of Hastings sometime after midnight. Ajay smiled at that. A new day, a new identity. That was the deal he'd made so long ago. His name always stayed the same, but his birthday was always today. It seemed a small bonus for such an odd complication. Leaving the surveillance world behind was harder than it had seemed. Sure, a person could find a house in the forest like Henry had done. That worked to some extent. Others disappeared by rewriting their lives and never drawing the attention of any authorities. Ever. Those people would make it only a few weeks before discovering that surveillance went deeper than they'd ever imagined. It was hard to buy anything without being tracked. Impossible to drive anywhere or call anyone.

But Ajay's solution was far cleverer. When he had wanted to disappear, he had used his access to the deepest parts of both government and private surveillance to create an algorithm that wiped him clean every day at midnight. He was a new man. A new Ajay Andersen with an all-new birthday and an all-new algorithmically rendered past.

That helped, but the key to his success had always been that damn black box. It was illegal but always helped him isolate himself when needed. People put computers and sensors everywhere, from carpet temperature sensors to ceiling fan rotations. Every aspect of modern life was monitored, and all that information was free for anyone to see. That was the Age of Honesty, and Ajay hated it. The diamond-optical device had formed a bubble around itself that prevented communication. It was a zone of privacy. The truck he drove probably had dozens of sensors, from location tracking to performance monitoring. Anybody could find that information if they knew where to look. With access to the Cube and the full power of quantum computing, it was probably possible to track him with even the faintest signal from any one of those sensors. But the black box could prevent that.

Which was why Ajay wished he had remembered to take it back from Jackson.

As he pulled into the tiny parking lot, at the base of the Hastings High Bridge across the Mississippi, a pair of harsh halogen headlights broke from the smattering of traffic that trickled through the town. He should have expected it. Any idiot could have predicted that Mack and his goons wouldn't wait to come looking for him. Their only delay had probably been the attempt to save their friends, and maybe rescue their employer. No, they were right there, lights glaring in his rearview mirror.

And he was trapped.

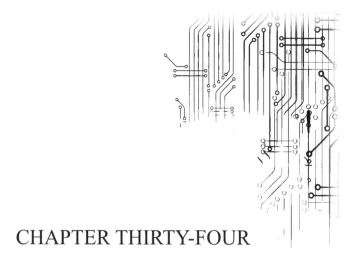

CHAPTER THIRTY-FOUR

Ajay drove through the parking lot in the shadow of the Hastings High Bridge, wheels rumbling against the ruined asphalt. The bridge loomed high in the dark sky, spanning steel and concrete across the Mississippi. The High Bridge led scenic U.S. 61 over the murky waters of the slow river. The metal buzz of cars crossing the river hummed in the night like a thousand angry wasps. Ajay listened through the broken windows of the faltering diesel truck. There was only one car parked on the cracked asphalt of the broken parking lot. There sat the sleek red car, covered in the dust from driving on gravel. It was Sashi's car, but it was empty.

"We have to move," he said, steering the truck next to the little car. "Get in the car and get out of here fast."

But when he stopped the truck, his muscles froze. He swallowed the hard lump in his throat. The truck following them into the lot stopped near the entrance.

Olivia's fingers brushed the back of his hand. "This place means something to you, doesn't it?"

He blinked back the tears in his eyes. "This is where I finally figured out that I was a terrible father." He swallowed back the lump in his throat. "Once, when Sashi ran away, this is where I found her. A bunch of local high school kids had a habit of hanging around here, and they'd always wrecked any surveillance attempts." He pointed at the bridge, where two shattered cameras hung like wilted flowers. "It's tradition, I think."

Olivia grasped his hand in hers. "They can still see us from the drones."

Ajay shrank deeper under his hood. "Sure, but with the bridge, the sightlines are terrible. Much lower chance of being observed. Gunshots will still be picked up by local sensors, but video's not going to be very good quality. It's a perfect place for kids to cause trouble."

She looked out her window. "Not much trouble to cause out here."

The foot of the bridge sat in the earth like the root of an ancient tree. Layers upon layers of graffiti covered the base, but really, there wasn't much else to do there. Kids probably came there for shitty drugs or uncomfortable sex in the backs of their parent's cars. Nobody was there right then, though, and for that Ajay was grateful.

"Get in the car as quickly and quietly as you can," said Ajay to Kylie. "And take Garrison with you."

Kylie's brow wrinkled with worry. "What about you?"

"I'll distract whoever's in that truck. If I can't stop them, then pull the door closed and the car will drive you back to your mother."

Kylie crossed her arms. "But I don't want to go back to my mother."

"We don't have time to discuss this," Ajay said. "We'll all go together and work things out. I'm sure there's an explanation that makes sense."

The truck dwarfed the little red car. It'd be easy to slip from the truck into the car, but if they did so, the other truck would likely just follow. Ajay had to stop that. Kylie climbed into the front seat of the truck and grasped Olivia's hand. Olivia blinked at the touch and then nodded. It almost felt like an unheard communication passed between the two.

Headlights shone into their cab as the other truck approached. Ajay opened the door and stepped out, leaning heavily on his cane. As he did, Kylie opened the door on the other side. He stood in the blinding halogen lights, letting the truck driver see that he was unarmed and injured. No threat at all. The truck stopped at the distance of a long putt. The passenger stepped out.

Mack's deep belly laugh had a mean edge to it. "I thought you looked like shit before, old man," he said. "Now you look like someone ground you up into sausage."

"Your boss tell you to follow us?" Ajay limped to one side, hovering at the edge of the stream of light. "Or are you off the leash?"

"Oh, I'm still getting paid for this, so don't worry about that." Mack cracked his knuckles. "But what's between you and me is personal now. See, I told you if you did anything to my truck, I'd do it right back to you." He nodded at the battered vehicle that Ajay had been driving. "I don't think you know what it means to be beat up yet."

The driver of the truck stepped out. He was the same lanky man Olivia had knocked out on the road, recognizable by the too-loose leather jacket, shaggy mustache, and the face-consuming purple bruise. He held himself like a baseball player stepping up to bat. His eyes darted around, scouring the shadows as if something might jump out at any second. He reached over into the bed of his truck and with a tremendous effort dragged a whale of a lump over the edge. It hit the ground like a bag of sand.

Then the lump groaned.

"Henry?" Ajay asked, shocked.

The thug pulled a sack off Henry's head. Half of Henry's massive beard had dissolved into ash, with red burns snaking up the left side of his face. One of his eyes was swollen shut, and his right ear oozed blood where the lobe was split.

"You son of a bitch," Ajay snarled at Mack. Before he knew what he was doing, he moved closer, swinging his cane like a madman and spitting curses. He closed half the distance.

Until the click-clack of a cocked pistol brought him up cold. Mack leveled the gun at him, finger on the trigger.

Mack smiled with the corner of his mouth. "This can go real easy, or real hard," he said. "Don't get me wrong. I'm going to kill you." He nudged Henry with his boot. "This fella here doesn't have to die, though."

The lanky thug drew a serrated hunting knife. He grinned through yellow teeth, took a handful of Henry's beard, and pressed the blade against his neck.

"What do you want?" Ajay asked. The walking stick felt like cold steel in his grip.

Mack's eyes darted to the truck. Something must have moved there.

Ajay took a step forward, and Mack's attention snapped back to him. "You want me to surrender?" Ajay asked. "Fine. I'm done, anyway."

Mack shook his head. "I think you owe us a good bit more than that, old man. We get paid when we deliver those girls, but I think maybe you know how to earn us a little bonus."

"How so?"

"You tell us how you brought in that Thunderhead, and we'll let this big fella live. How's that sound for a deal?"

Ajay narrowed his eyes and took another step forward. The gun followed his movement, but a medium putt still spanned between them. If they hadn't brought down the Thunderhead, then who?

He slipped his cheaters on. No use staying off-grid now, so he activated them so they would give him an outline of his adversary. They did so, showing Mack's massive form in amber outline. The big man limped as he walked, but was otherwise uninjured, noted the cheaters. Ajay wouldn't win a fight with that man. Didn't need cheaters to know that. The outlines of the tall thug and Henry showed in his glasses as well. The thug tensed every time Ajay moved, and the knife dug dangerously into his big friend's neck.

"I think we can work something out," Ajay said. "Let Henry up so I can see he'll live."

Mack spat. "He'll stay down till you give us the code."

"Then at least take your finger off that trigger. I can't concentrate."

The gangster's jaw set, and for a long while, Ajay didn't think he would respond. Then Mack backed over to the truck he'd arrived in and pulled a baseball bat out of the back. Then he stowed the pistol in his pants. "Better?"

The lanky thug loosened his grip on Henry, but the knife stayed in place.

Mack poked Ajay with the bat. Ajay turned on him, looking over the tops of his glasses at the angry man. His eyes adjusted to the dark, and moonlight gave the big man a bluish tone. Mack's face paint ran in streaks across his cheekbones, muddling into a mess in his beard. Even so, Ajay's cheaters couldn't properly lock facial recognition. Not that it mattered.

"Talk," Mack said.

"Garver must pay you well for all the shit you're bringing down on yourself."

"We can handle it." Mack took another step forward. He stood within swinging range now, his stink overpowering even the bitter wind. "And it was good coin."

Ajay hazarded a glance at Kylie and Olivia. Olivia was already in the other car, but Kylie struggled with Garrison. The big dog stared hard at Mack, showing his white teeth at the corners of his mouth. Ajay needed to buy more time so Kylie could get away with the dog. Once she was in the car, they could get away.

"How did you guess that I hacked the Thunderheads?" Thunderheads couldn't be hacked. They didn't communicate when they were in the sky. The drones flew such tight algorithms that they did all the thinking on their own without any connection. Some would stay up for months without any updates.

The lanky thug laughed. "Oh, you shoulda seen how pissed the boss was. Called every fed he knew after that hit."

"Shut up, Roy," snapped Mack. "How'd you do it, old man? You got a program for it?"

"If I give it to you," Ajay said, "will you let the girls go?"

Kylie pushed Garrison into the little red car. The big dog still fought her.

Mack's expression didn't change. "I'll think about it."

Ajay took a step back. He took out Jackson's fidget, turning it around in the headlights so Mack could see it. "One thing's bothering me, though."

"What's that?" asked Mack.

"You killed Ben," Ajay said, the bloody confrontation flashing before his eyes. He could still see his friend bleeding out in the front lobby of the Mississippi Prosthesis building. "You killed him and you didn't even need to." He tossed the fidget above the lanky thug's head.

Roy caught it, but his knife came away from Henry's neck. Henry twisted, caught the tall man on the side of the knee with a strong kick. Bones cracked, and the tall man screamed.

And all hell broke loose.

"Kylie," Ajay shouted, not taking his eyes off Mack. "Get in the car."

Roy slashed at Henry, but the big man rolled to one side and up. Henry shot out a jab. Blood and teeth pattered against the truck's bumper.

Mack let out a sharp, cruel laugh. Garrison barked: a low woof followed by an almost inaudible growl, taking Mack's attention.

Ajay swung the brass head of his cane, catching Mack with a glancing blow to the jaw. "Sorry about the truck," Ajay said.

"You're going to be," Mack snarled.

Henry laid into Roy, pounding him with meaty fists. The lanky thug slammed onto the hood, rolling over the side and falling to the ground.

Mack stepped up. Swung for the fences.

Ajay ducked. Pain flared in his shoulder. A fist hit his ribs. He fell.

Kylie shouted. Lights flickered. Ajay's hearing aid squelched, and his cheaters flashed. Vision went black, ruined by a sudden bright light. He drew breath to try to speak, to tell Kylie to run.

Henry shouted. Gurgled. Ajay caught a flash of blood bubbling from his throat.

Garrison. A deep growl rumbled in the dog's chest. He didn't attack, but he barreled into Ajay and stood between the old man and Mack.

Mack drew back his bat to swing.

Engine roared. Tires squealed.

Ajay grabbed Garrison with his good arm and pulled the dog back and away. The bat thunked into his back, slamming into his injured shoulder. He screamed.

Mack's truck lurched into motion squealing tires as it moved in reverse.

Kylie was gone. Where was she?

Ajay kicked out at Mack, but the big man was somehow light on his toes.

Ajay spotted Kylie near the little red car. She had the door open, but she stood by it, watching the truck with a laser focus. No, not the truck. She watched Olivia. Olivia drove the truck.

Mack left Ajay and turned to Olivia. He scrambled back, reaching into the bed of the other truck. Ajay saw the gun, and for a moment that vision froze before him. Mack, gun in hand. Olivia's hardened features behind the wheel of the truck. White steam billowing from the radiator. And the girl. Kylie watched with narrowed eyes.

The gun came up, Mack's finger on the trigger. He pointed at Olivia.

Ajay dove forward, swinging the cane. He missed, but his legs kept pumping him forward, into Mack. His body hit the bigger man the way a rabbit tackles a bear.

Gunshots.

Mack let out a grunt, shoving Ajay back. The old man stumbled and fell. All he could see was the black barrel of the gun as it pointed in his direction. Mack's paint-streaked face was a mask of madness and anger.

The truck hit Mack hard. He flew back, sprawling across the pavement.

Olivia didn't stop. She ran clear over the big man, then backed up and left the truck parked on his body.

Ajay patted Garrison on the shoulder, pulled himself up, and limped to Henry. The big man lay in a pool of his blood, the bleeding from his neck already down to a trickle. A short putt away, Roy lay in a similar pool, both men dead, their blood steaming in the cold air. Ajay found Jackson's fidget and put it back in his pocket.

Ajay crossed the lot to Kylie and the red car.

Kylie waved him forward. "Come on, Papa," she shouted waving for him to get in the little car.

"Not yet, Kylie," he said, struggling to hold breath. Every inhale sent hot sparks of pain through his ribs. His shoulder felt like it was bleeding again, but there was no time for that. "Not without Liv."

Olivia hopped down from the driver's side of the truck, black case held loosely in one hand. Her boots hit asphalt with a wet thump, blood smearing across them. She clutched her stomach with her other arm and limped forward, a grim expression on her face.

Ajay felt relief well up inside him. He leaned against the tiny car. They had done it. A short car ride, and then... then maybe they could fix everything. Make it all better. He forced himself to meet Olivia halfway to the car. Despite his injuries, he helped her move as best an injured old man could manage. It wasn't much, but it was all he could do. They shared the cane between them, hobbling like competitors in some three-legged race.

"You did it," he whispered to her. "You saved me."

She didn't speak but shook her head almost imperceptibly. He helped her climb into the car, and she slumped into the back seat so that she would face forward when the car drove away. As it should be.

Ajay leaned against the car and looked at his reflection in the mirror. A ghoul stared back at him with haunted eyes. His face was more bruise than not. His hair stuck up all over.

When had been his last shower? Garrison bumped into his leg, and the warmth of that dog by his side pulled him out of his self-absorbed reverie.

Odd flecks of metal flashed in the polished glass. The glass was thick. Olivia was visible inside the car, but only barely. Something was odd about that glass, and when he saw the door, its thick lining shone with a razor's edge. On the ceiling hung a dome camera, its light shining green.

"Wait," he tried to say, but his breath hitched and the wind tore the word from his lips.

Kylie climbed inside the car, flopping on the front seat, where she would face backward.

The door slammed shut on its own. Garrison woofed.

"No!" Ajay's raw voice burst from him with a wave of pain. He yanked at the door handle, but the door didn't open. "It's shielded."

Kylie stared at him in horror. She pulled at the handle on her side as the car powered up. She pounded on the shielded glass, but her little fists made no mark at all on it.

Nor would it.

The car pulled away, making its path around the now-burning trucks and cleanly avoiding the steaming, bloody corpses. Ajay dropped to his knees and watched the car leave the lot and disappear over the bridge.

They were gone. All of them. He'd failed to protect them. They protected him more than anything, and what good was he? What could he possibly do?

Ajay covered his face with his hands and wept.

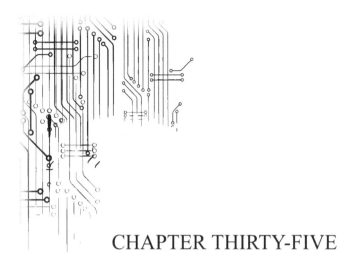

CHAPTER THIRTY-FIVE

Jackson's fidget buzzed in Ajay's pocket but answering the call fell into the priority list smack dab between eating a golf ball and wiping his ass with poison ivy. An old man had to admit failure at some point, right? As the body ages, at some point, it fails. This was his point. What could anyone want from him? Why would they call?

In the shadow of the High Pass bridge, Ajay pulled his coat close against the shivering night. The parking lot swarmed with police, lit by the flickering orange of fires burning in the two trucks and the red-white strobe of police vehicles. Someone spoke his name, and the voice resonated in his hearing aid. They searched for him, then. Passive searches so far, but they would come soon enough. All the more reason to avoid going anywhere. If any camera anywhere picked him up, they'd know it. They'd be there. Ajay drew his hood closer over his face. It lent him some protection, but not if they were really looking. The hood was only an answer so long as the police weren't asking questions. He dragged his finger through the Mississippi sludge and made a faint line along his cheekbone, then another at the center of his bottom lip. His identity wouldn't clear for another day, so he needed to trick facial recognition somehow.

If they thought him a murderer, this might be his only chance, but with no transportation, what good was it?

Ajay leaned against an old willow near the river. The sound of the mighty river's movement chattered behind him as he watched the boys in blue work. Boys. All of them. He was a fool to stay there. The cops would widen their search soon, and when they did, he wouldn't be able to move fast enough to avoid capture.

He stroked Garrison's head, scratching behind the ears. The big dog leaned into him, eager for the attention.

Hell, maybe it'd be better to let them capture him. Maybe they'd sort everything out. Whatever Sashi was up to might be illegal, and if it was, wouldn't they be interested?

Another vehicle hummed into the parking lot — a meat wagon, probably there for the bodies. That was fast. Two women hopped out and began loading Mack into their vehicle. A fireman blasted the trucks with a flame retardant foam.

Ajay leaned against the tree and bent his sore knees until his butt rested on a root. Garrison put his head in Ajay's lap, looking up at him with sad eyes. The cold air coming off the river chilled his bones, sinking so deep into his body that he feared his heart would freeze as it pumped cold blood. He turned his attention away from the police and gazed out upon the river.

A limp fog sat atop the lazy waves. The bitter breeze refused to pull away that hazy mist, and the bridge that towered high above hid in the fog's gray embrace. Sounds of speeding cars buzzed across that bridge, passing over the mighty river as if it were nothing more than an ancient speed bump. Careless of its frigid depths, those above worked frantically every day to avoid the implications of its movement. Still, the river cared even less for them. How could it? Men dammed it, harnessed it, polluted it. The mighty Mississippi rolled its length down to Louisiana, where it joined the greater sea. Whether people tried or not, it always went just where it was going. Ceaseless. Even frozen, it would move, for ice can only stop that thin veneer on the surface. It could only make that river appear to stop. Appear to give up its inevitable journey to the end.

The handheld buzzed again, pinging in his hearing aid. Sashi. Enough obfuscation shrouded the device that tracking him by his phone would be very difficult for the police — so long as he didn't answer. The notifications went through a million varying nodes on their way to his ever-changing digital ID. Once a conversation linked up, that ID would by necessity stay unchanging. He'd be trackable. Picking up was a risk for him.

So he didn't do it. Such was an old coward.

Despite the protest of his joints, Ajay forced himself up. "C'mon, Gare," he said as he limped along the river. His cane tapped against the frozen mud, in places cracking through the surface into the muck below. "They'll have drones out soon. We'd best make ourselves scarce."

Sashi's actions didn't make sense to him, though they never really had. Raising a kid in a world of constant surveillance presented its own challenges, most important of which was a pervasive lack of trust. Even before the so-called Age of Honesty, that problem had shaped kids. How could a father trust his daughter when her lies were so transparent? How could she ever learn to trust him with no true example of how trust worked? He always followed the "trust but verify" approach to parenting, but that wasn't really trust at all, was it?

Long ago, lack of trust drove kids to be more secretive. Kids were clever that way. They'd figured out how to hide the details of their lives. Not so with Sashi. Not really, anyway. Maybe some kids still managed. Other parents might be willfully ignorant of what their children were up to. Not Ajay. Not the greatest hacker to ever grace the American government. He was driven to know it all.

Then he didn't. All at once, she'd been able to keep secrets from him. She'd hidden from him, fooling him into thinking he knew everything. Yes, he'd found her eventually, but only after days. What kind of terrible father allowed his daughter to go missing for whole days?

What kind of father let his daughter stay estranged long enough to raise her own family? He could have stayed close to her. All it would have taken was effort — and a shred of humility.

But this wasn't the Sashi from so long ago. Something wasn't right and there had to be some piece of motivation that he was missing. The thought nagged at him. It itched in the back of his brain. What would make her act like that? Before answering a call from her, he needed to know why. What were her goals?

How much of what Jackson had said was true? He could have edited that video, but why? What plans did he have? Ajay had never liked the man, but that line of thought went nowhere. This wasn't a time to make decisions by emotion. Logic had to find a way.

Jackson wanted the girls, or at least he wanted Isabelle. Why? What was so special about her? Was it true that she had been raised with neurological modifications? Was she intended to be some kind of weapon? Ajay ground his teeth. Was Isabelle really not human?

"What'd you think of Isabelle, boy?" Ajay asked Garrison. Garrison gave no response except to walk a little closer to the old man. "Yeah, I like her, too. There's a good kid in there somewhere."

Ajay made his way under the bridge. Someone had constructed a wooden pathway down there, a small rickety structure that led to the other side of the highway. He picked his way past trash and broken glass. There were a few places where people had slept, but nobody was there on that cold night. The other side of the bridge opened into a row of boathouses, boats all raised out of the water for the season. His cheaters highlighted where online nodes were, so he avoided cameras by picking his way along the dock close to the shore.

Ajay didn't give a damn if Isabelle was genetically modified and mostly a computer. Hell, Ajay had been accused of being unemotional at times, and now he was angry as hell. Isabelle had definitely come across as cold at first, but once he'd learned how to talk to her, she was the same as any kid. Not warm or friendly, but vulnerable and adventurous. So they rewrote her brain so the areas that formed human emotion would be repurposed, but the human brain was a flexible thing. Other parts would compensate. The damage they did in her development might not have been as complete as they expected.

Jackson wanted to take her and train her to be a soldier and assassin. At this stage in her development, it wouldn't be hard to encourage her to develop in that way. She'd have skills that no normal human would ever have, especially if she could hack with a mere thought. Before encryption broke, she might have been unstoppable with such a power. Not as much anymore, but she could at least slip through the world undetected. And if there were others like her? Together they might be quite the deadly force.

For a time, anyway. The arms race would take years to catch up. Isabelle was years away from being an effective assassin, and presumably, any enemy wouldn't have even started such technology yet.

But what, then, did Sashi want? She'd at first seemed happy to leave Kylie, taking only Isabelle away. What did she want the older girl for?

The fidget in his pocket buzzed again. Insistent. Another call from Sashi. Asking her would be simple. Talk to the woman with plain words and simply trust her answer. He chewed on his lip until the buzzing stopped.

He was afraid of her. Always had been. Talking to her was like talking to an angry boss or a furious customer. He flinched at every word and always felt a failure no matter how the conversation came out. This wasn't something that had happened later in her life. This had always been the case. Ajay had skills in so many things, but parenting was not one of them.

So why didn't Kylie and Isabelle frighten him? Well, Isabelle did a little. Her standoffishness reminded him of

Sashi, but it didn't sting quite so much. After all, he didn't feel guilty for every mistake she made. She wasn't his kid, so her mistakes weren't his fault. There was a burden parents carried, whether they should or not.

With his granddaughters, he wanted the best for them. For his daughter, only perfection.

He drew a deep breath, and the cool air refreshed him. He pulled out Jackson's fidget to call Sashi. They would talk, and perhaps they could mend the divide between them. To hell with the police; he'd get away. He would ask her what was needed and then give it. Once she told him what had to happen, they could build trust.

But the phone buzzed before he could dial his daughter.

This time, Kylie's name flashed in the amber glow. Ajay knelt close to Garrison so that he could feel the dog's warmth. He needed it.

"Papa?" Her voice sounded so small. "Papa, they're going to take Olivia and they're going to hurt her."

"Who is, Kylie? Who's taking her?"

"It's Mom," she said in a whisper. "Mommy's going to hurt us."

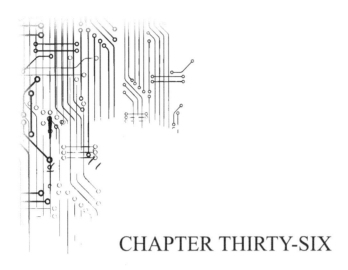

CHAPTER THIRTY-SIX

The drone came just as Ajay ducked into a thin stretch of forest along the river's edge. He almost swore at the sight of it, but then he remembered that he had Kylie on the line and it wouldn't do to curse in front of such a pleasant young lady. Maybe a person could learn to be a better role model.

"What's happening now, Kylie?"

"I did it," she said, her voice flat. "Like Isabelle does. I made the car go to a different building."

"You got away?"

"They're coming for us. Liv hit one of them and he didn't get up, but there are more of them. We're going to go hide."

The fidget pinged, then severed the call. The police must have started their search, and it was no longer safe to be on. He swore under his breath. Another few seconds and he might have learned where Kylie was or why she thought her mother was going to hurt them.

Jackson's fidget had some features he wasn't used to. He pulled them up, looking to see if anything might be useful. Nothing seemed relevant, but some curious routines drew his interest. "Direction protocols?" he muttered to himself. "What the hell is that?"

Holographic displays of an array of personality types and memory map imprints flashed in front of him. Incredibly detailed data profiles popped up, and he blinked, peering closer at them. What was all that for, and how did it stay on Jackson's fidget even after Ajay had replaced most of its software? It had to be locally stored, specific to this one device.

The bone-grating buzz of a drone drew Ajay back to the present. He pulled his hood closer over his face and found a place at the base of a tree, where the crook of its roots could mostly contain him. Making himself comfortable, he nestled in close, covered his face, and hoped for the best. That same technique had failed before, but it was his best chance. He couldn't bludgeon this drone, since doing so would bring a swarm of police within seconds.

Garrison nuzzled his face, pulling his hood back.

"Dammit, Gare." Ajay pulled his hood forward again and pushed the dog away.

The drone hovered closer, its rotors buzzing as it dipped from one side to the other. Ajay froze, every muscle aching in an effort to remain perfectly still. When the device passed close to his spot, it hesitated. He held his breath.

Garrison bumped up against him again. The drone was too close, so Ajay didn't dare respond. The dog nuzzled in, then leaned his whole weight over Ajay, flopping on top of him. Ajay didn't move, despite the stabbing pain in his shoulder.

Turning himself in might not be a bad strategy. After all, the police would want to know what was happening. Genetic modifications to infant children? That had to be illegal. And the use of viral biologics to significantly modify humans in strange experimentations? He expected it to be big news when it got out, but where would that leave his granddaughters? Was it true that they wouldn't even be treated as human?

People wouldn't believe him, even if he knew all the pieces to the puzzle. The information was too far-fetched. In all his days seeking secrets, he had never come across anything like this. Somehow it had stayed hidden from the general population, even though it was clearly funded by government contracts.

Or was it? Again, how much could he depend on Jackson's video? There were hints in there that led Ajay down the road of deep conspiracy. Powerful factions wanted Isabelle, but what evidence did he have that the government was really involved? Only that in Jackson's video.

The drone passed him, making its way farther along the shore.

Ajay followed the drone, careful not to get close enough to fall into its scanning range. His hip ached as he struggled to keep up with it, but that ache was old and familiar. It almost felt good to feel that particular pain instead of the dozen others that wracked his body, until he thought about how the cold kept the rest of his body unnaturally numb. Worryingly numb.

Where the tree line fell away to open beach, Ajay hung back, watching the drone zigzag its way across the stretch. It wasn't following any specific path. No doubt it was programmed to be unpredictable in its movements, to better find the clever criminal. It had the four rotors of a cheap hover drone, and as it passed the streetlamp over a parking lot, Ajay could see the telltale blue and white police colors. He tuned his hearing aid to pick up that type of drone's buzz and scanned the area for others. There weren't any closer, as far as he could tell.

But he needed shelter. Heart thumping, he set out across the field just as the drone dipped behind an old shed. It would normally only be a short jog across, being an easy seven iron. No, maybe a hard eight. But struggling with the ache of his hip and his other injuries, Ajay couldn't manage more than a stiff walk.

The drone buzzed, turning around behind the building. It moved up, then back. He wasn't going to make it, and there was nowhere to hide. His walking stick tapped against frozen earth, feet shuffling past broken corn stalks. Fat flakes of snow drifted down around him, but the chill fled from his bones. Breaths came in big gasps as he forced his way forward.

The drone stopped, hovering. He dared not look, but his ears couldn't tell him if it had rounded the corner. His ankle twisted on the frozen earth, his penny loafer scuffing against the ground. Instinct brought his arm out to protect him from a fall that wasn't going to happen. Icy hot pain flared in his shoulder, and he had to bite his tongue to keep from screaming.

He stood straight. Drew in a slow, ragged breath. Kept walking.

The hum shifted, and it took a few seconds before Ajay realized that it moved away. He closed the final distance into the woods again, leaning against a tree to catch his breath. Long before that breath was caught, he forced himself forward again, pressing through the rows of trees to find a line of houses. Their unfenced back yards faced the river, and in this black night, no lights shone against the dark line of trees.

He drew out the fidget, sending out some simple procedures. His cheaters showed him the locations of connected devices, either as distinct points or as big blobs. Devices that reported their own locations were distinct, like cameras, drones, or cars. Other items, like refrigerators, only showed as indistinct shapes. They didn't have location services because nobody really cares where their refrigerator is. If it wasn't where they'd left it, then they'd expect a different kind of message.

Location might not be specifically denoted, but a lot could be learned from a refrigerator. Jackson's fidget buzzed a quick cadence as the procedure completed. He scanned the data. Seven of the fridges along this row of houses had been opened in the last twelve hours. He could tell by fluctuations in temperature logs. Of the five others, three had been opened in the previous twenty-four hours. That left two, neither of which had been opened in the last week.

Zooming in on those two, Ajay discovered that one mostly saw use in the summer, and it usually contained steaks, salads, and beer. The other held sugary energy drinks, frozen dinners, and a shockingly wide variety of ketchups. It even had some still in it. Ajay chuckled to himself as he crossed the yard to that house. Under a fake rock near the door, he found a key. Security was a joke to young people, it turned out. Just a goddamn joke.

His hand froze an inch away from the door. He chewed his lip and submitted one more process via the handheld. Navigating existing procedures was easy, but developing any custom routines required a more complete interface. Luckily the task he wanted wasn't terribly far off the rails. All he needed to know was whether or not a device on this property ever contacted a certain type of security company.

It had. Cumberland Security Group out of Minneapolis had a ping only a week ago. That meant there was an offline device ready to connect the second he opened the door. From his access point, there wasn't any way to know what devices would come online with that first ping, but he could tell how they connected. They didn't have a dedicated uplink. The device worked through the house's network.

Ajay disabled the network router, looping it back in onto itself. Then he opened the door. The security system was trivial to disassemble from the inside. He wiped data from the cameras, unplugged the motion sensors, and disconnected the sound triggers. When his looped back router stopped receiving security alerts, he enabled it. The energy drinks in the fridge were nasty sugar bombs of caffeine and vitamins: abominations of processed chemicals that passed for sustenance in a modern palate. Horrid things.

They were delicious. Ajay pounded back a nutrient sludge like it was nectar of the gods. A bill on the countertop was addressed to Hank Mason Jr, and Ajay sent a thankful nod at a photo of three men magnetized to the fridge, even though he didn't know which of the three was Hank. He followed up the sludge with another energy drink and a glass of water just for good measure. The water reminded him of

Olivia's hydrophobia. He couldn't relax, so he went immediately to work.

His hunch about the energy drinks had been correct. The place was owned by someone who was not only well off, but also young enough to care about keeping the newest gaming rig. The computer occupied most of one room, with a holo-surface twice the size of Ajay's table back home, including the very best in twitch controllers and full voice-expressive interface. It was, of course, completely unlocked.

Ajay flexed the fingers of his good hand. He acclimated himself to the fancy unit, growing accustomed to its strange interface. The unit listened to his voice commands, which in a way was nice because he didn't have full use of both hands. It was also bad because it meant that when he muttered to himself, the computer would pick it up and try to interpret the words as commands. He connected the machine with his own set of personal preferences and slid into his own hacking routine. Garrison settled down in a corner, dreaming his big dog dreams.

"Let's try the easy stuff first," Ajay muttered to himself, reflexively dismissing the command error that popped up at the sound of his voice.

He searched surveillance of the street outside the parking lot, showing it in the hours prior to his arrival. He needed to find where that car went, and that was the obvious way to start. It wasn't there. Dozens of drones had data relating to that site, but all the information had been scrubbed — not only deleted but modified to remove the vehicle. Cameras around at the time the car went through town had had similar scrubs. He started a routine to find the other end of the timeline when the car arrived at the lot. Shunting that to one side, Ajay continued with a deeper information dive. Kylie's call was the next obvious solution. He checked his holographic display for contact information.

I'm trying to find you, he texted to her.

The message sucked itself into a void and disappeared. There was something very strange about her address. It wasn't a standard node address. The numbers didn't match any protocol he had ever seen. In fact, if he had been forced to guess, he would say that the address itself was in some kind of rapidly shifting encryption.

Jackson had mentioned Haveraptics, and while the name sounded familiar, Ajay didn't know what they did. A quick search brought up milspec cyberwarfare technology, robotics, and a whole pile of government contracts. He scanned the summaries of a few, noting where contracts alternated between Haveraptics and Trevan Pharma. An odd competition, but one that might play into his current predicament.

Ajay brought up the list he had compiled from the data Olivia had pulled when they were in the woods. It was an incomplete list, but he used it to help narrow his search. While his algorithms rooted out relationships between the two datasets, he perused some conspiracy theory sites. Most seemed related to cyborg technology, killer robots, and illegal soldier enhancements. Jackson's video confirmed several of those theories, but Ajay didn't take that as proof.

Jackson Garver's name appeared at the top of his correlation algorithm. Ajay flinched. He should have read through the list from his earlier dataset. The scripts didn't flag Jackson's name as particularly interesting, but Ajay would have noticed it right away. As it was, the name appeared on both sources at overlapping times. Jackson worked on two projects, one for each company. At Haveraptics, he was a flunky on a soldier enhancement project.

At Trevan, he worked on — Lyssameds. Ajay blinked at the display for several seconds as the pieces fell into place. Lyssameds, the same nanomachine virus that was failing Olivia, was also somehow involved in a soldier enhancement program. Or...

Soldier replacement.

They were building something that would replace the need for normal human soldiers. Was that what they thought Isabelle was? It didn't make sense that the girl was somehow their soldier of the future. Did it? Ajay's fists clenched at his sides. Whatever they thought she was, they couldn't have her.

"Open the Cube," Ajay said in his most authoritative tone. Garrison raised his head, blinked a few times, then went back to sleep.

Crack the address, find the node. It should be simple, and that Kylie had used heavy encryption gave him hope. The Cube interface rose on the display and he wrote some quick snippets of code to get the information into the right formats. Simple decryption like that wouldn't take long for an experienced hacker.

But it didn't work. The second he cracked the encryption, the original changed. He cracked it again, and again the original changed. It was as if the number itself were in some kind of quantum state and decrypting it changed it somehow.

"Fine," he muttered to himself. "Then let's figure out where the hell Jackson went."

Photos of Jackson were easy to find, and Ajay didn't stop there. He found a pre-processed recognition array of the man, a key to locate him in any video from any source. Using that, it should have been simple to track where Jackson ended up after leaving the woods.

The space over the reservation was a sparse stippling of images, blurry obfuscations covering most of the forest floor. Where sharp images filtered through, they were empty motion-capture shots of wildlife or unsecured traffic imagery. Nothing useful near Henry's house. Not even close.

Ajay scanned the edges of the rez, wheeling back through the past few hours in hope of finding the point in time when Jackson had left. Nothing.

Maybe he was still there.

Coopting the camera controls on a nearby Thunderhead, Ajay located, after significant effort, the little radio tower atop the bluff. He saw the concrete building and the trees next to it, but the angle didn't work. He couldn't see Jackson.

"Would Mack have just left him there?" Ajay asked.

Garrison made the monumental effort to raise his eyebrows but did not respond. He was right, of course. Mack had left Jackson there, otherwise, Jackson would have been in the truck at the High Bridge.

The fidget buzzed with an incoming call, and Ajay's hope spiked for a second before he realized that it was Sashi calling, not Kylie. He had not yet decided how to deal with his daughter, whether to scold or comfort or condemn. Still, there she was. An opportunity.

Swiping with his good hand and wincing with a spike of pain from his bad shoulder, Ajay cleared the screen and uplinked his call. Dozens of his pre-rendered routines could track an incoming call in seconds. He brought them all up. Different approaches, from response latency delays to network route analysis. Simple and complex. He'd track where his daughter was calling from, and from there he could find Isabelle, Kylie, and Olivia.

Every one of Ajay's processes crashed as Sashi's image rendered on the holographic display.

"Dammit," Ajay swore.

"Well, dammit to you, too, Dad." She flashed a weak smile at him, and he took in the bags under her eyes and her frazzled hair. Ajay's daughter looked as tired as he felt.

Beneath the display that showed Sashi, Ajay worked to recover his hacking utilities. They'd been wiped clean, obliterated within seconds. Every one of his tracking tools was gone from this system. He'd have to recover them from one of his online stashes. He struggled to keep the frown from his face.

"Did Kylie make it to you?" he asked, keeping his tone as conversational as possible.

"Yes, she did," responded Sashi. Her facial expression betrayed nothing of the lie. "In fact, both girls are here and I'm calling to thank you for your help. It means a lot to me, to be able to rely on you like this."

Ajay couldn't believe how casual she made it sound, as if he had simply watched a movie with the girls and not gone on a several-day hike through bluff country. "I'd like to speak with them," Ajay said.

"It's the middle of the night, Papa. I can't just wake them up to chat."

He couldn't tell her that he didn't think they were safe, so Ajay dropped the matter. She wasn't going to let him talk to them, anyway. His hands worked furiously, typing commands into the system by memory, navigating through his personal network to get just the routine that he needed.

"Well," he said, "it was good seeing you, Sash. Your mother would be proud of everything you've done."

Sashi's smile failed to wrinkle the corners of her eyes. "It's good to hear you say that."

Ajay closed his eyes and drew a deep breath. When he opened his eyes, Sashi looked at him, and below her image sat the full command that he had assembled to run. It might not work, but when he ran it, she would know. They would be done talking because she'd know that he was only trying to stall her, and as much as he did want to connect with his daughter, it was true. He was stalling.

"Can you tell me one thing, Sashi?" Ajay asked.

She raised an eyebrow and waited for him to continue.

"Are they really safe? The girls, I mean?" He cleared his throat. "And what about Olivia?"

Sashi licked her lips, taking a very long time to answer a simple question. But then, he hadn't expected a straight answer, anyway.

"Tell me," Ajay asked again, "is Olivia okay?"

"Did you break into a house?" Sashi asked, amusement in her voice. "You did, didn't you? You broke into someone's house. That's why the police drones aren't finding you in the woods."

"You called to trace me."

The shadow of sadness flashed over her face. "I'm sorry about this, Papa. I didn't want it to end like this."

A chill went through Ajay's veins. On another display, he brought up tracking of nearby drones. The police drones swarmed along the ground, still, apparently, searching for him. A mid-tier set of drones hovered around the city, no doubt taking measurements of local conditions and managing surveillance for important businesses. There weren't many in a small town like Hastings, but they did exist.

Then, high above, he saw the Thunderhead. It was fast, circling to point his direction. Had she launched it with orders to kill him? If so, he had seconds to live.

He met her gaze and saw no sadness there. She looked back at him with a lizard's calculation of predator or prey, and Ajay knew how he came out in the bottom of that ledger.

But not all prey is helpless.

Sometimes prey can be so prickly, it's not worth trying to take it down at all.

Ajay mashed the command and submitted his routine. The program piggybacked along the image stream, slipping nicely onto Sashi's node. Once there, it grabbed root authority, searched the local processes, and killed the kernel.

Sashi's image flickered surprise, then disappeared.

"Goodbye, Sash," he muttered, leaning against the console. He held his breath for several long seconds, but the Thunderhead strike never hit. It had needed her final confirmation, and he had disrupted that.

He brought up a quick news scan, keeping his filters common and untraceable. Seconds later, he saw what he needed. Reports came in that the Steaholtz Biomedics building lost power and connectivity. Emergency systems were underway and recovery was inevitable. According to the news feeds, the building's links all dropped at the exact second he'd deployed his kill routine.

He zoomed back on the map, seeing the building and all that lay between him and it. The roads were a swarm of drones and police. No path on land would get him there quickly, but when he saw that the towering building sat on a tiny island in the Mississippi River, he knew exactly how to get there.

Ajay needed a boat.

"But first," he said to Garrison, "I need a new shirt."

On the display, a control module for a textile printer flashed through a dozen fashion suggestions. Ajay swiped those away and found designs for a nicely tailored suit coat, long overcoat, and a shirt that buttoned down the side and sleeve so he wouldn't have to move his arm to get it on. When it finished printing, he struggled into the still-warm outfit and looked at himself in the mirror. With his hair combed, he almost looked respectable, so long as he ignored the bruising on his face and the unavoidable grimace every time he moved his arm.

It would do, though. It would have to.

CHAPTER THIRTY-SEVEN

Lock and Dam Number Two sat just north of the Hastings High bridge. Hank Mason Jr's shoreline house was north of the dam, where the Mississippi meandered among the bluffs.

Ajay saw a gap in patrol drones and hobbled his way down to shore. Hank Mason Jr's boat, the Hank Mason, sat in a little shelter by the river, suspended in the air by a winch. Ajay figured out how the mechanism worked and jimmied the lock. The fourteen-foot bass boat settled into the water, and after only a little fuss, the electronics came alive. He pulled away from shore as quickly and quietly as possible, the sleek electric motor humming. Ajay gave a silent thanks to Hank Mason Jr. as the boat thumped across the rolling waves.

The Minnesota shoreline sped by. Garrison sat at the front of the boat, wind whipping through his flopping ears. Forest and bluffs gave way quickly to suburbs and docks. Small towns held small businesses that sold their small wares. The great history of the place was written on its scenic overlooks and limestone brick buildings. Long ago, the Mississippi had cut an impassable barrier across the American wilderness, then later it grew to be a trade conduit all the way down to New Orleans. It still was, in many ways, though that late in the season the barges had stopped coming so far north. Soon the river would freeze. Ajay watched the water for signs of ice or other debris.

After a while, Garrison leaned against Ajay's leg, a kind of hip check that Ajay could only guess was the big dog's way of making sure his presence was still known. Garrison snuffed loudly at a pile of dog food, some of the stash that Ajay took from Hank Mason Jr's garage. The dog converted it into rancid gas, making Ajay grateful that the boat didn't have a complete enclosure, despite the biting wind that wound its way around the glass shield to nip at his gloved fingers.

Ajay didn't know how long the ride took, for he didn't bother to check the time. He moved as fast as he could and knowing the time didn't make any difference since it wouldn't make him move any faster. By the time he passed large buildings and the islands of Saint Paul, the sky twinkled with approaching dawn.

Raspberry Island stood as a shallow mud bank under the Wabasha Bridge, smack in the middle of the Mississippi. To either side, towering structures stretched right up to the banks of the rivers. The north bank had the active, bustling feel of a social city, the kind of place where a person would see a baseball game or bring the kids for a day of shopping. To the south, new development turned the scenic areas Ajay remembered into a sterile collection of office buildings, rideshare towers, and parking ramps.

But the Steaholtz Biomedics building on Raspberry Island — that was something to behold.

Steaholtz Biomedics stabbed like a great green horn from the earth, arcing up and over the Mississippi and mocking the river's gentle curve with the stiff angles of its own. The emerald glass angled so that it caught the new day's glow and bathed the earth below in green sparks of razor-sharp light. This was a building architected to show wealth and power. It wasn't some structure meant only to house offices and research. It was an affront to God, as if to say "I stab at Thee" with its massive shard of glass. It was one of many new additions to the landscape, brought about by not only the devastating Age of Honesty but also the boom of biomedical sciences. It was a structure that neurotech bought, paid for, and bought again. Steaholtz Biomedics was one of the few companies to solve the erasing death of Alzheimer's, and the world was happy to send their money to it.

But why was Sashi there? Her business was a competitor, running with similar derived technology, but never collaborating. What business could she have there?

Ajay steered the boat into a private set of docks along the south shore. The spot was as secluded as he could hope to get. A boat left floating downriver might raise questions too quickly, he thought. One here, among several other boats, might have a chance to remain undetected. Its tiny corner might avoid a camera's touch for most of a day if he was lucky, and from that spot, he could see the Steaholtz Biomedics building. It would only be a matter of disabling cameras and making his way across the bridge.

"C'mon, Gare," he said, setting off along the concrete path. Tapping his cane as he went, he made his slow way around. The city would wake soon if it had not already. He needed to find Isabelle and be gone before people discovered him. That meant crossing the bridge to Raspberry Island, somehow gaining entrance, and then figuring out where the girl was inside that massive building. "This isn't going to be easy," he muttered to his dog.

Ajay, dog at his heel, climbed the path to the bridge and started along the concrete walkway. Cars passed, lights glaring as the little machines zipped along the Wabasha Street bridge. The sky's light grew, stretching the long, cold morning as much as it possibly could. Might be another hour before the sun bothered to come up, but it was thinking about it and that was good enough for now. Shadows still sucked up against the aluminum walls of the bridgeworks. Ajay made his way along, not sure what he would do when he got there.

Kylie's voice rang loud in his ear as if she were standing next to him. "Papa," she said.

Ajay stopped. Looked around. "Was that you?" he asked of Garrison, who only looked back with head cocked to one side. Ajay shrugged the voice off as the final snapping of frayed nerves and started to continue.

"Wait," Kylie said. "Don't go yet. You have to go back."

"Where are you?" Ajay asked, muttering from the corner of his mouth. He realized then that her voice was coming from his hearing aid, but without any of the usual directional information. "Why can't I hear where you're coming from?"

He stood in silence for a long time. Somewhere the electric hum of a midrange drone called out into the night. He pulled his hoodie close, hunching down so it better covered his face. Wind bit at his gloved hands, freezing his old joints as if they were packed in ice. He looked out on the Steaholtz Building, seeing now its bustling activity and shining lights. Up close the building took on an even greener shade, or maybe that was the effect of the approaching dawn. Ajay wondered at the activity, but it made some sense. The procedure he'd used to drop the kernel probably had left a catastrophic level of chaos throughout their whole system. He'd punched the beehive right in the middle when he'd run that thing. They'd lose revenue by the millions every hour until they had everything up again.

"Papa, they're waiting for you," Kylie said. "The bad men."

Ajay slipped on his cheaters. "Can you show me, dearie?" he asked, still not knowing if she could really hear him.

"They tried to go inside before," she said. "But they came back out like they're waiting for something."

A moment later, red blips appeared on the lenses of his glasses. They tracked as he moved, showing him locations of figures he couldn't see due to darkness and the massive bridge in the way. There were at least a dozen dots, maybe more. Some kept blinking in and out, and others faded and disappeared. They formed a perimeter around the building entrance.

"Are you somewhere you can see these men?" Ajay asked.

"Yes."

"Do they look like the men who were after us before?"

Kylie seemed to consider this. "They're different. Not as scruffy, or anything, but they still have guns."

"They're Jackson's men from Haveraptics." He scratched his mustache. They would complicate things. "How do I get to you?"

"Turn around," she said.

He did. There, atop a ten-story rideshare building on the south side of the river, a small green dot blinked. Below, cars swarmed out of the building, like bees moving out to pollinate the flowering city.

Ajay said, "I'm coming to you."

Olivia's voice snapped his attention closer. "No," she said. "No, you're not. Not yet, Ajay."

He slipped off his cheaters. Olivia stood in the center of the walkway, quilted coat hugged close to her body. In one hand she held the black case she had picked up from Henry. Her eyes were grim and lucid, and her jaw set hard against the cold.

"I don't have much time," she said. "It comes and goes. Sometimes I don't even know who I am."

"You're here," he said.

"I waited too long, Ajay. I should have said something a long time ago. I'm sorry for that. I guess I always thought there was more time, but I knew there wasn't. There never was." She took his hands in her own. "Don't wait, Ajay. Do you understand me? Don't stop your life just because you fear that it might someday end."

She swept up close to him and planted a kiss on his lips the likes of which he hadn't felt in decades. The case clattered to the ground, and Ajay pulled her close, drinking in her warmth, her smell. Time slowed, and the biting wind stopped. Years of friendship turned to passion, burned in him, and he couldn't get enough of her. Touching her. Loving her. She was lucid again. Something had changed in her and her memory's return brought his Olivia back in full force.

Then she pulled away, swallowing breaths. Her eyes scanned him, and he felt their bright curiosity.

"Who are you?" she asked.

She was gone. Still in his arms, but gone. He drew her hands to his chest and showed her all the warmth and kindness he could manage. She watched him closely, tracking his expressions as he drew her hands together and warmed them in his.

"I'm your friend," he said in a whisper that would barely carry on the cold wind. "And I love you."

CHAPTER THIRTY-EIGHT

Ajay hugged Olivia close with his good arm. They sat in the lower waiting area for the rideshare tower immediately off the Wabasha bridge. The building had an open bottom that little cars flowed into at a steady rate. Olivia stared straight ahead, her vacant expression showing no reaction to the cars zipping through the building.

Time always stole either mind or body. Better the mind than the body, Ajay had always thought. A slipping mind could still find happiness, but a broken body knew only pain. Now, looking at Olivia, he wasn't so sure. The disease that gnawed so rapidly at her brain didn't seem to leave enough of her to make that claim to happiness. How long before she ceased to function at all?

"It scares me, Papa," Kylie said through his earpiece.

"It scares me, too, baby." Ajay touched the back of Olivia's hand, and she flinched away.

Olivia looked at him, brow furrowed with curiosity. "Even if I told you where it was," she said, "you'd never get it. Nobody climbs as high as me."

"You were able to bring her back before, right?" Ajay asked Kylie. "I mean, that was you?"

Kylie stayed silent for a long time before answering. "Mom always said Isabelle was something special."

"I'll see everything up there," said Olivia, pointing up toward the top of the tower. "Up on top of that tree, I can see all the way to town."

Ajay chewed on his lip. "We have to get her to a hospital," he said. "They can help."

Olivia's eyes locked on the black case. "No." She shook her head.

Ajay bent down so he could look at her eyes. "No? No hospitals, you mean?"

She gave an almost imperceptible nod. "We have to go up," she said. "The highest place we can get. The enemy will be looking for us there, but that's where we gotta go."

"This isn't a war," Ajay said.

Olivia's voice acquired a sharp edge. "When they come for your kids, it's war."

"For Isabelle, you mean?" Ajay asked.

"Isabelle!" Olivia grinned. "She's such a pretty girl, Ajay. Not so nice as the other one, but we have to do something."

Ajay gripped her hand. He didn't want to think about his granddaughters. He cursed himself for being selfish, but all he wanted to do was spend more time with Olivia. Lucid, coherent Olivia.

She looked up, finally meeting Ajay's gaze. "I don't have much time left, Ajay. Help me get up there."

Not knowing anything better to do, Ajay took her hand and guided her to the elevator. When they reached the top floor with public access, which was only Level 7, it was packed bumper to bumper with little electric cars. A short distance away, several open windows let cool air in from outside.

Kylie sat on the hood of an orange car, her head cradled in her hands. When she looked up and saw Ajay, her face brightened, and she rushed up to him, bowling into him hard with an aggressive hug. He winced at the tug at the stitches in his arm, but instead of pulling away, he pulled Kylie closer and patted the back of her head.

Olivia swallowed again, with a dry click in her throat. She was still dehydrated, but she edged away from the drinking fountain as she crossed the room. Her hydrophobia had to have been in full force, then. Once she reached the window, she peered out, squinting at the dimly lit ground below.

And the building above. The Steaholtz building loomed, its shining facets fracturing the lightening sky. The sun still hadn't risen, but it would be up soon, and Ajay expected the building and the ground below to be a blaze of light when it did. Any chance of sneaking past was probably already lost.

"There." Olivia pointed one arthritic finger at the island. "Soldiers ready to pounce."

Ajay squinted at the men down below. "Who are they, though?"

Their black coats and hoods kept them hidden well in the gloom, but whenever one moved, he was as visible as day. He counted three, but more wandered around the entrance. Would Sashi have left so many men just to stop her dear old dad? That didn't seem likely. They had to be Haveraptics mercenaries.

"They're not Steaholtz men," said Olivia, confirming his theory. She blinked a few times as if she needed to clear a fog from her brain. "Didn't see that Jackson character, but my guess is they're with him." She turned to Ajay. "I wouldn't expect them to take too kindly to your visit. They don't exactly look like the ask-questions-first type."

"We need a new plan," Ajay said. "What if we wait for Sashi and Isabelle to leave and intercept them then?"

Kylie answered. "Isabelle isn't coming out."

"What do you mean?" Ajay peered out the window again. "Kylie, what do you mean she won't come out?" He looked to Olivia, hoping she might have an answer.

Olivia only shrugged and knelt in front of her case, opening it. The matte black and steel pieces of the rifle shone like the sleek silhouettes of stealth-black drones. Olivia touched each piece in turn, snapping it in place and taking a deep breath at each satisfying click.

"Mom talked to us in the car. She said that this was the last option. She couldn't find anything else, but she knew somebody here who would save me."

"Save you?" Ajay asked.

Kylie sat down in an overstuffed orange chair, her eyes focused on something far, far away. "She said she wanted it to be anything else, but that this was the only way."

"What was? What was the only way?"

The young girl looked through the window at the towering emerald building. "That's the only scanner that can give them what they need. Isa said I had to get away, so she showed me how to hack the car." She pinched the bridge of her nose. "The car had to stop first, though, so we got this close before we could get away. Olivia had to fight some people while I hacked the car."

"You hacked it yourself?"

Kylie scuffed the floor with her shoes. "Yeah."

"Nice work." Ajay leaned heavily on his cane, trying to process everything Kylie was saying. "So, you talked to Isabelle?"

Kylie nodded.

"While you were in the car?"

"We've always talked in our heads, but Mom says not to tell anyone." She drew in a long, shaking breath. "Especially not Dad."

Ajay remembered the video Jackson had shown them. Young Isabelle had been able to control a truck with only her mind. How hard would it be for Kylie and Isabelle to figure out how to talk directly to each other if they both had the same abilities? They must have learned the trick at an early age.

"Can you talk to her now?"

Kylie shrugged.

"What— what does that mean?"

"She wanted me to go away."

Ajay scratched the stubble of his beard. "So that you would be safe."

"She said Momma wouldn't hurt me, but the others might."

"Listen to me," Ajay said. "Do you know where she is?"

Kylie nodded. "She's all the way on the top floor."

Olivia snapped another piece onto the rifle. In the truck, she'd assembled pieces in a mad flurry of activity, but Ajay wondered if she'd only put it part of the way together back then. Now that she'd assembled the whole thing it felt more... substantial.

If Kylie was communicating with computers, did that mean that Jackson's video was the truth? Did the younger sister have the same problems as the older? Kylie seemed so much more personable than Isabelle, but what had Isabelle been like at that age?

He opened his mouth to talk, but Olivia cut him off. "Don't, Ajay. The girl needs to come into this at her own pace. Just trust her to do what's right and things might work out."

"She's ten," he said.

"Ten's plenty."

Ajay chewed on his lip. He brought up his fidget, retrieving maps of the Steaholtz building. The top floors rotated in the holographic display, and he peered as closely as he could at the image. The elevator went all the way to the top, but the top four floors seemed to operate on their own secure grid. They had a utility elevator near the back of the building, and the offices were arranged in concentric circles around an enormous central device, which ran the entire height of the building.

"It's the gravitic scanner," he muttered to himself. He had known it was a huge device, but the scale of it was still staggering. Then to Kylie, he said, "I need you to run. Get away and get safe and take Garrison. Can you do that for me?"

"But you need my help." She nodded to Olivia. "She slips if I get too far away."

Ajay looked at Olivia, then at the men down below. With some cover, he might get into the building, but Olivia wouldn't give him any help at all if her mind slid away at the wrong moment. If Kylie could help her, then it made sense to keep Kylie close.

But she was only ten. Ajay couldn't even remember being ten, though the idea of it existed on a purely academic level. Ten meant candy and video games. Ten was the age before adolescence really complicated life. What kind of human subjected a ten-year-old to the horrors of combat? The thought of that violence twisted Ajay's gut. What effect would it have on Kylie?

What was it, though, compared to what she had already been through? Hadn't he always built up a wall around Sashi when she was young? He had coddled her and then sent her into the world unprepared because all through her youth he'd protected her and ignored her in equal parts. She had never been as weak as he'd assumed. Never.

"Stay, then," he said. "Only until I get into the building, then you run away as far as you can get. Find me later. You'll know how to do that, right?"

"Yes."

"Good girl. It won't be safe here. They'll shoot back at Liv, and when they do, I want you nowhere near that window." He waited for an affirmative from Kylie, then pressed several clips of crystal chits into her hand. "If Liv gets hit, I need you to shut down all your feelings. Just turn it off, and run away. Can you do that?"

"Yes."

Olivia stood, holding a dark rifle nearly as long as she was tall. Her eyes were shaded and dull — the spark slipping from them fast. Ajay touched her hand where she held the rifle. At first, she flinched from it, but then leaned into him. He held her close to his chest, wrapping her up in his warmth.

"The last ten years is catching up to me," Olivia whispered. "All that extra time is shaking under my feet like a big mudslide, just like they said it would."

Ajay pulled her closer. "We'll find a fix, Liv. Someone over there," he nodded at the Steaholtz building, "has the answer."

She shook her head, gray hair rubbing against his chin. "They've got nothing for me, Ajay. All that's left is a few memories and the strength in my arms."

"But you remember me, and you remember Kylie and Isabelle. It can't be so far gone, can it?"

"This cure," she said. "It lets me keep what's important to me, losing everything else first. But it's slipping, Ajay. It's slipping."

Ajay forced back the tear threatening to roll down his cheek. How could she be gone so quickly? They had known each other for years and she had shown no signs of memory problems. The cure had worked, but why would it abandon her now? Now, when the feelings they'd always felt for each other were finally coming to the surface. He held her for several minutes as the sky moved from a blackboard gray to a white with a hint of blood touching the eastern horizon. The sun would rise soon.

"You know what I have to do," Olivia said. She pulled away from him and stood in the window. Every muscle in her body moved like a coiled spring. This was Olivia, Army Ranger. This was Olivia of the First Battalion. Nobody messed with this warrior. Nobody. Her eyes narrowed as she picked out the figures below. "There's a traffic circle down there, where cars drop off passengers. Not fifty feet between that drop-off and the door." She smiled. "It's a long putt."

"I might chip that far."

"Not with that shoulder you won't." Olivia pulled back Ajay's hood, frowning at the tangle of his hair. She mussed it up, straightening it with a little spit. Then she pulled some makeup from her pocket and applied it to his face. "You just walk in there looking halfway respectable and nobody will even look twice. Hood down, eyes up. Got it? I'll be your distraction."

"They'll see me."

"They'll be distracted."

"Liv…"

"Don't you try to stop me." Olivia didn't move from her place at the window. She didn't even look back at Ajay.

"I won't." Ajay thought his voice might be too quiet for her to hear, so he spoke again, louder. "I won't try to stop you. Do you remember Oscar?"

After a long moment, she nodded. "He'll be the last person I forget." She looked at Ajay and winked. "No offense."

"None taken." Ajay removed his hearing aid from his ear. He set it to play Beethoven's Moonlight Sonata on repeat, the tense measures sounding in the tiny speaker. He fixed it to her ear and she closed her eyes. Her shoulders relaxed visibly. "This is it, Liv. It's that final chance you wanted. You can test your skills against those men below, and Liv? You can do this. Hold onto that memory hard as you can, and don't stop for nothing. You don't need to hit every shot. Hell, you don't even have to hit more than one."

"I don't shoot to miss, Ajay."

"I'm leaving Garrison with you," he said. "Keep him close, and keep Kylie safe. That's all I ask."

She nodded. Ajay doubted he could keep her from doing anything she put her mind to, no matter how much he wanted to stop her. He doubted anyone could.

"I'll find that cure if it's there, Liv. If there's any chance of getting you fixed up, I'll have it when I get back."

Olivia ran a finger along the curved stock of her rifle, eyes out of focus. "Play golf again, Ajay."

Ajay closed his eyes. "I can't. I'm too old, and my hip gives me trouble. Sometimes we have to move on."

"No. You're not too old." Olivia sighed. "You're afraid of finding out that you're not as good as you were twenty years ago. Trust me, you're not, but you just walked miles through hard terrain. You can manage a fairway once your shoulder heals a bit."

He laughed because if he didn't it would be a sob. "I won't be much on the fairway."

Her hand brushed his. "But try."

She was right, of course. "We'll go together. When this is done, we'll go out. You can be my caddy if you don't want to play."

Olivia gave no response but turned to look out the window. A chill wind rustled her silver and green hair.

"And Olivia?" Ajay said.

She turned and met his gaze.

"I love you." He kissed the corner of her mouth, turned, and walked to the elevator without looking back. By the time he got there, she was perched in position, pointing her rifle down at the traffic circle below. Garrison let out a single low woof, but Kylie hugged him close and he didn't try to follow.

"I love you, too, Ajay," Olivia said as the elevator doors slid shut. "Don't get yourself killed."

On the way down, Ajay busied himself with the work of creating the false identity of a sad old man who simply wanted a car to take him from the rideshare tower over to the Steaholtz building. The identity was a nice one — a kindly old man who never made big mistakes in his life. He loved his daughters and visited them often. The false identity led to an easy, dull life. He played golf often and sometimes bowled with a group of friends. He never hid from the law or falsified his records. The identity was everything Ajay wished for himself, but it wasn't him. By the time he stepped into the little blue button of a car, he'd tossed that identity into the trash.

Because who the hell needed that guy? Isabelle needed Ajay, hacker, charlatan. Cyberspy.

And he sure as hell wasn't going to let her down now.

CHAPTER THIRTY-NINE

The first gunshot rang out as the seal popped on the little car's door. A sharp whirl of wind slipped into the vehicle's warm bubble, spinning in a frigid little dance around Ajay's face. The fine crystals of a morning frost hung in that air, tugged along by the minuscule weather system that nipped at Ajay's wrinkled hand.

An easy chip-shot separated the drop-off circle from the dark double doors of the Steaholtz building. Three short sets of steps ran through a passage formed by concrete planters. Leafless maples clawed their way out of the urban landscape, framing the gauntlet he needed to walk. The great green tooth of the building curved up above Ajay, increasing the building's cruel grandeur. Emerald facets high above caught the first rays of sunrise, piercing light swept across the cold concrete.

"Shooter!" someone yelled, and dark shapes moved as one. The men in long coats broke for cover, rifles snapping up like springing snakes.

Ajay stopped trying to count, instead keeping his eyes focused on the door. His walking stick jabbed at the concrete, and when it found purchase, he leaned heavily upon it and hefted his tired body up out of the car. He felt naked with his hood down and the sky stretching away behind him. Above him. Everywhere, the sky watched.

The air filled with the pop-pop of small weapons. Someone pushed past him, using his car for cover. Shiny sunglasses covered the man's eyes. Ajay turned away, making his way to the door. He didn't see anyone injured from that first shot. Maybe Olivia hadn't hit anyone, or maybe she shot someone far from his line of sight. Regardless, he forced his legs to keep moving. One step, then another.

She shot again. The thunder-crack of her gunshot rang out like a bell, amplified by the cold glass of the building above. Out of the corner of his eye, Ajay saw a man drop, weapon skittering across the concrete. Stark, bright blood pooled around his twisting form, forming a shocking contrast with the cold white concrete. Someone ran to the man, tried to pull him away, but it was too late. He was too hurt.

The building above flashed like a flame as sunlight crept down its height. Orange and red flared in majestic glory around the great green tower. It was maybe more beautiful than anything Ajay had ever seen, but he didn't dare look long. He checked himself as his hands instinctively moved to pull his hood back over his face. The old man walked.

Stairs rose in front of him and stepping up to the first one sent a shock of pain through his body. His shoulder seized up, throwing his balance off. He ground his teeth, curled back his lips, and pushed forward. He wasn't going to fail at walking one goddamn chip-shot. No way in hell.

All around, men shouted. Someone drove away in the car Ajay had arrived in, but Ajay didn't care. It wasn't his car, after all, only a loaner from the rideshare tower. Voices mixed in a muddled mess in his ears, words mashing together in a mumbled-up soup. Without his hearing aid, he still could concentrate and hear voices up close, but in the hot mess of active combat, he was useless. More small weapons popped, but they had to know the effort was futile. Olivia wouldn't give them a good shot, and even those with rifles were wasting their time. Ajay conquered the first set of stairs. Two more to go.

Two men pushed past Ajay, ducking into the cover of the waist-high wall on the side of the steps. Ornamental grasses planted in the top of a burl gave them good visual cover, and the two men spoke in urgent voices.

Still, Ajay walked. His pace quickened a little, legs attaining the rhythm of a steady pace. Pain still plagued him, but as his muscles stretched he found a more natural gait. For once his hip caused him no trouble, choosing that moment to give him the mercy of full mobility.

The second man behind the grass loaded a long rifle. The gun was nothing like Olivia's. His was not a long arm to reach across a mile and touch death. It would handle the par-five to where Olivia struck with her even-handed justice, but only barely.

Ajay's heart pounded, and his palms grew sweaty despite the cold. That man could kill Olivia. Every protective instinct told Ajay to hit him. The urge to strike the man down grew so strong that Ajay's step faltered. He stopped.

No, Olivia could handle herself. She wanted this one last thing: to help Ajay succeed. If Ajay stopped there to fight the younger man, it was almost assuredly going to end in failure. Even if he somehow hit the man hard enough to drop him, others would see the struggle. People would notice Ajay. He needed to be the most ignored man on the battlefield.

The man snapped his rifle as Ajay mounted the second set of steps. Raising it, the man popped up, aimed, slipped a finger on the trigger—

His head exploded with another crack of judgment from above.

"Oh, shit!" shouted the other man. He scrambled backward, eyes wide with fear. He turned and ran, and several others ran, too.

But not all of them.

Atop the second set of stairs, Ajay saw that some of the men moved with the precision of well-trained militia. Those men wore gray fatigues. Their weapons were better, black rifles gripped in gloved hands.

Another gunshot and another dropped, but still, those men didn't run.

On the last staircase, Ajay stumbled, dropping to one knee. His chest hurt and the sky went dark. Shouts faltered, and he knew that any second, one of those professionals would turn his gaze to him. Someone would see that he didn't belong and that he was, in fact, the very man they were looking for. Worse, Jackson might show up.

And the sunrise struck his face like the blessing of the gods. Sky exploded into a wash of orange and pink, strangely disjointed rainbows dancing across the pavement and refracting against the emerald structure above. Ajay squinted at the light, feeling its warmth shatter the frozen air.

He gripped his walking stick and forced himself to his feet.

Another crack and a man only a short putt ahead of Ajay dropped in a spray of blood. Ajay defeated the steps and walked briskly to the big double doors, which he saw now loomed in the wall like the gate to a castle. He stopped at the doorway and drew in a deep breath, absorbing the outside air like it was his last life-giving breath before diving deep under the ocean. Another of Olivia's gunshots rang out as he pulled the door open and slipped inside. Before the door closed completely, he turned and looked across the river, sneaking one last look at Olivia in her perch.

She held her rifle high, waving it for all to see. Her distraction was finished, with half a dozen men dead on the ground. He silently thanked her, knowing the satisfaction she must have felt at one last job done well.

Rifle in hand, she stood in full view of the window up on the seventh floor of the rideshare tower, paying no attention to her safety. Her posture went slack, arms low at her sides. She was done, but the pop-pop of weapons still sounded from in front of the building.

A shot struck her in the chest.

She fell backward.

And then she was gone.

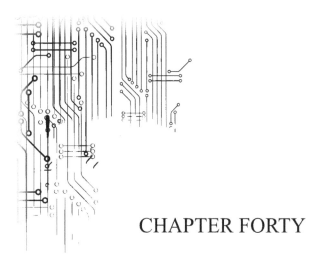

CHAPTER FORTY

When Kylie closed her eyes, she saw the world. Computers, machines, drones. Everything came to her like tingling at the tips of her fingers. Olivia was there, too, but still slippery. Still sticky. Worse than before, too. Much harder to get a good look at. Whatever system she ran in her head was failing, and all Kylie knew was she could hold it in place if she concentrated hard enough.

Which was why she was surprised when Olivia stopped being slippery at all.

Kylie opened her eyes to see Olivia falling backward, hitting the floor like a great big sack of laundry.

"Liv?" Kylie said, trying to keep the panic from her voice. "Ms. Olivia?" She crawled over to the woman and looked into her face.

Olivia's lips were bright red with blood, a stark contrast to her pale skin. Those lips parted, and a ragged breath sputtered blood. "Run, Kylie," Olivia said. "You get away now."

Kylie shook her head frantically. "I won't. I'll stay here."

Olivia reached out with a hand, her cold fingers brushing across Kylie's wrist. "You've done so much, baby. Your grandpa's so proud."

Kylie touched the wound on the woman's chest, her fingertips coming back bloody. "We can fix it," she said, tears blotting out her vision. "We can make it better."

Olivia coughed and closed her eyes.

"Papa will come back," Kylie said. "He'll make it better."

"Kylie, dear," Olivia said. Kylie had to lean forward to hear her words. "Never wait on a man to do anything." Her body shook with what Kylie guessed might be laughter. "It'll never get done."

Kylie wiped away her tears. The sticky blood on her hands wouldn't come off, and she didn't think it ever could. Her hands might always be red. Forever.

Olivia drew in a slow, bubbly breath. "Turn away," she said. "Turn away and shut off all your feelings. You need to escape. Can't do that with your head all messed up. Feel those feelings later. You will feel them later, whether you want it or not." She licked her lips. "For now, just shut that all off like your grandpa said."

Kylie retreated several feet. Turn off all those feelings and escape? What did they think was so bad about feelings? Why did old people think that how she felt made her stupid? Kylie wasn't dumb. She could handle this.

Kylie balled her hands into fists.

"Kylie, dear," Olivia said, but to Kylie, her tone now sounded condescending. "Run downstairs, grab a car, and get as far away as possible. If you're smart, you won't even wait for your grandpa. He'll find you no matter what."

"If he lives, you mean." Kylie realized that she was retreating again when her back hit the wall. "He could die up there." Her heart pounded. Images flashed in front of her blurry eyes, of Papa dying and Mama killing Isabelle.

Mama wouldn't kill Isa. She wouldn't!

Would she?

Fear rippled across Kylie's senses, sharpening her sight into all those things at the very edges of her view. She saw Olivia clearly, not one mushy source, but a million tiny ones. Beyond, she sensed the thousands of cars parked in the tower, and the cameras, and the elevator, and the heat sensors, and so many devices of so many people. Through the blue flame of her fear, she felt them all.

Then Olivia went silent. The woman's head lolled to one side, and her eyes closed. Kylie crawled forward, touching the woman's cheek. She sensed nothing there anymore. Nothing.

Tears mixed with blood. Kylie didn't know how long she wept, but through her grief, she sensed even more. The more she tried to close the world out, the more the world intruded. She saw through cameras as far away as the Steaholtz building. The lobby cameras showed her Papa working his way through a crowd. Closer, she sensed people walking through the parking tower.

There was a man with a pen. She sensed the pen, making its way slowly up the stairs. It wasn't a normal pen like they have at banks and in people's desks. This special pen helped the man spell words by listening and speaking back to him. He might not have known it, but the pen always listened, and so, too, could Kylie.

At first, she heard only footsteps. Then a gruff man's voice said, "Two more flights, go in hard. She's dangerous and might have backup."

"I thought they got her," said a second voice.

"Just do this by the book."

Kylie swallowed back her fear. She drew Garrison across the room, hiding with him behind one of the far row of cars. The men crept up the last few flights, and she stretched out her sense to them. The pen was not the only connected device. They had mil-spec fidgets, which gave her names and information. She pushed that aside. No time to read it all. They wore full vision gear, information from their allies constantly updating in each other's feeds. She saw what they saw. There were three of them and they were getting closer. Their guns were smart-data equipped, recording every shot and uploading tactical information to the team. The armor-piercing rounds carried digital ID tags, complete with constant updates of location data.

They were murderers. Dangerous thugs. The guns told her as much. They had shot people. Scared people. Lots of them.

Is that what they wanted to do to Isa?

The three men burst into the room, their boots eerily silent as they moved in pre-rehearsed patterns.

"Clear," said the guy with the pen. "Moving forward."

Kylie saw him approach Olivia's body, one step, then another. He moved as if he thought she might pounce up at him. Kylie wished she would. The two other men stood by the stairway, blocking both the stairs and the elevator. They covered their partner, their bodies tense, and fingers next to the triggers of their smart guns.

"Damn," said the man. He nudged Olivia with the toe of his boot. "It's just a fuckin' old lady." He let out a cruel laugh and kicked her hard on the side of the head. "Bitch."

And it made Kylie so mad. Her angry fists balled up so tight they hurt. She kept her eyes shut hard, seeing through the three men's helmets. The video glitched and spat. Sputtering noise flickered across their feeds. She knew she was doing it. She knew on some level that she could do what Isabelle had been learning to do.

"What the hell," said one of the guys by the elevator. "You seeing this?"

"Yeah," said the guy next to him. He tapped the side of his helmet. "Interference or something. Stay sharp."

Kylie read in his device that his biometrics were the tensest of the three. His heart rate slammed in his chest, almost as hard as Kylie's.

Her head hurt, and she curled herself tighter into a ball. Her rage ran free, and a thousand cars in the ramp honked and blinked, their alarms set off. She had no control.

No focus. Her vision flickered again. She must have made a noise because one of the men looked her way. He couldn't see her behind the cars, but he approached. Only a few more feet and he'd see her.

Shut it off, they had said. Don't panic, just do what needs to be done. Her fists, those little balls of stone, unfurled, and it took her whole will to do it. She swallowed the bile at the back of her throat, forcing herself to breathe one long, deep breath.

Those emotions, those feelings. Her self. All of it, in a flicker of static, went away. Kylie's life became the dull gray of logic. No fear, no grief. She knew what to do. Beside her, Garrison growled.

Videos from the network flashed before her eyes. She pulled what she needed, redirecting feeds and shuffling around data. Reaching out to the men's visors, she augmented what they saw. In their sight, the sky went black.

Olivia rose, staring at the closest man with her glassy eyes. She had a gun in her hand.

The seventh-floor lobby burst into a hurricane of noise. Gunshots tore across the room, ripping through furniture, windows, walls. Kylie curled as small as she could, feeling bullets tear through the cars above her. She didn't panic, not even a little. Logic required that she stay small for a minute, and so she did.

When she stood, she opened her eyes to see the bloody mess the men had left. It hadn't taken much to set them off. To fool them. They saw what they feared and they shot at it. Simple. Simple. Simple. One of them sputtered and whined in pain.

Kylie didn't even smile at her triumph. She summoned the elevator without bothering to touch the button. Her senses reached out again to the building on the island. What did they do over there? How could she get her sister back?

She saw a way.

Kylie knew what she needed to do. Garrison cocked his head at her, no doubt curious about her plans. She didn't need him. He would be in the way. It made no sense to bother with him now.

The elevator doors opened, and she stepped inside without calling the dog to her side. She left without saying goodbye.

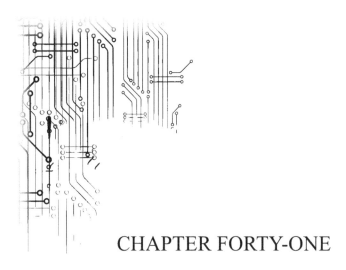

CHAPTER FORTY-ONE

Ajay sidestepped a pack of paramedics, narrowly avoiding being barreled over. He merged with the crowd inside the door, shuffling along as if he'd been there all along. The warm air in the building scoured his face and sent knives into the bones of his frozen hands. He stood for a long moment absorbing the heat like it could somehow give him the will to move forward. Ajay longed for his hearing aid so he could pinpoint conversations, but there probably was no real information there, anyway. They didn't know more than he did, in any case. These were sheep with a wolf in their midst — retreating with no real direction.

The lobby's marble floor reflected sunrise from windows that surrounded the entire lower level of the building. Green-tinted sunlight filtered through a jungle of vines, playing like a flickering green flame across the heavy, raised reception desk. People stood in clusters throughout the room, some chattering while others stared into the long distance. The lobby staff, including several uniformed guards, shuffled people around, with no apparent goal. Nobody was being allowed to the elevators, and from his vantage point near the window, Ajay could see that the elevator panels flashed red warning lights. Likely they had been disabled.

That would make a trip to the top floor difficult.

Ajay blended in with the crowd about as well as a lit firework blends in with a box of dynamite. He touched a finger to his numb cheek, drawing it away with a spot of blood. Not his own. The electric buzz of anxiety dug into that spot between his shoulder blades. People would notice him.

But they didn't. Days' worth of grime and injury and windburn meant that anyone who bothered to look at his face would know he didn't belong. How much blood did he have on him? He ducked into the lobby restroom, pushing past a weeping man huddled in the hallway.

In the mirror, an old, broken man stared back at Ajay through hollow eyes. Never had his wrinkles cut so deep, like fissures in craggy earth. Blood covered the left side of his face in tiny droplets. He splashed the filth away with warm water, but it hardly helped the deep bags under his eyes. His reflection looked so tired, so beaten down. Ajay leaned on the countertop, looking deep into his own bloodshot eyes.

There was no direction but forward. No solution but to find a way up that elevator to confront Sashi. Ajay kept his hood back, smoothing his nest of hair with his fingers. His smile almost made him look like a frazzled scientist. The new coat looked nice on him. Almost respectable. He swallowed, noticing how dry his throat was. He cupped his hands under the faucet and drank some water. The warm water felt good running down his throat, and he thought again of Olivia's hydrophobia.

He wept, tears mixing with the warm water.

Twice, he tried to gather himself and put on a brave face, but the mirror betrayed him. There was no brave face. The face that looked back at him held only grief and fear. It looked back at him with contempt for giving up on Olivia. For allowing her to sacrifice herself. He swallowed a lump in his throat.

"I don't need to be brave," he muttered to himself in the mirror. Fear and grief would take him, but they would need to wait. "There's work to do."

He straightened his back and brushed his coat clean as best he could. Running his fingers through his hair one last time, he made his way out of the bathroom and into the chaos.

The lobby was even more crowded than before. Guards hurried people to the stairs, sending them either up or down. Someone made an announcement over the PA, but the words muddled with background noise. They acted as if there were a continued threat, though that couldn't be. Ajay couldn't make out their words, lost in the masses as they were, but he understood the plan well enough. The lobby was too close to outside, and outside was full of enemy shooters. Violence. People needed to get to safety. Sheep needed to be herded.

Ajay found the nearest guard, touching the woman's arm to get her attention.

She turned to him and scowled. "We need people to go downstairs, sir," she said. "Get to the tornado shelter downstairs."

Ajay cupped his hand around his ear as if to amplify her words. "Tornado? There's a tornado?"

The guard shook her head. "Just move downstairs, sir. We'll explain later."

Ajay stepped forward, but his ankle twisted and he lurched. The guard caught him in two hands, her grasp jamming his injured shoulder. A lightning flash of agony burned down his arm. Stitches ripped at his flesh.

"Sorry," he said. "Sorry, sorry." He straightened up and shuffled away as best he could, smiling at the lump in his coat pocket. He only had to hope that the keys he'd taken from her were the right ones for the elevator.

The muddled voice came over the loudspeaker again, saying something about emergency procedures. Ajay pushed his way through the crowd, working against it toward the elevators.

"Excuse me," a deep voice said, too close. A burly man grabbed Ajay's bad arm, sending another jolt of pain through his shoulder. "We're having people go downstairs until we know it's safe up here."

Ajay ground his teeth. They didn't know the shooting had stopped. They were still in emergency mode for however long it took to verify that everything had settled down. Outside, the red and white strobe of police drones lit up the windows.

"Yes, I'm sorry," Ajay muttered. He turned to move with the crowd long enough to lose the man's attention. Then he angled to one side where he could lean against a pillar. His mouth tasted bitter, and his heart pounded in his chest. The lobby seemed even more crowded than before, though Ajay knew there couldn't be more people coming in. They just were all crammed to one side: the side opposite the elevators. It wouldn't be possible to cross that half of the room without drawing some attention, and his knees grew weak at the thought of it. If he walked out there, people would start asking questions, and he didn't have any answers.

The front door opened and three armed men entered the room. Those sleek, professional men who had killed Olivia now stood near the entrance, scanning the crowd through narrowed eyes.

Ajay couldn't help but think they were looking for him.

He needed a distraction, but there was no distraction to be had. The only way to stay anonymous was to make sure nobody ever bothered looking for him. It was what always worked. Never draw attention. Never step out of line. Control the questions.

But staying in line would see him shuffled down into the basement. There was no knowing how long he would have to stay there. A walk across the lobby would draw the attention of the men, but it wasn't a long walk, and he could partially obscure their view by moving where the marble columns would block their line of sight.

Ajay shook his head. That wouldn't work. He wasn't fast enough. They would catch him.

Before his brain processed what he was doing, Ajay's feet moved. He pushed his way to the back of the crowd, which was noticeably smaller already. Ducking past the big, burly man, Ajay muttered something about a lost hat so the man might think he was picking up something from behind the lines.

They would be looking for an old man using a cane if they were looking for him at all. Facial recognition would be a problem if they used it, but Ajay didn't give them a good angle for it. He tucked his cane up under his armpit so that it was hidden, and he walked.

And walked.

His penny loafers scuffed against the polished marble floor. Confidently, the old man chose the route that anyone would take to cross the empty lobby. A straight line, except for where he needed to dodge around a plant. He didn't walk fast but instead moved with the upright authority of someone who belonged. His jaw stiffened.

Every step, certainty rose that someone would stop him. He felt a dozen eyes on his back — knew that people were watching him. The men in black had to have seen him. Guards herding the crowds had to have spotted him. They would shout at any moment.

But they didn't.

Stepping into the elevator, he let out a breath, only then realizing that he'd been holding it. His hip ached from the abuse, but the reflection that looked back at him from the mirrored elevator walls was one triumphant. He now could go see his daughter.

And maybe rescue Isabelle.

A dozen keys jangled on the keyring. His hand shook from the adrenaline rush. He selected the first key on the ring, testing it in the elevator's lock. It wasn't even close. The next three didn't fit, and he had to stop to breathe. His heart raced in his chest and his head spun.

The next key fit, and he turned it, unlocking the elevator. The panel lit up, and he pushed the button for floor 57.

A wave of relief spread over Ajay as the doors slid.

But just as they were inches apart, a gloved hand slipped between them and stopped the elevator. The doors slid open again, and Ajay saw Jackson Garver's smug face.

"Mind if I join you?" Jackson asked as he stepped into the elevator. "I'd rather not wait for the next one."

The doors slid closed, and the elevator started upward.

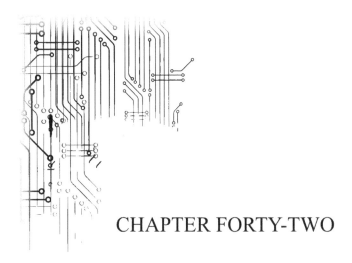

CHAPTER FORTY-TWO

"You and I are the same, Andersen. We both just want your granddaughters to be happy."

Ajay glared at the younger man as the elevator rushed upward. Numbers ticked as they rose to their destination.

Jackson rubbed the dark bruise under his hairline. "I'm willing to let it all go. Let's just help the girls and we can sort things out later."

Ajay lightly thumped Jackson in the chest with the brass handle of his cane. "I don't know what you did to those girls, but they're kids and ought to be left to grow up."

Jackson blew out some air. "So, we agree. They get to make decisions for themselves." He gestured at the space around them. "Look where that got them. Isabelle, perhaps one of the most talented hackers ever to live, has been duped by her crazy mother into killing herself."

"She wouldn't."

A smirk flashed across Jackson's face. "You don't know? This building is one big gravitic scanner. They use it to do destructive molecular-level three-dimensional maps of animals." He sighed. "Or in this case, people."

"But there's no way Isabelle will go willingly."

Jackson barked out a laugh. "You think Sashi could stand up to her daughter? You have no idea what Isabelle is capable of, do you?"

Ajay tapped Jackson on the chest again. "This is your fault."

Jackson shoved Ajay back. Ajay slammed hard into the panel of buttons, sending explosions of pain through his stitched arm. He winced and the black edges of his vision closed in.

The younger man grinned like a shark with a meal. "Who can we really say is to blame? Certainly not you. I mean, you haven't been involved in their lives at all, have you?" He gave Ajay another little shove. "Let it go, old man. You've had a rough couple of days, haven't you? Retire, already."

Ajay clutched his shoulder, and his fingers came away slick with blood.

The elevator stopped, and the door slid open. "Twenty-five," said the automated voice. Both Ajay and Jackson looked at the panel. Several more buttons were lit up.

"Dammit," Jackson muttered. The air seemed to go out of him. "A lot changed after you left the NSA, you know."

"Sure," Ajay said through gritted teeth, "they started letting the assholes run the show."

Jackson barked out a bitter laugh. "They'd been doing that for ages." He leaned back against the wall as the door slid shut and the elevator accelerated upward. "No, I mean once you broke encryption, the whole focus of the department changed. Sneaking around online was like lurking on an open street corner in broad daylight. Everything anyone did was out there for anyone to see. Only, people didn't stop committing crimes right on that street corner. For a long time, they just kept being surprised that they got caught. Spies, hackers, perverts." He shook his head. "Then they looked around and saw that everyone else was doing it."

"Sounds like your job got easy. Back in my day, it was hard work to uncover anything."

Jackson nodded as if understanding.

"Thirty-two," the elevator said, and the door opened again. This time a group of women in business suits stood outside, but Jackson stopped them when they tried to board.

"We're going up," Jackson explained. The women eyed Ajay uncomfortably. He became acutely aware of the blood seeping through his coat.

The doors slid shut.

"So, you got lazy," Ajay growled. "What's that got to do with me and my family?"

Jackson grabbed Ajay's wounded shoulder and squeezed until the old man dropped to one knee. "They're not your family, Ajay. Don't you see that? Sashi left you because you were too much of an ass to be a father to her." He drew several deep breaths through his nose, nostrils flaring. "We didn't get lazy. The game changed. Instead of spending all our time tracking down a hacker in his mom's basement, we spent time in the field, because if we did our search from a comfy base, we'd be too late by the time we got to that guy's basement. See, we could see them, but they could see us seeing them." He eased up on Ajay's wound, patting him on the back as if they were old chums. "It wasn't all at once. We didn't turn into a police force overnight. I mean, people kept trying to solve the broken encryption, so for a long time there was still hope."

"But every solution got shot down," Ajay said.

"Even some of the tricks you use, Mr. Anonymous."

Ajay slumped back against the wall, not even bothering to stand. "So, you know."

"Yeah, we know. How long did you think you could stay off the radar?"

Ajay rubbed the back of his spotted hands and looked at the wrinkles on the backs of his knuckles. "Long enough, I figured. So long as nobody was actively looking."

Jackson chuckled. "See—"

"Forty-five," said the elevator. Ajay bled quietly as the elevator cycled. Nobody waited outside the doors there, and the floor was the dim light of unused office space.

Ajay buried his face in his hands. "I have a headache, Jackson. Can we cut the crap?" He looked the other man in the eyes. "What does this have to do with my granddaughters?"

Jackson breathed out through his teeth. "Everything. I care about Isabelle. Really, I do. I want what's best for her."

"It just happens that what's best for her also happens to be what's best for you?"

"And more," Jackson paced the small space of the elevator as the door opened and closed again. "Isabelle was the first of many, but her success is critical to the success of the others. We're having..." He chewed his lip. "...unacceptable loss."

"You're killing kids with your experiments?"

"They're not human, Ajay. They've lived in a lab their whole life because they're products. It's not illegal."

"Illegal?" Spittle flew as Ajay talked. "Illegal? These are my granddaughters. I don't care if they're human or damned Muppets. They deserve to live their lives."

"We're training them to cope with abilities that you and I can't even understand. It's just that some of them aren't making the cut. They're going crazy instead of learning." He peered at Ajay for a long moment. "Isabelle figured it out. If we can study her, then we can help the others."

"And you'll have your army of hacker-assassins." Ajay scratched his chin. "You're really not making your case, you know."

"There'll be peace."

"There's already peace."

"Fifty-three," said the elevator voice. The doors cycled, revealing a stark-white lobby with lab coats hanging on hooks along one undecorated wall. Nobody waited in the empty room.

But Ajay didn't let the doors close. He jammed his cane in the track so that the door bounced back open. Ignoring the brilliant flash of pain in his shoulder, he forced himself to his feet. "This is my stop," he said.

Jackson drew a small pistol from his pocket. He shook his head. "Andersen..."

"Hear me out, Jackson. You say that you want the best for Isabelle, but I don't know that's true. My daughter says she wants what's best for the girls, but I don't think that's true, either. The only person here who knows what's best for Isabelle is Isabelle. You think you can force your way in and fix everything? Good luck. I'll have no part in it."

"You're not going to try to stop me?"

"What can I do?" Ajay nodded to the lobby outside the elevator door. "That area's nothing but a security airlock. Once I'm out there, I'm stuck until the elevator comes back, which I'm guessing isn't going to happen until you're long gone." He leaned out the elevator door, looking at the entrance to the lab. "The door there has a digital code, which I might hack, but also an air-gapped scanner and a physical keyed lock, one that probably has the best of the best in lockpick protection." Ajay pulled his cane from the door, keeping a hand out so the door didn't close. "The only tech I have to work with is a stick."

"And my fidget, you thieving old bastard."

Ajay drew out the device and handed it over. "Well, you stole my quantum computer. It only seemed fair."

Jackson patted his coat pocket. "Yes," he said. "I suppose that could come in handy."

"I'm no threat to you," Ajay said. "Once you leave this building, I don't think I'll be able to find you, even if I think of a good goddamn reason to try." He sagged, the ache penetrating his bones. "I'm old. I can't keep up like this, even if I don't agree with what you're doing."

Jackson looked outside the elevator door. The secure door appeared just as Ajay had described. There was access to the stairwell next to the elevator, but that wouldn't get him far, since the only unlocked door would be at the bottom.

"Fine." Jackson waved Ajay out of the elevator with his gun. "Nice working with you again, Andersen."

"Wish I could say the same." Ajay watched the elevator doors slide shut.

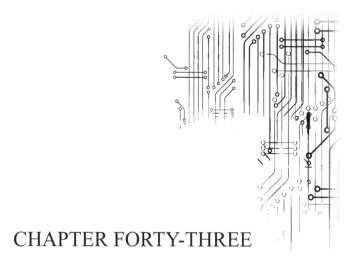

CHAPTER FORTY-THREE

As soon as the door closed, Ajay burst into a flurry of movement. He dropped his coat, flinging it into the corner. Slipping on his cheaters and a spare lab coat from the hook, the old man straightened his sore back. Respectable. Intelligent. This was a disguise he could pull off.

Because of course he wasn't going to give up.

He eyed the door. It really was the pinnacle of security. The wave-gapped digital and chromed physical locks would take hours to hack past, hours he didn't have. Ajay licked his lips, spit on the palms of his hands, and slicked back his hair.

With the bronze end of his cane, Ajay tapped on the door.

He waited, sour taste in the back of his mouth. The elevator wouldn't come again any time soon, and Jackson would be smart enough to watch the stairs. The son of a bitch might even blockade the doorway at the top of those stairs. Ajay wouldn't be able to go that way, but this was near enough to the top floor that he suspected there might be another way.

This door kept him away from Isabelle, and he would get through it. How afraid must that girl be? Ajay could only imagine what she was going through. Isabelle was hard to read, but inside she was still vulnerable. She was still a little girl in need of protection.

Protection from her mother. Sour bile rose in the back of Ajay's throat. How could Sashi betray her own family like that? Ajay shook his head. Maybe there existed some explanation for Sashi's actions. Maybe she wasn't going to hurt her daughter. She had sounded so cold when they spoke last. She had stalled him in order to catch him in a trap. The Sashi he knew would never hurt her daughter, but did he know her at all? A lot could happen in twenty years.

Ajay tapped on the door again, louder this time. He glanced up at the security camera. No use hiding now. If the security team wasn't still busy with Olivia's distraction, then they'd be all over him whether he hid his ugly mug or not. His only hope was to get Isabelle and then... Then.

It hurt not having a plan. Physically hurt. His chest constricted; the thought of being trapped weighed like a car parked on his sternum.

Ajay eyed the door's security systems. It'd be unhackable, even with time and his custom fidget. This system was advanced, far beyond anything he had ever worked on. Tension built in his shoulders. His cheaters gave him an overlay of the access console. Nope. No getting through that. Another tap with the cane, impatient this time.

The door opened a crack. A man in blue, flickering glasses and a white lab coat poked his head through the door. "Whaddya need?" he said, peering at Ajay over the top of his glasses.

Ajay muttered, "Forgot my badge," and hooked the door with his cane, pulling it open. Head down, he pushed his way past the other man, who gave way with no protest. "Thanks."

People always thought social engineering had to be an elaborate scheme. Sometimes the best hacks were as simple as asking politely and trusting human decency. Security was only as good as its weakest link, and often that link was the one that wore a lab coat and shied away from social situations. Ajay smiled to himself. It was too goddamn easy.

Once past the door, Ajay shuffled down the hallway until an intersection adjacent to an open conference room. He flipped the light on, pushed the door closed, and sat heavily on a chair.

The service elevator was near the back of the building, but the more Ajay tried to orient himself, the more confused he became. Theoretically, straight ahead from the open elevators would lead him to the large service elevators, but there didn't seem to be a path through the middle. After a few minutes, Ajay poked his head out of the room. Not seeing anyone, he walked down the hall, keeping his head down and muttering to himself. He passed three women in lab coats who paid him no heed.

Eventually, he figured out the problem with the map. The middle of this floor was dominated by the inner lab, and that lab stretched to encompass the back of the building, too. The massive machinery of the scanner spanned the outer curve of the building like a giant's spine, but between him and that lab sat another layer of security. Ajay located it with no trouble and followed a man through.

"Okay," he said to himself, "that was ridiculous." No wonder the security teams always hated working with scientists and engineers.

The center of the room was a hole encased in thick crystal. In the center of the vast empty space, a single thread flashed and wove, piercing the shattered black like a razor of light. The line flared blue and pink and orange, whipping around like a loose firehose. All around the circumference of the room, banks of computer displays stood, bathing the men and women who worked them with an eerie white flame.

"Almost back online," said a woman not a long putt from where Ajay stood. "Ten minutes until stabilization."

"Any word what caused the outage?" said the man Ajay had followed in. "We're going to be behind schedule for a week after this."

The woman shrugged. Ajay watched her from the corner of his eye. "The client's ready for us, so nobody's had time to investigate."

Ajay turned away from those two and made his way around the circle at the center. The central chamber was no larger than the green at a nice golf course, but the crystal around it was perfectly smooth, with no visible seams at all. He wondered how that vast tube had been constructed. It might have been grown. Warped through the thick, clear crystal, the long, curved void stretched down the height of the entire building. Farther up, the thread of light flicked and spun at least three more floors before embedding in a crystalline construct above.

This was what Sashi needed. This was the better scanner that would tell her everything she needed to know. This device would pick apart Isabelle's brain like a swarm of locusts. So Jackson had been telling the truth. This was the gravitic scanner and it would kill Isabelle.

Ajay's jaw tightened involuntarily. He fought the urge to smash the central tube with his cane, mostly because it wouldn't work, anyway. Maybe a quick hack could take down enough of their computers, but even though these lab techs weren't the bulkiest, they would likely stop him as soon as they suspected trouble.

The best way to remain free was to keep them from noticing him. The best way to do that was to make sure they were never looking for him. But how could he do that? Ajay shifted his weight. The walk across this busy computer lab wasn't going to be subtle. People would see him and they would notice him. If they had the right tech, they might even try to scan his face and figure out who he was.

Ajay smoothed his lab coat and straightened his back. He turned his chin up in a display of confidence so empty anyone could blow it apart with a stiff breeze.

He cleared his throat. Loudly.

A man whose rumpled lab coat bore black stains hurried to him.

"Surprise inspection," said Ajay. "Your name?"

The man looked Ajay up and down, clearly not sure how to proceed. He licked his lips. "Garrett, sir," he finally said. "Garrett Strouse."

Ajay stuck out a hand, which Garrett timidly shook. "I'm here for the full tour," he said. "Starting from up top."

Garrett hesitated. Ajay could see the questions lingering on the skinny man's lips. All he needed to do was doubt Ajay's story enough to ask and it would all be blown wide open. There was no telling who Garrett thought Ajay was. Maybe a company owner or someone in higher-up management.

Ajay didn't look like an intruder. Age lent Ajay credibility, and a deepening frown intimidated the young lab tech into compliance. Maybe being old wasn't always such a bad thing. Blood pulsed in his veins, and a rush of adrenaline quickened his step.

"This way, sir," Garrett said.

They made their way through the lab, Ajay's walking stick tapping against the raised floor where cables and wires ran underneath like snakes in a pit. In places the wires burst forth, connecting everything from computer displays to a docking station in which a shiny blue fidget sat.

"No wireless here at all?" asked Ajay.

"No, the tube has a Faraday cage and the lab itself sits inside another one." He flashed a quirky grin. "Double protection, you know?"

"Seems like overkill, don't you think?" Ajay intoned the question so that the man would think he was being baited.

"Not at all. Even though nothing here communicates wirelessly, we still generate a lot of signal. There's a lot of power pumping through some of these cables, and that emits noise." Garrett brushed his lab coat flat. "And this is important stuff. We can't afford any of this leaking out, since it's essentially the greatest trade secret since the recipe for Coca-Cola."

"It had cocaine in it," Ajay said.

"T-that's..." Garrett sputtered. "Okay."

Ajay nodded grimly, but inside he was smiling. That explained why Garrett hadn't run facial recognition immediately. These people were used to limited connectivity. If what they had was so secret, then they would do anything to keep the lab's information from having any connection to the outside world. Once again, security protocols hindered actual security.

The two continued around the tube, and the elevator's large red doors came into view. Flickering light from the computer displays and the pulse inside the tube flashed against the door's shining surface. Garrett pushed the button and stood back, fidgeting. Behind the doors, a mechanical thrum told of an incoming elevator.

Ajay struggled to hold his lofty poise. His neck hurt from keeping his chin up and his hip ached worse than it ever had with his back artificially straight. He cleared his throat. "Is it true the scan is completely destructive?"

Garrett flashed his quirky smile again. "Yes, sir. Completely. We mostly scan rats or mice, but sometimes we study monkeys or even pigs. It all depends on what the best model for the human disease is."

"You don't scan humans?"

Garrett barked a laugh. "It'd be the last scan they ever got." He glanced nervously at the tube, the line of light in the middle straightening into a single rigid slash. When he spoke again, it was almost too quiet to hear. "It'd be useful, though."

"I'm sure it would."

"I don't mean that in a grisly way. It's just that there are a lot of neurological problems that we can't figure out without a good model. This system models things like neurons and mitochondrial activity perfectly, even capturing their current state of charge and chemical activity. It's like a perfect snapshot that gives us fantastic insight into the inner workings of an unbelievably complex system." Garrett bounced, visibly excited.

The elevator doors slid open without fanfare. Garrett gestured for Ajay to step inside, and then followed him. As the doors slid closed, Garrett pushed the button to take the elevator to the top floor.

Ajay relaxed his stiff back, slouching forward once again. His fingers gripped the middle of his walking stick, its heavy bronze handle bobbing with his every heartbeat.

Garrett stood, facing the door's polished steel. Ajay closed his eyes and let out a deep sigh.

"Garrett?" Ajay said. His grip tightened, and all his muscles tensed.

"Yes, sir?"

"There's something I need to tell you." Ajay let his walking stick slip through his fingers until the end touched the ground. He leaned heavily on it as the elevator doors opened on the top floor. "It's something you're not going to like."

Garrett gave him a curious look.

"A woman up here is about to put a girl into that machine of yours. If what you say is true, then it's going to kill her." Ajay gave the man his best pleading look. "Will you help me stop this?"

But Garrett's expression hardened. His fists clenched at his sides, and his wiry muscles tensed. "So you know about that. Who are you, anyway?"

There it was. The question. Ajay ground his teeth. "You have a little business going on the side, or is this official Steaholtz business?"

Garrett's answer was a clumsy haymaker, but Ajay was ready for it. He dipped back, letting the blow glance harmlessly off his good shoulder.

Ajay stepped forward, poked Garrett in the chest hard enough to send him staggering backward out of the elevator. Ajay followed with a swing of the heavy bronze cane.

Garrett caught the cane in one hand, letting out a sharp yelp as the bones in his hand snapped. With his other hand, he grabbed Ajay's lab coat and tried to slam him against the wall, but Ajay was at an odd angle, and it ended up being a harmless shove. The elevator door started to close.

Ajay stuck out a foot, stopping the door. Garrett took advantage of the distraction and pulled back, only to find Ajay had a solid grip on his own coat, having let go of the cane. Garrett winced, holding his broken hand close. He shifted his grip on the walking stick and jabbed at Ajay's chest.

He missed the chest but poked the business end of the cane right into Ajay's bullet wound. Ajay bit back the scream and dropped to his knees. The elevator door started to close again, but Ajay fell in that direction and tripped the motion sensor, causing the door to slide open.

"Who are you?" asked Garrett. "I thought you were one of the bosses, but I think you're a spy. Who do you work for?"

Ajay said nothing but gently chuckled to himself.

"Who?" Garrett repeated. When Ajay didn't answer again, Garrett rapped him hard on the back of the head with the cane. "Who are you?"

Ajay whispered. "I'm nobody."

"What?"

Looking up at the lab tech through narrowed eyes, Ajay repeated, "I'm nobody." Blood bloomed through his white coat where his wound was open once again. "I prefer to remain anonymous."

Garrett took the cane in a baseball grip, pulling back as if to play tee-ball with Ajay's head. Ignoring flashes of pain, Ajay rolled onto his back and kicked up hard, hitting Garrett in mid-swing, right in the crotch. Garrett crumpled into a ball.

With effort, Ajay stood. He wrestled his cane from Garrett's weakened grip and slipped out of his lab coat. Using the coat to tie the other man's hands behind his back, Ajay pulled him over so that he would remain in the elevator door, keeping it open. It took several swings to knock Garrett senseless with his cane, but he got the job done, or at least well enough.

Ajay turned his attention to the top floor of the building and heard the voices echo through the halls.

CHAPTER FORTY-FOUR

The top floor of the Steaholtz building was much smaller than those below. Its hallways splayed out like the strands of a spiderweb, roughly circular with wedges where small offices and conference rooms broke the symmetry of the design. The service elevator did not open directly into the center of the circle, for which Ajay was grateful because that was where Sashi and Jackson stood. Ajay crept through the short hall, peeking out to see that a great crystalline chamber stood between him and the pair. Inside the chamber sat Isabelle on a small, white table.

Isabelle.

She stared into the far distance, head cocked to one side. Her eyes seemed never to blink, and her fingers twitched in her lap. What could be going through her head? Did she know what was coming for her?

"It is the only way," Sashi shouted at Jackson. They stood in front of a bank of computers along one side of the center chamber. "Why do you not see that?"

Jackson's voice was a threatening growl. "This will kill your daughter, Sashi."

"Daughter," Sashi spat. "You know yourself she's no daughter of mine."

"You carried her. You raised her. Hell, she's genetically your daughter."

Her glare practically spit fire at him. "Isabelle is not yours to care about. If I do this, I can save Kylie. Our Kylie."

"They both matter," Jackson said.

"To what? To your company with your army of information specialists?" She said the last words as if they were code for something else.

Jackson's expression hardened. "It's more than that."

"It's too late for Isabelle. Look at her." Sashi gestured to the girl sitting calmly in the center of the glass chamber. "She feels nothing. When their brains develop into adulthood they change, and their— their humanity slips away." Sashi's lip quivered. Tears flowed down her cheeks. "It is like they are dying, and we need to save our daughter. You must see that."

Jackson reached out to put a hand on her shoulder, but she shrugged it away. Ajay crept closer, using the center chamber to block their view of him. He could see from this angle that there was a glass door on one side of the chamber, sealed with some kind of plastic mechanism. He leaned his walking stick against the wall, crawling forward on hands and knees to stay low and out of view.

"You can't do this, Sashi," said Jackson. "It's murder."

Sashi spoke through her teeth. "Do you think I don't know what it is? Do you think I didn't try everything else that I could think of? I'm an expert at this, Jackson. I know the science. This is the only way to save Kylie." She shoved him back. "And what is it that you are doing? I'm sure everything you do is morally perfect and legal."

"No less legal than what you've done to these girls."

Sashi's sharp footsteps were Ajay's only warning, but he ducked behind a computer console just in time as she stalked across the room. The door was only a few feet away, but he didn't dare open it until he understood where Sashi was.

"You need to stop, Sashi," Jackson said.

A hum reverberated through Ajay's fingers where they touched the floor. The walls of the chamber lit up like the hot glow of an electric stove, and below Isabelle, the shielding slid away to reveal a crystalline floor and a thousand feet of jet black nothing.

"What is it you want, Jack?" Sashi asked, her voice silky smooth. "Are you chasing some romantic dream, or are you just here to do your job?"

"Sashi," Jackson said, resignation in his voice. "Sashi, you can't kill her. It's not right. Let me take her and work with her. She can do so much already. I just need her to help the others." He raised his fidget and flashed a sequence of commands.

In the chamber, Isabelle sat up straight. Her eyes went wide at the sight of his device.

"Others?" Sashi rasped. "Others? How many others?" She gasped. "Did you continue the program? Did you steal my virus after you left?"

"I stole it long before that."

"You bastard!" She swiped at his fidget, but he pulled away.

"I did what I needed to do, Sashi. You know that."

Ajay crept to the door, not confident at all that the two wouldn't look his way at any moment. He flipped the latch on the door and crawled inside. Isabelle's wide eyes tracked his movements.

"Come here," Ajay whispered. "We can sneak away while they argue."

Isabelle shook her head.

Sashi threw things at Jackson, which clattered to the floor behind him or thunked uselessly against him. She swore vile insults through angry tears, but the smug upward curl never left Jackson's lips.

Ajay swallowed. "Now is our chance, Isabelle. Granddaughter. Come and we can talk about this. You will die if you stay here." He stole a glance out of the chamber, but the warped view through the glass made it impossible to tell if Sashi or Jackson were looking his way. A flash of motion crossed the room on the opposite side of the room, and he wondered if it might only be a trick of the light.

Isabelle only responded with a quick shake of her head. Ajay crawled forward, letting the glass door close quietly behind him. An ultra-fine mesh of wire was embedded in thick crystal under him. Below, the dark chasm stretched out seemingly forever. Hell's maw gaped below them, and Ajay pulled himself up against the low table on which Isabelle sat. The slick texture under his fingers felt false to him, though it never pretended to be anything other than plastic. Whatever material made the things in this room probably were invisible to the exotic particles the machine below emitted. Ajay tried to stop himself from imagining what kind of mess a destructive scan would leave, but failed. Badly.

He took Isabelle's hand. "Tell me," he whispered, "why are you here? What do you hope to accomplish?"

She turned her cold eyes on him, appearing to calculate him like a particularly tricky equation. "Why won't you let me stop?" she asked.

"Stop? You mean stop living?" Ajay shook his head. "We'd all like to stop sometimes, but it's not right, Isabelle. There's so much good left for you."

"No," she said. "Not for me."

Ajay furrowed his brow. Looking into her eyes felt like looking at a particularly shiny pair of agates. She showed no emotion. There was no connection. "I don't believe that," he finally said.

"I'm dying," she said. "I don't have much time left." Isabelle's voice came out in a dusky monotone. "The world went gray and lost its flavor. At first, it was for a day or two at a time. Then it was weeks. Now..."

"But you've been better," Ajay said.

She shook her head. "I've been pretending."

"No." Ajay gripped her hand tighter. "I don't believe you. You were happy at Henry's place. For a little while, you had a life back again. You didn't want to—"

The corners of Isabelle's mouth twitched up.

"You've been trying to kill yourself."

Her smile faded. "This way I'll help Kylie, too. I— I don't know if that's good, but I think it is."

"The drone strikes," Ajay said. "At the tower and in the woods. You were responsible for both of them, weren't you?"

"The one at the tower surprised me. I only wanted to ask it to help scare those men away. Sometimes I can hear the sky."

"And the sky can hear you."

Isabelle nodded. "It answers me."

Ajay blinked. "How can that be? Nobody can hack a drone in flight. They're designed specifically to be unmodifiable in the air."

The corners of Isabelle's lips twitched up. Was that pride? "They don't like to listen, but I insist." Her eyes flicked to Jackson, who still waved his glowing display around with every emphatic gesture.

"Your father," Ajay said. "He has something that controls you, doesn't he?"

Isabelle nodded.

"On the day he left, he used it, didn't he?"

Her lower lip quivered, but when she spoke there was no weakness in her voice. "It was like he could change what I wanted. Like he could just poke at my brain and make me a different person." Her hands balled up into fists. "I'm nobody."

"That's not true."

Isabelle's eyes flashed with anger. "If I'm whoever he wants me to be, then I'm nobody."

"He wants you to be a weapon, Isa," Ajay said. "But that's not who you really are."

She pounded the table with a fist. "I can't! You just want to change me the same way he does. You'll never get it — never understand what it is to be me! You can't!"

Ajay's mouth ran dry. "No." His voice came out as a tired rasp. "I can't, can I?"

She pulled her knees up close to her chest. "I'm not leaving."

"Isabelle," Ajay said, "you can't let yourself go out like this. I promise we'll save Kylie, but you can't let your mother do this. There are other options."

Isabelle opened her mouth to answer, but something caught her eye. Ajay turned to see, catching a flash of red somewhere opposite where Sashi and Jackson still fought. He didn't see enough to know for sure, but that red was familiar. It was the deep red of a certain filthy sweater.

Kylie's filthy sweater.

"Shit," Ajay said.

Isabelle touched the back of his hand with the tips of her slender fingers. "Shit," she said.

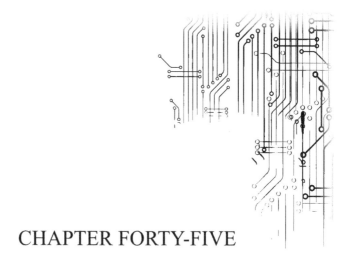

CHAPTER FORTY-FIVE

Kylie's flesh was numb, and her vision gray, but the world all around her flared in flashes of spectacular color. Her senses reached as far as she cared to stretch, and every little node bent to her wishes.

And yet, no thrill came with the power, no excitement or fear. In the back of her mind, there lurked an awareness of death and love. There might, by some strange abstraction, have been a hint at a comfortable future. A home. Those things didn't exist, though. Her cold logic told her that much.

Getting to the top floor had been so easy. The elevator behaved as told, politely speeding her to her destination. When she stepped out and saw her parents shouting, something in the deepest part of her mind hinted at the shadow of an idea of unhappiness. Discontent.

Maybe that was what Isabelle had felt a year ago when Dad left. That night he and Mom had shouted late into the night. Kylie and Isabelle had huddled together in their shared room, and Isabelle had comforted her sister as best she could. But that night hadn't gone as all the others had. Their parents hadn't stopped.

It had frightened Kylie, the way Isabelle's face had snapped from pure rage to absolute tranquility. The older sister had confronted her father, with a soft voice.

"Stop it," she had said, her hands balled up into fists. The lights flickered and dimmed. The music in the other room burst into static.

Dad had only smiled. "Oh, Isa, shouldn't it be up to you?"

"Jackson," Mom had said, a warning in her voice.

"She has a right to decide, Sashi. She's a teenager."

"Go. Away." Isabelle's face had turned beet red. There was a sharp pop and smoke came from Dad's fidget, and he shook it off. The video screen on the wall came alive with demonic images and a haunting howl.

Dad's eyes grew wide. "You're doing it." He touched Isabelle's arm, but she pulled away. "Honey, you've got it. You're controlling the information." He turned to Sashi. "How long has she been able to do this?"

"Go," Sashi shouted. "Get out, and don't come back!"

To Kylie's surprise, he'd backed out, hands raised. He had ignored Mom, keeping his gaze locked on Isa. "You can be so much better, Isa, dearie. We can help you and give you purpose. It's your choice."

Then he was gone and Mom had slid down the closed door, sitting in front of it for a long time with tears in her eyes. "I need to buy a gun," she had whispered to nobody in particular. "And we need to leave."

After that, Isabelle had never been the same.

Kylie wanted Isabelle back. Her sister, who she could see in the center of the lab, was somehow beyond her reach. Kylie had always known the warm glow of her sister's presence, but there, only a little way away from her, she was out of reach. Something blocked their signal. In fact, the whole glass room in the center was a black hole. Nothing transmitted from inside there. Kylie had never considered that her connection to her sister might be anything other than normal.

"You were nothing more than a spy!" Kylie's mother shouted. She had a gun in her hand and gestured with it. "I meant nothing to you, and you— you poisoned them!"

Her dad raised his hands, palms forward as if surrendering. "Sashi, please, understand. It wasn't like that."

Kylie didn't believe him. She sensed a muddy signal from her mother, the same kind she'd felt from Olivia. Through that signal, she felt a strong sense of anger and distrust for Dad. How could he have done those things? But what had he done? Kylie hid behind a computer console, knowing the advantages of hearing more, and understanding that the words might be devastating.

She didn't need to feel any more, though, so she listened.

"You were NSA, like my father," her mother spat. "A spy from the beginning, and once you went private, you kept being a spy. You knew that Trevan had a technology your people wanted, and you married me just to get close to it."

Her father sputtered. When he spoke again, it was a growl of anger. "You never cared about me or your girls. They were nothing more than experiments to you."

"What? How can you say that? You monster, you're the one who wants to put them in a war."

"I'm the one who wants to give them a good life, one where they can be exceptional at what they do."

Kylie's mother took a step back. "It's not your choice."

"Is it yours? You plan to kill Isabelle." He moved close. "How can you even consider that?"

Then something in Kylie's mother changed. Her expression went flat, as Isabelle's had. The sense of powerful emotion that Kylie read on her signal toned down to steely gray, with hardly a blip of feeling.

The woman raised her gun.

Kylie's father moved faster than Kylie had ever seen anyone move. The gun went off but missed. He stepped close, and with a chop, the gun went flying. Another gun appeared in his hand, and in a flash, he brought it down hard on her head.

She crumpled to the floor.

"No!" Kylie yelled.

He looked up at her, realizing she stood there. "Kylie," he said. He held the gun behind his back. "Kylie, how did you get here?"

Kylie felt a tightness in her chest. Breathing came hard for a moment, but she fought. Soon, the world turned gray and big again. She crossed the floor and stood in front of her father.

He kneeled and spoke on her level. "I want what's best for you and your sister," he said in a soft voice.

She shook her head slowly. "No, you don't. Neither does Mom."

"Kylie." He swallowed hard. "Your mother is very sick."

"Her brain is broken, too."

Looking back at the woman sprawled on the floor, he said, "The virus she used on you and your sister is hurting her. It's driving her insane. Maybe did a long time ago. She thought she could find a cure using this," he gestured at the enormous glass room, "to scan the changes in Isa's brain." He looked as if he might be considering his options. "But you don't need a cure. You're fine as you are."

Isa and Papa watched from inside the room. Isabelle looked serene, but Papa wore a look of deep anger. In some deep part of her mind, Kylie hoped that anger wasn't directed at her.

"You have to come back with me, Kylie," her father said. He set down his gun and opened his arms for an embrace. "We'll go away from this. Maybe you can convince your sister to come, too."

Kylie looked at him for a long time. He stayed open to her, a kind look on his face. Could he be trusted? What would happen if she opened herself up to him? Would he take care of her or would he want to use her? Both? The cold logic slipped around in her brain, but she knew she needed to have her feelings back. She didn't want them.

The tingle at the tips of her new senses flashed across her skin. Everything around them lit up with a technicolor glow. All those computers left a pure radio silence, but even though they didn't reach out to her, they were right there. She could control them. So much power flickered at the edge of her senses, but no answers.

Why didn't she want her feelings back?

Fear. The answer came to her, and the feeling crashed down hard.

Then came everything else. Olivia. The men she had killed so casually. Her mother. Garrison. How had she left Garrison?

Kylie wept. Her body, barely under her own control, flopped forward into her father's hug. She no longer cared if it was the right choice. How could there be anything else? He hugged her tight, and she breathed in his warmth.

"It'll be okay, honey," he said, patting her back. "You'll be okay."

She wiped at her tears, absolutely certain that it wouldn't.

"You go over and get the elevator open. I'll get your sister and grandfather."

Kylie nodded, pulling away from her father. He didn't have a kind face, but his stern face had kindness on it. Some small glimmer of hope sparked in her chest. She ran to the main elevator, certain that it was probably still on this floor. They could go down and escape that awful place, all together, and they would figure out the cure that Mama was looking for without killing Isa to do it.

She mashed the button on the elevator, and the door slid open.

Then she heard gunshots.

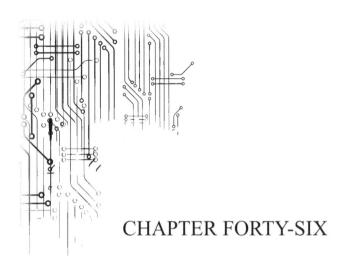

CHAPTER FORTY-SIX

Something banged against the glass chamber, sending a resonating boom through Ajay's skull. Jackson pounded on the glass with the butt of his gun. Through the warped view, Ajay saw him shouting, but the man's voice was swallowed by the thick walls.

Ajay scowled at the man, sure that anything involving Jackson had to be bad. Sashi lay on the floor, face bloodied by Jackson. What did he want?

Jackson yanked the plastic door open. "You!" he shouted at Ajay.

Ajay showed Jackson his one good fist. When he spoke, he aimed to project a confidence he didn't feel. "Stay back, young man."

Jackson tipped his chin at Isabelle. "Planning on keeping her, then? Will you take her and turn her into whatever kind of person you want, just like you did your crazy daughter?" He snapped up a routine on his fidget and ran it.

Isabelle stiffened, her body rigid with tense muscle.

Ajay swallowed back the lump in his throat. He stood between Jackson and Isabelle, blocking as much as possible with his body as if the gesture could do any good at all. What chance did he have to physically overpower the younger man?

"Hold him," Jackson said in a casual tone.

Isabelle, in a fluid movement, snatched up Ajay's good arm and held it up behind him in a joint lock.

"See, old man," Jackson said, "I told you I could make her happy. She'll enjoy what I tell her to enjoy."

"You," Ajay said. "You should be ashamed of yourself. What is wrong with you to experiment on people like this?"

Jackson's lip curled up in a sneer. He met Ajay's gaze for a long while, nostrils flaring in a barely contained rage. Finally, he said, "I loved Isabelle, you know. Loved Sashi. It's not your place, the estranged father, to judge me on those I care about."

Ajay clenched his fist tighter. "You never loved my daughter."

Taking a step back, Jackson raised his gun. "Get out here."

"No," Ajay said, jutting out his jaw.

Jackson's hand trembled, his muscles tense with fury. "I said, step out here. Isabelle, dear, please help your grandfather."

Ajay straightened his back, standing tall in the face of the gun. Isabelle wrenched his arm, but he stood against the pressure. "I will not come out. Isabelle, you don't need to do this."

"Sashi told me all about you. You were never there for her. Never trusted her." His breaths came in deep gasps. "She was paranoid when I met her. A nutcase because of you."

Isabelle touched Ajay's shoulder, but he brushed it off and took a step forward. "You never loved her, you goddamn spy. From the very moment you met her, you were only there to steal technology from her. The whole time." He gestured back at Isabelle. "And even now you want your precious product of years of spying. Your manufactured weapons of war."

"Weapon." Jackson's voice went calm, but his gun didn't waver. "Isabelle was the weapon. Kylie was our daughter. She had nothing to do with this."

"Didn't she?" Ajay stepped closer to the doorway, but not into it. "Didn't she have everything to do with the program? She got the modifications. She's more enhanced than her sister." He watched Jackson for the span of several breaths. "You didn't know."

Jackson pointed his pistol at the ground. "Not at first. When Sashi started showing symptoms, we guessed that it was in her blood. Only, Kylie didn't show it and by then, well, it was hard for me to get quality one-on-one time long enough to run any real tests."

"But you would still put her in a program to make her an assassin."

"Wouldn't you? If you could give her purpose and an active life? If you could give her a chance at being the greatest hacker in the world?" He ran a hand through his hair. His eyes were sunken, haunted. "Wouldn't you do that, no matter what it takes?"

"No," Ajay said, letting the word hang in the air before continuing. "Because I believe that what they want isn't always the right thing."

A smirk crossed Jackson's lips in a flash. "You see," he said, "that is where we differ." He raised his weapon.

Ajay clenched his eyes shut.

The gunshot reverberated in the little room, a deafening thunderclap of noise and power. Isabelle gasped and dropped Ajay's arm. His ears rang, but he heard her stumble back, away from him.

There was no pain. Ajay swayed on his feet, eyes still clenched shut. When, finally, he braved a look, he saw Jackson sprawled on the floor, the blue splash of neutralizing rounds sinking into his flesh.

"Sashi," Ajay said.

Sashi limped forward, clunky paintball gun trained on Ajay. Blood streaked the side of her face, matting her hair. Without taking her eyes from Ajay, she holstered her weapon, picked up Jackson's gun, and pumped several bullets into his brain. Blood and brain and skull flew in chunks across the floor. The crystalline wall of the chamber darkened with the spray.

Isabelle sobbed.

Sashi stood with a pistol leveled at Ajay. Her face was a mask of deep red, her blood forming a ragged scowl across her otherwise emotionless features. Her expression never flicked away from one of pure businesslike duty. She tried moving the body from several angles, then found that she could tug at one ankle to drag the body out of the way, leaving a long smear of blood on the crystalline floor. Once that was out of the way, she closed the outer door without another word. Ajay heard the distinct click of the door locking.

"Well, shit," Ajay said.

The corner of Isabelle's mouth tweaked up again. "Well, shit," she said.

CHAPTER FORTY-SEVEN

Ajay pulled himself up. There was no use trying to hide anymore. He watched as Sashi crossed to a control panel and touched some buttons. The low hum under their feet grew. The sequence started, and he wondered if it could be stopped. Ajay caught more movement out of the corner of his eye: a flash of red against the steel gray decor. When he looked, Kylie was gone.

"How do you feel?" Ajay asked Isabelle, his voice shaking.

"I'm sorry," she said. "It made me want to do what he said."

"But it doesn't anymore?"

She shook her head. "It's gone now."

Ajay put his good arm around Isabelle. "Well, Isa," he said. "If that signal's gone, then this must really be you."

"No," she said. "It stays with me."

"What have you always wanted out of life?" Ajay asked. "Think back as far as you can."

She licked her lips. Her expression had softened and real fear showed in her eyes. "I don't know."

"We're going to die here," he said, "but it would be nice to end with a pleasant thought, don't you think?"

For a long time, Sashi worked with the controls, her expression blank. The hum grew to a steady background of tension, and the glass walls flashed with color. It was a beautiful sight, and for a time Ajay was mesmerized by its scintillating colors. Sure, once the scan activated he'd be dead, but until then it was going to be breathtaking.

"I've always wanted to see a capybara," Isabelle said.

He raised an eyebrow. "Really?"

This time Isabelle's smile grew to touch her eyes. "Ever since I was little. They're so cute and fuzzy," she said. "I found videos of them online all the time when I wasn't supposed to. One time I asked Mom to take me to the zoo, but she wouldn't do it. We never got to leave to go anywhere."

"Why capybaras?"

"Why not? They don't give a shit what anyone thinks, so why should I?"

Ajay pulled her close as the hum's intensity shook his teeth. Light flashed across the plastic bed and glass walls. The metal mesh in the floor glowed in waves of orange and red. He looked to Sashi, who stood frozen with her hand above a button. He tried to silently plead with her. He might be too proud to beg for his own life, but for his granddaughter, he would do anything. How could his own daughter do such a terrible thing? The weight of his life's failure crushed him, putting such pressure on his chest that it was hard to breathe.

There she was, though. Hesitating, yes, but her eyes burned with stubborn determination. She would press that button.

"Do you know what reincarnation is, Isi?" Ajay asked.

"When you come back as something else?"

Ajay nodded. "My mother believed in it. She mostly left behind her religion when she came from India, but I think she always liked the idea of reincarnation. She'd threaten me with it, anyway."

Isabelle gnawed on her lip. "I don't want to die, Papa."

"I know, dear. I don't either, but let's both think of capybaras when we go." He looked her in the eye and for once she met his gaze. "Just in case."

Her brow furrowed in determination. Tears glistened in her eyes. "Just in case."

And in that moment, Isabelle seemed more warm and human than anyone Ajay had ever known. All those hours of thinking she was cold and strange melted away as her defenses crumbled. She was his granddaughter, and he felt more connected to her than he had ever been with Sashi. Despite the experimental changes to her DNA and the computer installed in her brain, Isabelle was still only a kid. There was still life in her and she still deserved saving. Ajay only wished there was something he could do to get them out.

But he didn't need to.

Kylie flew from hiding like a viper striking prey. She hit Sashi hard from the side, knocking her down. At the same time, the door to the chamber hissed and opened. Ajay pulled himself up and Isabelle helped him toward the door. He swayed, knees suddenly loose. Pressure pounded in his ears, and the flashes of color on the floor made it difficult to know how to stand. Isabelle helped him, pulling him along.

He pushed the door open the rest of the way and he and Isabelle emerged into the sharp ozone smell of the outer room.

"You can't kill her!" Kylie shouted at her mother.

Quick as lightning, Sashi grabbed Kylie's arm and twisted. "I'll do what I need to do," she said. "You're my baby girl, Kylie. I'll do what it takes."

"You killed Daddy," Kylie said. "You killed him!" She grabbed Sashi's thumb and twisted, locking her mother's elbow long enough to shove her away.

A look of confusion crossed Sashi's face but fell when she saw Jackson's body on the floor. She staggered back, blinking back tears. "I did," she said, determination leaving her voice. "It was necessary."

"No," Ajay said. "No, Sashi, it wasn't."

Sashi pushed Kylie away and drew her gun on Ajay. "What would you know?"

"I know you better than you think, Sash." Ajay raised his good palm in an act of surrender. "I know I wasn't the best for you, but you succeeded anyway. You were brilliant, and I was always proud of you. Proud, but not proud of myself. I could never give you what you needed. The work I did was too much, and then when that work was gone, I..." He lowered his hand because keeping it up was just too much work. Standing at all was almost too much. "Sashi," he said, "you tried the virus on yourself, didn't you?"

The light in the chamber grew to a steady golden glow, brighter and brighter, like a glimpse of a rising dawn over the ocean.

She shook her head, but her arm relaxed until her gun pointed at the ground. "It was accidental," she said. "For a long time, we didn't think the exposure had taken effect."

"But it did. You can hear signals, can't you? Parts of your brain have been rewritten to give you the same signal sense these girls were born with."

Sashi nodded. Kylie crept slowly away, staying back out of Sashi's line of sight. Kylie's eyes were wide with fear. Ajay wondered how much she knew.

"Is it true that Kylie was Jackson's daughter?" Ajay asked, "Or was she another experiment?"

Sashi's voice hardened. "Kylie wasn't supposed to be part of it."

Ajay said, "But she is part of it, isn't she? It's affecting you, too, Sashi. That same viral nanomachine that you designed to cross the blood-brain barrier crossed the placental barrier as well. You think that getting the scan of Isabelle will save Kylie, but you're trying to save yourself as well."

Sashi turned to Isabelle. "It's the only way," she said. "We need to see what the mitochondria are doing. There's so much activity in the brain that we don't fully understand, Papa. So much we can learn."

"It's killing you, isn't it?" Ajay took a step forward and looked down at Jackson's body at his feet. "That's what the scan at Mississippi Prosthetics was all about. You needed to know if the deep scan was necessary."

"Come," Sashi said to her eldest daughter. "You need to go now." She took hold of the girl's arm and pulled, but Isabelle didn't move.

Ajay spoke through his teeth. "This isn't the only way, is it? There are two of you with this particular virus. A scan of either one of you would suffice, wouldn't it?" Ajay swallowed hard. "Parenting is sometimes about self-sacrifice, Sashi."

Her face twisted in a sneer, and her grip on her daughter hardened. "What do you know of sacrifice, Papa? You never let me get in the way of your career, did you? You never gave a damn thing up for me. You expected me to conform to your every whim. You never let me make a decision on my own, preferring perfect obedience simply so you wouldn't have to deal with the inconvenience of being a father." She gave Isabelle another yank, but when the girl didn't move, Sashi screamed furious madness. "Move! The scan will trigger any second and you need to be in there!"

Isabelle's face was a mask of passivity.

Sashi wept angry tears. "Isabelle, you're not even human. The modifications they did to you. You were meant to be a killer, but please, save your sister. It's your only chance to do good."

"She is human and you know it." Ajay shook his cane at her. "Sashi, you know better. This girl is just as human as you or me, no matter what you did to her." He leaned heavily on his cane. "And you're right. I was no father to you. My idea of sacrifice was working harder, and that wasn't what you needed. It never was, and I didn't do it out of love, but out of fear. I was afraid of you. Afraid of trying my best with you and failing. Afraid of seeing you make mistakes and knowing that those were my mistakes." He let the golden light from the scanner play across his face for a moment, like the dying rays of a sunset. "But people make mistakes, Sashi. I know I made plenty. It's how we behave afterward that matters. How we try to make it better if we can. And how we forgive."

"I'll do it," said Isabelle.

Ajay blinked. "What did you say?"

Isabelle met Kylie's gaze but said nothing to her. Kylie nodded. To her mother, Isabelle said, "I'll do it, Momma."

The golden light grew, and the hum's pitch dropped a full octave.

Sashi swallowed, and like the flip of a switch, emotion dropped from her face. "Of course," she said. "You'd best hurry." She led Isabelle over to the open chamber door.

Ajay's blood pulsed in his ears. His head swam. "Sashi," he said, "don't do this." He stepped in front of them, blocking their way to the scanner.

"Let me make this choice, Papa," Sashi said. "Step aside."

Isabelle stopped his response with a hug. "No," he said weakly. He shook his head, but Isabelle kissed him on the head, anyway.

"I'm sorry, but this is the best. Don't forget about the capybaras."

She stood and walked with her mother to the chamber entrance. Isabelle was nearly as tall as the older woman, though considerably thinner. Sashi put away her gun and hugged her daughter. Isabelle pulled away a little so she could look into her mother's eyes.

Ajay knelt beside Jackson's body, feeling at the coat pockets where the quantum cube still lay. The diamond-optical device sat heavy in his hand. Activating it might bring the systems in there crashing down. The flood of signals would almost certainly cause problems with every system in the lab. It was his best chance to stop this, but he hesitated. It might stop their deaths, but it would definitely prevent data collection. Everything they did — the decision they were making — would be wasted.

"Mother," Isabelle asked, "would you forgive me if I made a mistake?"

Sashi blinked. "Yes, but—"

Isabelle broke her mother's nose with a vicious head-butt.

Sashi screamed and flailed, but Isabelle pulled her elbow joint taut. She spun her around to the crystal door and released her with a hard shove. Isabelle shouted so that her mother could hear. "Mother, thank you." And then Isabelle closed the door.

"No," said Ajay. He stood, but his knees buckled and he fell hard. He let the box slip from his hands, and he staggered toward the console.

He met Sashi's eyes through the chamber glass, and she held his gaze for a long time. Golden light played across her features, and he saw her flash through a range of emotions. Anger, fear, then finally resignation fell across her face. She mouthed, "I love you, Papa," before relaxing and lying down on the table in the middle of the room. All those years of rescuing his daughter and making decisions for her came to this. His final failure as a father.

And Sashi's decisions had killed her long ago. It had taken time for the virus to catch up with her, but there it was. If she'd told the truth, she would be dead either way and in doing this, she could at least give Kylie and Isabelle a chance.

It didn't make Ajay feel one bit better.

Kylie reached for the button, but Ajay took her hand in his. As strange and unemotional as she seemed, he couldn't let her kill her own mother. How could she live with that guilt? The burden would be too much to bear. He pulled Kylie close, wrapping her in his arms so she couldn't see. He pressed the button.

The room filled with yellow light, like the sharp intensity of the sun. Warmth rolled out across the room in flickering waves.

He saw that little girl, hair tied back, climbing the tree in their yard. She climbed and climbed, his little Sashi, and when she reached the top, she called out to the world in triumph. Sashi, the unstoppable girl. Sashi, the determined. Sashi, the fiercely independent. When, long ago, she had climbed that tree and broken her arm coming down — even that had not stopped her. She'd climbed it again before the bone had even set.

Yet, finally, there she was at her end. Finally stopped by the hand of her father. Ajay didn't know how he would be able to bear the burden of that guilt. It already crushed him. Kylie melted into his arms and hugged him close.

When at last the light died down, Sashi was gone. Nothing remained in the chamber save the transparent table at its center. Her body, her clothes, her tech — all of it had been picked apart at a molecular level and transported up and away.

There was nothing.

Grief washed across Kylie's face. "I'm sorry, Mama," she said over and over.

Ajay hugged her closer. She wept into his shoulder, tears mixing with his blood. For a long time, he couldn't think about what to do next. There was no world outside of his grief, and even twenty years apart from his daughter was nothing compared to losing her forever. She was gone. Really gone.

Movement across the room drew Ajay's attention. Isabelle stood inside the open elevator. She held up Jackson's fidget for him to see, and he nodded to her. She had what she needed. Maybe with that, she could find who she was. Wasn't that what kids her age always did?

The doors slid closed, and she was gone.

"The data," he said, failing to keep his voice from cracking.

Kylie understood. She ran back to the console, fiddled with it, and came away with a data stick. She flashed a weak smile to her grandfather before stuffing the drive in her pocket. On her way back to him, she picked up the diamond-optical device.

"Good," he said. "C'mon, then."

She got him to the elevator, and on the way down he bled and cried. The bleeding, he knew, would eventually stop, and he would heal, but he doubted he would ever really stop crying.

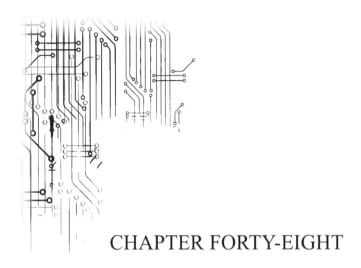

CHAPTER FORTY-EIGHT

"It's a nine iron," Ajay said, holding out the correct club from his comfortable seat on the golf cart.

Kylie shook her head. "It's not, Papa," she said. "I need the seven."

Sun shone on grandfather and granddaughter as they played the eighteen holes of the Castle Highlands Golf Course near Bemidji. They couldn't have asked for a better day to be out on the course. A gentle breeze tickled their backs.

Ajay's shoulder still hadn't fully healed, but his hip felt better. Still, he was perfectly happy living vicariously through his granddaughter. Kylie took immediately to golf, as she'd taken immediately to many things. She had even started school for a brief time after they had relocated to northern Minnesota. Bemidji still had real school: the kind where you actually showed up every day. It took some time to figure out identification, but Ajay was reasonably certain nobody was looking for them.

"It's eighty yards," said Kylie.

Ajay peered over the top of his dark sunglasses. "A seven's going to go too shallow. It'll roll past."

Garrison lay his head on Ajay's lap and whined until he was adequately scratched behind his ears. Dogs weren't normally allowed on the golf course, but what use was setting up a new identity if a person couldn't officially declare his dog to be a helper animal? Seemed like an abuse of a good system, but Ajay justified it by telling himself that Garrison really was helpful. After all, when a person needed to find the nearest hotdog vendor, Garrison's nose came in handy every time.

Kylie held the nine-iron in her hands, considering it carefully. "If I hit the seven lighter, it'll roll up onto the green."

"No, it won't. It'll roll up short. Plus, it's a greater risk to hit those bunkers."

"But—"

"Trust me on this."

"I'd have to swing too hard."

Ajay shook his head. "You don't have to swing hard. Just give it a good, full swing. Give it your best and it'll be good enough, even if it falls a little short."

Kylie took the seven-iron. Ajay let her. After all, it was ultimately her choice. She lined up her feet just as he had taught her, shifting back and forth to get the cleats settled. After a couple practice swings, she stepped up to the ball, lined up the club, and swung.

The ball soared through the air, launching up high into the blue sky. Ajay lost it for a moment in the sun, but when he looked down, blinking away the blind spots, he saw it land shy of the green and roll right up.

Kylie shook with joy, the smile beaming across her face competing in brightness with the sun above. With a flourish, she handed the club back to her grandfather, who stowed it in the bag. She slid onto the cart, sharing a seat with Garrison, who whined in complaint but shifted to give her enough room.

Ajay tipped his hat at Kylie, an acknowledgment that she'd done well.

"You're the best caddy," Kylie said as they bumped across the fairway.

Ajay grumbled in fake discontent. "Don't judge 'til you've tried some of the competition, now. Might be that someone else is much better at this than me. You have a whole lifetime to find a better caddy, young miss."

Kylie's gaze became distant. "Yeah."

"What is it?"

"Sometimes it's hard to focus." She flashed a weak smile. "I miss Isabelle."

Ajay scratched his mustache. "I know. We'll see her again, though. I bet she's keeping an eye on you and she'll be back when it's safe."

Kylie looked up at the skies, no doubt sensing the drones flying high above. "It's comforting, knowing she's watching."

"Sure," Ajay said. "A little." He still didn't like the level of surveillance over the golf course, but he did have to admit that knowing Isabelle might be watching helped some. It kept his anxiety in check, anyway.

"Am I going to get like her?" Kylie asked. "Mom thought it was because…"

"Because of your special talents?" Ajay pulled the cart up as close to the green as was allowed. "Maybe, but I don't think your mother knew exactly what she was talking about. Plus, we have a good scan that shows the changes in her whole neurological system. I've got my best contacts pulling apart the data. If there's a good fix, we'll find it."

"What if we don't?"

Ajay put an arm around her shoulder. "Well, Garrison and I won't stop loving you."

She flashed a weak smile.

Ajay continued, "Maybe we'll get you your own helper dog. Train it how to keep you from getting too far out there."

Kylie hugged Garrison's head, letting him slobber on her. "I'll take this one."

"Now wait a second."

Ajay set the brake on the cart and pulled Kylie in for an embrace. Ajay gave her some time. She'd lost her parents. Maybe Sashi and Jackson hadn't been the best people, but most parents probably weren't all that great. After a while, he twisted around and pulled two putters from her golf bag.

He held one out to Kylie. "Better get up there and putt."

The young girl looked at his second putter. "You're coming, too?" She wiped tears from her eyes.

"Might as well. Gotta get back into the game sometime, right?" He hopped out of the cart and tossed a ball onto the green.

She swished the club back and forth. When she hopped out of the cart, Garrison lumbered out as well, following her as far as the edge of the green. She took a few steps, thought better of it, and circled to where Ajay stood.

Kylie kissed him on the cheek. "I love you, Papa."

"I love you, too, Kylie," Ajay said, trying to stop his tears from flowing. "Now get up there and putt."

So, she did.

ACKNOWLEDGMENTS

I would be remiss to not acknowledge my own grandpa as the inspiration for this book. He was very different from Ajay, but there are some fundamental similarities that I'd like to bring up.

Yes, grandfathers can be stubborn. They're often these stubborn, vital old men who just keep going at whatever their chosen thing is no matter what. That was Grandpa Eichenlaub. He was the kind of guy who played tennis until he was eighty and never, ever stopped inventing.

It's easy to look at the characters in my books and argue that nobody has their ridiculously high pain tolerance, but, ok, listen. There was this time playing tennis with Grandpa Eichenlaub. He stumbled going for a ball, because even as an old man playing against a teenager he was super competitive. He fell and rolled, bending two fingers on his right hand far enough back that the skin ripped open and the knuckles came out of joint.

"Oh, flub," was as much of a curse as we got from him. He popped his fingers back into joint, accepted (grudgingly) a ride to the hospital, and really, really wanted to play the last game of our set later that afternoon.

With two heavily bandaged and stitched fingers on his primary hand.

I mean, we didn't let him, but he was definitely up for it.

I never met the grandpa on my other side. Or, at least, I was too young to really remember anything about him. Luckily, I had a bonus grandpa by marriage. His name was Homer, and he didn't have the kind of pain tolerance Grandpa Eichenlaub had, but he had a level of kindness and sensitivity that I consider to be the hallmark of a truly great person. I hope some of that comes through in the characters I write.

When we're young, we worship them. When they're gone, we miss them. Here's to all the badass grandpas out there. Don't let anyone tell you to slow down.

-Anthony W. Eichenlaub

On the cutting edge of humanity, rules are made for one thing.

No, it is not "to be broken."

Biologist Ash Morgan loves breaking rules, but this is ridiculous. Edge is humanity's bastion on the frontier of space and science. She plays fast and loose with the Edge's ultra-strict governing AI, but even she's willing to admit that maybe there are some laws not meant to be broken.

When a fellow colonist asks for help delivering a child, Ash agrees against her better judgment.

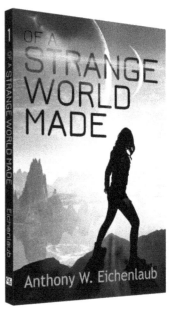

But something's not right.

The birth will exceed the precise population cap set by the colony AI. Somehow those numbers need to balance.

And the child is born strange. Too strange. What experiments could produce a child like this? Who would do this?

When the mother descends into depression and madness, Ash must decide which rules can be broken, which rules must be obeyed, and which rules will inevitably lead to the colony's ultimate destruction.

On the cutting edge of humanity, rules are made for one thing: to be followed perfectly with zero deviation.

Always.

Or else.

Of a Strange World Made

https://oakleafbooks.com

Metal and Men

There are some problems all the tech in Texas can't solve.

Things aren't always easy for the Sheriff of Dead Oak, Texas. Cybernetically modified biker gangs roam the skies, dangerous outlaws prowl the streets, and gunslingers threaten the delicate balance of a Texas gone sour. J.D. doesn't mind. He'll hold hard the line of justice, no matter what it takes.

Sometimes things aren't so simple.

When a rancher is murdered, it's going to take all of J.D.'s skills as a Texas Ranger to track the killer. Every turn he makes he find more threads of a massive conspiracy that could tear his town apart. Every discovery leads him down the darker path of his own past.

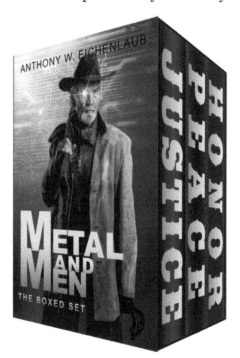

And he's not the only one doing some tracking. A man in black is on his trail.

There's only one thing J.D. knows for sure: One way or another, there's going to be Justice in an Age of Metal and Men.

https://oakleafbooks.com

Lightning Source UK Ltd.
Milton Keynes UK
UKHW010035070223
416578UK00002B/305